THE DARK HEART OF AFRICA

SHORT STORIES OF HORROR, BLACK MAGIC AND HUNTING FROM THE SEARING DESERT TO THE DARKEST JUNGLE

British Library Cataloguing-in-Publication Data
A catalogue record for this book is available from
the British Library

Contents

Short Autobiographies of the Authors

The magician
Lord Lytton

It was deep night, and the Magician suddenly stood before me.
'Arise,' said he, 'and let us go forth upon the surface of the
world.' I rose, and followed the sorcerer until we arrived at the
entrance of a cavern. Pursuing its subterranean course for some
minutes, with the rushing sound of imprisoned waters loud and
wild upon the ear, we came at length into a colder and fresher
atmosphere; and presently, through a fissure in the rock, the
sudden whiteness of the moon broke in, and partially lit up
walls radiant with spars, and washed by a deep stream that
wound its mysterious way to the upper air. And now, gliding
through the chasm, we stood in a broad cell, with its lofty arch
open to the sea. Column and spire, brilliant with various crys-
tallizations – spars of all hues, sprang lightly up on either side
of this cavern; and with a leap and a mighty voice, the stream,
whose course we had been tracking, rushed into the arms of the
great sea. Upon that sea, star after star mirrored its solemn
lustre; and the moon, clad in a fuller splendour than I had ever
before seen gathered round her melancholy orb, filled the
cavern with a light, which was to the light of day what the life
of a spirit is to that of a mortal. Passionless, yet tender – stead-
fast – mystic – unwavering – she shone upon the glittering
spars; and in a long line, from the cavern to the verge of
heaven, her sweet face breathed a quiet joy into the rippling
billows – 'smiles of the sea'. A few thin and fleecy clouds alone
varied the clear expanse of the heavens. And,
    'Beautiful,' said I, 'is this outward world! – your dim realms
beneath have nothing to compare with it. There are no stars in
the temples of the hidden earth – and one glimpse from the
lovely moon is worth all the witchfires and meteors of the giant
palaces below.'

'Young mortal,' said the Wizard in his mournful voice, 'thou beholdest my native shore. Beside that sea stood my ancestral halls – and beneath that moon first swelled within my bosom the deep tides of human emotion – and in this cavern, whence we now look forth on the seas and heavens, my youth passed some of its earnest hours in contemplations never known to your lesser race clogged with the mire of ages: for that epoch lies remote in primeval times, which even tradition scarcely pierces. Your first fathers – what of their knowledge know ye? – what of their secrets have ye retained? Their vast and solemn minds were never fathomed by the plummet of your researches. The waves of the black Night have swept over the ancient world; and you can only guess of its buried glories by the shivered fragments which, ever and anon, Chance casts upon the shores of the modern Time.'

'Do we sink, then,' said I, 'by comparison with the men of those distant dates? Is not our lore deeper and more certain? Was not their knowledge the imperfect offspring of confused conjecture? Did they not live among dreams and shadows, and make Truth herself the creature of fantastic Fable?'

'Nay,' replied the shrouded and uncertain form beside me, 'their knowledge pierced into the heart of things. They consulted the stars – but it was to measure the dooms of earth; and could we recall from the dust their perished scrolls, you would behold the mirror of the living times. Their prophecies, wrung from the toil and rapture of those powers which ye suffer to sleep, quenched, within the soul, traversed the wilds of ages, and pointed out among savage hordes the cities and laws of empires yet to be. Ten thousand arts have mouldered from the earth, and Science is the shadow of what it was. Young mortal, thou hast set thine heart upon Wisdom – thou hast wasted the radiant hours of opening life amidst the wearisome thoughts of doting sages: thou hast laboured after Knowledge, and in that labour the healthful hues have left thy cheek, and the worm of decay creeps into the core of thy youth while the dew is yet upon its leaf: and for this labour – and in the transport and the vision that the soul's labour nurtures – thy spirit is now rapt from its fleshly career on earth, wandering at will among the chasms and mines wombed within the world – breathing a vital air among the dead, comraded by Spirits and the Powers that are not of flesh, and catching, by imperfect glimpse and shadowy type, some knowledge of the arch mysteries of Creation; and thou beholdest in me and in my science that which thy learning and thy fancy tracked not before. No legend ever chanced upon my strange and solemn being: nor does aught of my nature resemble the tales of wizard or sorcerer that the vulgar fantasies of superstition have embodied. Thou hast journeyed over a land without a chart, and in which even fable has hackneyed not the truth. Thou wouldst learn something of the Being thus permitted to thy wonder; be it so. Under these sparkling arches – and before my ancestral sea – and beneath the listening ear of the halting moon – thou shalt learn a history of the antique world.'

The tale of Kosem Kesamin

Along the shores which for thirty centuries no human foot has trod, and upon plains where now not one stone stands upon another, telling even of decay – was once the city and the empire of the Wise Kings; for so termed by their neighbours were the monarchs that ruled this country. Generation after generation they had toiled to earn and preserve that name. Amidst the gloom of mysterious temples and the oracular learning of the star-read priests, the youth of each succeeding king was reared into a grave and brooding manhood. Their whole lives were mystery. Wrapped in the sepulchral grandeur of the imperial palace; seen rarely, like gods, they sent forth, as from a cloud, the light of their dread but benignant laws: the courses of their life were tracked not – but they were believed to possess a power over the seasons and elements, and to summon, at their will, the large-winged spirits that flit to and fro across the earth, governing, like dreams, with a vague and unpenetrated power the destiny of nations and the career of kings.

There was born to this imperial race a son, to whom seer and king alike foretold a strange and preternatural fate. His childhood itself was of a silent, stern, and contemplative nature. And his learning, even in his boyish youth, had ransacked all that the grey priests could teach him.

But when wind encounters wind the meeting is warfare – the warfare is storm. Wind meets with wind when the mind of youth soars from earth to seek wisdom and the heart of youth ranges heaven to find love.

The Magician paused for a moment, and then, in a voice far different from the cold and solemn tone in which his accents were usually clothed, he broke forth:

Oh, beautiful, beyond the beauty of these sicklied and hoary times, was the beauty of Woman in the young world! The glory of Eden had not yet departed from her face, and the lustre of unwearied Nature glowed alike upon earth and earth's majestic daughters. Age after age Man invents and deserts some worship of idols in his yearning for symbols of a Power beyond the reach of his vision and the guess of his reason. But never yet has he forsaken the oldest idolatry of all – the adoration of earthly beauty as the fairest image of celestial good. Yet to me, for I am that prince of whose throne and whose people no record in Time remains, to me even the love of Beauty was a passion less ardent than the desire of Knowledge! My mind launched itself into the depth of things – I loved step after step to trace effect to its first cause. Reason was a chain from heaven to earth, and every link led me to aspire to the stars themselves. And the wisdom of my wise fathers was mine; I knew the secret of the elements, and could charm them into slumber, or arouse them into war. The mysteries of that dread chemistry which is now among the sciences that sleep – by which we can command the air and walk on its viewless paths, by which we can wake the thunder, and summon the cloud, and rive the earth; the exercise of that high faculty – the Imagining Power – by which Fancy itself creates what it wills, and which, trained and exercised, can wake the spectres of the dead – and bring visible to the carnal eye the Genii that walk the world; the watchful, straining, sleepless science, that can make a sage's volume of the stars; these were mine, and yet I murmured – I repined! – what higher mysteries were yet left to learn! The acquisition of today was but the disappointment of the morrow, and the dispensation of my ambition was – to *desire*!

It was evening, and I went from the groves of the sacred temple to visit one whom I loved. The way spread over black and rugged masses of rock, amidst which the wild shrub and dark weed sprung rife and verdant; for the waste as yet was eloquent of some great revolution in the earlier epochs of the world – when change often trod the heels of change; and Earth was scarcely reconciled to the sameness of her calm career. And I stood beneath the tree where SHE was to meet me; my heart leaped within me as I saw her footsteps bounding along – she came with her sweet lips breathing the welcome of human love, and I laid my head on her bosom and was content.

And, 'Oh,' said she, 'art thou proud of thy dawning fame? The seers speak of thee with wonder, and the priests bow their heads before thy name.'

Then the passion of my soul broke forth, and I answered, 'What is this petty power that I possess, and what this barren knowledge? The great arch secret of all, I have toiled night after night to conquer, and I cannot attain it. What is it to command even the dark Spirits at war with Heaven – if we know not the nature of those whom we command? What I desire is not knowledge, but the source of knowledge. I wish that my eye should penetrate at once into the germ and cause of things: that when I look upon the outward beauty of the world, my sight should pierce within, and see the mechanism which causes and generates the beauty working beneath. Enough of my art have I learned to know that there is a film over human eyes which prevents their penetrating beyond the surface; it is to remove that film, and dart into the essence, and survey the One Great Productive Spirit of all Things, that I labour and yearn in vain. All other knowledge is a cheat; this is the high prerogative which mocks at conjecture and equals us with a God![x]

Then Lyciah saw that I was moved, and she soothed me into rest with the coo of her sweet songs.

Midnight had crept over the earth as I returned homeward across that savage scene. Rock heaped on rock bordered and broke upon the lonely valley that I crossed; and the moon was still, and shining, as at this hour, when its life is four thousand years nearer to its doom. Then suddenly I saw moving before me, with a tremulous motion, a meteoric Fire of an exceeding brightness. Ever as it moved above the seared and sterile soil, it soared and darted restlessly to and fro; and I thought, as it danced and quivered, that I heard it laugh from its burning centre with a wild and frantic joy. I fancied, as I gazed upon the Fire, that in that shape sported one of the children of the Elementary Genii; and, addressing it in their language, I bade it assume a palpable form. But the Fire darted on unheedingly, save that now the laugh from amidst the flame came distinctly and fearfully on my ear. Then my hair stood erect, and my veins curdled, and my knees knocked together; I was under the influence of an awe; for I felt that the Power was not of this world, nor of any world of which the knowledge ye call magic had yet obtained a glimpse. My voice faltered, and thrice I strove to speak to the Light – but in vain: and when at length I addressed it in the solemn adjuration by which the sternest of the Fiends are bound, the Fire sprang up from the soil – towering aloft – with a livid but glorious lustre, bathing the whole atmosphere in its glare, quenching, with an intenser ray, the splendours of the moon, and losing its giant crest in the far Invisible of Heaven!

And a voice came forth, saying – 'Thou callest upon inferior Spirits; I am that which thou has pined to behold – I am The Living Principle of the World!'

I bowed my face, and covered it with my hands, and my voice left me; when again I looked round, behold, the Fire had shrunk from its momentary height, and was (now dwarfed and humble) creeping before me in its wavering and snakelike course. But fear was on me, and I fled, and fast fled the Fire by my side; and oft, but faint, from its ghastly heart came the laugh that thrilled the marrow of my bones. The waste was past, and the giant temple of the One God rose before me; I rushed forward, and fell breathless by its silent altar. And there sat the High Priest; for night and day some one of the sacred host watched by the altar; he was of great age, and the tide of human emotion had ebbed from his veins; but even he was struck with my fear, and gazed upon me with his rayless eyes, and bade me be of cheer, for the place was holy. I looked round; the Fire was not visible, and I breathed freely; but I answered not the Priest, for years had dulled him into stone, and when I rose his eye followed me not. I gained the purple halls set apart for the king's son. And the pillars were of ivory inlaid with gold; the gems and perfumes of the East gave light and fragrance to the air; the gorgeous banquet was spread; and music from unseen hands swelled from floor to roof as I passed along. But lo! by the throne, crouching beneath the purple canopy, I saw the laughing Fire; and it seemed, lowly and paled, to implore protection. I paused, and took the courtiers aside, and asked them to mark the flame; but they saw it not –

only for me did it gleam and burn. Then knew I that it was indeed a Spirit of that high race, which, even when they take visible form, are *not* visible save to the students of the Dread Science! And I trembled but revered.

And the Fire stayed by me night and day, and I grew accustomed to its light. But never, by charm nor spell, could I draw further word from it; and it followed my steps with a silent and patient homage. By degrees there came over me a vain and proud delight to think that I was so honoured; and I looked upon the changeful face of the Fire as upon the face of a friend.

There was a man who had told years beyond the memory of the living – a revered and famous soothsayer – to whom, in times of dread and omen, our priests and monarchs themselves repaired for warning and advice. I sought his abode. The Seer was not of our race – he came from the distant waters of the Nile, banished by the hierophants of Egypt for solutions more clear than their own of the mysteries of Osiris and Naith. It was in the very cavern in which we now stand that the Seer held his glittering home – lamp upon lamp then lighted up, from an unfailing naphtha, these dazzling spars, hailed as a beacon by the seamen who brought the merchandise of the world into yonder bay, then so loud and swarming, now so desolate and still. Hither had my feet often turned in boyhood, and from the shrivelled lips of the old Egyptian had much of my loftiest learning been gleaned; for he loved me; and seeing with a prophet eye far down the lengths of Time, he foretold the dates at which Nations should be no more; and yet, far as he could look, beheld me living still; me, the infant he had cradled on his lap.

It was on that night, when the new moon scatters its rank and noxious influence over the foliage and life of earth, that I sought the Egyptian. The Fire burned with a fiercer and redder light than its wont, as it played and darted by my side. And when, winding by the silver sands, I passed into the entrance of the cave, I saw the old man sitting on a stone. As I entered, the Seer started from his seat in fear and terror – his eyes rolled – his thin grey hairs stood erect – a cold sweat broke from his brow – and the dread master stood before his pupil in agony and awe.

'Thou comest,' muttered he with white lips. 'What is by thy side? Hast thou dared to seek knowledge with the Soul of all Horror – with the ghastly Leper of—? Avaunt! bid the fiend begone!'

His voice seemed to leave the old man, and with a shriek he fell upon his face on the ground.

'Is it,' said I, appalled by his terror – 'is it the Fire that haunts my steps at which thou tremblest? Behold, it is harmless as a dog; it burns not while it shines: if a fiend, it is a merry fiend, for I hear it laugh while I speak. But it is for this, dread sire, that I have sought thee. Canst thou tell me the nature of the Spirit? – for a Spirit it surely is. Canst thou tell me its end and aim?'

I lifted the old man from the earth, and his kingly heart returned to him: he took the wizard crown from the wall, and he placed it on his brows; for he was as a monarch among the Things that are not of clay. And he said to the Fire – 'Approach!' The Fire glided to his knees. And he said, 'Art thou the Spirit of the Element, and was thy cradle in the Flint's heart?'

And a voice from the flame answered 'No.'

And again the Egyptian trembled.

'What art thou, then?' said he.

And the Fire answered, 'Thy Lord.'

And the limbs of the Egyptian shook as if in the grasp of death.

And he said, 'Art thou a Demon of *this* world?'

And the Fire answered, 'I am the Life of this world – and I am *not* of other worlds.'

'I know thee – I fear thee – I acknowledge thee!' said the Egyptian; 'and in thy soft lap shall this crowned head soon be laid.'

And the Fire laughed.

'But tell me,' said I – for, though my blood stood still, my soul was brave and stern – 'Tell me, O seer! what hath this Thing with me?'

'It is the Great Ancestor of us all!' said the Egyptian, groaning.

'And knows it the secrets of the Past?'

'The secrets of the Past are locked within it.'

'Can it teach me that which I pine to know? Can it teach me the essence of things – the nature of all I see? Can it raise the film from the human gaze?'

'Hush, rash prince!' cried the Egyptian. 'Seek not to know that which will curse thee with the knowledge. Ask not a power that would turn life into a living grave. All the lore that man ever knew is mine; but that secret have I shunned, and that power have I cast from me, as the shepherd casts the viper from his hand. Be moderate and be wise. And bid me exorcise the Spirit that accosts thee from the Fire!'

'Can it teach me the arch mystery? When I gaze upon the herb or flower, can it gift my gaze with the power to pierce into the cause and workings of its life?'

'I can teach thee this,' said the Fire; and it rose higher, and burned more fiercely, as it spoke, till the lamps of naphtha paled before it.

'Then abide by me, O Spirit!' said I; 'and let us not be severed.'

'Miserable boy!' cried the Egyptian; 'was this, then, the strange and preternatural doom which my Art foresaw was to be thine, though it deciphered not its nature? Knowest thou that this Fire, so clear – so pure – so beautiful – is—'

'Beware!' cried the voice from the Fire; and the crest of the flame rose, as the crest of a serpent about to spring upon its prey.

'Thou awest me not,' said the Egyptian, though the blood fled from his shrivelled and tawny cheeks. 'Thou art—'

'The Principle of the Living World,' interrupted the voice.

'And thine other name?' cried the Egyptian.

'Thy Conqueror!' answered the voice; and straight as the answer went forth, the Egyptian fell, blasted as by lightning, a corpse at my feet. The light of the Fire played with a blue and tremulous lustre upon the carcase, and presently I beheld by that light that the corpse was already passed into the loathsomeness of decay – the flesh was rotting from the bones – and the worm and the creeping thing which the rottenness generates, twined in the very jaws and temples of the Sage.

I sickened and gasped for breath. 'Is this thy work, oh fearful fiend?' said I, shuddering. And the Fire, passing from the corpse, crept humbly to my feet; and its voice answered – 'Whatever my power, it is thy slave!'

'Was that death thy work?' repeated my quivering lips.

'Thou knowest,' answered the Fire, 'that death is not the will of any Power – save One. The death came from His will, and I but exulted over the blow!'

I left the cavern; my art, subtle as it was, gave me no glimpse into the causes of the Egyptian's death. I looked upon the Fire, as it crept along the herbage, with an inquisitive, yet timorous eye. I felt an awe of the Demon's power; and yet the proud transport I had known in the subjection of that power was increased, and I walked with a lofty step at the thought that I should have so magnificent a slave. But the words of the mysterious Egyptian still rang in my ear – still I shuddered and recoiled before his denunciation of the secret I desired to know. And, as I passed along the starry solitude, the voice of the Fire addressed me with a sweet and persuasive tone. 'Shrink not, young Sage,' it said, or rather sang, 'from a power beyond that of which thy wisest ancestors ever dreamed; lose not thy valour at the drivelling whispers of age: when did age ever approve what youth desires? Thou art formed for the destiny which belongs to royal hearts – the destiny courts thee. Why dost thou play the laggard?'

'Knowledge,' said I, musingly, 'can never be productive of woe. If it be knowledge thou canst give me, I will not shrink. Lo! I accept thy gift!'

The Fire played cheerily to and fro. And from the midst of it there stepped forth a pale and shadowy form, of female shape and of exceeding beauty; her face was indeed of no living wanness, and the limbs were indistinct, and no roundness swelled from their vapoury robes; but the features were lovely as a dream, and long yellow hair – glowing as sunlight – fell adown her neck. 'Thou wouldst pierce,' said she, 'to the Principle of the World. Thou wouldst that thine eye should penetrate into my fair and mystic dominion. But not yet; there is an ordeal to pass. To the Whole Knowledge thou must glide through the Imperfect!' Then the female kissed my eyes, and vanished, and with it vanished also the Fire.

Oh, beautiful! – Oh, wondrous! – Oh, divine! A scale had fallen from my sight – and a marvellous glory was called forth upon the face of earth. I saw millions and millions of spirits shooting to and fro athwart the air – spirits that my magic had never yet invoked – spirits of rainbow hues, and quivering with the joy which made their nature. Wherever I turned my gaze, life upon life was visible. Every blade of grass swarmed with myriads invisible to the common eye – but performing with mimic regularity all the courses of the human race; every grain of dust, every drop of water, was a world – mapped into countless tribes, all fulfilling mortal destinies through the agency of mortal instincts – hunger and love and hate and contest. There was no void in space, no solitude in creation. Bending my eyes below, I saw emerging from the tiny hollows of the earth those fantastic and elfin shapes that have been chiefly consecrated by your Northern Bards: forth they came merrily, merrily – now circling in choral dances, now chasing gossamers whose airy substance eludes the glass of science. If all around was life, it was the life of enchantment and harmony – a subtle, pervading element of delight. Speech left me for very joy, and I gazed, thrilled and breathless, around me – entered, as it were, into the innermost temple of the great system of the universe.

I looked round for the Fire – it was gone. I was alone amidst this new and populous creation, and I stretched myself voluptuously beneath a tree, to sate my soul with wonder. As a Poet in the height of his delirium was my rapture – my veins were filled with Poesy, which is intoxication – and my eyes had been touched with Poesy, which is the creative power – and the miracles before me were the things of Poesy, which is the enchanter's wand.

Days passed, and the bright Demon which had so gifted me appeared not, nor yet did the spell cease; but every hour, every moment, new marvels rose. I could not touch stone nor herb without coming into a new realm utterly different from those I had yet seen, but equally filled with life – so that there was never a want of novelty; and had I been doomed to pass my whole existence upon three feet of earth, I might have spent that existence in perpetual variety – in unsatisfied and eternally new research. But most of all, when I sought Lyciah I rejoiced in the gift I possessed; for in conversing with her my sense penetrated to her heart, and I felt, as with a magnetic sympathy, moving through its transparent purity, the thoughts and emotions which were all my own.

By degrees I longed indeed to make her a sharer in my discovered realms; for I now slowly began to feel the weariness of a conqueror who reigns alone – none to share my power or partake the magnificence in which I dwelt.

One day, even in the midst of angelic things that floated

blissfully round me – so that I heard the low melodies they hymned as they wheeled aloft – one day this pining, this sense of solitude in life – of satiety in glory – came on me with intense increase of force. And I said, 'But this is the Imperfect state; why not achieve the Whole? Why not ascend to that high and empyreal Knowledge which admits of no dissatisfaction, because in itself complete? Bright Spirit,' cried I aloud, 'to whom I already owe so great a benefit, come to me now – why hast thou left me? Come and complete thy gifts. I see yet only the wonders of the secret portions of the world – touch mine eyes that I may see *the cause* of the wonders. I am surrounded with an air of life; let me pierce into the principle of that life. Bright Spirit, minister to thy servant!' Then I heard the sweet voice that had spoken in the Fire – but I saw not the Fire itself. And the voice said unto me—

'Son of the Wise Kings, I am here!'

'I see thee not,' said I. 'Why hidest thou thy lustre?'

'Thou seest the Half, and that very sight blinds thee to the Whole. This redundant flow of life gushes from me as from its source. When the midcourse of the river is seen, who sees also its distant spring? In thee, not myself, is the cause that thou beholdest me not. I am as I was when I bowed my crest to thy feet; but thine eyes are not what then they were!'

'Thou tellest me strange things, O Demon!' said I; 'for why, when admitted to a clearer sight of things, should my eyes be only darkened when they turn to thee?'

'Does not all knowledge, save the one right knowledge, only lead men from the discovery of the primal cause? As Imagination may soar aloft, and find new worlds, yet lose the solid truths of this one – so thou mayest rise into the regions of a preternatural lore, yet recede darklier and darklier from the clue to Nature herself.'

I mused over the words of the Spirit, but their sense seemed dim.

'Canst thou not appear to me in thine old, wan, and undulating brightness?' said I after a pause.

'Not until thine eyes receive power to behold me.'

'And when may I be worthy that power?'

'When thou art thoroughly dissatisfied with thy present gifts.'

'Dread Demon, I am so now!'

'Wilt thou pass from this pleasant state at a hazard – not knowing that which may ensue? Behold, all around thee is full of glory, and musical with joy! Wilt thou abandon that state for a dark and perilous Unknown?'

'The Unknown is the passion of him who aspires to know.'

'Pause; for there is terror in thy choice,' said the Invisible.

'My heart beats steadily. I brave whatsoever be the penalty that attends on my desire!'

'Thy wish is granted,' said the Spirit.

Then straightway a pang, quick, sharp, agonizing, shot through my heart. I felt the stream in my veins stand still, hardening into a congealed substance – my throat rattled, I struggled against the grasp of some iron power. A terrible sense of my own impotence seized me – my muscles refused my will, my voice fled – I was in the possession of some authority that had entered, and claimed, and usurped the citadel of my own self. Then came a creeping of the flesh, a numbing sensation of ice and utter coldness; and lastly, a blackness, deep and solid as a mass of rock, fell over the whole earth – I had entered DEATH!

From this state I was roused by the voice of the Demon. 'Awake, look forth! – Thou hast thy desire! – Abide the penalty!' The darkness broke from the earth; the ice thawed from my veins; once more my senses were my servants.

I looked, and behold, I stood in the same spot, but how changed! The earth was one crawling mass of putridity; its rich verdure, its lofty trees, its sublime mountains, its glancing waters, had all been the deceit of my previous blindness; the very green of the grass and the trees were rottenness, and the leaves (not each leaf one and inanimate as they seemed to the common eye) were composed of myriads of insects and puny reptiles, battened on the corruption from which they sprang. The waters swarmed with a leprous life – those beautiful shapes that I had seen in my late delusion were corrupt in their several parts, and from that corruption other creatures were generated living upon them. Every breath of air was *not* air, a thin and healthful fluid, but a wave of animalculae, poisonous and foetid; for the Air is the Arch Corrupter, hence all who breathe die; it is the slow, sure venom of Nature, pervading and rotting all things; the light of the heavens was the sickly, loathsome glare that steamed from the universal Death in Life. The World was one dead carcase, from which everything the World bore took its being. There was not such a thing as beauty! – there was not such a thing as life that did not generate from its own corruption a loathsome life for others! I looked down upon myself, and saw that my very veins swarmed with a motelike creation of shapes, springing into hideous existence from mine own disease, and mocking the Human Destiny with the same career of life, love, and death. Methought it must be a spell, which change of scene would annul. I shut my eyes with a frantic horror, and I fled, fast, fast, but blinded; and ever as I fled a laugh rang in my ears. I stopped not till I was at the feet of Lyciah, for she was my first involuntary thought. Whenever a care or fear possessed me, I had been wont to fly to her bosom, and charm my heart by the magic of her sweet voice. I was at the feet of Lyciah – I clasped her knees – I looked up imploringly into her face – God of my Fathers! the same curse attended me still! Her beauty was gone. There was no whole, no one life in that Being whom I had so adored. Her life was composed of a million lives; her stately shape, of atoms crumbling from each other, and so bringing about the ghastly state of corruption which reigned in all else around. Her delicate hues, her raven hair, her fragrant lips— Pah! What, what was my agony! I turned from her again, I shrank in loathing from her embrace, I fled once more, on – on. I ascended a mountain, and looked down on the various leprosies of Earth. Sternly I forced myself to the task; sternly I inhaled the knowledge I had sought; sternly I drank in the horrible penalty I had dared.

'Demon!' I cried, 'appear, and receive my curse!'

'Lo, I am by thy side evermore,' said the voice. Then I gazed, and, behold, the Fire was by my side; and I saw that it was the livid light which the jaws of Rottenness emits; and in the midst of the light which was as its shroud and garment, stood a Giant shape – which was the shape of a Corpse that had been for months buried. I gazed upon the Demon with an appalled yet unquailing eye, and, as I gazed, I recognized in those ghastly lineaments a resemblance to the Female Spirit that had granted me the first fatal gift. But exaggerated, enlarged, dead, Beauty rotted into Horror.

'I am that which thou didst ask to see face to face. I am the Principle of Life.'

'Of Life! Out, horrible mocker! – hast thou no other name?'

'I have! and that name – CORRUPTION!'

'Bright Lamps of Heaven!' I cried, lifting my eyes in anguish from the loathly charnel of the universal earth; 'and is this which men call Nature, is this the sole Principle of the World?'

As I spoke, the huge carcase beneath my feet trembled. And over the face of the corpse beside me there fell a fear. And lo! the heavens were lit up with a pure and glorious light, and from the midst of them there came forth a Voice which rolled slowly over the charnel earth as the voice of thunder above the valley of the shepherd. 'SUCH,' said the Voice, 'IS NATURE, IF THOU ACCEPTEST NATURE AS THE FIRST CAUSE – SUCH IS THE UNIVERSE WITHOUT A GOD!'

The Kiss of Fate

There came a man to Philae. Watching from a pylon top whither I had gone to pray alone, I saw him land upon the island and from far off noted that he was a godlike man, clad in armour such as the Grecians used, over which was thrown a common cloak, hooded as though to disguise him; one who had the air of a warrior. At a distance from the temple gate he halted and looked upward as though something drew his glance to me standing high above him upon the pylon top. I could not see his face because of the shadow thrown by the great walls behind which the sun was sinking, but doubtless he could see me well enough, whose shape was outlined against the veil of golden light that must have touched me with its glory, though, as that light was behind me, my face also would be hidden from him. At least he stood a little while as though amazed, staring upward steadily, then bowed his head and passed into the temple, followed by men bearing burdens.

Some pilgrim to the shrine, I thought to myself, then turned my mind to other matters, remembering that with men I had no more to do. Thus for the first time here in the body, all unknowing, I looked upon Kallikrates and he looked on me, but often I have thought that there was a veiled lesson or a parable in the fashion of this meeting.

For did I not stand far above him, clothed in the glory of heaven's gold, and did he not stand far beneath in the gloom of the shadows that lay upon the lowly earth, so that between us there was space unclimbable? And has it not been ever thus throughout the centuries, for am I not still upon the pylon top clad in the splendour of the spirit, and is he not still far beneath me wrapped with the shadows of the flesh? And since as yet the secret of the pylon stair is hidden from him, must I not descend to earth if we would meet, leaving the light and my pride of place that I may walk humbly with him in the shadow? And is it not often so between those that love, that one is set far above the other, though still this rope of love draws them together, uplift-ing the one, or dragging down the other?

The man passed into the temple and that night I heard he was a Grecian captain of high blood, one who though young had seen much service in the wars and done great deeds, Kallikrates by name, who had come to seek the counsel of the goddess, bringing precious gifts of gold and Eastern silks, the spoils of battle in which he had fought.

I asked why such a one sought the wisdom of Isis, and was told that it was because his heart was troubled. It seemed that he had been dwelling at Pharaoh's court as a captain of the Grecian guard, and that there he had quarrelled with and slain one who was as a brother to him, if indeed he were not his very brother. This ill deed, it was said, preyed upon his soul and drove him into the arms of Mother Isis, seeking for pardon and that comfort which he could not find at the hand of any of the gods of the Greeks.

Again I asked idly enough why this Kallikrates had killed his familiar friend or his brother, whichever it might be. The answer was — because of some highly-placed maiden whom both of them loved, so that they fought from jealousy, after the fashion of men. For this reason the life of Kallikrates was held to be forfeit according to the stern military law of the Grecian soldiers, and he must fly. Also the deed had tarnished that great lady's name; also his heart was broken with remorse and hither he came to pray Isis to mend it of her mercy, he who had forsaken the world.

The tale moved a little, but again I cast it from my mind, for are not such common among men? Always the story is the same; two men and a woman, or two women and a man, and bloodshed and remorse and memories which will not die and the cry for pardon that is so hard to find.

Yes, I cast it from my mind, saying lightly — oh! those evil-omened words — that doubtless his own blood in a day to come would pay for that which he had spilt.

For a while, some months indeed, this Grecian Kallikrates vanished from my sight and even from my thoughts, save when, from time to time, I heard of him as studying the Mysteries among the priests, having, it was said, determined to renounce the world and be sworn to the service of the goddess. Noot, the high priest, told me that he was very earnest in this design and made great progress in the faith, which pleased the priests who desired above everything to convert those that served Grecian gods with whom the deities of Egypt, and most of all Isis, were at war. Therefore they hastened his preparation, so that as soon as might be he should be bound to the heavenly Queen by bonds that could not be loosed.

At length his fasts and instruction were finished; his trials had been passed and the hour came when he must make his last confession to the goddess and swear the awful oaths to her very self.

Now as Isis did not descend to earth to stand face to face with every neophyte, it was needful in this great ceremony that one filled with her spirit should take her place and, as may be guessed, that one was I, Ayesha the Arab. To speak truth, in all Egypt because of my beauty, my learning and the grace that was given to me, there was none so fitting to wear her mantle as myself. Indeed afterward this was acknowledged when, with a single voice, the Colleges of her servants throughout the land, men and women together promoted me to be her high-priestess, and gave me, who at first among them was known by the title of Wisdom's Daughter, the new name of *Isis come to earth*, or in shorter words, *The Isis*. For my own name of Ayesha I kept hid lest it should be discovered that I was that chieftainess, the child of Yarab, who had defeated the army of Nectanebes.

Therefore at a certain hour of the night, draped in the holy robes, wearing on my brow the vulture cap and the bent symbol of the moon, holding in my hands the *sistrum* and the cross of Life, I was conducted to the pillared sanctuary and seated alone upon a throne of blackest marble, with the round symbol of the world for my footstool.

Thus, having learned my part and the ancient hallowed words that I must say, I sat awhile, wondering in my heart whether Isis herself could be more glorious or more fair. So indeed did the priests and priestesses who saw me thus arrayed and bent the knee to me as though I were the very goddess, which in truth some of the humbler among them half believed.

Thus I sat in the moonlight that flowed from the unroofed hall beyond, while the carven gods watched me with their quiet eyes.

At length I heard the sound of footsteps whereon there came a priestess and flung over me the white veil of innocence sewn with golden stars that, until the appointed moment, must hide Isis from her worshipper. The priestess withdrew and, wrapped in the dark, hooded robe that signified the stained flesh about to be cast away, which hid all of him so that his face could not be seen, appeared that tall neophyte led by two priests who held his right hand and his left. I noted those hands because they were so white against the blackness of the robe, and even by the moonlight saw that they were beautiful, long, thin and shapely, though one, the right, was somewhat broadened as though by the long handling of the tools of war.

The priests led him to the entrance to the shrine and in hushed whispers bade him kneel upon a footstool and make his sacrifice and confession to the goddess as he had been taught to do. Then they departed leaving us alone.

There followed silence which at length I broke, whispering: .

'Who is this that comes to visit the Mother in her earthly shrine and what is his prayer to the Queen of Heaven and Earth?'

Though I spoke so gently and so low, perhaps because of their quiet sweetness, my words seemed to frighten him; or perhaps he believed that he stood in the very presence of the goddess; at least he answered in a trembling voice:

'O holy Queen adored, in the world I was named Kallikrates the comely. But the priests, O Queen, have given me a new name, and it is, *Lover of Isis.*'

'What have you to say to Isis, O Lover of Isis?'

'O Queen eternal, I come to tell my sins and ask her pardon for them, I who have passed the Trials and am accepted by her servants. If it is granted, then to her I must make the oath, binding myself eternally to love and serve her, her and no other in heaven or on earth.'

'Set out those sins, O Lover of Isis, that my Majesty may judge of them, whether they can be forgiven or are beyond forgiveness,' I answered in the words of the appointed ritual.

Then he began and told a tale that made me redden behind my veil, for all of it had to do with women, and never before had I learned what wantons those Greeks could be. Also he told me of men whom he had slain in war, one of them in the battle against my tribe, in which strangely enough it seemed he had fought as a lad, for this man was a great warrior. Of these killings, however, I took no account, because they had been of those who were the enemies of himself or of his cause.

In stern silence I listened, noting that save for these matters of light love and fightings, the man seemed innocent enough, for in his story there was naught of baseness or of betrayal. Moreover it seemed that he was one in whom the spirit had striven against the flesh, and who, however much his feet were tangled in the bitter snares of earth, from time to time had set his eyes on Heaven.

At length he paused and I asked of him:

'Is the black count finished? Tell now the truth and dare to hold nothing back from the goddess who notes all.'

'Nay, O Queen,' he answered, 'the worst is yet to speak. I came to Egypt as a captain of the Grecian guard that watches the House of Pharaoh of Sais. With me came another captain, my half-brother, for our father was the same, with whom I was brought up and loved as never I loved any other man, and who loved me. He was a glorious warrior, though some held that I was more handsome in my person. Tisisthenes by name, that in my Grecian tongue in which I speak, means the Avenger. Thus was he called because my father, whose firstborn he was, desired that he might grow up to work vengeance upon the Persians who slew his father named like myself, Kallikrates, the most beauteous Spartan that was ever born. Foully they slew him before the battle of Plataea, whilst he was aiding the great Pausanius to make sacrifice to the gods. This Tisisthenes my brother I killed with my own hand.'

'For what cause did you kill him?'

'There was a royal maiden at that Court, one fairer than any woman has been, is or will be — ask not her name, O Mother, though doubtless it is known to you already. This lady both of us saw at the same time and by the decree of Aphrodite, both of us loved. As it chanced it was I who won her favour, not my brother. We were spied upon; the tale was told; trouble fell upon that royal maiden who, when she should be old enough, was sworn in marriage to a distant king. To save her name she made denial, as she must do. She swore there was naught between her and me, and to prove it turned her face from me and towards my brother. I came upon them together in a garden. She had plucked a flower which she gave to him and he kissed the hand that held the flower. She saw me and fled away. I, maddened with jealousy, smote my beloved brother in the face and forced him to fight with me. We fought. He guarded himself but ill, as though he cared nothing of the end of that fray. I cut him down. He lay before me dying, but before he died he spoke:

' "This is a very evil business," he said. "Know, Kallikrates, my most beloved brother, that what you saw in the garden between that royal maid and myself was but a plot to save you both, since thereby I proposed to take on to my own head the weight of your transgression against the law of this land, because she prayed it and it was my wish. This I have done and for this reason I suffered you to slay me, though during that fight twice I could have pierced you, because you were blind with rage and forgot your swordsmanship. Now it will be said that you found me pursuing this royal maiden and rightly slew me according to your duty and that it was I who loved her and not you, as has been commonly reported. Yet in truth I love her well and am glad to die because it was to you that her heart turned and not to me; also because thereby I save both her and you. Yet, Kallikrates, my brother, in this the hour of my death, the gods give me wisdom and foresight and I say that you will do well to have done with this lady and all women, and to seek rest in the bosom of the gods, since if you do not, great trouble will come upon you, and through this same curse of jealousy, such a death as mine shall be yours also. Now let us who are the victims of Fate, kiss each other on the brow as we used to do when we were children playing together in the happy fields of Greece, from whom death was yet a long way off, forgiving each other all and hoping that we may meet once more in the region of the Shades."

'So we embraced and my brother Tisisthenes gave up his spirit in my arms and looking on him I wished that I were dead in his place. Then as I turned to go the soldiers of our company found me and seeing that I had slain my brother, would have brought me to trial, not because we had fought together, but because he was my superior in rank and therefore I who, being under his command, drew sword on him, by the law of the Greeks must die. Yet before I could be put upon my trial, some of those who loved me and guessed the truth of the business, thrust me out of our camp disguised, with all the treasure that I had won in war, bidding me hide myself awhile till the matter was forgotten. O Queen, I did not desire to go; nay, I desired to stay and to pay the price of my sin. But they would not have it so. I think indeed that there were others behind, great ones of Egypt, moving in this matter; at least I was thrust forth all being made easy for me, and all eyes growing blind.'

Again he paused and I, Ayesha, clothed as the goddess, asked:

'And what did you then, you who could slay your brother for the sake of a woman?'

'Then, divine One, I fled up Nile where, because of the trouble that was in the land, Pharaoh's arm could not reach me, nor the arm of the commander of the Greeks. Tarrying not and without speech with that high maiden who was the cause of my sin, I fled up Nile.'

'Why did you fly up Nile and not back to your own people, O most sinful man?'

'Because my heart was broken, Queen, and I desired to seek the mercy of Isis whose law I had learned already and to become her priest. I knew that those who bow themselves to her may look no more on woman, but henceforth must live virgin to the death, and it was my own will to look no more on woman, since woman had stained my hands with a brother's blood, and therefore I hated her.'

Now I, Ayesha, asked:

'What gods did you worship before your heart was turned to Isis, Queen of Heaven?'

'I worshipped the gods of Greece and first among them Aphrodite, Lady of Love.'

'Who has paid you well for your service, making of you a murderer of one of your own blood who, before she blinded your eyes, was more to you than any on the earth. Do you then renounce this wanton Aphrodite?'

'Aye, Queen, I renounce her for ever. Never more will I offer at her altars or look on woman in the way of love. If I may have pardon for my sins, here and now I vow myself to Isis as her faithful priest and servant. Here and now I blot out the name of Aphrodite; yea, I reject her gifts and tread down all her memories beneath my aspiring feet that at last shall bear my heart to peace.'

Thus the man spoke in a quivering and earnest voice, and was silent. Yes, deep silence reigned in that holy place, whilst I, Ayesha, although it is true that as a woman I misdoubted me of such rash oaths, as the minister of the goddess, prepared myself to grant pardon to this seeker in the hallowed, immemorial words, and to open to his troubled soul the doors of purity and eternal rest.

Then suddenly in that silence clearly I heard the sound of silvern laughter; soft, sweet laughter that seemed to come from the skies above and though it was so low to fill the shrine and all the hall beyond. I looked about me but could see nothing. It would seem that the Greek heard also, for he turned his head and glanced behind him, then once more let it fall upon his hands.

Whence came that sound? Could it be that the queen of love. . .? Nay, it was impossible, and not thus would I be turned from my office, I who was clothed with the robe and for that hour wielded the might of Isis.

'Hearken, O man, in the world named Kallikrates,' I said. 'On behalf of Isis, the All-Mother, Goddess of virtue and of wisdom, speaking with her voice, hearing with her ears, and filled with her soul, I wash you clean of all your sins and accept you as her priest, promising to you light burdens on the earth and beyond the earth great rewards for ever. First swear the oath that may not be broken, and then draw near that I may kiss you on the brow, accepting you as the slave and lover of Isis, from this day until the moon, her heavenly throne, shall crumble into nothingness.'

Having spoken thus, letting the words fall one by one, slowly as the tears of that penitent fell upon the ground, I uttered the oath, the form of which even now I will not write.

It was a dreadful oath covering all things, and binding him who took it to Isis alone, an oath that if it were forgot, wrought upon the traitor the age-long doom of death in this world and woe in the worlds to come, till by slow steps, with pierced heart and bleeding feet, the holy height from which he had fallen should be climbed again.

At length it was finished and he said faintly:

'I swear! With fear and trembling still I swear!'

Then I beckoned to him with the *sistrum* of which the little shaken bells made a faint compelling music that already he had learned to follow, and he came and kneeled before me. There I laid the Cross of Life upon his head and gave him blessing, laid it upon his lips and gave him wisdom, laid it upon his heart and gave him breath for thousands upon thousands of years. All these things I did in the name and with the strength of Isis the Mother.

Came the last rite, the greeting of the Mother to her child new born in spirit, the rite of the Kiss of Welcome. At that moment supreme a light fell on me from above: perchance it came from Heaven, perchance it was but an art of the watching priests; I do not know. At least it fell upon me illumining my glittering robes and jewelled head-dress with a soft splendour in the darkness of that shrine. At that moment, too, at a touch my veil fell down, so that the moonlight struck full upon my face making it mystical and lovely in the frame of my flowing hair.

The priest new-ordained lifted his bent head that I might consecrate his brow with the kiss of welcome, and his hood fell back. The moonlight shone on his face also, his beautiful face like that of a sculptured Grecian god; shapely, fine-featured, large-eyed and crowned with little golden curls — for as yet he was unshorn; yes, a face more beautiful than that which I had seen on any man, set above a warrior's tall and sinewy form.

By Isis! I knew this face; it was that which had haunted me from my childhood, that which often I had seen in a dream of halls beyond the earth, that of a man who in this dream had been sworn to me to complete my womanhood. Oh! I could not doubt, it was the same, the very same, and looking on it, the curse of Aphrodite fell upon me and for the first time I knew the madness of our mortal flesh. Yea, my being was rent and shattered like a cedar beneath the lightning stroke; I was smitten through and through. I, the priestess of Isis, proud and pure, was as lost as any village maid within her lover's arms.

The man, too! He saw me and his aspect changed; the holy fervour went out of his eyes and into them entered something more human, something more fateful. It was as though he too remembered — I know not what.

By a mighty effort of the will, aware that the eyes of the

goddess and perhaps of her priests also were upon me, I conquered myself and with beating heart and heaving breast bent down to touch his brow with the Kiss of Ceremony. Yet, I know not how — I know not if the fault were his or mine or perchance that of both of us — I touched his *lips* and not his brow, just touched them and no more.

It was nothing, or at any rate but a little thing, in one instant come and gone, and yet to me it was all. For in that touch I broke my holy vows, and he, new-sworn to the worship of the goddess, broke his, yes, in the very act of sacrifice. What drove us to it? I do not know, but once again I thought I heard that low, triumphant laughter and it came into my mind that we were the sport of an indomitable power greater than ourselves and all the oaths that mortals swear to gods or men.

I waved my sceptre. The new-made priest rose, bowed and withdrew, I wondering of whom he was the priest — of Isis or of Aphrodite. The singing of a distant choir broke out upon the silence, the heirophants came and led him away to be of their company till his death: the ceremony was ended. My attendants, arrayed as the goddesses Hathor and Nut, conducted me from the shrine. I was unrobed of my sacred panoplies and once more from a goddess became a woman. Then as a woman I sought my couch and wept and wept.

For in my heart, had I not at the first temptation broken the law and betrayed the trust of her who, as then I believed, is and was and shall be; her whose veil no mortal man had lifted, the Mother of the sun and all its stars?

The Tale of Philo

This tale is a sequel to that called The Kiss of Fate. *Egypt has been invaded; Noot, the high priest of Isis, and the new priest Kallikrates have sailed away down the Nile. Ayesha, high priestess of Isis, guided by the sea captain Philo, is endeavouring to find them.*

Once more it was the night of full moon. As we had done for many days, we were sailing before that steady wind along the coast of Libya, having this upon our right hand, and upon our left at a distance a line of rocky reef upon which breakers fell continually.

It was a very splendid moon that turned the sea to silver and lit up the palm-grown shore almost as brightly as does the sun. I sat upon the deck near to my cabin and by me stood Philo watching that shore.

'For what do you seek, Philo? Are you in fear of sunken rocks?'

'Nay, child of Isis, yet it is true that I seek a certain rock of which, by my reckoning, we should now be in sight. Ah!'

Then suddenly he ran foward and shouted an order. Men leaped and sprang to the ropes while the rowers began to get out the sweeps. As they did this the *Hapi* came round so that her bow pointed to the shore and the great sail sank to the deck. Then the long oars drove us shorewards.

Philo returned.

'Look, lady,' he said. 'Now that the moon has risen higher you can see well,' and he pointed to a headland in front of us.

Following his outstreched hand with my eyes I perceived a great rock many cubits in height and, carvèn on the crest of it, a head far larger than that of the huge Sphinx of Egypt. Or perchance it was not carved; perchance Nature had fashioned it thus. At least there it stood and will stand, a terrible and hideous

---

Hutchinson's Magazine, September 1922.

thing, having the likeness of an Ethiopian's head gazing eternally across the sea.

'What is it?' I asked.

'Lady, it is the guardian of the gate of the land whither we go. Legend tells that it is shaped to the likeness of the first king of that land who lived thousands upon thousands of years before the pyramids were built; also that his bones lie in it, or at least, that it is haunted by his spirit. For this reason none dare to touch and much less to climb yonder monstrous rock.'

Then he left me to see to the matters of the ship, because, as he said in going, the entrance to the place was narrow and dangerous. But I sat on alone upon the deck watching this strange new sight.

Within an hour, rowing carefully, we entered the mouth of a river, having the rock shaped like a negro's head upon our right. Then it was that I saw something which put me in mind of Philo's tale about an ancient king. For there, unless I dreamed, upon the very point of the skull of the effigy, of a sudden I perceived a tall form clad in armour which shone silvery bright in the moon's rays. It leaned upon a great spear and when we were opposite to it, it straightened itself and bent forward as though to stare at our ship beneath. Next, thrice it lifted the spear in salutation; thrice it bowed, as I thought in obeisance to me, and having done so, threw its arms wide and was gone.

Afterwards I asked Philo if he also had seen this shape.

'Nay,' he answered in a doubtful voice as though the matter were one of which he did not wish to talk, adding:

'It is not the custom of mariners to study that head in moonlight, because the story goes that if they do and chance to see some such ghost as that you tell of, it casts a spear towards them, who then are doomed to die within the year. Yet at you, child of Isis, he cast no spear, only bowed and gave the salute of kings, or so you tell me. Therefore doubtless neither you nor any of us, your companions, are marked for death.'

I smiled and said that I whose soul was in touch with heaven, feared not the wraith of any ancient king, nor did we speak more of this matter. Yet in the after ages it came into my mind that there was truth in the story and that this long-dead chieftain appeared thus to give greeting to her who was destined to rule his land through many generations; also that perchance he was not dead at all, but, having drunk of a certain cup of life of which I was to learn, lived eternally there upon the rock.

I laid me down and slept and when I woke in the bright morning, it was to find that we had passed from that river into a canal dug by man, which, though deep, was too narrow for the sweeps to work. Therefore the *Hapi* must be pushed along with poles and towed by ropes dragged at by the mariners from a path that ran upon the bank.

For three days we travelled thus making but slow progress, since the toil of dragging so large a ship was great, and at night we tied up to the bank, as boats do upon the Nile. All this while we saw no habitation though of ruins there were many. Indeed, that country was very desolate and full of great swamps that were tenanted by wild beasts, the haunt of owls and bitterns, where lions roared and serpents crept, great serpents such as I had never seen.

At length at noon on the fourth day we came to a lake where the canal ended, which lake once had been a harbour, for we saw stone quays to which were tied some boats that seemed to be little used. Here Philo said that we must disembark and travel on by land. So we left the *Hapi*, sadly enough for my part, because those were happy, quiet days that I had spent on board of her, veritable oases in the storm-swept desert of my life.

Scarcely had we set foot upon the land when appeared, I knew not whence, a company of men, handsome, hook-nosed, sombre men, such as I had seen among the crew upon the *Hapi*. These men, though so fierce of countenance, were not barbarians for they wore linen garments that gave to them the aspects of priests. Moreover, their leaders could speak Arabic in its most ancient form which, having studied it as it chanced, I knew. With this army, who bore bows and spears, came a multitude of folk of a baser sort that carried litters, or burdens, also a guard of great fellows who, Philo told me, were my escort. Now my patience failed so that I turned to Philo saying angrily,

'Hitherto, friend, I have trusted myself to you, because it seemed decreed that I should do so. Tell me, I pray you, for what reason I journey over countless leagues of sea into a land untrod, and whither I go in the fellowship of these barbarians? Because you brought me a certain writing in an acceptable hour, I gave myself into your keeping, nor did I so much as ask light from the goddess or seek to solve the mystery of its spells. Yet, now, as the Prophetess of Isis, I demand the truth of you, her humbler servant.'

'Lady divine,' answered Philo, bowing himself before me, 'what I have withheld is by command, the command of a very great one, of none less than Noot, the aged and holy. You go to an old land that is yet new, to find Noot, your master and mine.'

'In the flesh or in the spirit?' I asked.

'In the flesh, prophetess, if he lives, as these men say, and see, I accompany you, I whom you have found faithful in the past. If I fail you, let my life pay forfeit, and for the rest, ask it of the holy Noot.'

'It is enough,' I said. 'Lead on.'

We entered the litters; we laded the bearers with the treasures of Isis and with my own peculiar wealth, and having placed the ship *Hapi* under guard, marched into the unknown, like to some great caravan of merchants. For days we marched, following a broad road that was broken down in places, over plains and through vast swamps, at night sleeping in caves, or covered by tents which we had brought with us.

This was a strange journey which I made surrounded by that host of hook-nosed, silent, ghost-like men, who, as I noted, loved the night better than they did the day. Almost I might have thought that they had been sent from Hades to conduct us to those gates from which for mortals there is no return. My fellowship of the priests and priestesses grew afraid and clustered round me at night, praying to be led back to familiar lands and faces.

I answered them that what I dared, they must dare also, and that the goddess was as near to us here as she had been in Egypt, nor could death be closer to us than it was in Egypt. Yea, I bade them have faith, since without faith we could not be at peace one hour, who, lacking it, must be overwhelmed with terrors, even within the walls of citadels.

They listened, bowing their heads and saying that whatever else they might doubt, they trusted themselves to me.

So we went on, passing through a country where more of these half-savage men, that I learned were called *Amahagger*, surrounded by their cattle, dwelt in villages or by colonies in caves. At last there arose before us a mighty mountain whose towering cliffs had the appearance of a wall so vast that the eye could not compass it. By a gorge we penetrated that mountain and found within it an enormous, fertile plain, and on the plain a city larger than Memphis or than Thebes, but a city half in ruins.

Passing over a great bridge spanning a wide moat, once filled with water, that now here and there was dry, we entered the walls of that city and by a street broader than any I had ever seen, bordered by many noble, broken houses, though some of these seemed still to be inhabited, came to a glorious temple like to those of Egypt, only greater, and with taller columns. Across its grass-grown courts that were set one within another, we were carried to an inner sanctuary. Here we descended from the litters and were led to sculptured chambers that seemed to have been made ready to receive us, where we cleansed ourselves of the dust of travel, and ate. Then came Philo who conducted me to a little lamp-lit hall, for now the night had fallen, where was a chair of state such as high-priests used, in which at his bidding I sat myself.

I think that being weary with travel, I must have slept in that chair, since I dreamed or seemed to dream, that I received worship such as is given to a queen, or even to a goddess. Heralds hailed me, sweet voices sang to me, spirits appeared in troops to talk to me, the spirits of those who thousands of years before had departed from the earth. They told me strange stories of the past and of the future; tales of a fallen people, of a worship and a glory that had gone by and been swallowed in the gulfs of time. Then gathering in a multitude they seemed to hail me, crying,

'Welcome, appointed queen! Build thou up that which has fallen. Discover thou that which is lost. Thine is the strength, thine the opportunity, yet beware of the temptations, beware of the flesh, lest the flesh should overcome the spirit and by its fall add ruin unto ruin, the ruin of the soul to the ruin of the body.'

I awoke from my vision and saw Philo standing before me.

'Hearken, Philo,' I said. 'I can bear no more of these mysteries. The time has come when you must speak, or face my wrath. Why have I been brought to this strange and distant land where it seems that I must dwell in a place of ruins?'

'Because the holy Noot so commanded, O child of wisdom,'

he answered. 'Was it not set down in the writing I gave you at the Isle of Reeds upon the Nile?'

'Where then is the holy Noot?' I asked. 'I see him not. Is he dead?'

'I do not think that he is dead, lady. Yet to the world he is dead. He has become a hermit, one who dwells in a cave in a perilous place not very far from this city. Tomorrow I will bring you to him, if that be your will. Thus only can you see him who now for years has never left that cave, or so I think, unless it be to fetch the food which is prepared for him.'

'A strange tale, Philo, though that Noot should become a hermit does not amaze me, for such was ever his desire. Now tell me how he came here, and you with him?'

'Lady, you will remember that in the bygone years when Nectanebes, he who was Pharaoh, fled up Nile, the holy Noot embarked upon my ship, the *Hapi*, to sail to the northern cities, that there he might treat with the Persians for the ransom of those temples of Egypt that remained unravished.'

'I remember, Philo. What chanced to you upon that journey?'

'This, lady: that we were very nearly slain, every one of us, for whom the Persians had set a trap, thinking to snare Noot and his company, and torture him till he revealed where the treasures of the temples of Isis were buried. Nevertheless, because I am a good sailor and because that warrior priest, Kallikrates, was brave, we escaped into the canal which is called the *Road of Rameses*, and so at last out to sea, for to return up Nile was impossible. Then Noot commanded that I should sail on southerly upon a course he seemed to know well enough; or perhaps the goddess taught it to him; I cannot say. At least I obeyed, so that in the end we reached that harbour which is guarded by a rock carved to the likeness of an Ethiopian's head, and thence travelled to this place, still guided by the wisdom of Noot who knew the road.'

'And Kallikrates? What chanced to Kallikrates — who, it seems, was with you?' I asked in an indifferent voice, though my heart burned to hear his answer.

'Lady, so far as it is known to me, this is the story of Kallikrates and the Princess Amenartas.'

'*The Princess Amenartas!* By all the gods, what is your meaning, Philo? She went up Nile with Nectanebes her father, he who was Pharaoh.'

'Nay, lady, she went *down* Nile with Kallikrates, or perhaps with Noot, or perhaps with herself alone. I do not know with whom she hid, since I never saw her, nor learned that she was aboard my ship until we were two days' journey out to sea, with the coasts of Egypt far behind us.'

'Is it so?' I asked coldly, though I was filled with bitter anger. 'And what did the holy Noot when he found that this woman was aboard his vessel?'

'Nothing, lady, except look on her somewhat doubtfully . and lead her to the cabin – that which was yours.'

'And the priest, Kallikrates? Did he strive to be rid of her?'

'Nay, lady, indeed that would have been impossible, unless he had cast her overboard. He, too, did nothing except talk with her – that is, so far as I saw.'

'Then, Philo, where is she now, and where is Kallikrates? I do not see him in this place?'

'Lady, I cannot tell you, but I think it probable that they are dead and in the fellowship of Osiris. When we had been some weeks at sea we were driven by storm to an island off the coast under the lee of which we took shelter, a very fertile and beautiful island, peopled by kindly folk. After we had sailed again from that island it was discovered that the priest Kallikrates and the royal Princess Amenartas were missing from the ship, nor because of the strong wind that blew us forward, was it possible for us to return to seek for them. I enquired of the matter and the sailors told me that they had been fishing together and that a shark which took their bait, pulled them both into the sea; in which case doubtless they were drowned.'

'And did you believe that story, Philo?'

'Nay, lady. I understood at once that it was one which the sailors had been bribed to tell. Myself I think that they went to the island in one of the boats of the people who dwell there; perhaps because they could no longer bear the cold eyes of Noot fixed upon them, or perhaps to gather fruit, for which those who have been long upon the sea often conceive a great desire. But,' he added simply, 'I do not know why they should have done this, seeing that the island-dwellers brought us aplenty of fruits in their boats.'

'Doubtless they preferred to pluck them fresh with their own hands, Philo.'

'Perhaps, lady; or perhaps they wished to stay awhile upon that island. At least I noted that the Princess took her garments and her jewels with her, which she could scarcely have done if the shark had dragged her into the sea.'

'Are you so sure, Philo, that she did not leave some of those jewels behind – in *your* keeping, Philo? It is very strange to me that the Princess Amenartas could have come aboard your ship and have left your ship and you know nothing.'

Now Philo looked up innocently and said,

'Surely it is lawful for a captain to receive faring money from his passengers, and that I admit I did. But I do not understand why the child of wisdom is so wroth because a Greek and a great lady were by chance left together upon an island where, for aught I know, one or other of them may have had friends.'

'Am I not the guardian of the honour of the goddess?' I answered. 'And do you not know that under our law Kallikrates was sworn to her alone?'

'If so, prophetess, doubtless that captain, or that priest, remembers his oaths and deals with this princess as though she were his sister or his mother. At the least, the goddess can guard her own honour, so why should you fret your soul concerning it, prophetess? Lastly, it is probable that by now both of them are dead and have made all things clear to Isis in the heavenly halls.'

Thus he prattled on, adding lie to lie as only a Greek can do. I listened until I could bear no more. Then I said but one word. It was 'Begone!'.

He went humbly, yet, as I thought, smiling.

Oh! now I understood. Noot had made a plot to remove Kallikrates far from me, so that I might never look upon him again. Philo knew of this plot, and through him Amenartas knew it also. Unknown to Noot, she bribed Philo to hide her upon his ship till they were far from land, though whether the plan was known to Kallikrates I could not say, nor did it greatly matter. Then the rest followed. Amenartas appeared upon the ship and cast her net about Kallikrates who had sworn to have done with her, and the end can be guessed. Noot was wroth with them, so wroth that when the chance came, they fled away, purposing to stay upon that island until they could find a ship to take them back to Egypt, or elsewhere. Thus I was sure, ran the story, and, as it proved afterwards, I was right.

Well, they were gone and as I hoped, dead, since only death could cover up such a sin, and for my part I was glad that I had done with Kallikrates and his light-of-love. And yet there, seated on the couch of state, I wept — because of the outrage done to Isis whom I served. Or was it for myself that I wept? I cannot say, I only know that my tears were bitter. Also I was very lonely in this strange and desolate place. Why had I been brought here, I wondered. Because Noot had commanded it, sending for me from afar, and what he commanded, that I must obey. Where, then, was Noot, who Philo swore, still lived? Why had he not appeared to greet me? I covered my eyes with my hands and threw out my soul to Noot, saying,

'Come to me, Noot. Come to me, my beloved master.'

Lo! a voice, a well-remembered voice answered.

'Daughter, I am here.'

I let fall my hands. I gazed with my tear-stained eyes, and behold! before me, white-robed, gold-filleted, snowy-bearded; grown very ancient and ethereal, stood the prophet and high-priest, my master. For a moment I thought that it was his spirit which I saw. Then he moved and I heard his white robes rustle, and knew that there stood Noot himself whom I had travelled far to find.

I rose; I ran to him; I seized his thin hand and kissed it, while he, murmuring, 'My daughter, at last, at last!' leaned forward and with his lips touched me on the brow.

'Far away your summons reached me in an hour of peril,' I said. 'Behold! I obeyed, I came. In faith I came, asking no questions, and I am here in safety, for I think the goddess herself was with me on that journey. Tell me all, O Noot. What is this place? How were you brought to it and why have you called me to you?'

'Hearken, daughter,' he said, seating himself beside me on the throne-like couch. 'This city is named Kôr. Once she was queen of the world, as after her Babylon, Tyre, Thebes, and Athens are, or have been queens. From Kôr thousands of years ago in the black, lost ages Egypt was peopled, as were other lands. In those dim days, by another title, her citizens worshipped Isis, queen of heaven, only they named her *Truth* whom in Egypt you know as Maat. Then apostasy arose and many of

36

this great people, abandoning the pure and gentle worship of Isis wrapped in the veil of truth, set up another god under the name of Rezu, a fierce sun-demon, to whom they made human sacrifices, as the Sidonians did to Moloch. Yea, they sacrificed men, women, and children by thousands, and even learned to eat their flesh, first as a sacred rite, and afterwards to satisfy their appetites. Heaven saw and grew wrath. Heaven smote the people with a mighty pestilence, so that they perished and perished till few were left. Thus Kôr fell by the sword of God as, for like cause, fell Sidon.'

'Of all this afterwards,' I answered impatiently. 'Tell me first, how came you here? Long years ago you sailed down Nile to treat with the Persians for the ransom of the temples of Isis, a mission in which it seems you failed, my father.'

'Aye, Ayesha, I failed. It was but a trap, since those false-hearted fire-worshippers thought to take me captive and hold my life in gage against all the treasures of Isis. By the cunning and seamanship of Philo and the courage of a priest named Kallikrates, whom you may still remember after all these years . . .' here he glanced at me sharply, 'I escaped when a gang of them disguised as envoys, strove to snare me. But the road up Nile being barred, we were forced to fly south, down Pharaoh's great ditch, till at length, after many wanderings and adventures, we came to this land, as it was fated that I should do. You will remember daughter that I told you I believed that we were parting for a long while, although I believed also that we should meet again in the flesh.'

'I remember well,' I answered, 'also that I swore to come to you at the appointed hour.'

'I came to this land,' went on Noot, 'but Kallikrates, the Greek captain who was a priest of Isis, never reached it. He was lost on the way.'

'With another, my father. I have heard that story from Philo.'

'With another who caused him to break his vows. Be sure, daughter, that I knew nothing of her plot or that she was hidden aboard the ship, though perchance Philo knew. The goddess hid it from me, doubtless for her own purposes.'

'Are this pair dead, or do they still live, my father?'

'I cannot say; that also is hidden from me. Better for them

if they are dead, since soon or late for such sacrilege vengeance will fall upon the head of one, if not of both of them. Peace be to them. May they be forgiven! At least, as I think they loved each other much and, since love is very strong, all should have pity on them who have ever loved where they ought not,' and again his questioning eyes played upon my face.

THE NAMELESS CITY

by H. P. Lovecraft

WHEN I drew nigh the nameless city I knew it was accursed. I was travelling in a parched and terrible valley under the moon, and afar I saw it protruding uncannily above the sands as parts of a corpse may protrude from an ill-made grave. Fear spoke from the age-worn stones of this hoary survivor of the deluge, this great-grandmother of the oldest pyramid; and a viewless aura repelled me and bade me retreat from antique and sinister secrets that no man should see, and no man else had ever dared to see.

Remote in the desert of Araby lies the nameless city, crumbling and inarticulate, its low walls nearly hidden by the sands of uncounted ages. It must have been thus before the first stones of Memphis were laid, and while the bricks of Babylon were yet unbaked. There is no legend so old as to give it a name, or to recall that it was ever alive; but it is told of in whispers around campfires and muttered about by grandmas in the tents of sheiks so that all the tribes shun it without wholly knowing why. It was of this place that Abdul Alhazred, the mad poet, dreamed on the night before he sang his unexplainable couplet :

"That is not dead which can eternal lie,
And with strange aeons even death may die."

I should have known that the Arabs had good reason for

shunning the nameless city, the city told of in strange tales but seen by no living man, yet I defied them and went into the untrodden waste with my camel. I alone have seen it, and that is why no other face bears such hideous lines of fear as mine; why no other man shivers so horribly when the night wind rattles the windows. When I came upon it in the ghastly stillness of unending sleep it looked at me, chilly from the rays of a cold moon amidst the desert's heat. And as I returned its look I forgot my triumph at finding it, and stopped still with my camel to wait for the dawn.

For hours I waited, till the east grew grey and the stars faded, and the grey turned to roseate light edged with gold. I heard a moaning and saw a storm of sand stirring among the antique stones though the sky was clear and the vast reaches of the desert still. Then suddenly above the desert's far rim came the blazing edge of the sun, seen through the tiny sandstorm which was passing away, and in my fevered state I fancied that from some remote depth there came a crash of musical metal to hail the fiery disc as Memnon hails it from the banks of the Nile. My ears rang and my imagination seethed as I led my camel slowly across the sand to that unvocal stone place; that place too old for Egypt and Meroe to remember; that place which I alone of living men had seen.

In and out amongst the shapeless foundations of houses and places I wandered, finding never a carving or inscription to tell of these men, if men they were, who built this city and dwelt therein so long ago. The antiquity of the spot was unwholesome, and I longed to encounter some sign or device to prove that the city was indeed fashioned by mankind. There were certain *proportions* and *dimensions* in the ruins which I did not like. I had with me many tools, and dug much within the walls of the obliterated edifices; but progress was slow, and nothing significant was revealed. When night and the moon returned I felt a chill wind which brought new fear, so that I did not dare to remain in the city. And as I went outside the antique walls to sleep, a small sighing sandstorm gathered behind me, blowing over the grey stones though the moon was bright and most of the desert still.

I awakened just at dawn from a pageant of horrible dreams, my ears ringing as from some metallic peal. I saw the sun peering redly through the last gusts of a little sandstorm that hovered over the nameless city, and marked the quietness of the rest of the landscape. Once more I ventured within those brooding ruins that swelled beneath the sand like an ogre under a coverlet, and again dug vainly for relics of the forgotten race. At noon I rested, and in the afternoon I spent much time tracing the walls and bygone streets, and the outlines of the nearly vanished buildings. I saw that the city had been mighty indeed, and wondered at the sources of its greatness. To myself I pictured all the splendours of an age so distant that Chaldaea could not recall it, and thought of Sarnath the Doomed, that stood in the land Mnar when mankind was young, and of Ib, that was carven of grey stone before mankind existed.

All at once I came upon a place where the bed rock rose stark through the sand and formed a low cliff; and here I saw with joy what seemed to promise further traces of the antediluvian people. Hewn rudely on the face of the cliff were the unmistakable façades of several small, squat rock houses or temples; whose interiors may preserve many secrets of ages too remote for calculation, though sandstorms had long since effaced any carvings which may have been outside.

Very low and sand-choked were all of the dark apertures near me, but I cleared one with my spade and crawled through it, carrying a torch to reveal whatever mysteries it might hold. When I was inside I saw that the cavern was indeed a temple, and beheld plain signs of the race that had lived and worshipped before the desert was a desert. Primitive altars, pillars, and niches, all curiously low, were not absent; and though I saw no sculptures nor frescoes, there were many singular stones clearly shaped into symbols by artificial means. The lowness of the chiselled chamber was very strange, for I could hardly kneel upright; but the area was so great that my torch showed only part of it at a time. I shuddered oddly in some of the far corners; for certain altars and stones suggested forgotten rites of terrible, revolting, and inexplicable nature and made me wonder what manner of men could have made and frequented such a temple. When I had seen all that the place contained, I crawled out again, avid to find what the other temples might yield.

Night had now approached, yet the tangible things I had seen made curiosity stronger than fear, so that I did not flee from the long moon-cast shadows that had daunted me when first I saw the nameless city. In the twilight I cleared another aperture and with a new torch crawled into it, finding more vague stones and symbols, though nothing more definite than the other temple had contained. The room was just as low, but much less broad, ending in a very narrow passage crowded with obscure and cryptical shrines. About these shrines I was prying when the noise of a wind and my camel outside broke through the stillness and drew me forth to see what could have frightened the beast.

The moon was gleaming vividly over the primitive ruins, lighting a dense cloud of sand that seemed blown by a strong but decreasing wind from some point along the cliff ahead of me. I knew it was this chilly, sandy wind which had disturbed the camel, and was about to lead him to a place of better shelter when I chanced to glance up and saw that there was no wind atop the cliff. This astonished me and made me fearful again, but I immediately recalled the sudden local winds that I had seen and heard before at sunrise and sunset, and judged it was a normal thing. I decided it came from some rock fissure leading to a cave, and watched the troubled sand to trace it to its source; soon perceiving that it came from the black orifice of a temple a long distance south of me, almost out of sight. Against the choking sand-cloud I plodded towards this temple, which as I neared it loomed larger than the rest, and showed a doorway far less clogged with caked sand. I would have entered had not the terrific force of the icy wind almost quenched my torch. It poured madly out of the dark door, sighing uncannily as it ruffled the sand and spread among the weird ruins. Soon it grew fainter and the sand grew more and more still, till finally all was at rest again; but a presence seemed stalking among the spectral stones of the city, and when I glanced at the moon it seemed to quiver as though mirrored in unquiet water. I was more afraid than I could explain, but not enough to dull my thirst for wonder; so as soon as the wind was quite gone I crossed into the dark chamber from which it had come.

This temple, as I had fancied from the outside, was larger than either of those I had visited before; and was presumably a natural cavern since it bore winds from some region beyond. Here I could stand quite upright, but saw that the stones and altars were as low as those in the other temples. On the walls and roof I beheld for the first time some traces of the pictorial art of the ancient race, curious curling streaks of paint that had almost faded or crumbled away; and on two of the altars I saw with rising excitement a maze of well-fashioned curvilinear carvings. As I held my torch aloft it seemed to me that the shape of the roof was too regular to be natural, and I wondered what the prehistoric cutters of stone had first worked upon. Their engineering skill must have been vast.

Then a brighter flare of the fantastic flame showed that for which I had been seeking, the opening to those remoter abysses whence the sudden wind had blown; and I grew faint when I saw that it was a small and plainly artificial door chiselled in the solid rock. I thrust my torch within, beholding a black tunnel with the roof arching low over a rough flight of very small, numerous and steeply descending steps. I shall always see those steps in my dreams, for I came to learn what they meant. At the time I hardly knew whether to call them steps or mere footholds in a precipitous descent. My mind was whirling with mad thoughts, and the words and warnings of Arab prophets seemed to float across the desert from the land that men know to the nameless city that men dare not know. Yet I hesitated only a moment before advancing through the portal and commencing to climb cautiously down the steep passage, feet first, as though on a ladder.

It is only in the terrible phantasms of drugs of delirium that any other man can have such a descent as mine. The narrow passage led infinitely down like some hideous haunted well, and the torch I held about my head could not light the unknown depths towards which I was crawling. I lost track of the hours and forgot to consult my watch, thought I was frightened when I thought of the distance I must be traversing. There were changes of direction and of steepness; and once I came to a long, low, level passage where I had to wriggle feet first along the rocky floor, holding the torch at arm's length beyond my head. The place was not high enough for kneeling. After that were more of the steep steps, and I was still scrambling down interminably when my failing torch died out. I do not think I noticed it at the time, for when I did notice it I was still holding it above me as if it were ablaze. I was quite unbalanced with that instinct for the strange and the unknown which had made me a wanderer upon earth and a haunter of far, ancient, and forbidden places.

In the darkness there flashed before my mind fragments of my cherished treasury of daemoniac lore; sentences from Alhazred the mad Arab, paragraphs from the apocryphal nightmares of Damascius, and infamous lines from the delirious "Image du Monde" of Gauthier de Metz. I repeated queer extracts, and muttered of Afrasiab and the daemons

that floated with him down the Oxus; later chanting over
and over again a phrase from one of Lord Dunsany's tales –
"The unreverberate blackness of the abyss." Once when the
descent grew amazingly steep I recited something in sing-
song from Thomas Moore until I feared to recite more :

> "A reservoir of darkness, black
>   As witches' cauldrons are, when fill'd
> With moon-drugs in th' eclipse distill'd.
> Leaning to look if foot might pass
> Down thro' that chasm, I saw, beneath,
> As far as vision could explore,
> The jetty sides as smooth as glass,
> Looking as if just varnished o'er
> With that dark pitch the Seat of Death
> Throws out upon its slimy shore."

Time had quite ceased to exist when my feet again felt
a level floor, and I found myself in a place slightly higher
than the rooms in the two smaller temples now so incal-
culably far above my head. I could not quite stand, but
could kneel upright, and in the dark I shuffled and crept
hither and thither at random. I soon knew that I was in a
narrow passage whose walls were lined with cases of wood
having glass fronts. As in that Palaeozoic and abysmal
place I felt of such things as polished wood and glass I
shuddered at the possible implications. The cases were
apparently ranged along each side of the passage at regular
intervals, and were oblong and horizontal, hideously like
coffins in shape and size. When I tried to move two or three
for further examination, I found that they were firmly
fastened.

I saw that the passage was a long one, so floundered ahead
rapidly in a creeping run that would have seemed horrible
had any eye watched me in the blackness; crossing from side
to side occasionally to feel of my surroundings and be sure
the walls and rows of cases still stretched on. Man is so used

to thinking visually that I almost forgot the darkness and pictured the endless corridor of wood and glass in its low-studded monotony as though I saw it. And then in a moment of indescribable emotion I did see it.

Just when my fancy merged into real sight I cannot tell : but there came a gradual glow ahead, and all at once I knew that I saw the dim outlines of the corridor and the cases, revealed by some unknown subterranean phosphorescence. For a little while all was exactly as I had imagined it, since the glow was very faint; but as I mechanically kept stumbling ahead into the stronger light I realized that my fancy had been but feeble. This hall was no relic of crudity like the temples in the city above, but a monument of the most magnificent and exotic art. Rich, vivid, and daringly fantastic designs and pictures formed a continuous scheme of mural painting whose lines and colours were beyond description. The cases were of a strange golden wood, with fronts of exquisite glass, and containing the mummified forms of creatures outreaching in grotesqueness the most chaotic dreams of man.

To convey any idea of these monstrosities is impossible. They were of the reptile kind, with body lines suggesting sometimes the crocodile, sometimes the seal, but more often nothing of which either the naturalist or the palaeontologist ever heard. In size they approximated a small man, and their fore-legs' bore delicate and evident feet curiously like human hands and fingers. But strangest of all were their heads, which presented a contour violating all known biological principles. To nothing can such things be well compared – in one flash I thought of comparisons as varied as the cat, the bulldog, the mythic Satyr, and the human being. Not Jove himself had had so colossal and protuberant a forehead, yet the horns and the noselessness and the alligator-like jaw placed the things outside all established categories. I debated for a time on the reality of the mummies, half-suspecting they were artificial idols; but soon decided they were indeed some palaeogean species which had lived when the nameless city was alive. To crown their grotesqueness, most of them were gorgeously enrobed in the costliest of fabrics, and lavishly laden with ornaments of gold, jewels, and unknown shining metals.

The importance of these crawling creatures must have been vast, for they held first place among the wild designs on the frescoed walls and ceiling. With matchless skill had the artist drawn them in a world of their own, wherein they had cities and gardens fashioned to suit their dimensions; and I could not help but think that their pictured history was allegorical, perhaps showing the progress of the race that worshipped them. These creatures, I said to myself, were to the men of the nameless city what the she-wolf was to Rome, or some totem-beast is to a tribe of Indians.

Holding this view, I could trace roughly a wonderful epic of the nameless city; the tale of a mighty sea-coast metropolis that ruled the world before Africa rose out of the waves, and of its struggles as the sea shrank away, and the desert crept into the fertile valley that held it. I saw its wars and triumphs, its troubles and defeats, and afterwards its terrible fight against the desert when thousands of its people – here represented in allegory by the grotesque reptiles – were driven to chisel their way down through the rocks in some marvellous manner to another world whereof their prophets had told them. It was all vividly weird and realistic, and its connection with the awesome descent I had made was unmistakable. I even recognized the passages.

As I crept along the corridor toward the brighter light I saw later stages of the painted epic – the leave-taking of the race that had dwelt in the nameless city and the valley around for ten million years; the race whose souls shrank from quitting scenes their bodies had known so long where they had settled as nomads in the earth's youth, hewing in the virgin rock those primal shrines at which they had never ceased to worship. Now that the light was better I studied the pictures more closely and, remembering that the strange reptiles must represent the unknown men, pondered upon the customs of the nameless city. Many things were peculiar and inexplicable. The civilization, which included a written alphabet, had seemingly risen to a higher order than those immeasurably later civilizations of Egypt and Chaldea, yet there were curious omissions. I could, for example, find no pictures to represent deaths or funeral customs, save such as were related to wars, violence, and plagues; and I wondered at the reticence shown concerning natural death. It was as though an ideal of immortality had been fostered as a cheering illusion.

Still nearer the end of the passage were painted scenes of the utmost picturesqueness and extravagance : contrasted views of the nameless city in its desertion and growing ruin, and of the strange new realm of paradise to which the race had hewed its way through the stone. In these views the city and the desert valley were shown always by moonlight, a golden nimbus hovering over the fallen walls and half-revealing the splendid perfection of former times, shown spectrally and elusively by the artist. The paradisal scenes were almost too extravagant to be believed; portraying a hidden world of eternal day filled with glorious cities and ethereal hills and valleys. At the very last I thought I saw signs of an artistic anticlimax. The paintings were less skilful, and much more bizarre than even the wildest of the earlier scenes. They seemed to record a slow decadence of the ancient stock, coupled with a growing ferocity towards the outside world from which it was driven by the desert. The forms of the people – always represented by the sacred reptiles – appeared to be gradually wasting away, though their spirit was shewn hovering about the ruins by moonlight gained in proportion. Emaciated priests, displayed as reptiles in ornate robes, cursed the upper air and all who breathed it; and one terrible final scene showed a primitive-looking man, perhaps a pioneer of ancient Irem, the City of Pillars, torn to pieces by members of the elder race. I remember how the Arabs fear the nameless city, and was glad that beyond this place the grey walls and ceiling were bare.

As I viewed the pageant of mural history I had approached very closely the end of the low-ceilinged hall, and was aware of a gate through which came all of the illuminating phosphorescence. Creeping up to it, I cried aloud in transcendent amazement at what lay beyond; for instead of other and brighter chambers there was only an illimitable void of uniform radiance, such as one might fancy when gazing down from the peak of Mount Everest upon a sea of sunlit mist. Behind me was a passage so cramped that I could not stand upright in it; before me was an infinity of subterranean effulgence.

Reaching down from the passage into the abyss was the head of a steep flight of steps – small numerous steps like those of the black passages I had traversed – but after a few feet the glowing vapours concealed everything. Swung back open against the left-hand wall of the passage was a massive door of brass, incredibly thick and decorated with fantastic bas-reliefs, which could if closed shut the whole inner world of light away from the vaults and passages of rock. I looked at the steps, and for the nonce dared not try them. I touched the open brass door, and could not move it. Then I sank prone to the stone floor, my mind aflame with prodigious reflections which not even a death-like exhaustion could banish.

As I lay still with closed eyes, free to ponder, many things I had lightly noted in the frescoes came back to me with new and terrible significance – scenes representing the nameless city in its heyday – the vegetation of the valley around it, and the distant lands with which its merchants traded. The allegory of the crawling creatures puzzled me by its universal prominence, and I wondered that it would be so closely followed in a pictured history of such importance.

In the frescoes the nameless city had been shown in proportions fitted to the reptiles. I wondered what its real proportions and magnificence had been, and reflected a moment on certain oddities I had noticed in the ruins. I thought curiously of the lowness of the primal temples and of the underground corridor, which were doubtless hewn thus out of deference to the reptiles deities there honoured; though it perforce reduced the worshippers to crawling. Perhaps the very rites here involved a crawling in imitation of the creatures. No religious theory, however, could easily explain why the level passages in that awesome descent should be as low as the temples – or lower, since one could not even kneel in it. As I thought of the crawling creatures, whose hideous mummified forms were so close to me, I felt a new throb of fear. Mental associations are curious, and I shrank from the idea that except for the poor primitive man torn to pieces in the last painting, mine was the only human form amidst the many relics and symbols of primordial life.

But as always in my strange and roving existence, wonder soon drove out fear; for the luminous abyss and what it might contain presented a problem worthy of the greatest explorer. That a weird world of mystery lay far down that flight of peculiarly small steps I could not doubt, and I hoped to find there those human memorials which the painted corridor had failed to give. The frescoes had pictured unbelievable cities, and valleys in this lower realm, and my fancy dwelt on the rich and colossal ruins that awaited me.

My fears, indeed, concerned the past rather than the future. Not even the physical horror of my position in that cramped corridor of dead reptiles and antediluvian frescoes, miles below the world I knew and faced by another world of eerie light and mist, could match the lethal dread I felt at the abysmal antiquity of the scene and its soul. An ancientness so vast that measurement is feeble seemed to leer down from the primal stones and rock-hewn temples of the nameless city, while the very latest of the astounding maps in the frescoes showed oceans and continents that man has forgotten, with only here and there some vaguely familiar outline. Of what could have happened in the geological ages since the paintings ceased and the death-hating race resentfully succumbed to decay, no man might say. Life had once teemed in these caverns and in the luminous realm beyond; now I was alone with vivid relics, and I trembled to think of the countless ages through which these relics had kept a silent deserted vigil.

Suddenly there came another burst of that acute fear which had intermittently seized me ever since I first saw the terrible valley and the nameless city under a cold moon, and despite my exhaustion I found myself starting frantically to a sitting posture and gazing back along the black corridor toward the tunnels that rose to the outer world. My sensations were like those which had made me shun the nameless city at night, and were as inexplicable as they were poignant. In another moment, however, I received a still greater shock in the form of a definite sound – the first which had broken the utter silence of these tomb-like depths. It was a deep, low moaning, as of a distant throng of condemned spirits, and came from the direction in which I was staring. Its volume rapidly grew, till soon it reverberated frightfully through the low passage, and at the same time I became conscious of an increasing draught of cold air, likewise flowing from the tunnels and the city above. The touch of this air seemed to restore my balance, for I instantly recalled the sudden gusts which had risen around the mouth of the abyss each sunset and sunrise, one of which had indeed revealed the hidden tunnels to me. I looked at my watch and saw that sunrise was near, so braced myself to resist the gale that was sweeping down to its cavern home as it had swept forth at evening. My fear again waned low, since a natural phenomenon tends to dispel broodings over the unknown.

More and more madly poured the shrieking, moaning

night wind into that gulf of the inner earth. I dropped prone again and clutched vainly at the floor for fear of being swept bodily through the open gate into the phosphorescent abyss. Such fury I had not expected, and as I grew aware of an actual slipping of my form toward the abyss I was beset by a thousand new terrors of apprehension and imagination. The malignancy of the blast awakened incredible fancies; once more I compared myself shudderingly to the only human image in that frightful corridor, the man who was torn to pieces by the nameless race, for in the fiendish clawing of the swirling currents there seemed to abide a vindictive rage all the stronger because it was largely impotent. I think I screamed frantically near the last – I was almost mad – but if I did so my cries were lost in the hell-born babel of the howling wind-wraiths. I tried to crawl against the murderous invisible torrent, but I could not even hold my own as I was pushed slowly and inexorably towards the unknown world. Finally reason must have wholly snapped; for I fell to babbling over and over that unexplainable couplet of the mad Arab Alhazred, who dreamed of the nameless city :

"That is not dead which can eternal lie,
And with strange aeons even death may die."

Only the grim brooding desert gods know what really took place – what indescribable struggles and scrambles in the dark I endured or what Abaddon guided me back to life, where I must always remember and shiver in the night wind till oblivion – or worse – claims me. Monstrous, unnatural, colossal, was the thing – too far beyond all the ideas of man to be believed except in the silent damnable small hours of the morning when one cannot sleep.

I have said that the fury of the rushing blast was infernal – cacodaemoniacal – and that its voices were hideous with the pent-up viciousness of desolate eternities. Presently these voices, while still chaotic before me, seemed to my beating brain to take articulate form behind me; and down there in the grave of unnumbered aeon-dead antiquities, leagues below the dawn-lit world of men, I heard the ghastly cursing and snarling of strange-tongued fiends. Turning, I saw outlined against the luminous aether of the abyss that could not be seen against the dusk of the corridor – a nightmare horde of rushing devils; hate-distorted, grotesquely panoplied, half-transparent devils of a race no man might mistake – the crawling reptiles of the nameless city.

And as the wind died away I was plunged into the ghoul-pooled darkness of earth's bowels; for behind the last of the creatures the great brazen door clanged shut with a deafening peal of metallic music whose reverberations swelled out to the distant world to hail the rising sun as Memnon hails it from the banks of the Nile.

MONKEYS

by E F Benson

Dr Hugh Morris, while still in the early thirties of his age, had justly earned for himself the reputation of being one of the most dexterous and daring surgeons in his profession, and both in his private practice and in his voluntary work at one of the great London hospitals his record of success as an operator was unparalleled among his colleagues. He believed that vivisection was the most fruitful means of progress in the science of surgery, holding, rightly or wrongly, that he was justified in causing suffering to animals, though sparing them all possible pain, if thereby he could reasonably hope to gain fresh knowledge about similar operations on human beings which would save life or mitigate suffering; the motive was good, and the gain already immense. But he had nothing but scorn for those who, for their own amusement, took out packs of hounds to run foxes to death, or matched two greyhounds to see which would give the death-grip to a single terrified hare: that, to him, was wanton torture, utterly unjustifiable. Year in and year out, he took no holiday at all, and for the most part he occupied his leisure, when the day's work was over, in study.

He and his friend Jack Madden were dining together one warm October night at his house looking on to Regent's Park. The windows of his drawing-room on the ground-floor were open, and they sat smoking, when dinner was done, on the broad window-seat. Madden was starting next day for Egypt, where he was engaged in archæological work, and he would be engaged throughout the winter in the excavation of a newly-discovered cemetery across the river from Luxor, near Medinet Habu. But it was no good.

'When my eye begins to fail and my fingers to falter,' said Morris, 'it will be time for me to think of taking my ease. What do I want with a holiday? I should be pining to get back to my work all the time. I like work better than loafing. Purely selfish.'

'Well, be unselfish for once,' said Madden. 'Besides, your work would benefit. It can't be good for a man never to relax. Surely freshness is worth something.'

'Precious little if you're as strong as I am. I believe in continual concentration if one wants to make progress. One may be tired, but why not? I'm not tired when I'm actually engaged on a dangerous operation, which is what matters. And time's so short. Twenty years from now I shall be past my best, and I'll have my holiday then, and when my holiday is over, I shall fold my hands and go to sleep for ever and ever. Thank God, I've got no fear that there's an after-life. The spark of vitality that has animated us burns low and then goes out like a windblown candle, and as for my body, what do I care what happens to that when I have done with it? Nothing will survive of me except some small contribution I may have made to surgery, and in a few years' time that will be superseded. But for that I perish utterly.'

Madden squirted some soda into his glass.

'Well, if you've quite settled that – ' he began.

'I haven't settled it, science has,' said Morris. 'The body is transmuted into other forms, worms batten on it, it helps to feed the grass, and some animal consumes the grass. But as for the survival of the individual spirit of a man, show me one title of scientific evidence to support it. Besides, if it did survive, all the evil and malice in it must surely survive too. Why should the death of the body purge that away? It's a nightmare to contemplate such a thing, and oddly enough, unhinged people like spiritualists want to persuade us for our consolation that the nightmare is true. But odder still are those old Egyptians of yours, who thought that there was something sacred about their bodies, after they were quit of them. And didn't you tell me that they covered their coffins with curses on anyone who disturbed their bones?'

'Constantly,' said Madden. 'It's the general rule in fact. Marrowy curses written in hieroglyphics on the mummy-case or carved on the sarcophagus.'

'But that's not going to deter you this winter from opening as many tombs as you can find, and rifling from them any objects of interest or value.'

Madden laughed.

'Certainly it isn't,' he said. 'I take out of the tombs all objects of art, and I unwind the mummies to find and annex their scarabs and jewellery. But I make an absolute rule always to bury the bodies again. I don't say that I believe in the power of those curses, but anyhow a mummy in a museum is an indecent object.'

'But if you found some mummied body with an interesting malformation, wouldn't you send it to some anatomical institute?' asked Morris.

'It has never happened to me yet,' said Madden, 'but I'm pretty sure I shouldn't.'

'Then you're a superstitious Goth and an anti-educational Vandal,' remarked Morris . . . 'Hullo, what's that?' He leant out of the window as he spoke. The light from the room vividly illuminated the square of lawn outside, and across it was crawling the small twitching shape of some animal. Hugh Morris vaulted out of the window, and presently returned, carrying carefully in his spread hands a little grey monkey, evidently desperately injured. Its hind legs were stiff and outstretched as if it was partially paralysed.

Morris ran his soft deft fingers over it.

'What's the matter with the little beggar, I wonder,' he said. 'Paralysis of the lower limbs: it looks like some lesion of the spine.'

The monkey lay quite still, looking at him with anguished appealing eyes as he continued his manipulation.

'Yes, I thought so,' he said. 'Fracture of one of the lumbar vertebræ. What luck for me! It's a rare injury, but I've often wondered. . . . And perhaps luck for the monkey too, though that's not very probable. If he was a man and a patient of mine, I shouldn't dare to take the risk. But, as it is . . .'

Jack Madden started on his southward journey next day, and

by the middle of November was at work on this newly-discovered cemetery. He and another Englishman were in charge of the excavation, under the control of the Antiquity Department of the Egyptian Government. In order to be close to their work and to avoid the daily ferrying across the Nile from Luxor, they hired a bare roomy native house in the adjoining village of Gurnah. A reef of low sandstone cliff ran northwards from here towards the temple and terraces of Deir-el-Bahari, and it was in the face of this and on the level below it that the ancient graveyard lay. There was much accumulation of sand to be cleared away before the actual exploration of the tombs could begin, but trenches cut below the foot of the sandstone ridge showed that there was an extensive area to investigate.

The more important sepulchres, they found, were hewn in the face of this small cliff: many of these had been rifled in ancient days, for the slabs forming the entrances into them had been split, and the mummies unwound, but now and then Madden unearthed some tomb that had escaped these marauders, and in one he found the sarcophagus of a priest of the nineteenth dynasty, and that alone repaid weeks of fruitless work. There were nearly a hundred *ushaptiu* figures of the finest blue glaze; there were four alabaster vessels in which had been placed the viscera of the dead man removed before embalming: there was a table of which the top was inlaid with squares of variously coloured glass, and the legs were of carved ivory and ebony: there were the priest's sandals adorned with exquisite silver filagree: there was his staff of office inlaid with a diaper-pattern of cornelian and gold, and on the head of it, forming the handle, was the figure of a squatting cat, carved in amethyst, and the mummy, when unwound, was found to be decked with a necklace of gold plaques and onyx beads. All these were sent down to the Gizeh Museum at Cairo, and Madden reinterred the mummy at the foot of the cliff below the tomb. He wrote to Hugh Morris describing this find, and laying stress on the unbroken splendour of these crystalline winter days, when from morning to night the sun cruised across the blue, and on the cool nights when the stars rose and set on the vapourless rim of the desert. If by chance Hugh should change his mind, there was ample room for him in this house at Gurnah, and he would be very welcome.

A fortnight later Madden received a telegram from his friend. It stated that he had been unwell and was starting at once by long sea to Port Said, and would come straight up to Luxor. In due course he announced his arrival at Cairo and Madden went across the river next day to meet him: it was reassuring to find him as vital and active as ever, the picture of bronzed health. The two were alone that night, for Madden's colleague had gone for a week's trip up the Nile, and they sat out, when dinner was done, in the enclosed courtyard adjoining the house. Till then Madden had shied off the subject of himself and his health.

'Now I may as well tell you what's been amiss with me,' he said, 'for I know I look a fearful fraud as an invalid, and physically I've never been better in my life. Every organ has been functioning perfectly except one, but something suddenly went wrong there just once. It was like this.'

He paused a moment.

'After you left,' he said, 'I went on as usual for another month or so, very busy, very serene and, I may say, very successful. Then one morning I arrived at the hospital when there was one perfectly ordinary but major operation waiting for me. The patient, a man, was wheeled into the theatre anæsthetized, and I was just about to make the first incision into the abdomen, when I saw that there was sitting on his chest a little grey monkey. It was not looking at me, but at the fold of skin which I held between my thumb and finger. I knew, of course, that there was no monkey there, and that what I saw was a hallucination, and I think you'll agree that there was nothing much wrong with my nerves when I tell you that I went through the operation with clear eyes and an unshaking hand. I had to go on: there was no choice about the matter. I couldn't say: "Please take that monkey away," for I knew there was no monkey there. Nor could I say: "Somebody else must do this, as I have a distressing hallucination that there is a monkey sitting on the patient's chest." There would have been an end of me as a surgeon and no mistake. All the time I was at work it sat there absorbed in the most part in what I was doing and peering into the wound, but now and then it looked up at me, and chattered with rage. Once it fingered a spring-forceps which clipped a severed vein, and that was the worst moment of all. . . At the end it was carried out still balancing itself on the man's chest. . . I think I'll have a drink. Strongish, please. . . Thanks.'

'A beastly experience,' he said when he had drunk. 'Then I went straight away from the hospital to consult my old friend Robert Angus, the alienist and nerve-specialist, and told him exactly what had happened to me. He made several tests, he examined my eyes, tried my reflexes, took my bood-pressure: there was nothing wrong with any of them. Then he asked me questions about my general health and manner of life, and among these questions was one which I am sure has already occurred to you, namely, had anything occurred to me lately, or even remotely, which was likely to make me visualize a monkey. I told him that a few weeks ago a monkey with a broken lumbar vertebra had crawled on to my lawn, and that I had attempted an operation – binding the broken vertebra with wire – which had occurred to me before as a possibility. You remember the night, no doubt?'

'Perfectly,' said Madden, 'I started for Egypt next day. What happened to the monkey, by the way?'

'It lived for two days: I was pleased, because I had expected it would die under the anæsthetic, or immediately afterwards from shock. To get back to what I was telling you. When Angus had asked all his questions, he gave me a good wigging. He said that I had persistently overtaxed my brain for years, without giving it any rest or change of occupation, and that if I wanted to be of any further use in the world, I must drop my work at once for a couple of months. He told me that my brain was tired out and that I had persisted in stimulating it. A man like me, he said, was no better than a confirmed drunkard, and that, as a warning, I had had a touch of an appropriate delirium tremens. The cure was to drop work, just as a drunkard must drop drink. He laid it on hot and strong: he said I was on the verge of a breakdown, entirely owing to my own foolishness, but that I had wonderful physical health, and that if I did break down I should be a disgrace. Above all – and this seemed to me awfully sound advice – he told me not to attempt to avoid thinking about what had happened to me.

If I kept my mind mind off it, I should be perhaps driving it into the subconscious, and then there might be bad trouble. "Rub it in: think what a fool you've been," he said. "Face it, dwell on it, make yourself thoroughly ashamed of yourself." Monkeys, too: I wasn't to avoid the thought of monkeys. In fact, he recommended me to go straight away to the Zoological Gardens, and spend an hour in the monkey-house.'

'Odd treatment,' interrupted Madden.

'Brilliant treatment. My brain, he explained, had rebelled against its slavery, and had hoisted a red flag with the device of a monkey on it. I must show it that I wasn't frightened at its bogus monkeys. I must retort on it by making myself look at dozens of real ones which could bite and maul you savagely, instead of one little sham monkey that had no existence at all. At the same time I must take the red flag seriously, recognize there was danger, and rest. And he promised me that sham monkeys wouldn't trouble me again. Are there any real ones in Egypt, by the way?'

'Not so far as I know,' said Madden. 'But there must have been once, for there are many images of them in tombs and temples.'

'That's good. We'll keep their memory green and my brain cool. Well, there's my story. What do you think of it?'

'Terrifying,' said Madden. 'But you must have got nerves of iron to get through that operation with the monkey watching.'

'A hellish hour. Out of some disordered slime in my brain there had crawled this unbidden thing, which showed itself, apparently substantial, to my eyes. It didn't come from outside: my eyes hadn't told my brain that there was a monkey sitting on the man's chest, but my brain had told my eyes so, making fools of them. I felt as if someone whom I absolutely trusted had played me false. Then again I have wondered whether some instinct in my subconscious mind revolted against vivisection. My reason says that it is justified, for it teaches us how pain can be relieved and death postponed for human beings. But what if my subconscious persuaded my brain to give me a good fright, and reproduce before my eyes the semblance of a monkey, just when I was putting into practice what I had learned from dealing out pain and death to animals?'

He got up suddenly.

'What about bed?' he said. 'Five hours' sleep was enough for me when I was at work, but now I believe I could sleep the clock round every night.'

Young Wilson, Madden's colleague in the excavations, returned next day and the work went steadily on. One of them was on the spot to start it soon after sunrise, and either one or both of them were superintending it, with an interval of a couple of hours at noon, until sunset. When the mere work of clearing the face of the sandstone cliff was in progress and of carting away the silted soil, the presence of one of them sufficed, for there was nothing to do but to see that the workmen shovelled industriously, and passed regularly with their baskets of earth and sand on their shoulders to the dumping-grounds, which stretched away from the area to be excavated, in lengthening peninsulas of trodden soil. But, as they advanced along the sandstone ridge, there would now and then appear a chiselled smoothness in the cliff and then both must be alert. There was great excitement to see if, when they exposed the hewn slab that formed the door into the tomb, it had escaped ancient marauders, and still stood in place and intact for the modern to explore. But now for many days they came upon no sepulchre that had not already been opened. The mummy, in these cases, had been unwound in the search for necklaces and scarabs, and its scattered bones lay about. Madden was always at pains to reinter these.

At first Hugh Morris was assiduous in watching the excavations, but as day after day went by without anything of interest turning up, his attendance grew less frequent: it was too much of a holiday to watch the day-long removal of sand from one place to another. He visited the Tomb of the Kings, he went across the river and saw the temples at Karnak, but his appetite for antiquities was small. On other days he rode in the desert, or spent the day with friends at one of the Luxor hotels. He came home from there one evening in rare good spirits, for he had played lawn-tennis with a woman on whom he had operated for malignant tumour six months before and she had skipped about the court like a two-year-old. 'God, how I want to be at work again,' he exclaimed. 'I wonder whether I ought not to have stuck it out, and defied my brain to frighten me with bogies.'

The weeks passed on, and now there were but two days left before his return to England, where he hoped to resume work at once: his tickets were taken and his berth booked. As he sat over breakfast that morning with Wilson, there came a workman from the excavation, with a note scribbled in hot haste by Madden, to say that they had just come upon a tomb which seemed to be unrifled, for the slab that closed it was in place and unbroken. To Wilson, the news was like the sight of a sail to a marooned mariner, and when, a quarter of an hour later, Morris followed him, he was just in time to see the slab prised away. There was no sarcophagus within, for the rock walls did duty for that, but there lay there, varnished and bright in hue as if painted yesterday, the mummycase roughly following the outline of the human form. By it stood the alabaster vases containing the entrails of the dead, and at each corner of the sepulchre there were carved out of the sandstone rock, forming, as it were, pillars to support the roof, thick-set images of squatting apes. The mummy-case was hoisted out and carried away by workmen on a bier of boards into the courtyard of the excavators' house at Gurnah, for the opening of it and the unwrapping of the dead.

They got to work that evening directly they had fed: the face painted on the lid was that of a girl or young woman, and presently deciphering the hieroglyphic inscription, Madden read out that within lay the body of A-pen-ara, daughter of the overseer of the cattle of Senmut.

'Then follow the usual formulas,' he said. 'Yes, yes . . . ah, you'll be interested in this, Hugh, for you asked me once about it. A-pen-ara curses any who desecrates or meddles with her bones, and should anyone do so, the guardians of her sepulchre will see to him, and he shall die childless and in panic and agony; also the guardian of her sepulchre will tear the hair from his head and scoop his eyes from their sockets, and pluck the thumbs from his right hand, as a man plucks the young blade of corn from its sheath.'

Morris laughed.

'Very pretty little attentions,' he said. 'And who are the

guardians of this sweet young lady's sepulchre? Those four great apes carved at the corners?'

'No doubt. But we won't trouble them, for to-morrow I shall bury Miss A-pen-ara's bones again with all decency in the trench at the foot of her tomb. They'll be safer there, for if we put them back where we found them, there would be pieces of her hawked about by half the donkey-boys in Luxor in a few days. "Buy a mummy hand, lady? . . . Foot of a Gyppy Queen, only ten piastres, gentlemen" . . . Now for the un-winding.'

It was dark by now, and Wilson fetched out a paraffin lamp, which burned unwaveringly in the still air. The lid of the mummy-case was easily detached, and within was the slim, swaddled body. The embalming had not been very thoroughly done, for all the skin and flesh had perished from the head, leaving only bones of the skull stained brown with bitumen. Round it was a mop of hair, which with the ingress of the air subsided like a belated *soufflé*, and crumbled into dust. The cloth that swathes the body was as brittle, but round the neck, still just holding together, was a collar of curious and rare workmanship: little ivory figures of squatting apes alternated with silver beads. But again a touch broke the thread that strung them together, and each had to be picked out singly. A bracelet of scarabs and cornelians still clasped one of the fleshless wrists, and then they turned the body over in order to get at the members of the necklace which lay beneath the nape. The rotted mummy-cloth fell away altogether from the back, disclosing the shoulder-blades and the spine down as far as the pelvis. Here the embalming had been better done, for the bones still held together with re-mnants of muscle and cartilage.

Hugh Morris suddenly sprang to his feet.

'My God, look there!' he cried, 'one of the lumbar vertebræ, there at the base of the spine, has been broken and clamped together with a metal band. To hell with your antiquities: let me come and examine something much more modern than any of us!'

He pushed Jack Madden aside, and peered at this marvel of surgery.

'Put the lamp closer,' he said, as if directing some nurse at an operation. 'Yes: that vertebra has been broken right across and has been clamped together. No one has ever, as far as I know, attempted such an operation except myself, and I have only performed it on that little paralysed monkey that crept into my garden one night. But some Egyptian surgeon, more than three thousand years ago, performed it on a woman. And look, look! She lived afterwards, for the broken vertebra put out that bony efflorescence of healing which has encroached over the metal band. That's a slow process, and it must have taken place during her lifetime, for there is no such energy in a corpse. The woman lived long: probably she recovered completely. And my wretched little monkey only lived two days and was dying all the time.'

Those questing hawk-visioned fingers of the surgeon perceived more finely than actual sight, and now he closed his eyes as the tip of them felt their way about the fracture in the broken vertebra and the clamping metal band.

'The band doesn't encircle the bone,' he said, 'and there are no studs attaching it. There must have been a spring in it, which, when it was clasped there, kept it tight. It has been clamped round the bone itself: the surgeon must have scraped the verebra clean of flesh before he attached it. I would give two years of my life to have looked on, like a student, at that masterpiece of skill, and it was worth while giving up two months of my work only to have seen the result. And the injury itself is so rare, this breaking of a spinal vertebra. To be sure, the hangman does something of the sort, but there's no mending that! Good Lord, my holiday has not been a waste of time!'

Madden settled that it was not worth while to send the mummy-case to the museum at Gizeh, for it was of a very ordinary type, and when the examination was over they lifted the body back into it, for reinterment next day. It was now long after midnight and presently the house was dark.

Hugh Morris slept on the ground-floor in a room adjoining the yard where the mummy-case lay. He remained long awake marvelling at that astonishing piece of surgical skill performed, according to Madden, some thirty-five centuries ago. So occupied had his mind been with homage that not till now did he realize that the tangible proof and witness of the operation would to-morrow be buried again and lost to science. He must persuade Madden to let him detach at least three of the vertebræ, the mended one and those immediately above and below it, and take them back to England as demonstration of what could be done: he would lecture on his exhibit and present it to the Royal College of Surgeons for example and incitement. Other trained eyes beside his own must see what had been successfully achieved by some unknown operator in the nineteenth dynasty ... But supposing Madden refused? He always made a point of scrupulously reburying these remains: it was a principle with him, and no doubt some superstition-complex – the hardest of all to combat with because of its sheer unreasonableness – was involved. Briefly, it was impossible to risk the chance of his refusal.

He got out of bed, listened for a moment by his door, and then softly went out into the yard. The moon had risen, for the brightness of the stars was paled, and though no direct rays shone into the walled enclosure, the dusk was dispersed by the toneless luminosity of the sky, and he had no need of a lamp. He drew the lid off the coffin, and folded back the tattered cerements which Madden had replaced over the body. He had thought that those lower vertebræ of which he was determined to possess himself would be easily detached, so far perished were the muscle and cartilage which held them together, but they cohered as if they had been clamped, and it required the utmost force of his powerful fingers to snap the spine, and as he did so the severed bones cracked as with the noise of a pistol-shot. But there was no sign that anyone in the house had heard it, there came no sound of steps, nor lights in the windows. One more fracture was needed, and then the relic was his. Before he replaced the ragged cloths he looked again at the stained fleshless bones. Shadow dwelt in the empty eye-sockets, as if black sunken eyes still lay there, fixedly regarding him, the lipless mouth snarled and grimaced. Even as he looked some change came over its aspect, and for one brief moment he fancied that there lay staring up at him the face of a great brown ape. But instantly that illusion vanished, and replacing the lid he went back to his room.

The mummy-case was reinterred next day, and two evenings after Morris left Luxor by the night train for Cairo, to join a homeward-bound P & O at Port Said. There were some hours to spare before his ship sailed, and having deposited his luggage, including a locked leather despatch-case, on board, he lunched at the Café Tewfik near the quay. There was a garden in front of it with palm trees and trellises gaily clad in bougainvillias: a low wooden rail separated it from the street, and Morris had a table close to this. As he ate he watched the polychromatic pageant of Eastern life passing by: there were Egyptian officials in broad-cloth frock coats and red fezzes; barefooted splay-toed fellahin in blue gabardines; veiled women in white making stealthy eyes at passers-by; half-naked gutter-snipes, one with a sprig of scarlet hibiscus behind his ear; travellers from India with solar topees and an air of aloof British superiority; dishevelled sons of the Prophet in green turbans; a stately sheik in a white *burnous*; French painted ladies of a professional class with lace-rimmed parasols and provocative glances; a wild-eyed dervish in an accordion-pleated skirt, chewing betel-nut and slightly foaming at the mouth. A Greek boot-black with box adorned with brass plaques tapped his brushes on it to encourage customers, an Egyptian girl squatted in the gutter beside a gramophone, steamers passing into the Canal hooted on their syrens.

Then at the edge of the pavement there sauntered by a young Italian harnessed to a barrel-organ: with one hand he ground out a popular air by Verdi, in the other he held out a tin can for the tributes of music-lovers: a small monkey in a yellow jacket, tethered to his wrist, sat on the top of his instrument. The musician had come opposite the table where Morris sat: Morris liked the gay tinkling tune, and feeling in his pocket for a piastre, he beckoned to him. The boy grinned and stepped up to the rail.

Then suddenly the melancholy-eyed monkey leaped from its place on the organ and sprang on to the table by which Morris sat. It alighted there, chattering with rage in a crash of broken glass. A flower-vase was upset, a plate clattered on to the floor. Morris's coffee-cup discharged its black contents on the tablecloth. Next moment the Italian had twitched the frenzied little beast back to him, and it fell head downwards on the pavement. A shrill hubbub arose, the waiter at

Morris's table hurried up with voluble execrations, a policeman kicked out at the monkey as it lay on the ground, the barrel-organ tottered and crashed on the roadway. Then all subsided again, and the Italian boy picked up the little body from the pavement. He held it out in his hands to Morris.

'*E morto,*' he said.

'Serves it right, too,' retorted Morris. 'Why did it fly at me like that?'

He travelled back to London by long sea, and day after day that tragic little incident, in which he had had no responsible part, began to make a sort of colouring matter in his mind during those hours of lazy leisure on ship-board, when a man gives about an equal inattention to the book he reads and to what passes round him. Sometimes if the shadow of a seagull overhead slid across the deck towards him, there leaped into his brain, before his eyes could reassure him, the ludicrous fancy that this shadow was a monkey springing at him. One day they ran into a gale from the west: there was a crash of glass at his elbow as a sudden lurch of the ship upset a laden steward, and Morris jumped from his seat thinking that a monkey had leaped on to his table again. There was a cinematograph show in the saloon one evening, in which some naturalist exhibited the films he had taken of wild life in Indian jungles: when he put on the screen the picture of a company of monkeys swinging their way through the trees Morris involuntarily clutched the sides of his chair in hideous panic that lasted but a fraction of a second, until he recalled to himself that he was only looking at a film in the saloon of a steamer passing up the coast of Portugal. He came sleepy into his cabin one night and saw some animal crouching by the locked leather despatch-case. His breath caught in his throat before he perceived that this was a friendly cat which rose with gleaming eyes and arched its back . . .

These fantastic unreasonable alarms were disquieting. He had as yet no repetition of the hallucination that he saw a monkey, but some deep-buried 'idea,' to cure which he had taken two months' holiday, was still unpurged from his mind. He must consult Robert Angus again when he got home, and seek further advice. Probably that incident at Port Said had rekindled the obscure trouble, and there was this added to it, that he knew he was now frightened of real monkeys: there was terror sprouting in the dark of his soul. But as for it having any connection with his pilfered treasure, so rank and childish a superstition deserved only the ridicule he gave it. Often he unlocked his leather case and sat poring over that miracle of surgery which made practical again long-forgotten dexterities.

But it was good to be back in England. For the last three days of the voyage no menace had flashed out on him from the unknown dusks, and surely he had been disquieting himself in vain. There was a light mist lying over Regent's Park on this warm March evening, and a drizzle of rain was falling. He made an appointment for the next morning with the specialist, he telephoned to the hospital that he had returned and hoped to resume work at once. He dined in very good spirits, talking to his manservant, and, as subsequently came out, he showed him his treasured bones, telling him that he had taken the relic from a mummy which he had seen unwrapped and that he meant to lecture on it. When he went up to bed he carried the leather case with him. Bed was comfortable after the ship's berth, and through his open window came the soft hissing of the rain on to the shrubs outside.

His servant slept in the room immediately over his. A little before dawn he woke with a start, roused by horrible cries from somewhere close at hand. Then came words yelled out in a voice that he knew:

'Help! Help!' it cried. 'O my God, my God! Ah – h – ' and it rose to a scream again.

The man hurried down and clicked on the light in his master's room as he entered. The cries had ceased: only a low moaning came from the bed. A huge ape with busy hands was bending over it; then taking up the body that lay there by the neck and the hips he bent it backwards and it cracked like a dry stick. Then it tore open the leather case that was on a table by the bedside, and with something that gleamed white in its dripping fingers it shambled to the window and disappeared.

A doctor arrived within half an hour, but too late. Handfuls of hair with flaps of skin attached had been torn from the head of the murdered man, both eyes were scooped out of their sockets, the right thumb had been plucked off the hand, and the back was broken across the lower vertebræ.

Nothing has since come to light which could rationally explain the tragedy. No large ape had escaped from the neighbouring Zoological Gardens, or, as far as could be ascertained, from elsewhere, nor was the monstrous visitor of that night ever seen again. Morris's servant had only had the briefest sight of it, and his description of it at the inquest did not tally with that of any known simian type. And the sequel was even more mysterious, for Madden, returing to England at the close of the season in Egypt, had asked Morris's servant exactly what it was that his master had shown him the evening before as having been taken by him from a mummy which he had seen unwrapped, and had got from him a sufficiently conclusive account of it. Next autumn he continued his excavations in the cemetery at Gurnah, and he disinterred once more the mummy-case of A-pen-ara and opened it. But the spinal vertebræ were all in place and complete: one had round it the silver clip which Morris had hailed as a unique achievement in surgery.

A PROFESSOR OF EGYPTOLOGY

by Guy Boothby

From seven o'clock in the evening until half past, that is to say for the half-hour preceding dinner, the Grand Hall of the Hôtel Occidental, throughout the season, is practically a lounge, and is crowded with the most fashionable folk wintering in Cairo. The evening I am anxiuos to describe was certainly no exception to the rule. At the foot of the fine marble staircase – the pride of its owner– a well-known member of the French Ministry was chatting with an English Duchess whose pretty, but somewhat delicate, daughter was flirting mildly with one of the Sirdar's Bimbashis, on leave from the Soudan. On the right-hand lounge of the Hall an Italian Countess, whose antecedents were as doubtful as her diamonds, was apparently listening to a story a handsome Greek *attaché* was telling her; in reality, however, she was endeavouring to catch scraps of a conversation being carried on, a few feet away, between a witty Russian and an equally clever daughter of the United States. Almost every nationality was represented there, but unfortunately for our prestige, the majority were English. The scene was a brilliant one, and the sprinkling of military and diplomatic uniforms (there was a Reception at the Khedivial Palace later) lent an additional touch of colour to the picture. Taken altogether, and regarded from a political point of view, the gathering had a significance of its own.

At the end of the Hall, near the large glass doors, a hand-some, elderly lady, with grey hair, was conversing with one of the leading English doctors of the place – a grey-haired, clever-looking man, who possessed the happy faculty of being able to impress everyone with whom he talked with the idea that he infinitely preferred his or her society to that of any other member of the world's population. They were discussing the question of the most suitable clothing for a Nile voyage, and as the lady's daughter, who was seated next her, had been conversant with her mother's ideas on the subject ever since their first visit to Egypt (as indeed had been the Doctor), she preferred to lie back on the divan and watch the people about her. She had large, dark, contemplative eyes. Like her mother she took life seriously, but in a somewhat different fashion. One who has been bracketed third in the Mathematical Tripos can scarcely be expected to bestow very much thought on the comparative merits of Jæger, as opposed to dresses of the Common or Garden flannel. From this, however, it must not be inferred that she was in any way a blue stocking, that is, of course, in the vulgar acceptation of the word. She was thorough in all she undertook, and for the reason that mathematics interested her very much the same way that Wagner, chess, and, shall we say, croquet, interest other people, she made it her hobby, and it must be confessed she certainly succeeded in it. At other times she rode, drove, played tennis and hockey, and looked upon her world with calm, observant eyes that were more disposed to find good than evil in it. Contradictions that we are, even to ourselves, it was only those who knew her intimately, and they were few and far between, who realised that, under that apparently sober, matter-of-fact personality, there existed a strong leaning towards the mysterious, or, more properly speaking, the occult. Possibly she herself would have been the first to deny this – but that I am right in my surmise this story will surely be sufficient proof.

Mrs Westmoreland and her daughter had left their comfortable Yorkshire home in September, and, after a little dawdling on the Continent, had reached Cairo in November – the best month to arrive, in my opinion, for then the rush has not set in, the hotel servants have not had sufficient time to become weary of their duties, and what is better still, all the best rooms have not been bespoken. It was now the middle of December, and the fashionable caravanserai, upon which they had for many years bestowed their patronage, was crowded from roof to cellar. Every day people were being turned away, and the manager's continual lament was that he had not another hundred rooms wherein to place more guests. He was a Swiss, and for that reason regarded hotel-keeping in the light of a profession.

On this particular evening Mrs Westmoreland and her daught Cecilia had arranged to dine with Dr Forsyth – that is to say, they were to eat their meal at his table in order that they might meet a man of whom they had heard much, but whose acquaintance they had not as yet made. The individual in question was a certain Professor Constanides – reputed one of the most advanced Egyptologists, and the author of several well-known works. Mrs Westmoreland was not of an exacting nature, and so long as she dined in agreeable company did not trouble herself very much whether it was with an English earl or a distinguished foreign *savant*.

'It really does not matter, my dear,' she was wont to observe to her daughter. 'So long as the cooking is good and the wine above reproach, there is absolutely nothing to choose between them. A Prime Minister and a country vicar are, after all, only men. Feed them well and they'll lie down and purr like tame cats. They don't want conversation.' From this it will be seen that Mrs Westmoreland was well acquainted with her world. Whether Miss Cecilia shared her opinions is another matter. At any rate, she had been looking forward for nearly a fortnight to meeting Constanides, who was popularly supposed to possess an extraordinary intuitive knowledge – instinct, perhaps, it should be called – concerning the localities of tombs of the Pharaohs of the Eleventh, Twelfth and Thirteenth Dynasties.

'I am afraid Constanides is going to be late,' said the Doctor, who had consulted his watch more than once. 'I hope, in that case, as his friend and your host, you will permit me to offer you my apologies.'

The Doctor at no time objected to the sound of his own voice, and on this occasion he was even less inclined to do so. Mrs Westmoreland was a widow with an ample income, and Cecila, he felt sure, would marry ere long.

'He has still three minutes in which to put in an

appearance,' observed that young lady, quietly. And then she added in the same tone, 'Perhaps we ought to be thankful if he comes at all.'

Both Mrs Westmoreland and her friend the Doctor regarded her with mildly reproachful eyes. The former could not understand anyone refusing a dinner such as she felt sure the Doctor had arranged for them; while the latter found it impossible to imagine a man who would dare to disappoint the famous Dr Forsyth, who, having failed in Harley Street, was nevertheless coining a fortune in the land of the Pharaohs.

'My good friend Constanides will not disappoint us, I feel sure,' he said, consulting his watch for the fourth time. 'Possibly I am a little fast, at any rate I have never known him to be unpunctual. A remarkable – a very remarkable man is Constanides. I cannot remember ever to have met another like him. And such a scholar!'

Having thus bestowed his approval upon him the worthy Doctor pulled down his cuffs, straightened his tie, adjusted his *pince-nez* in his best professional manner, and looked round the hall as if searching for someone bold enough to contradict the assertion he had just made.

'You have, of course, read his *Mythological Egypt,*' observed Miss Cecilia, demurely, speaking as if the matter were beyond doubt.

The Doctor looked a little confused.

'Ahem! Well, let me see,' he stammered, trying to find a way out of the difficulty. 'Well, to tell the truth, my dear young lady, I'm not quite sure that I have studied that particular work. As a matter of fact, you see, I have so little leisure at my disposal for any reading that is not intimately connected with my profession. That, of course, must necessarily come before everything else.'

Miss Cecilia's mouth twitched as if she were endeavouring to keep back a smile. At the same moment the glass doors of the vestibule opened and a man entered. So remarkable was he that everyone turned to look at him – a fact which did not appear to disconcert him in the least.

He was tall, well shaped, and carried himself with the air of one accustomed to command. His face was oval, his eyes large and set somewhat wide apart. It was only when they

73

were directed fairly at one that one became aware of the power they possessed. The cheek bones were a trifle high, and the forehead possibly retreated towards the jet-black hair more than is customary in Greeks. He wore neither beard nor moustache, thus enabling one to see the wide, firm mouth, the compression of the lips which spoke for the determination of their possessor. Those who had an eye for such things noted the fact that he was faultlessly dressed, while Miss Cecila, who had the precious gift of observation largely developed, noted that, with the exception of a single ring and a magnificent pearl stud, the latter strangely set, he wore no jewellery of any sort.

He looked about him for Dr Forsyth, and, when he had located him, hastened forward.

'My dear friend,' he said in English, which he spoke with scarcely a trace of foreign accent, 'I must crave your pardon a thousand times if I have kept you waiting.'

'On the contrary,' replied the Doctor, effusively, 'you are punctuality itself. Permit me to have the pleasure – the very great pleasure – of introducing you to my friends, Mrs Westmoreland and her daughter, Miss Cecilia, of whom you have often heard me speak.'

Professor Constanides bowed and expressed the pleasure he experienced in making their acquaintance. Though she could not have told you why, Miss Cecilia found herself undergoing very much the same sensation as she had done when she had passed up the Throne Room at her presentation. A moment later the gong sounded, and, with much rustling of skirts and fluttering of fans, a general movement was made towards the dining-room.

As host, Dr Forsyth gave his arm to Mrs Westmoreland, Constanides following with Miss Cecilia. The latter was conscious of a vague feeling of irritation; she admired the man and his work, but she wished his name had been anything rather than what it was.

(It should be here remarked that the last Constanides she had encountered had swindled her abominably in the matter of a turquoise brooch, and in consequnce the name had been an offence to her ever since.)

Dr Forsyth's table was situated at the further end, in the

window, and from it a good view of the room could be obtained. The scene was an animated one, and one of the party, at least, I fancy, will never forget it – try how she may.

During the first two or three courses the conversation was practically limited to Cecilia and Constanides; the Doctor and Mrs Westmoreland being too busy to waste time on idle chatter. Later, they became more amenable to the discipline of the table – or, in other words, they found time to pay attention to their neighbours.

Since then I have often wondered with what feelings Cecilia looks back upon that evening. In order, perhaps, to punish me for my curiosity, she has admitted to me since that she had never known, up to that time, what it was to converse with a really clever man. I submitted to the humiliation for the reason that we are, if not lovers, at least old friends, and, after all, Mrs Westmoreland's cook is one in a thousand.

From that evening forward, scarcely a day passed in which Constanides did not enjoy some portion of Miss Westmoreland's society. They met at the polo ground, drove in the Gezîreh, shopped in the Muski, or listened to the band, over afternoon tea, on the balcony of Shepheard's Hotel. Constanides was always unobtrusive, always picturesque and invariably interesting. What was more to the point, he never failed to command attention whenever or wherever he might appear. In the Native Quarter he was apparently better known than in the European. Cecilia noticed that there he was treated with a deference such as one would only expect to be shown to a king. She marvelled, but said nothing. Personally, I can only wonder that her mother did not caution her before it was too late. Surely she must have seen how dangerous the intimacy was likely to become. It was old Colonel Bettenham who sounded the first note of warning. In some fashion or another he was connected with the Westmorelands, and therefore had more or less right to speak his mind.

'Who the man is, I am not in a position to say,' he remarked to the mother; 'but if I were in your place I should be very careful. Cairo at this time of year is full of adventurers.'

'But, my dear Colonel,' answered Mrs Westmoreland, 'you surely do not mean to insinuate that the Professor is an adventurer. He was introduced to us by Dr Forsyth, and he has written so many clever books.'

'Books, my dear madam, are not everything,' the other replied judicially, and with that fine impartiality which marks a man who does not read. 'As a matter of fact I am bound to confess that Phipps – one of my captains – wrote a novel some years ago, but only one. The mess pointed out to him that it wasn't good form, don't you know, so he never tried the experiment again. But as for this man, Constanides, as they call him, I should certainly be more than careful.'

I have been told since that this conversation worried poor Mrs Westmoreland more than she cared to admit, even to herself. To a very large extent she, like her daughter, had fallen under the spell of the Professor's fascination. Had she been asked, point blank, she would doubtless have declared that she preferred the Greek to the Englishman – though, of course, it would have seemed flat heresy to say so. And yet – well, doubtless you can understand what I mean without my explaining further.

I am inclined to believe that I was the first to notice that there was serious trouble brewing. I could see a strained look in the girl's eyes for which I found if difficult to account. Then the truth dawned upon me, and I am ashamed to say that I began to watch her systematically. We have few secrets from each other now, and she has told me a good deal of what happened during that extraordinary time – for extraordinary it certainly was. Perhaps none of us realised what a unique drama we were watching – one of the strangest, I am tempted to believe, that this world of ours has ever seen.

Christmas was just past and the New Year was fairly under way when the beginning of the end came. I think by that time even Mrs Westmoreland had arrived at some sort of knowledge of the case. But it was then too late to interfere. I am as sure that Cecilia was not in love with Constanides as I am of anything. She was merely fascinated by him, and to a degree that, happily for the peace of the world, is as rare as the reason for it is perplexing.

To be precise, it was on Tuesday, January the 3rd, that the

crisis came. On the evening of that day, accompanied by her daughter and escorted by Dr Forsyth, Mrs Westmoreland attended a reception at the palace of a certain Pasha, whose name I am obviously compelled to keep to myself. For the purposes of my story it is sufficient, however, that he is a man who prides himself on being up-to-date in most things, and for that and other reasons invitations to his receptions are eagerly sought after. In his drawing-room one may meet some of the most distinguished men in Europe, and on occasion it is even possible to obtain an insight into certain political intrigues that, to put it mildly, afford one an opportunity of reflecting on the instability of mundane affairs and of politics in particular.

The evening was well advanced before Constanides made his appearance. When he did, it was observed that he was more than usually quiet. Later, Cecilia permitted him to conduct her into the balcony, whence, since it was a perfect moonlight night, a fine view of the Nile could be obtained. Exactly what he said to her I have never been able to discover; I have, however, her mother's assurance that she was visibly agitated when she rejoined her. As a matter of fact, they returned to the hotel almost immediately, when Cecilia, pleading weariness, retired to her room.

And now this is the part of the story you will find as difficult to believe as I did. Yet I have indisputable evidence that it is true. It was nearly midnight and the large hotel was enjoying the only quiet it knows in the twenty-four hours. I have just said that Cecilia had retired, but in making that assertion I am not telling the exact truth, for though she had bade mother 'Goodnight' and had gone to her room, it was not to rest. Regardless of the cold night air she had thrown open the window, and was standing looking out into the moonlit street. Of what she was thinking I do not know, nor can she re-member. For my own part, however, I incline to the belief that she was in a semi-hypnotic condition and that for the time being her mind was a blank.

From this point I will let Cecilia tell the story herself.

How long I stood at the window I cannot say; it may have been only five minutes, it might have been an hour. Then, suddenly, an extraordinary thing happened. I knew that it was imprudent, I was aware that it was even wrong, but an overwhelming craving to go out seized me. I felt as if the house were stifling me and that if I did not get out into the cool night air, and within a few minutes, I should die. Stranger still, I felt no desire to battle with the temptation. It was as if a will infinitely stronger than my own was dominating me and that I was powerless to resist. Scarcely conscious of what I was doing I changed my dress, and then, throwing on a cloak, switched off the electric light and stepped out into the corridor. The white-robed Arab servants were lying about on the floor as is their custom; they were all asleep. On the thick carpet of the great staircase my steps made no sound. The hall was in semi-darkness and the watchman must have been absent on his rounds, for there was no one there to spy upon me. Passing through the vestibule I turned the key of the front door. Still success attended me, for the lock shot back with scarcely a sound and I found myself in the street. Even then I had no thought of the folly of this escapade. I was merely conscious of the mysterious power that was dragging me on. Without hesitation I turned to the right and hastened along the pavement, faster I think than I had ever walked in my life. Under the trees it was comparatively dark, but out in the roadway it was well-nigh as bright as day. Once a carriage passed me and I could hear its occupants, who were French, conversing merrily – otherwise I seemed to have the city to myself. Later I heard a *muezzin* chanting his call to prayer from the minaret of some mosque in the neighbourhood, the cry being taken up and repeated from other mosques. Then at the corner of a street I stopped as if in obedience to a command. I can recall the fact that I was trembling, but for what reason I could not tell. I say this to show that while I was incapable of returning to the hotel, or of exercising my normal will power, I still possessed the faculty of observation.

I had scarcely reached the corner referred to, which, as a matter of fact, I believe I should recognise if I saw it again, when the door of a house opened and a man emerged. It was Professor Constanides, but his appearance at such a place and at such an hour, like everything else that happened that night, did not strike me as being in any way extraordinary.

'You have obeyed me,' he said by way of greeting. 'That is well. Now let us be going – the hour is late.'

As he said it there came the rattle of wheels and a carriage drove swiftly round the corner and pulled up before us. My companion helped me into it and took his place beside me. Even then, unheard-of as my action was, I had no thought of resisting.

'What does it mean?' I asked. 'Oh, tell me what it means? Why am I here?'

'You will soon know,' was his reply, and his voice took a tone I had never noticed in it before.

We had driven some considerable distance, in fact, I believe we had crossed the river, before either of us spoke again.

'Think,' said my companion, 'and tell me whether you can remember ever having driven with me before?'

'We have driven together many times lately,' I replied. 'Yesterday to the polo, and the day before to the Pyramids.'

'Think again,' he said, and as he did so he placed his hand on mine. It was as cold as ice. However, I only shook my head.

'I cannot remember,' I answered, and yet I seemed to be dimly conscious of something that was too intangible to be a recollection. He uttered a little sigh and once more we were silent. The horses must have been good ones for they whirled us along at a fast pace. I did not take much interest in the route we followed, but at last something attracted my attention and I knew that we were on the road to Gizeh. A few moments later the famous Museum, once the palace of the ex-Khedive Ismail, came into view. Almost immediately the carriage pulled up in the shadow of the *Lebbek* trees and my companion begged me to alight. I did so, whereupon he said something, in what I can only suppose was Arabic, to his coachman, who whipped up his horses and drove swiftly away.

'Come,' he said, in the same tone of command as before, and then led the way towards the gates of the old palace. Dominated as my will was by his I could still notice how beautiful the building looked in the moonlight. In the daytime it presents a faded and unsubstantial appearance, but now, with its Oriental tracery, it was almost fairylike. The Professor halted at the gates and unlocked them. How he had admitted us, I cannot say. It suffices that, almost before I was aware of it, we had passed through the garden and were ascending the steps to the main entrance. The doors behind us, we entered the first room. It is only another point in this extraordinary adventure when I declare that even now I was not afraid; and yet to find oneself in such a place and at such an hour at any other time would probably have driven me beside myself with terror. The moonlight streamed in upon us, revealing the ancient monuments and the other indescribable memorials of those long-dead ages. Once more my conductor uttered his command and we went on through the second room, passed the Skekh-El-Beled and the Seated Scribe. Room after room we traversed, and to do so it seemed to me that we ascended stairs innumerable. At last we came to one in which Constanides paused. It contained numerous mummy cases and was lighted by a skylight through which the rays of the moon streamed in. We were standing before one which I remembered to have remarked on the occasion of our last visit. I could distinguish the paintings upon it distinctly. Professor Constanides, with the deftness which showed his familiarity with the work, removed the lid and revealed to me the swathed-up figure within. The face was uncovered and was strangely well-preserved. I gazed down on it, and as I did so a sensation that I had never known before passed over me. My body seemed to be shrinking, my blood to be turning to ice. For the first time I endeavoured to exert myself, to tear myself from the bonds that were holding me. But it was in vain. I was sinking – sinking – sinking – into I knew not what. Then the voice of the man who had brought me to the place sounded in my ears as if he were speaking from a long way off. After that a great light burst upon me, and it was as if I were walking in a dream; yet I knew it was too real, too true to life to be a mere creation of my fancy.

It was night and the heavens were studded with stars. In the distance a great army was encamped and at intervals the calls of the sentries reached me. Somehow I seemed to feel no wonderment at my position. Even my dress caused me no surprise. To my left, as I looked towards the river, was a large tent, before which armed men paced continually. I looked about me as if I expected to see someone, but there was no one to greet me.

'It is for the last time,' I told myself. 'Come what may, it shall be the last time!'

Still I waited, and as I did so I could hear the night wind sighing through the rushes on the river's bank. From the tent near me – for Usirtasen, son of Amenemhait – was then fighting against the Libyans and was commanding his army in person – came the sound of revelry. The air blew cold from the desert and I shivered, for I was but thinly clad. Then I hid myself in the shadow of a great rock that was near at hand. Presently I caught the sound of a footstep, and there came into view a tall man, walking carefully, as though he had no desire that the sentries on guard before the Royal tent should become aware of his presence in the neighbourhood. As I saw him I moved from where I was standing to meet him. He was none other than Sinûhît – younger son of Amenemhait and brother of Usirtasen – who was at that moment conferring with his generals in the tent.

I can see him now as he came towards me, tall, handsome, and defiant in his bearing as a man should be. He walked with the assured step of one who has been a soldier and trained to warlike exercises from his youth up. For a moment I regretted the news I had to tell him – but only for a moment. I could hear the voice of Usirtasen in the tent, and after that I had no thought for anyone else.

'Is it thou, Nofrît?' he asked as soon as he saw me.

'It is I!' I replied. 'You are late, Sinûhît. You tarry too long over the wine cups.'

'You wrong me, Nofrît,' he answered, with all the fierceness for which he was celebrated. 'I have drunk no wine this night. Had I not been kept by the Captain of the Guard I should have been here sooner. Thou art not angry with me, Nofrît?'

'Nay, that were presumption on my part, my lord,' I answered. 'Art thou not the King's son, Sinûhît?'

'And by the Holy Ones I swear that it were better for me if I were not,' he replied. 'Usirtasen, my brother, takes all and I am but the jackal that gathers up the scraps wheresoever he may find them.' He paused for a moment. 'However, all goes well with our plot. Let me but have time and I will yet be ruler of this land and of all the Land of Khem beside.' He drew himself up to his full height and looked towards the sleeping camp. It was well known that between the brothers there was but little love, and still less trust.

'Peace, peace,' I whispered, fearing lest his words might be overheard. 'You must not talk so, my lord. Should you by chance be heard you know what the punishment would be!'

He laughed a short and bitter laugh. He was well aware that Usirtasen would show him no mercy. It was not the first time he had been suspected, and he was playing a desperate game. He came a step closer to me and took my hand in his. I would have withdrawn it – but he gave me no opportunity. Never was a man more in earnest than he was then.

'Nofrît,' he said, and I could feel his breath upon my cheek, 'what is my answer to be? The time for talking is past; now we must act. As thou knowest, I prefer deeds to words, and to-morrow my brother Usirtasen shall learn that I am as powerful as he.'

Knowing what I knew I could have laughed him to scorn for his boastful speech. The time, however, was not yet ripe, so I held my peace. He was plotting against his brother, whom I loved, and it was his desire that I should help him. That, however, I would not do.

'Listen,' he said, drawing even closer to me, and speaking in a voice that showed me plainly how much in earnest he was, 'thou knowest how much I love thee. Thou knowest that there is nought I would not do for thee or for thy sake. Be but faithful to me now and there is nothing thou shalt ask in vain of me hereafter. All is prepared, and ere the moon is gone I shall be Pharaoh and reign beside Amenemhait, my father.'

'Are you so sure that your plans will not miscarry?' I asked, with what was almost a sneer at his recklessness – for recklessness it surely was to think that he could induce an army that had been admittedly successful to swerve in its allegiance to the general who had won its battles for it, and to desert in the face of the enemy. Moreover, I knew that he was wrong in believing that his father cared more for him than for Usirtasen, who had done so much for the kingdom, and who was beloved by high and low alike. But it was not in Sinûhît's nature to look upon the dark side of things. He had complete confidence in himself and in his power to bring his conspiracy against his father and brother to a successful issue. He revealed to me his plans, and, bold though they were, I could see that it was impossible that they could succeed. And in the event of his failing,what mercy could he hope to receive? I knew Usirtasen too well to think that he would show any. With all the eloquence I could command I implored him to abandon the attempt, or at least to delay it for a time. He seized my wrist and pulled me to him, peering fiercely into my face.

'Art playing me false?' he asked. 'If it is so it were better that you should drown yourself in yonder river. Betray me and nothing shall save you – not even Pharaoh himself.'

That he meant what he said I felt convinced. The man was desperate; he was staking all he had in the world upon the issue of his venture. I can say with truth that it was not my fault that we had been drawn together, and yet on this night of all others it seemed as if there were nothing left for me but to side with him or to bring about his downfall.

'Nofrît,' he said, after a short pause, 'is it nothing, thinkest thou, to be the wife of a Pharaoh? Is it not worth striving for, particularly when it can be so easily accomplished?'

I knew, however, that he was deluding himself with false hopes. What he had in his mind could never come to pass. I was like dry grass between two fires. All that was required was one small spark to bring about a conflagration in which I should be consumed.

'Harken to me, Nofrît,' he continued. 'You have means of learning Usirtasen's plans. Send me word to-morrow as to what is in his mind and the rest will be easy. Your reward shall be greater than you dream of.'

Though I had no intention of doing what he asked, I knew that in his present humour it would be little short of madness to thwart him. I therefore temporised with him, and allowed him to suppose that I would do as he wished, and then, bidding him good-night, I sped away towards the hut where I was lodged. I had not been there many minutes when a messenger came to me from Usirtasen, summoning me to his presence. Though I could not understand what it meant I hastened to obey.

On arrival there I found him surrounded by the chief officers of his army. One glance at his face was sufficient to tell me that he was violently angry with someone, and I had the best of reasons for believing that that someone was myself. Alas! it was as I had expected. Sinûhît's plot had been discovered; he had been followed and watched, and my meeting with him that evening was known. I protested my innocence in vain. The evidence was too strong against me.

'Speak, girl, and tell what thou knowest,' said Usirtasen, in a voice I had never heard him use before. 'It is the only way by which thou canst save thyself. Look to it that thy story tallies with the tales of others!'

I trembled in every limb as I answered the questions he put to me. It was plain that he no longer trusted me, and that the favour I had once found in his eyes was gone, never to return.

'It is well,' he said when I had finished my story. 'And now we will see thy partner – the man who would have put me – the Pharaoh who is to be – to the sword had I not been warned in time.'

He made a sign to one of the officers who stood by, whereupon the latter left the tent, to return a few moments later with Sinûhît.

'Hail, brother!' said Usirtasen, mockingly, as he leaned back in his chair and looked at him through half-shut eyes. 'You tarried but a short time over the wine cup this night. I fear it pleased thee but little. Forgive me; on another occasion better shall be found for thee lest thou shouldst deem us lacking in our hospitality.'

'There were matters that needed my attention and I could not stay,' Sinûhît replied, looking his brother in the face. 'Thou wouldst not have me neglect my duties.'

'Nay! nay! Maybe they were matters that concerned our personal safety?' Usirtasen continued, still with the same gentleness. 'Maybe you heard that there were those in our army who were not well disposed towards us? Give me their names, my brother, that due punishment may be meted out to them.'

Before Sinûhît could reply, Usirtasen had sprung to his feet.

'Dog!' he cried, 'darest thou prate to me of matters of importance when thou knowest thou hast been plotting against me and my father's throne. I have doubted thee these many months and now all is made clear. By the Gods, the Holy Ones, I swear that thou shalt die for this ere cock-crow.'

It was at this moment that Sinûhît became aware of my presence. A little cry escaped him, and his face told me as plainly as any words could speak that he believed that I had betrayed him. He was about to speak, probably to denounce me, when the sound of voices reached us from outside. Usirtasen bade the guards to ascertain what it meant, and presently a messenger entered the tent. He was travel-stained and weary. Advancing towards where Usirtasen was seated, he knelt before him.

'Hail, Pharaoh,' he said. 'I come to three from the Palace of Titoui.'

An anxious expression came over Usirtasen's face as he heard this. I also detected beads of perspiration on the brow of Sinûhît. A moment latter it was known to us that Amenemhait was dead, and, therefore, Usirtasen reigned in his stead. The news was so sudden, and the consequences so vast, that it was impossible to realise quite what it meant. I looked across at Sinûhît and his eyes met mine. He seemed to be making up his mind about something. Then with lightning speed he sprang upon me; a dagger gleamed in the air; I felt as if a hot iron had been thrust into my breast, and after that I remember no more.

As I felt myself falling I seemed to wake from my dream – if dream it were – to find myself standing in the Museum by the mummy case, and with Professor Constanides by my side.

'You have seen,' he said. 'You have looked back across the centuries to that day when, as Nofrît, I believed you had betrayed me, and killed you. After that I escaped from the camp and fled into Kaduma. There I died; but it was decreed that my soul should never know peace till we had met again and you had forgiven me. I have waited all these years, and see – we meet at last.'

Strange to say, even then the situation did not strike me as being in any way improbable. Yet now, when I see it set down in black and white, I find myself wondering that I dare to ask anyone in their sober senses to believe it to be true. Was I in truth that same Nofrît who, four thousand years before, had been killed by Sinûhît, son of Amenemhait, because he believed that I had betrayed him? It seemed incredible, and yet, if it were a creation of my imagination, what did the dream mean? I fear it is a riddle of which I shall probably never know the answer.

My failure to reply to his question seemed to cause him pain.

'Nofrît,' he said, and his voice shook with emotion, 'think what your forgiveness means to me. Without it I am lost both here and hereafter.'

His voice was low and pleading and his face in the moonlight was like that of a man who knew the uttermost depths of despair.

'Forgive – forgive,' he cried again, holding out his hands to me. 'If you do not, I must go back to the sufferings which have been my portion since I did the deed which wrought my ruin.'

I felt myself trembling like a leaf.

'If it is as you say, though I cannot believe it, I forgive you freely,' I answered, in a voice that I scarcely recognised as my own.

For some moments he was silent, then he knelt before me and took my hand, which he raised to his lips. After that, rising, he laid his head upon the breast of the mummy before which we were standing. Looking down at it he addressed it thus:

'*Rest, Sinûhît, son of Amenemhait* – for that which was foretold for thee is now accomplished, and the punishment which was decreed is at an end. Henceforth thou mayest sleep in peace.'

After that he replaced the lid of the coffin, and when this was done he turned to me.

'Let us be going,' he said, and we went together through the rooms by the way we had come.

Together we left the building and passsed through the gardens out into the road beyond. There we found the carriage waiting for us, and we took our places in it. Once more the horses sped along the silent road, carrying us swiftly back to Cairo. During the drive not a word was spoken by either of us. The only desire I had left was to get back to the hotel and lay my aching head upon my pillow. We crossed the bridge and entered the city. What the time was I had no idea, but I was conscious that the wind blew chill as if in anticipation of the dawn. At the same corner whence we had started, the coachman stopped his horses and I alighted, after which he drove away as if he had received his orders before-hand.

'Will you permit me to walk with you as far as your hotel?' said Constanides, with his customary politeness.

I tried to say something in reply, but my voice failed me. I would much rather have been alone, but as he would not allow this we set off together. At the corner of the street in which the hotel is situated we stopped.

'Here we must part,' he said. Then, after a pause, he added, 'And for ever. From this moment I shall never see your face again.'

'You are leaving Cairo?' was the only thing I could say.

'Yes, I am leaving Cairo,' he replied with peculiar emphasis. 'My errand here is accomplished. You need have no fear that I shall ever trouble you again.'

'I have no fear,' I answered, though I am afraid it was only a half truth.

He looked earnestly into my face.

'Nofrît,' he said, 'for, say what you will, you are the Nofrît I would have made my Queen and have loved beyond all other women, never again will it be permitted you to look into the past as you did to-night. Had things been ordained otherwise we might have done great things together, but the gods willed that it should not be. Let it rest therefore. And now – farewell! To-night I go to the rest for which I have so long been seeking.'

Without another word he turned and left me. Then I went on to the hotel. How it came about I cannot say, but the door was open and I passed quickly in. Once more, to my joy, I found the watchman was absent from the hall.

Trembling lest anyone might see me, I sped up the stairs and along the corridor, where the servants lay sleeping just as I had left them, and so to my room. Everything was exactly as I had left it, and there was nothing to show that my absence had been suspected. Again I went to the window, and, in a feeling of extraordinary agitation, looked out. Already there were signs of dawn in the sky. I sat down and tried to think over all that had happened to me that evening, endeavouring to convince myself, in the face of indisputable evidence, that it was not real and that I had only dreamt it. Yet it would not do! At last, worn out, I retired to rest. As a rule I sleep soundly; it is scarcely, however, a matter for wonderment that I did not do so on this occasion. Hour after hour I tumbled and tossed – thinking – thinking – thinking. When I rose and looked into the glass I scarcely recognised myself. Indeed, my mother commented on my fagged appearance when we met at the breakfast table.

'My dear child, you look as if you had been up all night,' she said, and little did she guess, as she nibbled her toast, that there was a considerable amount of truth in her remark.

Later she went shopping with a lady staying in the hotel, while I went to my room to lie down. When we met again at lunch it was easy to see that she had some news of importance to communicate.

'My dear Cecilia,' she said, 'I have just seen Dr Forsyth, and he has given me a terrible shock. I don't want to frighten you, my girl, but have you heard that *Professor Constanides was found dead in bed this morning?* It is a most terrible affair! He must have died during the night!'

I am not going to pretend that I had any reply ready to offer her at that moment.

IMPRISONED WITH THE PHARAOHS

by Houdini & H P Lovecraft

Mystery attracts mystery. Ever since the wide appearance of my name as a performer of unexplained feats, I have encountered strange narratives and events which my calling has led people to link with my interests and activities. Some of these have been trivial and irrelevant, some deeply dramatic and absorbing, some productive of weird and perilous experiences and some involving me in extensive scientific and historical research. Many of these matters I have told and shall continue to tell very freely; but there is one of which I speak with great reluctance, and which I am now relating only after a session of grilling persuasion from the publishers of this magazine, who had heard vague rumours of it from other members of my family.

The hitherto guarded subject pertains to my non-professional visit to Egypt fourteen years ago, and has been avoided by me for several reasons. For one thing, I am averse to exploiting certain unmistakably actual facts and conditions obviously unknown to the myriad tourists who throng about the pyramids and apparently secreted with much diligence by the authorities at Cairo, who cannot be wholly ignorant of them. For another thing, I dislike to recount an incident in which my own fantastic imagination must have played so great a part. What I saw – or thought I saw – certainly did not take place; but is rather to be viewed as a result of my then recent readings in Egyptology, and of the speculations anent this theme which my environment naturally prompted. These imaginative stimuli, magnified by the excitement of an actual event terrible enough in itself, undoubtedly gave rise to the culminating horror of that grotesque night so long past.

In January, 1910, I had finished a professional engagement in England and signed a contract for a tour of Australian theatres. A liberal time being allowed for the trip, I determined to make the most of it in the sort of travel which chiefly interests me; so accompanied by my wife I drifted pleasantly down the Continent and embarked at Marseilles on the P & O Steamer *Malwa*, bound for Port Said. From that point I proposed to visit the principal historical localities of lower Egypt before leaving finally for Australia.

The voyage was an agreeable one, and enlivened by many of the amusing incidents which befall a magical performer apart from his work. I had intended, for the sake of quiet travel, to keep my name a secret; but was goaded into betraying myself by a fellow-magician whose anxiety to astound the passengers with ordinary tricks tempted me to duplicate and exceed his feats in a manner quite destructive of my incognito. I mention this because of its ultimate effect – an effect I should have foreseen before unmasking to a shipload of tourists about to scatter throughout the Nile valley. What it did was to herald my identity wherever I subsequently went, and deprive my wife and me of all the placid inconspicuousness we had sought. Travelling to seek curiosities, I was often forced to stand inspection as a sort of curiosity myself!

We had come to Egypt in search of the picturesque and the mystically impressive, but found little enough when the ship edged up to Port Said and discharged its passengers in small boats. Low dunes of sand, bobbing buoys in shallow water, and a drearily European small town with nothing of interest save the great De Lesseps statue, made us anxious to get on to something more worth our while. After some discussion we decided to proceed at once to Cairo and the Pyramids, later going to Alexandria for the Australian boat and for whatever Greco-Roman sights that ancient metropolis might present.

The railway journey was tolerable enough, and consumed only four hours and a half. We saw much of the Suez Canal, whose route we followed as far as Ismailiya and later had a taste of Old Egypt in our glimpse of the restored fresh-water canal of the Middle Empire. Then at last we saw Cairo glimmering through the growing dusk; a winking constellation which became a blaze as we halted at the great Gare Centrale.

But once more disappointment awaited us, for all that we beheld was European save the costumes and the crowds. A prosaic subway led to a square teeming with carriages, taxicabs, and trolley-cars and gorgeous with electric lights shining on tall buildings; whilst the very theatre where I was vainly requested to play and which I later attended as a spectator, had recently been renamed the 'American Cosmograph'. We stopped at Shepheard's Hotel, reached in a taxi that sped along broad, smartly built-up streets; and amidst the perfect service of its restaurant, elevators, and generally Anglo-American luxuries the mysterious East and immemorial past seemed very far away.

The next day, however, precipitated us delightfully into the heart of the *Arabian Nights* atmosphere; and in the winding ways and exotic skyline of Cairo, the Bagdad of Harun-al-Rashid seemed to live again. Guided by our Baedeker, we had struck east past the Ezbekiyeh Gardens along the Mouski in quest of the native quarter, and were soon in the hands of a clamorous cicerone who – notwithstanding later developments – was assuredly a master at his trade.

Not until afterward did I see that I should have applied at the hotel for a licenced guide. This man, a shaven, peculiarly hollow-voiced and relatively cleanly fellow who looked like a Pharaoh and called himself 'Abdul Reis el Drogman', appeared to have much power over others of his kind; though subsequently the police professed not to know him, and to suggest that *reis* is merely a name for any person in authority, whilst 'Drogman' is obviously no more than a clumsy modification of the word for a leader of tourists parties – *dragoman*.

Abdul led us among such wonders as we had before only read and dreamed of. Old Cairo is itself a story-book and a dream – labyrinths of narrow alleys redolent of aromatic secrets; Arabesque balconies and oriels nearly meeting above the cobbled streets; maelstroms of Oriental traffic with strange cries, cracking whips, rattling carts, jingling money, and braying donkeys; kaleidoscopes of polychrome robes, veils, turbans, and tarbushes; water-carriers and dervishes, dogs and cats, soothsayers and barbers; and over all the whining of blind beggars crouched in alcoves, and the sonorous chanting of muezzins from minarets limned delicately against a sky of deep, unchanging blue.

The roofed, quieter bazaars were hardly less alluring. Spice, perfume, incense beads, rugs, silks, and brass – old Mahmoud Suleiman squats cross-legged amidst his gummy bottles while chattering youths pulverize mustard in the hollowed-out capital of an ancient classic column – a Roman Corinthian, perhaps from neighboring Heliopolis, where Augustus stationed one of his three Egyptian legions. Antiquity begins to mingle with exoticism. And then the mosques and the museum – we saw them all, and tried not to let our Arabian revel succumb to the darker charm of Pharaonic Egypt which the museum's priceless treasures offered. That was to be our climax, and for the present we concentrated on the mediaeval Saracenic glories of the Califs whose magnificent tomb-mosques form a glittering faery necropolis on the edge of the Arabian Desert.

At length Abdul took us along the Sharia Mohammed Ali to the ancient mosque of Sultan Hassan, and the tower-flanked Babel-Azab, beyond which climbs the steep-walled pass to the mighty citadel that Saladin himself built with the stones of forgotten pyramids. It was sunset when we scaled that cliff, circled the modern mosque of Mohammed Ali, and looked down from the dizzy parapet over mystic Cairo – mystic Cairo all golden with its carven domes, its ethereal minarets and its flaming gardens.

Far over the city towered the great Roman dome of the new museum; and beyond it – across the cryptic yellow Nile that is the mother of eons and dynasties – lurked the menacing sands of the Libyan Desert, undulant and iridescent and evil with older arcana.

The red sun sank low, bringing the relentless chill of Egyptian dusk; and as it stood poised on the world's rim like that ancient god of Heliopolis – Re-Harakhte, the Horizon-Sun – we saw silhouetted against its vermeil holocaust the black outlines of the Pyramids of Gizeh – the palaeogean tombs there were hoary with a thousand years when Tut-

Ankh-Amen mounted his golden throne in distant Thebes. Then we knew that we were done with Saracen Cairo, and that we must taste the deeper mysteries of primal Egypt – the black Kem of Re and Amen, Isis and Osiris.

The next morning we visited the Pyramids, riding out in a Victoria across the island of Chizereh with its massive lebbakh trees, and the smaller English bridge to the western shore. Down the shore road we drove, between great rows of lebbakhs and past the vast Zoological Gardens to the suburb of Gizeh, where a new bridge to Cairo proper has since been built. Then, turning inland along the Sharia-el-Haram, we crossed a region of glassy canals and shabby native villages till before us loomed the objects of our quest, cleaving the mists of dawn and forming inverted replicas on the roadside pools. Forty centuries, as Napoleon had told his campaigners there, indeed looked down upon us.

The road now rose abruptly, till we finally reached our place of transfer between the trolley station and the Mena House Hotel. Abdul Reis, who capably purchased our Pyramid tickets, seemed to have an understanding with the crowding, yelling and offensive Bedouins who inhabited a squalid mud village some distance away and pestiferously assailed every traveller; for he kept them very decently at bay and secured an excellent pair of camels for us, himself mounting a donkey and assigning the leadership of our animals to a group of men and boys more expensive than useful. The area to be traversed was so small that camels were hardly needed, but we did not regret adding to our experience this troublesome form of desert navigation.

The pyramids stand on a high rock plateau, this group forming next to the northernmost of the series of regal and aristocratic cemeteries built in the neighbourhood of the extinct capital Memphis, which lay on the same side of the Nile, somewhat south of Gizeh, and which flourished between 3400 and 2000 B.C. The greatest pyramid, which lies nearest the modern road, was built by King Cheops or Khufu about 2800 B.C., and stand more than 450 feet in perpendicular height. In a line southwest from this are successively the Second Pyramid, built a generation later by King Khephren, and though slightly smaller, looking even larger because set on higher ground, and the radically smaller Third Pyramid of King Mycerinus, built about 2700 B.C. Near the edge of the plateau and due east of the Second Pyramid, with a face probably altered to form a colossal portrait of Khephren, its royal restorer, stands the monstrous Sphinx – mute, sardonic, and wise beyond mankind and memory.

Minor pyramids and the traces of ruined minor pyramids are found in several places, and the whole plateau is pitted with the tombs of dignitaries of less than royal rank. These latter were originally marked by *mastabas*, or stone bench-like structures about the deep burial shafts, as found in other Memphian cemeteries and exemplified by Perneb's Tomb in the Metropolitan Museum of New York. At Gizeh, however, all such visible things have been swept away by time and pillage; and only the rock-hewn shafts, either sand-filled or cleared out by archaeologists, remain to attest their former existence. Connected with each tomb was a chapel in which priests and relatives offered food and prayer to the hovering *ka* or vital principle of the deceased. The small tombs have their chapels contained in their stone *mastabas* or superstructures, but the mortuary chapels of the pyramids, where regal Pharaohs lay, were separate temples, each to the east of its corresponding pyramid, and connected by a causeway to a massive gate-chapel or propylon at the edge of the rock plateau.

The gate-chapel leading to the Second Pyramid, nearly buried in the drifting sands, yawns subterraneously south-east of the Sphinx. Persistent tradition dubs it the 'Temple of the Sphinx'; and it may perhaps be rightly called such if the Sphinx indeed represents the Second Pyramid's builder Khephren. There are unpleasant tales of the Sphinx before Khephren – but whatever its elder features were, the monarch replaced them with his own that men might look at the colossus without fear.

It was in the great gateway-temple that the life-size diorite statue of Khephren now in the Cairo museum was found; a statue before which I stood in awe when I beheld it. Whether the whole edifice is now excavated I am not certain, but in 1910 most of it was below ground, with the entrance heavily barred at night. Germans were in charge of the work, and the war or other things may have stopped them. I would give much, in view of my experience and of certain Bedouin whisperings discredited or unknown in Cairo, to know what has developed in connection with a certain well in a transverse gallery where statues of the Pharaoh were found in curious juxtaposition to the statues of baboons.

The road, as we traversed it on our camels that morning, curved sharply past the wooden police quarters, post office, drug store and shops on the left, and plunged south and east in a complete bend that scaled the rock plateau and brought us face to face with the desert under the lee of the Great Pyramid. Past Cyclopean masonry we rode, rounding the eastern face and looking down ahead into a valley of minor pyramids beyond which the eternal Nile glistened to the east, and the eternal desert shimmered to the west. Very close loomed the three major pyramids, the greatest devoid of outer casing and showing its bulk of great stones, but the others retaining here and there the neatly fitted covering which had made them smooth and finished in their day.

Presently we descended towards the Sphinx, and sat silent beneath the spell of those terrible unseeing eyes. On the vast stone breast we faintly discerned the emblem of Re-Harakhte, for whose image the Sphinx was mistaken in a late dynasty; and though sand covered the tablet between the great paws, we recalled what Thutmosis IV inscribed thereon, and the dream he had when a prince. It was then that the smile of the Sphinx vaguely displeased us, and made us wonder about the legends of subterranean passages beneath the monstrous creature, leading down, down, to depths none might dare hint at – depths connected with mysteries older than the dynastic Egypt we excavate, and having a sinister relation to the persistence of abnormal, animal-headed gods in the ancient Nilotic pantheon. Then, too, it was I asked myself an idle question whose hideous significance was not to appear for many an hour.

Other tourists now began to overtake us, and we moved on to the sand-choked Temple of the Sphinx, fifty yards to the southeast, which I have previously mentioned as the great gate of the causeway to the Second Pyramid's mortuary chapel on the plateau. Most of it was still underground, and although we dismounted and descended through a modern passage to its alabaster corridor and pillared hall, I felt that Adul and the local German attendant had not shown us all there was to see.

After this we made the conventional circuit of the pyramid plateau, examining the Second Pyramid and the peculiar ruins of its mortuary chapel to the east, the Third Pyramid and its miniature southern satellites and ruined eastern chapel, the rock tombs and the honeycombings of the Fourth and Fifth dynasties, and the famous Campbell's Tomb whose shadowy shaft sinks precipitously for fifty-three feet to a sinister sarcophagus which one of our camel drivers divested of the cumbering sand after a vertiginous descent by rope.

Cries now assailed us from the Great Pyramid, where Bedouins were besieging a party of tourists with offers of speed in the performance of solitary trips up and down. Seven minutes is said to be the record for such an ascent and descent, but many lusty shieks and sons of shieks assured us they could cut it to five if given the requisite impetus of liberal *baksheesh*. They did not get this impetus, though we did let Abdul take us up, thus obtaining a view of unprecedented magnificence which included not only remote and glittering Cairo with its crowned citadel background of gold-violet hills, but all the pyramids of the Memphian district as well, from Abu Roash on the north to the Dashur on the south. The Sakkara step-pyramid, which marks the evolution of the low *mastaba* into the true pyramid, showed clearly and alluringly in the sandy distance. It is close to this transition-monument that the famed tomb of Perneb was found – more than four hundred miles north of the Theban rock valley where Tut-Ankh-Amen sleeps. Again I was forced to silence through sheer awe. The prospect of such antiquity, and the secrets each hoary monument seemed to hold and brood over, filled me with a reverence and sense of immensity nothing else ever gave me.

Fatigued by our climb, and disgusted with the importunate Bedouins whose actions seemed to defy every rule of taste, we omitted the arduous detail of entering the cramped interior pasages of any of the pyramids, though we saw several of the hardiest tourists preparing for the suffocating crawl through Cheops' mightiest memorial. As we dismissed and overpaid our local bodyguard and drove back to Cairo with Abdul Reis under the afternoon sun, we half regretted the omission we had made. Such fascinating things were whispered about lower pyramid passages not in the guide books; passages whose entrances had been hastily blocked up and concealed by certain uncommunicative archaeologists who had found and begun to explore them.

Of course, this whispering was largely baseless on the face of it; but it was curious to reflect how persistently visitors were forbidden to enter the Pyramids at night, or to visit the lowest burrows and crypt of the Great Pyramid. Perhaps in the latter case it was the psychological effect which was feared – the effect on the visitor of feeling himself huddled down beneath a gigantic world of solid masonry; joined to the life he has known by the merest tube, in which he may only crawl, and which any accident or evil design might block. The whole subject seemed so weird and alluring that we resolved to pay the pryamid plateau another visit at the earliest possible opportunity. For me this opportunity came much earlier than I expected.

That evening, the members of our party feeling somewhat tired after the strenuous programme of the day, I went alone with Abdul Reis for a walk through the picturesque Arab quarter. Though I had seen it by day, I wished to study the alleys and bazaars in the dusk, when rich shadows and mellow gleams of light would add to their glamour and fantastic illusion. The native crowds were thinning, but were still very noisy and numerous when we came upon a knot of revelling Bedouins in the Suken-Nahhasin, or bazaar of the coppersmiths. Their apparent leader, an insolent youth with heavy features and saucily cocked tarbush, took some notice of us, and evidently recognized with no great friendliness my competent but admittedly supercilious and sneeringly disposed guide.

Perhaps, I thought, he resented that odd reproduction of the Sphinx's half-smile which I had often remarked with amused irritation; or perhaps he did not like the hollow and sepulchral resonance of Abdul's voice. At any rate, the ex-change of ancestrally opprobrious language became very brisk; and before long Ali Ziz, as I heard the stranger called when called by no worse name, began to pull violently at

Abdul's robe, an action quickly reciprocated and leading to a spirited scuffle in which both combatants lost their sacredly cherished headgear and would have reached an even direr condition had I not intervened and separated them by main force.

My interference, at first seemingly unwelcome on both sides, succeeded at last in effecting a truce. Sullenly each belligerent composed his wrath and his attire, and with an assumption of dignity as profound as it was sudden, the two formed a curious pact of honour which I soon learned is a custom of great antiquity in Cairo – a pact for the settlement of their difference by means of a nocturnal fist fight atop the Great Pyramid, long after the departure of the last moonlight sightseer. Each duellist was to assemble a party of seconds, and the affair was to begin at midnight, proceeding by rounds in the most civilized possible fashion.

In all this planning there was much which excited my interest. The fight itself promised to be unique and spectacular, while the thought of the scene on the hoary pile overlooking the antediluvian plateau of Gizeh under the wan moon of the pallid small hours appealed to every fibre of imagination in me. A request found Abdul exceedingly willing to admit me to his party of seconds; so that all the rest of the early evening I accompanied him to various dens in the most lawless regions of the town – mostly northeast of the Ezbekiyeh – where he gathered one by one a select and formidable band of congenial cutthroats as his pugilistic background.

Shortly after nine our party, mounted on donkeys bearing such royal or tourist-reminiscent names as 'Rameses,' 'Mark Twain,' 'J P Morgan,' and 'Minnehaha,' edged through street labyrinths both Oriental and Occidental, crossed the muddy and mast-forested Nile by the bridge of the bronze lions, and cantered philosophically between the lebbakhs on the road to Gizeh. Slightly over two hours was consumed by the trip, toward the end of which we passed the last of the returning tourists, saluted the last inbound trolley-car, and were alone with the night and the past and the spectral moon.

Then we saw the vast pyramids at the end of the avenue, ghoulish with a dim atavistical menace which I had not seemed to notice in the daytime. Even the smallest of them held a hint of the ghastly – for was it not in this that they had buried Queen Nitocris alive in the Sixth Dynasty; subtle Queen Nitocris, who once invited all her enemies to a feast in a temple below the Nile, and drowned them by opening the water-gates? I recalled that the Arabs whisper things about Nitocris, and shun the Third Pyramid at certain phases of the moon. It must have been over her that Thomas Moore was brooding when he wrote a thing muttered about by Memphian boatmen:

'The subterranean nymph that dwells
'Mid sunless gems and glories hid –
The lady of the Pyramid!'

Early as we were, Ali Ziz and his party were ahead of us; for we saw their donkeys outlined against the desert plateau at Kafrel-Haram; toward which squalid Arab settlement, close to the Sphinx, we had diverged instead of following the regular road to the Mena House, where some of the sleepy, inefficient police might have observed and halted us. Here, where filthy Bedouins stabled camels and donkeys in the rock tombs of Khephren's courtiers, we were led up the rocks and over the sand to the Great Pyramid, up whose time-worn sides the Arabs swarmed eagerly, Abdul Reis offering me the assistance I did not need.

As most travellers know, the actual apex of this structure has long been worn away, leaving a reasonably flat platform twelve yards square. On this eery pinnacle a squared circle was formed, and in a few moments the sardonic desert moon leered down upon a battle which, but for the quality of the ringside cries, might well have occurred at some minor athletic club in America. As I watched it, I felt that some of our less desirable institutions were not lacking; for every blow, feint, and defence bespoke 'stalling' to my inexperienced eye. It was quickly over, and despite my misgivings as to methods I felt a sort of proprietary pride when Abdul Reis was adjudged the winner.

Reconciliation was phenomenally rapid, and amidst the singing, fraternizing and drinking which followed, I found it difficult to realize that a quarrel had ever occurred. Oddly enough, I myself seemed to be more a centre of notice than the antagonists; and from my smattering of Arabic I judged that they were discussing my professional performances and escapes from every sort of manacle and confinement, in a manner which indicated not only a surprising knowledge of me, but a distinct hostility and scepticism concerning my feats of escape. It gradually dawned on me that the elder magic of Egypt did not depart without leaving traces, and that fragments of a strange secret lore and priestly cult-practices have survived surreptitiously amongst the fellaheen to such an extent that the prowess of a strange *hahwi* of magician is resented and disputed. I thought of how much my hollow-voiced guide Abdul Reis looked like an old Egyptian priest of Pharaoh or smiling Sphinx . . . and wondered.

Suddenly something happened which in a flash proved the correctness of my reflections and made me curse the denseness whereby I had accepted this night's events as other than the empty and malicious 'frame-up' they now showed themselves to be. Without warning, and doubtless in answer to some subtle sign from Abdul, the entire band of Bedouins precipitated itself upon me; and having produced heavy ropes, soon had me bound as securely as I was ever bound in the course of my life, either on the stage or off.

I struggled at first, but soon saw that one man could make no headway against a band of over twenty sinewy barbarians. My hands were tied behind my back, my knees bent to their fullest extent, and my wrists and ankles stoutly linked together with unyielding cords. A stifling gag was forced into my mouth, and a blindfold fastened tightly over my eyes. Then, as Arabs bore me aloft on their shoulders and began a jouncing descent of the pyramid, I heard the taunts of my late guide Adbul, who mocked and jeered delightedly in his hollow voice, and assured me that I was soon to have my 'magic powers' put to a supreme test which would quickly remove any egotism I might have gained through triumphing over all the tests offered by America and Europe. Egypt, he reminded me, is very old, and full of inner mysteries and antique powers not even conceivable to the experts of today, whose devices had so uniformly failed to entrap me.

How far or in what direction I was carried, I cannot tell; for the circumstances were all against the formation of any accurate judgment. I know, however, that it could not have been a great distance; since my bearers at no point hastened beyond a walk, yet kept me aloft a surprisingly short time. It is this perplexing brevity which makes me feel almost like shuddering whenever I think of Gizeh and its plateau – for one is oppressed by hints of the closeness to everyday tourist routes of what existed then and must exist still.

The evil abnormality I speak of did not become manifest at first. Setting me down on a surface which I reconized as sand rather than rock, my captors passed a rope around my chest and dragged me a few feet to a ragged opening in the ground, into which they presently lowered me with much rough handling. For apparent eons I bumped against the stony irregular sides of a narrow hewn well which I took to be one of the numerous burial-shafts of the plateau until the prodigious, almost incredible depth of it robbed me of all bases of conjecture.

The horror of the experience deepened with every dragging second. That any descent through the sheer solid rock could be so vast without reaching the core of the planet itself, or that any rope made by man could be so long as to dangle me in these unholy and seemingly fathomless profundities of nether earth, were beliefs of such grotesqueness that it was easier to doubt my agitated senses than to accept them. Even now I am uncertain, for I know how deceitful the sense of time becomes when one is removed or distorted. But I am quite sure that I preserved a logical consciousness that far; that at least I did not add any fullgrown phantoms of imagination to a picture hideous enough in its reality, and explicable by a type of cerebral illusion vastly short of actual hallucination.

All this was not the cause of my first bit of fainting. The shocking ordeal was cumulative, and the beginning of the later terrors was a very perceptible increase in my rate of descent. They were paying out that infinitely long rope very swiftly now, and I scraped cruelly against the rough and constricted sides of the shaft as I shot madly downward. My clothing was in tatters, and I felt the trickle of blood all over, even above the mounting and excruciating pain. My nostrils, too, were assailed by a scarcely definable menace: a creeping odour of damp and staleness curiously unlike anything I had ever smelled before, and having faint overtones of spice and incense that lent an element of mockery.

Then the mental cataclysm came. It was horrible – hideous beyond all articulate description because it was all of the soul, with nothing of detail to describe. It was the ecstasy of nightmare and the summation of the fiendish. The suddenness of it was apocalyptic and demoniac – one moment I was plunging agonizingly down that narrow well of million-toothed torture, yet the next moment I was soaring on bat-wings in the gulfs of hell; swinging free and swoopingly through illimitable miles of boundless, musty space; rising dizzily to measureless pinnacles of chilling ether, then diving gaspingly to sucking nadirs of ravenous, nauseous lower vacua. . . . Thank God for the mercy that shut out in oblivion those clawing Furies of consciousness which half unhinged my faculties, and tore harpy-like at my spirit! That one respite, short as it was, gave me the strength and sanity to endure those still greater sublimations of cosmic panic that lurked and gibbered on the road ahead.

It was very gradually that I regained my senses after that eldritch flight through stygian space. The process was infinitely painful, and coloured by fantastic dreams in which my bound and gagged condition found singular embodiment. The precise nature of these dreams was very clear while I was experiencing them, but became blurred in my recollection almost immediately afterwards, and was soon reduced to the merest outline by the terrible events – real or imaginary – which followed. I dreamed that I was in the grasp of a great and horrible paw; a yellow, hairy, five-clawed paw which had reached out of the earth to crush and engulf me. And when I stopped to reflect what the paw was, it seemed to me that it was Egypt. In the dream I looked back at the events of the preceding weeks, and saw myself lured and enmeshed little by little, subtly and insidiously, by some hellish ghoul-spirit of the elder Nile sorcery; some spirit that was in Egypt before ever man was, and that will be when man is no more.

I saw the horror and unwholesome antiquity of Egypt, and the grisly alliance it has always had with the tombs and temples of the dead. I saw phantom processions of priests with the heads of bulls, falcons, cats, and ibises; phantom processions marching interminably through subterraneous labyrinths and avenues of titanic propylaea beside which a man is as a fly, and offering unnamable sacrifice to indescribable gods. Stone colossi marched in endless night and drove herds of grinning androsphinxes down to the shores of illimitable stagnant rivers of pitch. And behind it all I saw the ineffable malignity of primordial necromancy, black and amorphous, and fumbling greedily after me in the darkness to choke out the spirit that had dared to mock it by emulation.

In my sleeping brain there took shape a melodrama of sinister hatred and pursuit, and I saw the black soul of Egypt singling me out and calling me in audible whispers; calling and luring me, leading me on with the glitter and glamour of a Saracenic surface, but ever pulling me down to the age-mad catacombs and horrors of its *dead* and abysmal pharaonic heart.

Then the dream faces took on human resemblances, and I saw my guide Abdul Reis in the robes of a king, with the sneer of the Sphinx on his features. And I knew that those features were the features of Khephren the Great, who raised the Second Pyramid, carved over the Sphinx's face in the likeness of his own and built that titanic gateway temple whose myriad corridors the archaeologists think they have dug out of the cryptical sand and the uninformative rock. And I looked at the long, lean, rigid hand of Khephren; the long, lean, rigid hand as I had seen it on the diorite statue in the Cairo Museum – the statue they had found in the terrible gateway temple – and wondered that I had not shrieked when I saw it on Abdul Reis . . . That hand! It was hideously cold, and it was crushing me; it was the cold and cramping of the sarcophagus . . . the chill and constriction of unrememberable Egypt . . . It was nighted, necropolitan Egypt itself . . . that yellow paw . . . and they whisper such things of Khephren. . . .

But at this juncture I began to awake – or at least, to assume a condition less completely that of sleep than the one just preceding. I recalled the fight atop the pyramid, the treacherous Bedouins and their attack, my frightful descent by rope through endless rock depths, and my mad swinging and plunging in a chill void redolent of aromtic putrescence. I perceived that I now lay on a damp rock floor, and that my bonds were still biting into me with unloosened force. It was very cold, and I seemed to detect a faint current of noisome air sweeping across me. The cuts and bruises I had received from the jagged sides of the rock shaft were paining me woefully, their soreness enhanced to a stinging or burning acuteness by some pungent quality in the faint draft, and the mere act of rolling over was enough to set my whole frame throbbing with untold agony.

As I turned I felt a tug from above, and concluded that the rope whereby I was lowered still reached the surface. Whether or not the Arabs still held it, I had no idea; nor had I any idea how far within the earth I was. I knew that the darkness around me was wholly or nearly total, since no ray of moonlight penetrated my blindfold; but I did not trust my senses enough to accept as evidenc of extreme depth the sensation of vast duration which had characterized my descent.

Knowing at least that I was in a space of considerable extent reached from the surface directly above by an opening in the rock, I doubtfully conjectured that my prison was perhaps the buried gateway chapel of old Khephren – the Temple of the Sphinx – perhaps some inner corridor which the guides had not shown me during my morning visit, and from which I might easily escape if I could find my way to the barred entrance. It would be a labyrinthine wandering, but no worse than others out of which I had in the past found my way.

The first step was to get free of my bonds, gag, and blindfold; and this I knew would be no great task, since subtler experts than these Arabs had tried every known species of fetter upon me during my long and varied career as an exponent of escape, yet had never succeeded in defeating my methods.

Then it occurred to me that the Arabs might be ready to meet and attack me at the entrance upon any evidence of my probable escape from the binding cords, as would be furnished by any decided agitation of the rope which they probably held. This, of course, was taking for granted that my place of confinement was indeed Khephren's Temple of the Sphinx. The direct opening in the roof, wherever it might lurk, could not be beyond easy reach of the ordinary modern entrance near the Sphinx; if in truth it were any great distance at all on the surface, since the total area known to visitors is not at all enormous. I had not noticed any such opening during my daytime pilgrimage, but knew that these things are easily overlooked amidst the drifting sands.

Thinking these matters over as I lay bent and bound on the rock floor, I nearly forgot the horrors of abysmal descent and cavernous swinging which had so lately reduced me to a coma. My present thought was only to outwit the Arabs, and I accordingly determined to work myself free as quickly as possible, avoiding any tug on the descending line which might betray an effective or even problematical attempt at freedom.

This, however, was more easily determined than effected. A few preliminary trials made it clear that little could be accomplished without considerable motion; and it did not surprise me when, after one especially energetic struggle, I began to feel the coils of falling rope as they piled up about me and upon me. Obviously, I thought, the Bedouins had felt my movements and released their end of the rope; hastening no doubt to the temple's true entrance to lie murderously in wait for me.

The prospect was not pleasing – but I had faced worse in my time without flinching, and would not flinch now. At present I must first of all free myself of bonds, then trust to ingenuity to escape from the temple unharmed. It is curious how implicitly I had come to believe myself in the old temple of Khephren beside the Sphinx, only a short distance below the ground.

That belief was shattered, and every pristine apprehension of preternatural depth and demoniac mystery revived, by a circumstance which grew in horror and significance even as I formulated my philosophical plan. I have said that the falling rope was piling up about and upon me. Now I saw that it was continuing to pile, as no rope of normal length could possibly do. It gained in momentum and became an avalanche of hemp, accumulating mountainously on the floor and half burying me beneath its swiftly multiplying coils. Soon I was completely engulfed and gasping for breath as the increasing convulsions submerged and stifled me.

My senses tottered again, and I vainly tried to fight off a menace desperate and ineluctable. It was not merely that I was tortured beyond human endurance – not merely that life and breath seemed to be crushed slowly out of me – it was the knowledge of what those unnatural lengths of rope implied, and the consciousness of what unknown and incalculable gulfs of inner earth must at this moment be surrounding me. My endless descent and swinging flight through goblin space, then, must have been real, and even now I must be lying helpless in some nameless cavern world toward the core of the planet. Such a sudden confirmation of ultimate horror was insupportable, and a second time I lapsed into merciful oblivion.

When I say oblivion, I do not imply that I was free from dreams. On the contrary, my absence from the conscious world was marked by visions of the most unutterable hideousness. God! . . . If only I had not read so much Egyptology before coming to this land which is the fountain of all darkness and terror! This second spell of fainting filled my sleeping mind anew with shivering realization of the country and its archaic secrets, and through some damnable chance my dreams turned to the ancient notions of the dead and their sojournings in soul and body beyond those mysterious tombs which were more houses than graves. I recalled, in dream-shapes which it is well that I do not remember, the peculiar and elaborate construction of Egyptian sepulchers; and the exceedingly singular and terrific doctrines which determined this construction.

All these people thought of was death and the dead. They conceived of a literal resurrection of the body which made them mummify it with desperate care, and preserve all the vital organs in canopic jars near the corpse; whilst besides the body they believed in two other elements, the soul, which after its weighing and approval by Osiris dwelt in the land of the blest, and the obscure and portentous *ka* or life-principle which wandered about the upper and lower worlds in a horrible way, demanding occasional access to the preserved body, consuming the food offerings brought by priests and pious relatives to the mortuary chapel, and sometimes – as men whispered – taking its body or the wooden double always buried beside it and stalking noxiously abroad on errands peculiarly repellent.

For thousands of years those bodies rested gorgeously encased and staring glassily upward when not visited by the *ka*, awaiting the day when Osiris should restore both *ka* and soul, and lead forth the stiff legions of the dead from the sunken houses of sleep. It was to have been a glorious rebirth – but not all souls were approved, nor were all tombs inviolate, so that certain grotesque *mistakes* and fiendish *abnormalities* were to be looked for. Even today the Arabs murmur of unsanctified convocations and unwholesome worship in forgotten nether abysses, which only winged invisible *kas* and soulless mummies may visit and return unscathed.

Perhaps the most leeringly blood-congealing legends are those which relate to certain perverse products of decadent priestcraft – *composite mummies* made by the artificial union of human trunks and limbs with the heads of animals in imitation of the elder gods. At all stages of history the sacred animals were mummified, so that consecrated bulls, cats, ibises, crocodiles and the like might return some day to greater glory. But only in the decadence did they mix the human and animal in the same mummy – only in the decadence, when they did not understand the rights and prerogatives of the *ka* and the soul.

What happened to those composite mummies is not told of – at least publicly – and it is certain that no Egyptologist ever found one. The whispers of Arabs are very wild, and cannot be relied upon. They even hint that old Khephren – he of the Sphinx, the Second Pyramid and the yawning gateway temple – lives far underground wedded to the ghoul-queen Nitocris and ruling over the mummies that are neither of man nor of beast.

It was of these – of Khephren and his consort and his strange armies of the hybrid dead – that I dreamed, and that is why I am glad the exact dream-shapes have faded from my memory. My most horrible vision was connected with an idle question I had asked myself the day before when looking at the great carven riddle of the desert and wondering with what unknown depth the temple close to it might be secretly connected. That question, so innocent and whimsical then, assumed in my dream a meaning of frenetic and hysterical madness . . . *what huge and loathsome abnormality was the Sphinx originally carven to represent?*

My second awakening – if awakening it was – is a memory of stark hideousness which nothing else in my life – save one thing which came after – can parallel; and that life has been full and adventurous beyond most men's. Remember that I had lost consciousness whilst buried beneath a cascade of falling rope whose immensity revealed the cataclysmic depth of my present position. Now, as perception returned, I felt the entire weight gone; and realized upon rolling over that although I was still tied, gagged and blindfolded, *some agency had removed completely the suffocating hempen landslide which had overwhelmed me.* The significance of this condition, of course, came to me only gradually; but even so I think it would have brought unconsciousness again had I not by this time reached such a state of emotional exhaustion that no new horror could make much difference. I was alone . . . *with what?*

Before I could torture myself with any new reflection, or make any fresh effort to escape from my bonds, an additional circumstance became manifest. Pains not formerly felt were racking my arms and legs, and I seemed coated with a profusion of dried blood beyond anything my former cuts and abrasions could furnish. My chest, too, seemed pierced by a hundred wounds, as though some malign, titanic ibis had been pecking at it. Assuredly the agency which had removed the rope was a hostile one, and had begun to wreak terrible injuries upon me when somehow impelled to desist. Yet at the time my sensations were distinctly the reverse of what one might expect. Instead of sinking into a bottomless pit of despair, I was stirred to a new courage and action; for now I felt that the evil forces were physical things which a fearless man might encounter on an even basis.

On the strength of this thought I tugged again at my bonds, and used all the art of a lifetime to free myself as I had so often done amidst the glare of lights and the applause of vast crowds. The familiar details of my escaping process commenced to engross me, and now that the long rope was gone I half regained my belief that the supreme horrors were hallucinations after all, and that there had never been any terrible shaft, measureless abyss or interminable rope. Was I after all in the gateway temple of Khephren beside the Sphinx, and had the sneaking Arabs stolen in to torture me as I lay helpless there? At any rate, I must be free. Let me stand up unbound, ungagged, and with eyes open to catch any glimmer of light which might come trickling from any source, and I could actually delight in the combat against evil and treacherous foes!

How long I took in shaking off my encumbrances I cannot tell. It must have been longer than in my exhibition performances, because I was wounded, exhausted, and enervated by the experiences I had passed through. When I was finally free, and taking deep breaths of a chill, damp, evilly spiced air all the more horrible when encountered without the screen of gag and blindfolded edges, I found that I was too cramped and fatigued to move at once. There I lay, trying to stretch a frame bent and mangled, for an indefinite period, and straining my eyes to catch a glimpse of some ray of light which would give a hint as to my position.

By degrees my strength and flexibility returned, but my eyes beheld nothing. As I staggered to my feet I peered diligently in every direction, yet met only an ebony blackness as great as that I had known when blindfolded. I tried my legs, blood-encrusted beneath my shredded trousers, and found that I could walk; yet could not decide in what direction to go. Obviously I ought not to walk at random, and perhaps retreat directly from the entrance I sought; so I paused to note the direction of the cold, fetid, natron-scented air-current which I had never ceased to feel. Accepting the point of its source as the possible entrance to the abyss, I strove to keep track of this landmark and to walk consistently toward it.

I had a match-box with me, and even a small electric flashlight; but of course the pockets of my tossed and tattered clothing were long since emptied of all heavy articles. As I walked cautiously in the blackness, the draft grew stronger and more offensive, till at length I could regard it as nothing less than a tangible stream of detestable vapour pouring out of some aperture like the smoke of the genie from the fisherman's jar in the Eastern tale. The East . . . Egypt . . .

truly, this dark cradle of civilization was ever the wellspring of horrors and marvels unspeakable!

The more I reflected on the nature of this cavern wind, the greater my sense of disquiet became; for although despite its odour I had sought its source as at least an indirect clue to the outer world, I now saw plainly that this foul emanation could have no admixture or connection whatsoever with the clean air of the Libyan Desert, but must be essentially a thing vomited from sinister gulfs still lower down. I had, then, been walking in the wrong direction!

After a moment's reflection I decided not to retrace my steps. Away from the draft I would have no landmarks, for the roughly level rock floor was devoid of distinctive configurations. If, however, I followed up the strange current, I would undoubtedly arrive at an aperture of some sort, from whose gate I could perhaps work round the walls to the opposite side of this Cyclopean and otherwise unnavigable hall. That I might fail, I well realized. I saw that this was no part of Khephren's gateway temple which tourists know, and it struck me that this particular hall might be unknown even to archaeologists, and merely stumbled upon by the inquisitive and malignant Arabs who had imprisoned me. If so, was there any present gate of escape to the known parts or to the outer air?

What evidence, indeed, did I now possess that this was the gateway temple at all? For a moment all my wildest speculations rushed back upon me, and I thought of that vivid melange of impressions – descent, suspension in space, the rope, my wounds, and the dreams that were frankly dreams. Was this the end of life for me? Or indeed, would it be merciful if this moment *were* the end? I could answer none of my own questions, but merely kept on, till Fate for a third time reduced me to oblivion.

This time there were no dreams, for the suddenness of the incident shocked me out of all thought either conscious or subconscious. Tripping on an unexpected descending step at a point where the offensive draft became strong enough to offer an actual physical resistance, I was precipitated headlong down a black flight of huge stone stairs into a gulf of hideousness unrelieved.

That I ever breathed again is a tribute to the inherent vitality of the healthy human organism. Often I look back to that night and feel a touch of actual humour in those repeated lapses of consciousness; lapses whose succession reminded me at the time of nothing more than the crude cinema melodramas of that period. Of course, it is possible that the repeated lapses never occurred; and that all the features of that underground nightmare were merely the dreams of one long coma which began with the shock of my descent into that abyss and ended with the healing balm of the outer air and of the rising sun which found me stretched on the sands of Gizeh before the sardonic and dawn-flushed face of the Great Sphinx.

I prefer to believe this latter explanation as much as I can, hence was glad when the police told me that the barrier to Khephren's gateway temple had been found unfastened, and that a sizable rift to the surface did actually exist in one corner of the still buried part. I was glad, too, when the doctors pronounced my wounds only those to be expected from my seizure, blindfolding, lowering, struggling with bonds, falling some distance – perhaps into a depression in the temple's inner gallery – dragging myself to the outer barrier and escaping from it, and experiences like that . . . a very soothing diagnosis. And yet I know that there must be more than appears on the surface. That extreme descent is too vivid a memory to be dismissed – and it is odd that no one has ever been able to find a man answering the description of my guide, Abdul Reis el Drogman – the tomb-throated guide who looked and smiled like King Khephren.

I have digressed from my connected narrative – perhaps in the vain hope of evading the telling of that final incident; that incident which of all is most certainly an hallucination. But I promised to relate it, and I do not break promises. When I recovered – or seemed to recover – my senses after that fall down the black stone stairs, I was quite as alone and in darkness as before. The windy stench, bad enough before, was now fiendish; yet I had acquired enough familiarity by this time to bear it stoically. Dazedly I began to crawl away from the place whence the putrid wind came, and with my bleeding hands felt the colossal blocks of a mighty pavement. Once my head struck against a hard object, and when I felt of it I learned that it was the base of a column – a column of unbelievably immensity – whose surface was covered with gigantic chiseled hieroglyphics very perceptible to my touch.

Crawling on, I encountered other titan columns at incomprehensible distances apart; when suddenly my attention was captured by the realization of something which must have been impinging on my subconscious hearing long before the conscious sense was aware of it.

From some still lower chasm in earth's bowels were proceeding certain *sounds*, measured and definite, and like nothing I had ever heard before. That they were very ancient and distinctly ceremonial I felt almost intuitively; and much reading in Egyptology led me to associate them with the flute, the sambuke, the sistrum, and the tympanum. In their rhythmic piping, droning, rattling and beating I felt an element of terror beyond all the known terrors of earth – a terror peculiarly dissociated from personal fear, and taking the form of a sort of objective pity for our planet, that it should hold within its depths such horrors as must lie beyond these aegipanic cacophonies. The sounds increased in volume, and I felt that they were approaching. Then – and may all the gods of all pantheons unite to keep the like from my ears again – I began to hear, faintly and afar off, the morbid and millennial tramping of the marching things.

It was hideous that footfalls so dissimilar should move in such perfect rhythm. The training of unhallowed thousands of years must lie behind that march of earth's inmost monstrosities . . . padding, clicking, walking, stalking, rumbling, lumbering, crawling . . . and all to the abhorrent discords of those mocking instruments. And then – God keep the memory of those Arab legends out of my head! – the mummies without souls . . . the meeting-place of the wandering *kas* . . . the hordes of the devil-cursed pharaonic dead of forty centuries . . . the *composite mummies* led through the uttermost onyx voids by King Khephren and his ghoul-queen Nitocris . . .

The tramping drew nearer – Heaven save me from the sound of those feet and paws and hooves and pads and talons as it commenced to acquire detail! Down limitless reaches of sunless pavement a spark of light flickered in the malodorous wind and I drew behind the enormous circumference of a Cyclopic column that I might escape for a while the horror that was stalking million-footed toward me through gigantic hypostyles of inhuman dread and phobic antiquity. The flickers increased, and the tramping and dissonant rhythm grew sickeningly loud. In the quivering orange light there stood faintly forth a scene of such stony awe that I gasped from sheer wonder that conquered even fear and repulsion. Bases of columns whose middles were higher than human sight . . . mere bases of things that must each dwarf the Eiffel Tower to insignificance . . . hieroglyphics carved by un- thinkable hands in caverns where daylight can be only a remote legend . . .

I *would not* look at the marching things. That I desperately resolved as I heard their creaking joints and nitrous wheezing above the dead music and the dead tramping. It was merciful that they did not speak . . . but God! *their crazy torches began to cast shadows on the surface of those stupendous columns. Hippopotami should not have human hands and carry torches . . . men should not have the heads of crocodiles . . .*

I tried to turn away, but the shadows and the sounds and the stench were everywhere. Then I remembered something I used to do in half-conscious nightmares as a boy, and began to repeat to myself, 'This is a dream! This is a dream!' But it was of no use, and I could only shut my eyes and pray . . . at least, that is what I think I did, for one is never sure in visions – and I know this can have been nothing more. I wondered whether I should ever reach the world again, and at times would furtively open my eyes to see if I could discern any feature of the place other than the wind of spiced putrefaction, the topless columns, and the thaumatropically grotesque shadows of abnormal horror. The sputtering glare of multiplying torches now shone, and unless this hellish place were wholly without walls, I could not fail to see some boundary or fixed landmark soon. But I had to shut my eyes again when I realized how many of the things were assembling – and when I glimpsed a certain object walking solemnly and steadily *without any body above the waist.*

A fiendish and ululant corpse-gurgle or death-rattle now

split the very atmosphere – the charnel atmosphere poisonous with naftha and bitumen blasts – in one concerted chorus from the ghoulish legion of hybrid blasphemies. My eyes, perversely shaken open, gazed for an instant upon a sight which no human creature could even imagine without panic, fear and physical exhaustion. The things had filed ceremonially in one direction, the direction of the noisome wind, where the light of their torches showed their bended heads – or the bended heads of such as had heads. They were worshipping before a great black fetor-belching aperture which reached up almost out of sight, and which I could see was flanked at right angles by two giant staircases whose ends were far away in shadow. One of these was indubitably the staircase I had fallen down.

The dimensions of the hole were fully in proportion with those of the columns – an ordinary house would have been lost in it, and any average public building could easily have been moved in and out. It was so vast a surface that only by moving the eye could one trace its boundaries . . . so vast, so hideously black, and so aromatically stinking . . . Directly in front of this yawning Polyphemus-door the things were throwing objects – evidently sacrifices or religious offerings, to judge by their gestures. Khephren was their leader; sneering King Khephren *or the guide Abdul Reis*, crowned with a golden pshent and intoning endless formulae with the hollow voice of the dead. By his side knelt beautiful Queen Nitocris, whom I saw in profile for a moment, noting that the right half of her face was eaten away by rats or other ghouls. And I shut my eyes again when I saw what objects were being thrown as offerings to the fetid aperture or its possible local deity.

It occurred to me that, judging from the elaborateness of this worship, the concealed deity must be one of considerable importance. Was it Osiris or Isis, Horus or Anubis, or some vast unknown God of the Dead still more central and supreme? There is a legend that terrible altars and colossi were reared to an Unknown One before even the known gods were worshipped. . . .

And now, as I steeled myself to watch the rapt and sepulchral adorations of those nameless things, a thought of escape flashed upon me. The hall was dim, and the columns heavy with shadow. With every creature of that nightmare throng absorbed in shocking raptures, it might be barely possible for me to creep past to the far-away end of one of the staircases and ascend unseen; trusting to Fate and skill to deliver me from the upper reaches. Where I was, I neither knew nor seriously reflected upon – and for a moment it struck me as amusing to plan a serious escape from that which I knew to be a dream. Was I in some hidden and unsuspected lower realm of Khephren's gateway temple – that temple which generations have persistently called the Temple of the Sphinx? I could not conjecture, but I resolved to ascend to life and consciousness if wit and muscle could carry me.

Wriggling flat on my stomach, I began the anxious journey toward the foot of the left-hand staircase, which seemed the more accessible of the two. I cannot describe the incidents and sensations of that crawl, but they may be guessed when one reflects on what I had to watch steadily in that malign, wind-blown torchlight in order to avoid detection. The bottom of the staircase was, as I have said, far away in shadow, as it had to be to rise without a bend to the dizzy parapeted landing above the titanic aperture. This placed the last stages of my crawl at some distance from the noisome herd, though the spectacle chilled me even when quite remote at my right.

At length I succeeded in reaching the steps and began to climb; keeping close to the wall, on which I observed decorations of the most hideous sort, and relying for safety on the absorbed, ecstatic interest with which the monstrosities watched the foul-breezed aperture and the impious objects of nourishment they had flung on the pavement before it. Though the staircase was huge and steep, fashioned of vast porphyry blocks as if for the feet of a giant, the ascent seemed virtually interminable. Dread of discovery and the pain which renewed exercise had brought to my wounds combined to make that upward crawl a thing of agonizing memory. I had intended, on reaching the landing, to climb immediately onward along whatever upper staircase might mount from there; stopping for no last look at the carrion abominations that pawed and genuflected some seventy or eighty feet below – yet a sudden repetition of that thunderous corpse-gurgle and death-rattle chorus, coming as I had nearly gained the top of the flight and showing by its ceremonial rhythm that it was not an alarm of my discovery, caused me to pause and peer cautiously over the parapet.

The monstrosities were hailing something which had poked itself out of the nauseous aperture to seize the hellish fare proffered it. It was something quite ponderous, even as seen from my height; something yellowish and hairy, and endowed with a sort of nervous motion. It was as large, perhaps, as a good-sized hippopotamus, but very curiously shaped. It seemed to have no neck, but five separate shaggy heads springing in a row from a roughly cylindrical trunk; the first very small, the second good-sized, the third and fourth equal and largest of all, and the fifth rather small, though not so small as the first.

Out of these heads darted curious rigid tentacles which seized ravenously on the excessively great quantities of unmentionable food placed before the aperture. Once in a while the thing would leap up, and occasionally it would retreat into its den in a very odd manner. Its locomotion was so inexplicable that I stared in fascination, wishing it would emerge farther from the cavernous lair beneath me.

Then it *did emerge* . . . it *did* emerge, and at the sight I turned and fled into the darkness up the higher staircase that rose behind me; fled unknowingly up incredible steps and ladders and inclined planes to which no human sight or logic guided me, and which I must ever relegate to the world of dreams for want of any confirmation. It must have been a dream, or the dawn would never have found me breathing on the sands of Gizeh before the sardonic dawn-flushed face of the Great Sphinx.

The Great Sphinx! God! That idle question I asked myself on that sun-blest morning before . . . *what huge and loathsome abnormality was the Sphinx originally carven to represent?* Accursed is the sight, be it in dream or not, that revealed to me the supreme horror – the unknown God of the Dead, which licks its colossal chops in the unsuspected abyss, fed hideous morsels by soulless absurdities that should not exist. The five-headed monster that emerged . . . that five-headed monster as large as a hippopotamus . . . the five-headed monster – *and that of which it is the merest forepaw* . . .

But I survived, and I know it was only a dream.

MY NEW YEAR'S EVE AMONG
THE MUMMIES

by Grant Allen

I have been a wanderer and a vagabond on the face of the earth for a good many years now, and I have certainly had some odd adventures in my time; but I can assure you, I never spent twenty-four queerer hours than those which I passed some twelve months since in the great unopened Pyramid of Abu Yilla.

The way I got there was itself a very strange one. I had come to Egypt for a winter tour with the Fitz-Simkinses, to whose daughter Editha I was at that precise moment engaged. You will probably remember that old Fitz-Simkins belonged originally to the wealthy firm of Simkinson and Stokoe, worshipful vintners; but when the senior partner retired from the business and got his knighthood, the College of Heralds opportunely discovered that his ancestors had changed their fine old Norman name for its English equivalent some time about the reign of King Richard I; and they immediately authorized the old gentleman to resume the patronymic and the armorial bearings of his distinguished forefathers. It's really quite astonishing how often these curious coincidences crop up at the College of Heralds.

Of course it was a great catch for a landless and briefless barrister like myself – dependent on a small fortune in South American securities, and my precarious earnings as a writer of burlesque – to secure such a valuable prospective property as Editha Fitz-Simkins. To be sure, the girl was undeniably plain; but I have known plainer girls than she was, whom forty thousand pounds converted into My Ladies: and if Editha hadn't really fallen over head and ears in love with me, I suppose old Fitz-Simkins would never have consented to such a match. As it was, however, we had flirted so openly and so desperately during the Scarborough season, that it would have been difficult for Sir Peter to break it off: and so I had come to Egypt on a tour of insurance to secure my prize, following in the wake of my future mother-in-law, whose lungs were supposed to require a genial climate – though in my private opinion they were really as creditable a pair of pulmonary appendages as ever drew breath.

Nevertheless, the course of true love did not run so smoothly as might have been expected. Editha found me less ardent than a devoted squire should be; and on the very last night of the old year she got up a regulation lovers' quarrel, because I had sneaked away from the boat that afternoon under the guidance of our dragoman, to witness the seductive performances of some fair Ghawázi, the dancing girls of a neighbouring town. How she found it out heaven only knows, for I gave that rascal Dimitri five piastres to hold his tongue: but she did find it out somehow, and chose to regard it as an offence of the first magnitude: a mortal sin only to be expiated by three days of penance and humiliation.

I went to bed that night, in my hammock on deck, with feelings far from satisfactory. We were moored against the bank at Abu Yilla, the most pestiferous hole between the cataracts and the Delta. The mosquitoes were worse than the ordinary mosquitoes of Egypt, and that is saying a great deal. The heat was oppressive even at night, and the malaria from the lotus beds rose like a palpable mist before my eyes. Above all, I was getting doubtful whether Editha Fitz-Simkins might not after all slip between my fingers. I felt wretched and feverish: and yet I had delightful interlusive recollections, in between, of that lovely little Gháziyah, who danced that exquisite, marvellous, entrancing, delicious, and awfully oriental dance that I saw in the afternoon.

By Jove, she *was* a beautiful creature. Eyes like two full moons; hair like Milton's Penseroso; movements like a poem of Swinburne's set to action. If Editha was only a faint picture of that girl now! Upon my word, I was falling in love with a Gháziyah!

Then the mosquitoes came again. Buzz – buzz – buzz. I make a lunge at the loudest and biggest, a sort of prima donna in their infernal opera. I kill the prima donna, but ten more shrill performers come in its place. The frogs croak dismally in the reedy shallows. The night grows hotter and hotter still. At last, I can stand it no longer. I rise up, dress myself lightly, and jump ashore to find some way of passing the time.

Yonder, across the flat, lies the great unopened Pyramid of Abu Yilla. We are going to-morrow to climb to the top; but I will take a turn to reconnoitre in that direction now. I walk across the moonlit fields, my soul still divided between Editha and the Gháziyah, and approach the solemn mass of huge, antiquated granite blocks standing out so grimly against the pale horizon. I feel half awake, half asleep, and altogether feverish: but I poke about the base in an aimless sort of way, with a vague idea that I may perhaps discover by chance the secret of its sealed entrance, which has ere now baffled so many pertinacious explorers and learned Egyptologists.

As I walk along the base, I remember old Herodotus's story, like a page from the 'Arabian Nights', of how King Rhampsinitus built himself a treasury, wherein one stone turned on a pivot like a door; and how the builder availed himself of this his cunning device to steal gold from the king's storehouse. Suppose the entrance to the unopened Pyramid should be by such a door. It would be curious if I should chance to light upon the very spot.

I stood in the broad moonlight, near the north-east angle of the great pile, at the twelfth stone from the corner. A random fancy struck me, that I might turn this stone by pushing it inward on the left side. I leant against it with all my weight, and tried to move it on the imaginary pivot. Did it give way a fraction of an inch? No, it must have been mere fancy. Let me try again. Surely it is yielding! Gracious Osiris, it has moved an inch or more! My heart beats fast, either with fever or excitement, and I try a third time. The rust of centuries on the pivot wears slowly off, and the stone turned ponderously round, giving access to a low dark passage.

It must have been madness which led me to enter the

forgotten corridor, alone, without torch or match, at that hour of the evening; but at any rate I entered. The passage was tall enough for a man to walk erect, and I could feel, as I groped slowly along, that the wall was composed of smooth polished granite, while the floor sloped away downward with a slight but regular descent. I walked with trembling heart and faltering feet for some forty or fifty yards down the mysterious vestibule: and then I felt myself brought suddenly to a standstill by a block of stone placed right across the pathway. I had had nearly enough for one evening, and I was preparing to return to the boat, agog with my new discovery, when my attention was suddenly arrested by an incredible, a perfectly miraculous fact.

The block of stone which barred the passage was faintly visible as a square, by means of a struggling belt of light streaming through the seams. There must be a lamp or other flame burning within. What if this were a door like the outer one, leading into a chamber perhaps inhabited by some dangerous band of outcasts? The light was a sure evidence of human occupation: and yet the outer door swung rustily on its pivot as though it had never been opened for ages. I paused a moment in fear before I ventured to try the stone: and then, urged on once more by some insane impulse, I turned the massive block with all my might to the left. It gave way slowly like its neighbour, and finally opened into the central hall.

Never as long as I live shall I forget the ecstasy of terror, astonishment, and blank dismay which seized upon me when I stepped into that seemingly enchanted chamber. A blaze of light first burst upon my eyes, from jets of gas arranged in regular rows tier above tier, upon the columns and walls of the vast apartment. Huge pillars, richly painted with red, yellow, blue and green decorations, stretched in endless succession down the dazzling aisles. A floor of polished syenite reflected the splendour of the lamps, and afforded a base for red granite sphinxes and dark purple images in porphyry of the cat-faced goddess Pasht, whose form I knew so well at the Louvre and the British Museum. But I had no eyes for any of these lesser marvels, being wholly absorbed in the greatest marvel of all: for there, in royal state and with mitred head, a living Egyptian king, surrounded by his coiffured court, was banqueting in the flesh upon a real throne, before a table laden with Memphian delicacies!

I stood transfixed with awe and amazement, my tongue and my feet alike forgetting their office, and my brain whirling round and round, as I remember it used to whirl when my health broke down utterly at Cambridge after the Classical Tripos. I gazed fixedly at the strange picture before me, taking in all its details in a confused way, yet quite incapable of understanding or realizing any part of its true import. I saw the king in the centre of the hall, raised on a throne of granite inlaid with gold and ivory; his head crowned with the peaked cap of Rameses, and his curled hair flowing down his shoulders in a set and formal frizz. I saw priests and warriors on either side, dressed in the costumes which I had often carefully noted in our great collections; while bronze-skinned maids, with light garments round their waists, and limbs displayed in graceful picturesqueness, waited upon them, half nude, as in the wall paintings which we had lately examined at Karnak and Syene. I saw the ladies, clothed from head to foot in dyed linen garments, sitting apart in the background, banqueting by themselves at a separate table; while dancing girls, like older representatives of my yesternoon friends, the Ghawázi, tumbled before them in strange attitudes, to the music of four-stringed harps and long straight pipes. In short, I beheld as in a dream the whole drama of everyday Egyptian royal life, playing itself out anew under my eyes, in its real original properties and personages.

Gradually, as I looked, I became aware that my hosts were no less surprised at the appearance of their anachronistic guest than was the guest himself at the strange living panorama which met his eyes. In a moment music and dancing ceased; the banquet paused in its course, and the king and his nobles stood up in undisguised astonishment to survey the strange intruder.

Some minutes passed before any one moved forward on either side. At last a young girl of royal appearance, yet strangely resembling the Gháziyah of Abu Yilla, and recalling in part the laughing maiden in the foreground of Mr Long's great canvas at the previous Academy, stepped out before the throng.

'May I ask you,' she said in Ancient Egyptian, 'who you are, and why you come hither to disturb us?'

I was never aware before that I spoke or understood the language of the hieroglyphics: yet I found I had not the slightest difficulty in comprehending or answering her question. To say the truth, Ancient Egyptian, though an extremely tough tongue to decipher in its written form, becomes as easy as love-making when spoken by a pair of lips like that Pharaonic princess's. It is really very much the same as English, pronounced in a rapid and somewhat indefinte whisper, and with all the vowels left out.

'I beg ten thousand pardons for my intrusion,' I answered apologetically: 'but I did not know that this Pyramid was inhabited, or I should not have entered your residence so rudely. As for the points you wish to know, I am an English tourist, and you will find my name upon this card;' saying which I handed her one from the case which I had fortunately put into my pocket, with conciliatory politeness. The princess examined it closely, but evidently did not understand its import.

'In return,' I continued, 'may I ask you in what august presence I now find myself by accident?'

A court official stood forth from the throng, and answered in a set heraldic tone: 'In the presence of the illustrious monarch, Brother of the Sun, Thothmes the Twenty-seventh, king of the Eighteenth Dynasty.'

'Salute the Lord of the World,' put in another official in the same regulation drone.

I bowed low to his Majesty, and stepped out into the hall. Apparently my obeisance did not come up to Egyptian standards of courtesy, for a suppressed titter broke audibly from the ranks of bronze-skinned waiting-women. But the king graciously smiled at my attempt, and turning to the nearest nobleman, observed in a voice of great sweetnes and self-contained majesty: 'This stranger, Ombos, is certainly a very curious person. His appearance does not at all resemble that of an Ethiopian or other savage, nor does he look like the pale-faced sailors who come to us from the Achaian land beyond the sea. His features, to be sure, are not very different from theirs; but his extraordinary and singularly inartistic dress shows him to belong to some other barbaric race.'

I glanced down at my waistcoat, and saw that I was wearing my tourist's check suit, of grey and mud colour, with which a Bond Street tailor had supplied me just before leaving town, as the latest thing out in fancy tweeds. Evidently these Egyptians must have a very curious standard of taste not to admire our pretty and graceful style of male attire.

'If the dust beneath your Majesty's feet may venture upon a suggestion,' put in the officer whom the king had addressed, 'I would hint that this young man is probably a stray visitor from the utterly uncivilized lands of the North. The headgear which he carries in his hand obviously betrays an Arctic habitat.'

I had instinctively taken off my round felt hat in the first moment of surprise, when I found myself in the midst of this strange throng, and I was standing now in a somewhat embarrassed posture, holding it awkwardly before me like a shield to protect my chest.

'Let the stranger cover himself,' said the king.

'Barbarian intruder, cover yourself,' cried the herald. I noticed throughout that the king never directly addressed anybody save the higher officials around him.

I put on my hat as desired. 'A most uncomfortable and silly form of tiara indeed,' said the great Thothmes.

'Very unlike your noble and awe-spiring mitre, Lion of Egypt,' answered Ombos.

'Ask the stranger his name,' the king continued.

It was useless to offer another card, so I mentioned   in a clear voice.

'An uncouth and almost unpronounceable designation truly,' commented his Majesty to the Grand Chamberlain beside him. 'These savages speak strange languages, widely different from the flowing tongue of Memnon and Sesostris.'

The chamberlain bowed his assent with three low genuflexions. I began to feel a little abashed at these personal remarks, and I *almost* think (though I shouldn't like it to be mentioned in the Temple) that a blush rose to my cheek.

The beautiful princess, who had been standing near me meanwhile in an attitude of statuesque repose, now appeared anxious to change the current of the conversation. 'Dear father,' she said with a respectful inclination, 'surely the stranger, barbarian though he be, cannot relish such pointed allusions to his person and costume. We must let him feel the grace and delicacy of Egyptian refinement. Then he may perhaps carry back with him some faint echo of its cultured beauty to his northern wilds.'

'Nonsense, Hatasou,' replied Thothmes XXVII testily. 'Savages have no feelings, and they are as incapable of appreciating Egyptian sensibility as the chattering crow is incapable of attaining the dignified reserve of the sacred crocodile.'

'Your Majesty is mistaken,' I said, recovering my self-possession gradually and realizing my position as a freeborn Englishman before the court of a foreign despot – though I must allow that I felt rather less confident than usual, owing to the fact that we were not represented in the Pyramid by a British Consul – 'I am an English tourist, a visitor from a modern land whose civilization far surpasses the rude culture of early Egypt; and I am accustomed to respectful treatment from all other nationalities, as becomes a citizen of the First Naval Power in the World.'

My answer created a profound impression. 'He has spoken to the Brother of the Sun,' cried Ombos in evident perturbation. 'He must be of the Blood Royal in his own tribe, or he would never have dared to do so!'

'Otherwise,' added a person whose dress I recognized as that of a priest, 'he must be offered up in expiation to Amon-Ra immediately.'

As a rule I am a decent truthful person, but under these alarming circumstances I ventured to tell a slight fib with an air of nonchalant boldness. 'I am a younger brother of our reigning king,' I said without a moment's hesitation; for there was nobody present to gainsay me, and I tried to salve my conscience by reflecting that at any rate I was only claiming consanguinity with an imaginary personage.

'In that case,' said King Thothmes, with more geniality in his tone, 'there can be no impropriety in my addressing you personally. Will you take a place at our table next to myself, and we can converse together without interrupting a banquet which must be brief enough in any circumstances? Hatasou, my dear, you may seat yourself next to the barbarian prince.'

I felt a visible swelling to the proper dimensions of a Royal Highness as I sat down by the king's right hand. The nobles resumed their places, the bronze-skinned waitresses left off standing like soldiers in a row and staring straight at my humble self, the goblets went round once more, and a comely maid soon brought me meat, bread, fruits and date wine.

All this time I was naturally burning with curiosity to inquire who my strange host might be, and how they had preserved their existence for so many centuries in this undiscovered hall; but I was obliged to wait until I had satisfied his Majesty of my own nationality, the means by which I had entered the Pyramid, the general state of affairs throughout the world at the present moment, and fifty thousand other matters of a similar sort. Thothmes utterly refused to believe my reiterated assertion that our existing civilization was far superior to the Egyptian; 'because,' he said, 'I see from your dress that your nation is utterly devoid of taste or invention;' but he listened with great interest to my account of modern society, the steam-engine, the Permissive Prohibitory Bill, the telegraph, the House of Commons, Home Rule, and other blessings of our advanced era, as well as to a brief *résumé* of European history from the rise of the Greek culture to the Russo-Turkish war. At last his questions were nearly exhausted, and I got a chance of making a few counter inquiries on my own account.

'And now,' I said, turning to the charming Hatasou, whom I thought a more pleasing informant than her august papa, 'I should like to know who *you* are.'

'What, don't you know?' she cried with unaffected surprise. 'Why, we're mummies.'

She made this astonishing statement with just the same quiet unconsciousness as if she had said, 'we're French,' or 'we're Americans.' I glanced round the walls, and observed behind the columns, what I had not noticed till then – a large number of empty mummy-cases, with their lids placed carelessly by their sides.

'But what are you doing here?' I asked in a bewildered way.

'Is it possible,' said Hatasou, 'that you don't really know

the object of embalming? Though your manners show you to be an agreeable and well-bred young man, you must excuse my saying that you are shockingly ignorant. We are made into mummies in order to preserve our immortality. Once in every thousand years we wake up for twenty-four hours, recover our flesh and blood, and banquet once more upon the mummied dishes and other good things laid by for us in the Pyramid. To-day is the first day of a millennium, and so we have waked up for the sixth time since we were first embalmed.'

'The *sixth* time?' I inquired incredulously. 'Then you must have been dead six thousand years.'

'Exactly so.'

'But the world has not yet existed so long,' I cried, in a fervour of orthodox horror.

'Excuse me, barbarian prince. This is the first day of the three hundred and twenty-seven thousandth millennium.'

My orthodoxy received a severe shock. However, I had been accustomed to geological calculations, and was somewhat inclined to accept the antiquity of man; so I swallowed the statement without more ado. Besides, if such a charming girl as Hatasou had asked me at that moment to turn Mohammedan, or to worship Osiris, I believe I should incontinently have done so.

'You wake up only for a single day and night, then?' I said.

'Only for a single day and night. After that, we go to sleep for another millennium.'

'Unless you are meanwhile burned as fuel on the Cairo Railway,' I added mentally. 'But how,' I continued aloud, 'do you get these lights?'

'The Pyramid is built above a spring of inflammable gas. We have a reservoir in one of the side chambers in which it collects during the thousand years. As soon as we awake, we turn it on at once from the tap, and light it with a lucifer match.'

'Upon my word,' I interposed, 'I had no notion you Ancient Egyptians were acquainted with the use of matches.'

'Very likely not. "There are more things in heaven and earth, Cephrenes, than are dreamt of in your philosophy," as the bard of Philæ puts it.'

Further inquiries brought out all the secrets of that strange tomb-house, and kept me fully interested till the close of the banquet. Then the chief priest solemnly rose, offered a small fragment of meat to a deified crocodile, who sat in a meditative manner by the side of his deserted mummy-case, and declared the feast concluded for the night. All rose from their places, wandered away into the long corridors or side-aisles, and formed little groups of talkers under the brilliant gas-lamps.

For my part, I strolled off with Hatasou down the least illuminated of the colonnades, and took my seat beside a marble fountain, where several fish (gods of great sanctity, Hatasou assured me) were disporting themselves in a porphyry basin. How long we sat there I cannot tell, but I know that we talked a good deal about fish, and gods, and Egyptian habits, and Egyptian philosophy, and, above all, Egyptian love-making. The last-named subject we found very interesting, and when once we got fully started upon it, no diversion afterwards occurred to break the even tenour of the conversation. Hatasou was a lovely figure, tall, queenly, with smooth dark arms and neck of polished bronze: her big black eyes full of tenderness, and her long hair bound up into a bright Egyptian headdress, that harmonized to a tone with her complexion and her robe. The more we talked, the more desperately did I fall in love, and the more utterly oblivious did I become of my duty to Editha Fitz-Simkins. The mere ugly daughter of a rich and vulgar brand-new knight, for-sooth, to show off her airs before me, when here was a Princess of the Blood Royal of Egypt, obviously sensible to the attentions which I was paying her, and not unwilling to receive them with a coy and modest grace.

Well, I went on saying pretty things to Hatasou, and Hatasou went on deprecating them in a pretty little way, as who should say, 'I don't mean what I pretend to mean one bit;' until at last I may confess that we were both evidently as far gone in the disease of the heart called love as it is possible for two young people on first acquaintance to become. There-fore, when Hatasou pulled forth her watch – another piece of mechanism with which antiquaries used never to credit the Egyptian people – and declared that she had only three more hours to live, at least for the next thousand years, I fairly broke down, took out my handkerchief, and began to sob like a child of five years old.

Hatasou was deeply moved. Decorum forbade that she should console me with too much *empressement*; but she ventured to remove the handkerchief gently from my face, and suggested that there was yet one course open by which we might enjoy a little more of one another's society. 'Suppose,' she said quietly, 'you were to become a mummy. You would then wake up, as we do, every thousand years; and after you have tried it once, you will find it just as natural to sleep for a millennium as for eight hours. Of course,' she added with a slight blush, 'during the next three or four solar cycles there would be plenty of time to conclude any other arrangements you might possibly contemplate, before the occurrence of another glacial epoch.'

This mode of regarding time was certainly novel and somewhat bewildering to people who ordinarily reckon its lapse by weeks and months; and I had a vague consciousness that my relations with Editha imposed upon me a moral necessity of returning to the outer world, instead of becoming a millennial mummy. Besides, there was the awkward chance of being converted into fuel and dissipated into space before the arrival of the next waking day. But I took one look at Hatasou, whose eyes were filling in turn with sympathetic tears, and that look decided me. I flung Editha, life, and duty to the dogs, and resolved at once to become a mummy.

There was no time to be lost. Only three hours remained to us, and the process of embalming, even in the most hasty manner, would take up fully two. We rushed off to the chief priest, who had charge of the particular department in question. He at once acceded to my wishes, and briefly explained the mode in which they usually treated the corpse.

That word suddenly aroused me. 'The corpse!' I cried; 'but I am alive. You can't embalm me living,'

'We can,' replied the priest, 'under chloroform.'

'Chloroform!' I echoed, growing more and more astonished: 'I had no idea you Egyptians knew anything about it.'

'Ignorant barbarian!' he answered with a curl of the lip; 'you imagine yourself much wiser than the teachers of the world. If you were versed in all the wisdom of the Egyptians, you would know that chloroform is one of our simplest and commonest anæsthetics.'

I put myself at once under the hands of the priest. He brought out the chloroform, and placed it beneath my nostrils, as I lay on a soft couch under the central court. Hatasou held my hand in hers, and watched my breathing with an anxious eye. I saw the priest leaning over me, with a clouded phial in his hand, and I experienced a vague sensation of smelling myrrh and spikenard. Next, I lost myself for a few moments, and when I again recovered my senses in a temporary break, the priest was holding a small greenstone knife, dabbled with blood, and I felt that a gash had been made across my breast. Then they applied the chloroform once more; I felt Hatasou give my hand a gentle squeeze; the whole panorama faded finally from my view; and I went to sleep for a seemingly endless time.

When I awoke again, my first impression led me to believe that the thousand years were over, and that I had come to life once more to feast with Hatasou and Thothmes in the Pyramid of Abu Yilla. But second thoughts, combined with closer observation of the surroundings, convinced me that I was really lying in a bedroom of Shepheard's Hotel at Cairo. An hospital nurse leant over me, instead of a chief priest; and I noticed no tokens of Editha Fitz-Simkins's presence. But when I endeavoured to make inquiries upon the subject of my whereabouts, I was peremptorily informed that I mustn't speak, as I was only just recovering from a severe fever, and might endanger my life by talking.

Some weeks later I learned the sequel of my night's adventure. The Fitz-Simkinses, missing me from the boat in the morning, at first imagined that I might have gone ashore for an early stroll. But after breakfast time, lunch time, and dinner time had gone past, they began to grow alarmed, and sent to look for me in all directions. One of their scouts, happening to pass the Pyramid, noticed that one of the stones near the north-east angle had been displaced, so as to give access to a dark passage, hitherto unknown. Calling several of his friends, for he was afraid to venture in alone, he passed down the corridor, and through a second gateway into the central hall. There the Fellahin found me, lying on the ground, bleeding profusely from a wound on the breast, and in an advanced stage of malarious fever. They brought me back to the boat, and the Fitz-Simkinses conveyed me at once to Cairo, for medical attendance and proper nursing.

Editha was at first convinced that I had attempted to commit suicide because I could not endure having caused her pain, and she accordingly resolved to tend me with the utmost care through my illness. But she found that my delirious remarks, besides bearing frequent reference to a princess, with whom I appeared to have been on unexpectedly intimate terms, also related very largely to our *casus belli* itself, the dancing girls of Abu Yilla. Even this trial she might have borne, setting down the moral degeneracy which led me to patronize so degrading an exhibition as a first symptom of my approaching malady: but certain unfortunate observations, containing pointed and by no means flattering allusions to her personal appearance – which I contrasted, much to her disadvantage, with that of the unknown princess – these, I say, were things which she could not forgive; and she left Cairo abruptly with her parents for the Riviera, leaving behind a stinging note, in which she denounced my perfidy and emptyheartedness with all the flowers of feminine eloquence. From that day to this I have never seen her.

When I returned to London and proposed to lay this account before the Society of Antiquaries, all my friends dissuaded me on the grounds of its apparent incredibility. They declare that I must have gone to the Pyramid already in a state of delirium, discovered the entrance by accident, and sunk exhausted when I reached the inner chamber. In answer, I would point out three facts. In the first place, I undoubtedly found my way into the unknown passage – for which achievement I afterwards received the gold medal of the Société Khédiviale, and of which I retain a clear recollection, differing in no way from my recollection of the subsequent events. In the second place, I had in my pocket, when found, a ring of Hatasou's, which I drew from her finger just before I took the chloroform, and put into my pocket as a keepsake. And in the third place, I had on my breast the wound which I saw the priest inflict with a knife of greenstone, and the scar may be seen on the spot to the present day. The absurd hypothesis of my medical friends, that I was wounded by falling against a sharp edge of rock, I must at once reject as unworthy of a moment's consideration.

My own theory is either that the priest had not time to complete the operation, or else that the arrival of the Fitz-Simkins' scouts frightened back the mummies to their cases an hour or so too soon. At any rate, there they all were, ranged around the walls undisturbed, the moment the Fellahin entered.

Unfortunately, the truth of my account cannot be tested for another thousand years. But as a copy of this book will be preserved for the benefit of posterity in the British Museum, I hereby solemnly call upon Collective Humanity to try the veracity of this history by sending a deputation of archæologists to the Pyramid of Abu Yilla, on the last day of December, Two thousand eight hundred and seventy-seven. If they do not then find Thothmes and Hatasou feasting in the central hall exactly as I have described, I shall willingly admit that the story of my New Year's Eve among the Mummies is a vain hallucination, unworthy of credence at the hands of the scientific world.

Smith and the Pharaohs

Scientists, or some scientists – for occasionally one learned person differs from other learned persons – tell us they know all that is worth knowing about man, which statement, of course, includes woman. They trace him from his remotest origin; they show us how his bones changed and his shape modified, also how, under the influence of his needs and passions, his intelligence developed from something very humble. They demonstrate conclusively that there is nothing in man which the dissecting-table will not explain; that his aspirations towards another life have their root in the fear of death, or, say others of them, in that of earthquake or thunder; that his affinities with the past are merely inherited from remote ancestors who lived in that past, perhaps a million years ago; and that everything noble about him is but the fruit of expediency or of a veneer of civilisation, while everything base must be attributed to the instincts of his dominant and primeval nature. Man, in short, is an animal who, like every other animal, is finally subdued by his environment and takes his colour from his surroundings, as cattle do from the red soil of Devon. Such are the facts, they (or some of them) declare; all the rest is rubbish.

At times we are inclined to agree with these sages, especially after it has been our privilege to attend a course of lectures by one of them. Then perhaps something comes within the range of our experience which gives us pause and causes doubts, the old divine doubts, to arise again deep in our hearts, and with them a yet diviner hope.

Perchance when all is said, so we think to ourselves, man *is* something more than an animal. Perchance he has known the past, the far past, and will know the future, the far, far future. Perchance the dream is true, and he does indeed possess what for convenience is called an immortal soul, that may manifest itself in one shape or another; that may sleep for ages, but, waking or sleeping, still remains itself, indestructible as the matter of the Universe.

An incident in the career of Mr James Ebenezer Smith might well occasion such reflections, were any acquainted with its details, which until this, its setting forth, was not the case. Mr Smith is a person who knows when to be silent. Still, undoubtedly it gave cause for thought to one individual – namely, to him to whom it happened. Indeed, James Ebenezer Smith is still thinking over it, thinking very hard indeed.

J.E. Smith was well born and well educated. When he was a good-looking and able young man at college, but before he had taken his degree, trouble came to him, the particulars of which do not matter, and he was thrown penniless, also friendless, upon the rocky bosom of the world. No, not quite friendless, for he had a godfather, a gentleman connected with business whose Christian name was Ebenezer. To him, as a last resource, Smith went, feeling that Ebenezer owed him something in return for the awful appellation wherewith he had been endowed in baptism.

To a certain extent Ebenezer recognised the obligation. He did nothing heroic, but he found his godson a clerkship in a bank of which he was one of the directors – a modest clerkship, no more. Also, when he died a year later, he left him a hundred pounds to be spent upon some souvenir.

Smith, being of a practical turn of mind, instead of adorning himself with memorial jewellery for which he had no use, invested the hundred pounds in an exceedingly promising speculation. As it happened, he was not misinformed, and his talent returned to him multiplied by ten. He repeated the experiment, and, being in a position to know what he was doing, with considerable success. By the time that he was thirty he found himself possessed of a fortune of something over twenty-five thousand pounds. Then (and this shows the wise and practical nature of the man) he stopped speculating and put out his money in such a fashion that it brought him a safe and clear four per cent.

By this time Smith, being an excellent man of business, was well up in the service of his bank – as yet only a clerk, it is true, but one who drew his four hundred pounds a year, with prospects. In short, he was in a position to marry had he wished to do so. As it happened, he did not wish – perhaps because, being very friendless, no lady who attracted him crossed his path; perhaps for other reasons.

Shy and reserved in temperament, he confided only in himself. None, not even his superiors at the bank or the Board of Management, knew how well off he had become. No one visited him at the flat which he was understood to occupy somewhere in the neighbourhood of Putney; he belonged to no club, and possessed not a single intimate. The blow which the world had dealt him in his early days, the harsh repulses and the rough treatment he had then experienced, sank so deep into his sensitive soul that never again did he seek close converse with his kind. In fact, while still young, he fell into a condition of old-bachelorhood of a refined type.

Soon, however, Smith discovered – it was after he had given up speculating – that a man must have something to occupy his mind. He tried philanthropy, but found himself too sensitive for a business which so often resolves itself into rude inquiry as to the affairs of other people. After a struggle, therefore, he compromised with his conscience by setting aside a liberal portion of his income for anonymous distribution among deserving persons and objects.

While still in this vacant frame of mind Smith chanced one day, when the bank was closed, to drift into the British Museum, more to escape the vile weather that prevailed without than for any other reason. Wandering hither and thither at hazard, he found himself in the great gallery devoted to Egyptian stone objects and sculpture. The place bewildered him somewhat, for he knew nothing of Egyptology; indeed, there remained upon his mind only a sense of wonderment not unmixed with awe. It must have been a great people, he thought to himself, that executed these works, and with the thought came a desire to know more about them. Yet he was going away when suddenly his eye fell on the sculptured head of a woman which hung upon the wall.

Smith looked at it once, twice, thrice, and at the third look he fell in love. Needless to say, he was not aware that such was his condition. He knew only that a change had come over him, and never, never could he forget the face which that carven mask portrayed. Perhaps it was not really beautiful save for its wondrous and mystic smile; perhaps the lips were too thick and the nostrils too broad. Yet to him that face was Beauty itself, beauty which drew him as with a cart-rope, and awoke within him all kinds of wonderful imaginings, some of them so strange and tender that almost they partook of the nature of memories. He stared at the image, and the image smiled back sweetly at him, as doubtless it, or rather its original – for this was but a plaster cast – had smiled at nothingness in some tomb or hiding-hole for over thirty centuries, and as the woman whose likeness it was had once smiled upon the world.

A short, stout gentleman bustled up and, in tones of authority, addressed some workmen who were arranging a base for a neighbouring statue. It occurred to Smith that he must be someone who knew about these objects. Overcoming his natural diffidence with an effort, he raised his hat and asked the gentleman if he could tell him who was the orginal of the mask.

The official – who, in fact, was a very great man in the Museum – glanced at Smith shrewdly, and, seeing that his interest was genuine, answered:

'I don't know. Nobody knows. She has been given several names, but none of them have authority. Perhaps one day the rest of the statue may be found, and then we shall learn – that is, if it is inscribed. Most likely, however, it has been burnt for lime long ago.'

'Then you can't tell me anything about her?' said Smith.

'Well, only a little. To begin with, that's a cast. The original is in the Cairo Museum. Mariette found it, I believe at Karnak, and gave it a name after his fashion. Probably she was a queen – of the eighteenth dynasty, by the work. But you can see her rank for yourself from the broken *uroeus*.' (Smith did not stop him to explain that he had not the faintest idea what a *uroeus* might be, seeing that he was utterly unfamiliar with the snake-headed crest of Egyptian royalty.) 'You should go to Egypt and study the head for yourself. It is one of the most beautiful things that ever was found. Well, I must be off. Good day.'

And he bustled down the long gallery.

Smith found his way upstairs and looked at mummies and other things. Somehow it hurt him to reflect that the owner of yonder sweet, alluring face must have become a mummy long, long before the Christian era. Mummies did not strike him as attractive.

He returned to the statuary and stared at his plaster cast till one of the workmen remarked to his fellow that if he were the gent he'd go and look at 'a live'un' for a change.

Then Smith retired abashed.

On his way home he called at his bookseller's and ordered 'all the best works on Egyptology'. When, a day or two later, they arrived in a packing-case, together with a bill for thirty-eight pounds, he was somewhat dismayed. Still, he tackled those books like a man, and, being clever and industrious, within three months had a fair working knowledge of the subject, and had even picked up a smattering of hieroglyphics.

In January – that was, at the end of those three months – Smith astonished his Board of Directors by applying for ten weeks' leave, he who had hitherto been content with a fortnight in the year. When questioned he explained that he had been suffering from bronchitis, and was advised to take a change in Egypt.

'A very good idea,' said the manager; 'but I'm afraid you'll find it expensive. They fleece one in Egypt.'

'I know,' answered Smith; 'but I've saved a little and have only myself to spend it upon.'

So Smith went to Egypt and saw the original of the beauteous head and a thousand other fascinating things. Indeed, he did more. Attaching himself to some excavators who were glad of his intelligent assistance, he actually dug for a month in the neighbourhood of ancient Thebes, but without finding anything in particular.

It was not till two years later that he made his great discovery, that which is known as Smith's Tomb. Here it may be explained that the state of his health had become such as to necessitate an annual visit to Egypt, or so his superiors understood.

However, as he asked for no summer holiday, and was always ready to do another man's work or to stop overtime, he found it easy to arrange for these winter excursions.

On this, his third visit to Egypt, Smith obtained from the Director-General of Antiquities at Cairo a licence to dig upon his own account. Being already well known in the country as a skilled Egyptologist, this was granted upon the usual terms — namely, that the Department of Antiquities should have a right to take any of the objects which might be found, or all of them, if it so desired.

Such preliminary matters having been arranged by correspondence, Smith, after a few days spent in the Museum at Cairo, took the night train to Luxor, where he found his headman, an ex-dragoman named Mahomet, waiting for him and his fellaheen labourers already hired. There were but forty of them, for his was a comparatively small venture. Three hundred pounds was the amount that he had made up his mind to expend, and such a sum does not go far in excavations.

During his visit of the previous year Smith had marked the place where he meant to dig. It was in the cemetery of old Thebes, at the wild spot not far from the temple of Medinet Habu, that is known as the Valley of the Queens. Here, separated from the resting-places of their royal lords by the bold mass of the intervening hill, some of the greatest ladies of Egypt have been laid to rest, and it was their tombs that Smith desired to investigate. As he knew well, some of these must yet remain to be discovered. Who could say? Fortune favours the bold. It might be that he would find the holy grave of that beauteous, unknown Royalty whose face had haunted him for three long years!

For a whole month he dug without the slightest success. The spot that he selected had proved, indeed, to be the mouth of a tomb. After twenty-five days of laborious exploration it was at length cleared out, and he stood in a rude unfinished cave. The queen for whom it had been designed must have died quite young and been buried elsewhere, or she had chosen herself another sepulchre, or mayhap the rock had proved unsuitable for sculpture.

Smith shrugged his shoulders and moved on, sinking trial pits and trenches here and there, but still finding nothing. Two-thirds of his time and money had been spent when at last the luck turned. One day, towards evening, with some half-dozen of his best men he was returning after a fruitless morning of labour, when something seemed to attract him towards a little *wadi*, or bay, in the hillside that was filled with tumbled rocks and sand. There were scores of such places, and this one looked no more promising than any of the others had proved to be. Yet it attracted him. Thoroughly dispirited, he walked past it twenty paces or more, then turned.

'Where go you, sah?' asked his head-man, Mahomet.

He pointed to the recess in the cliff.

'No good, sah,' said Mahomet. 'No tomb there. Bed-rock too near top. Too much water run in there; dead queen like keep dry!'

But Smith went on, and the others followed obediently.

He walked down the little slope of sand and boulders and examined the cliff. It was virgin rock; never a tool mark was to be seen. Already the men were going, when the same strange instinct which had drawn him to the spot caused him to take a spade from one of them and begin to shovel away the sand from the face of the cliff — for here, for some unexplained reason, were no boulders or débris. Seeing their master, to whom they were attached, at work, they began to work too, and for twenty minutes or more dug on cheerfully enough, just to humour him, since all were sure that here there was no tomb. At length Smith ordered them to desist, for, although now they were six feet down, the rock remained of the same virgin character.

With an exclamation of disgust he threw out a last shovelful of sand. The edge of his spade struck on something that projected. He cleared away a little more sand, and there appeared a rounded ledge which seemed to be a cornice. Calling back the men, he pointed to it, and without a word all of them began to dig again. Five minutes more of work made it clear that it was a cornice, and half an hour later there appeared the top of the doorway of a tomb.

'Old people wall him up,' said Mahomet, pointing to the flat stones set in mud for mortar with which the doorway had been closed, and to the undecipherable impress upon the mud of the scarab seals of the officials whose duty it had been to close the last resting-place of the royal dead for ever.

'Perhaps queen all right inside,' he went on, receiving no answer to his remark.

'Perhaps,' replied Smith, briefly. 'Dig, man, dig! Don't waste time in talking.'

So they dug on furiously till at length Smith saw something

which caused him to groan aloud. There was a hole in the masonry — the tomb had been broken into. Mahomet saw it too, and examined the top of the aperture with his skilled eye.

'Very old thief,' he said. 'Look, he try build up wall again, but run away before he have time finish.' And he pointed to certain flat stones which had been roughly and hurriedly replaced.

'Dig . . . dig!' said Smith.

Ten minutes more and the aperture was cleared. It was only just big enough to admit the body of a man.

By now the sun was setting. Swiftly, swiftly it seemed to tumble down the sky. One minute it was above the rough crests of the western hills behind them; the next, a great ball of glowing fire, it rested on their topmost ridge. Then it was gone. For an instant a kind of green spark shone where it had been. This too went out, and the sudden Egyptian night was upon them.

The fellaheen muttered among themselves, and one or two of them wandered off on some pretext. The rest threw down their tools and looked at Smith. 'Men say they no like stop here. They afraid of ghost! Too many *afreet* live in these tomb. That what they say. Come back finish tomorrow morning when it light. Very foolish people, these common fellaheen,' remarked Mahomet, in a superior tone.

'Quite so,' replied Smith, who knew well that nothing that he could offer would tempt his men to go on with the opening of a tomb after sunset. 'Let them go away. You and I will stop and watch the place till morning.'

'Sorry, sah,' said Mahomet, 'but I not feel quite well inside; I think I got fever. I go to camp and lie down and pray under plenty blanket.'

'All right, go,' said Smith; 'but if there is anyone who is not a coward, let him bring me my big coat, something to eat and drink, and the lantern that hangs in my tent. I will meet him there in the valley.'

Mahomet, though rather doubtfully, promised that this should be done, and, after begging Smith to accompany them, lest the spirit of whoever slept in the tomb should work him a mischief during the night, they departed quickly enough.

Smith lit his pipe, sat down on the sand, and waited. Half

an hour later he heard a sound of singing, and through the darkness, which was dense, saw lights coming up the valley.

'My brave men,' he thought to himself, and scrambled up the slope to meet them.

He was right. These were his men, no less than twenty of them, for with a fewer number they did not dare to face the ghosts which they believed haunted the valley after nightfall. Presently the light from the lantern which one of them carried (not Mahomet, whose sickness had increased too suddenly to enable him to come) fell upon the tall form of Smith, who, dressed in his white working clothes, was leaning against a rock. Down went the lantern, and with a howl of terror the brave company turned and fled.

'Sons of cowards!' roared Smith after them, in his most vigorous Arabic. 'It is I, your master, not an *afreet*.'

They heard, and by degrees crept back again. Then he perceived that in order to account for their number each of them carried some article. Thus one had the bread, another the lantern, another a tin of sardines, another the sardine-opener, another a box of matches, another a bottle of beer, and so on. As even thus there were not enough things to go round, two of them bore his big coat between them, the first holding it by the sleeves and the second by the tail as though it were a stretcher.

'Put them down,' said Smith, and they obeyed. 'Now', he added, 'run for your lives; I thought I heard two *afreets* talking up there just now of what they would do to any followers of the Prophet who mocked their gods, if perchance they should meet them in their holy place at night.'

This kindly counsel was accepted with much eagerness. In another minute Smith was alone with the stars and the dying desert wind.

Collecting his goods, or as many of them as he wanted, he thrust them into the pockets of the greatcoat and returned to the mouth of the tomb. Here he made his simple meal by the light of the lantern, and afterwards tried to go to sleep. But sleep he could not. Something always woke him. First it was a jackal howling amongst the rocks; next a sand-fly bit him on the ankle so sharply that he thought he must have been stung by a scorpion. Then, notwithstanding his warm coat, the cold got hold of him, for the clothes beneath were wet through with perspiration, and it occurred to him that unless he did something he would probably contract an internal chill or perhaps fever. He rose and walked about.

By now the moon was up, revealing all the sad, wild scene in its every detail. The mystery of Egypt entered his soul and oppressed him. How much dead majesty lay in the hill upon which he stood? Were they all really dead, he wondered, or were those fellaheen right? Did their spirits still come forth at night and wander through the land where once they ruled? Of course that was the Egyptian faith according to which the *Ka*, or Double, eternally haunted the place where its earthly counterpart had been laid to rest. When one came to think of it, beneath a mass of unintelligible symbolism there was much in the Egyptian faith which it was hard for a Christian to disbelieve. Salvation through a Redeemer, for instance, and the resurrection of the body. Had he, Smith, not already written a treatise upon these points of similarity which he proposed to publish one day, not under his own name? Well, he would not think of them now; the occasion seemed scarcely fitting – they came home too pointedly to one who was engaged in violating a tomb.

His mind, or rather his imagination – of which he had plenty – went off at a tangent. What sights had this place seen thousands of years ago! Once, thousands of years ago, a procession had wound up along the roadway which was doubtless buried beneath the sand whereon he stood towards the dark door of this sepulchre. He could see it as it passed in and out between the rocks. The priests, shaven-headed and robed in leopards' skins, or some of them in pure white, bearing the mystic symbols of their office. The funeral sledge drawn by oxen, and on it the great rectangular case that contained the outer and the inner coffins, and within them the mummy of some departed Majesty; in the Egyptian formula, 'the hawk that had spread its wings and flown into the bosom of Osiris', God of Death. Behind, the mourners, rending the air with their lamentations. Then those who bore the funeral furniture and offerings. Then the high officers of State and the first priests of Amen and of the other gods. Then the sister queens, leading by the hand a wondering child or two. Then the sons of Pharaoh, young men carrying the emblems of their rank.

Lastly, walking alone, Pharaoh himself in his ceremonial

robes, his apron, his double crown of linen surmounted by the golden snake, his inlaid bracelets and his heavy, tinkling earrings. Pharaoh, his head bowed, his feet travelling wearily, and in his heart — what thoughts? Sorrow, perhaps, for her who had departed. Yet he had other queens and fair women without count. Doubtless she was sweet and beautiful, but sweetness and beauty were not given to her alone. Moreover, was she not wont to cross his will and to question his divinity? No, surely it is not only of her that he thinks, her for whom he had prepared this splendid tomb with all things needful to unite her with the gods. Surely he thinks also of himself and that other tomb on the farther side of the hill whereat the artists labour day by day — yes, and have laboured these many years; that tomb to which before so very long he too must travel in just this fashion, to seek his place beyond the doors of Death, who lays his equal hand on king and queen and slave.

The vision passed. It was so real that Smith thought he must have been dreaming. Well, he was awake now, and colder than ever. Moreover, the jackals had multiplied. There were a whole pack of them, and not far away. Look! One crossed in the ring of the lamplight, a slinking, yellow beast that smelt the remains of dinner. Or perhaps it smelt him. Moreover, there were bad characters who haunted these mountains, and he was alone and quite unarmed. Perhaps he ought to put out the light which advertised his whereabouts. It would be wise and yet in this particular he rejected wisdom. After all, the light was some company.

Since sleep seemed to be out of the question, he fell back upon poor humanity's other anodyne, work, which has the incidental advantage of generating warmth. Seizing a shovel, he began to dig at the doorway of the tomb, whilst the jackals howled louder than ever in astonishment. They were not used to such a sight. For thousands of years, as the old moon above could have told, no man, or at least no solitary man, had dared to rob tombs at such an unnatural hour.

When Smith had been digging for about twenty minutes something tinkled on his shovel with a noise which sounded loud in that silence.

'A stone which may come in handy for the jackals,' he thought to himself, shaking the sand slowly off the spade until it appeared. There it was, and not large enough to be of much service. Still, he picked it up, and rubbed it in his hands to clear off the encrusting dirt. When he opened them he saw that it was no stone, but a bronze.

'Osiris,' reflected Smith, 'buried in front of the tomb to hallow the ground. No, an Isis. No, the head of a statuette, and a jolly good one, too – at any rate, in moonlight. Seems to have been gilded.' And, reaching out for the lamp, he held it over the object.

Another minute, and he found himself sitting at the bottom of the hole, lamp in one hand and statuette, or rather head, in the other.

'The Queen of the Mask!' he gasped. 'The same – the same! By heavens, the very same!'

Oh, he could not be mistaken. There were the identical lips, a little thick and pouted; the identical nostrils, curved and quivering, but a little wide; the identical arched eyebrows and dreamy eyes set somewhat far apart. Above all, there was the identical alluring and mysterious smile. Only on this master-piece of ancient art was set a whole crown of *uræi* surrounding the entire head. Beneath the crown and pressed back behind the ears was a full-bottomed wig or royal head-dress, of which the ends descended to the breasts. The statuette, that, having been gilt, remained quite perfect and uncorroded, was broken just above the middle, apparently by a single violent blow, for the fracture was very clean.

At once it occurred to Smith that it had been stolen from the tomb by a thief who thought it to be gold; that outside of the tomb doubt had overtaken him and caused him to break it upon a stone or otherwise. The rest was clear. Finding that it was but gold-washed bronze he had thrown away the fragments, rather than be at the pains of carrying them. This was his theory, probably not a correct one, as the sequel seems to show.

Smith's first idea was to recover the other portion. He searched quite a long while, but without success. Neither then nor afterwards could it be found. He reflected that perhaps this lower half had remained in the thief's hand, who, in his vexa-tion, had thrown it far away, leaving the head to lie where it fell. Again Smith examined this head, and more closely. Now he saw that just beneath the breasts was a delicately cut cartouche.

Being by this time a master of hieroglyphics, he read it without trouble. It ran: 'Ma-Mee, Great Royal Lady. Beloved of . . .' Here the cartouche was broken away.

'Ma-Mé, or it might be Ma-Mi,' he reflected. 'I never heard of a queen called Ma-Mé, or Ma-Mi, or Ma-Mu. She must be quite new to history. I wonder of whom she was beloved? Amen, or Horus, or Isis, probably. Of some god, I have no doubt, at least I hope so!'

He stared at the beautiful portrait in his hand, as once he had stared at the cast on the Museum wall, and the beautiful portrait, emerging from the dust of ages, smiled back at him there in the solemn moonlight as once the cast had smiled from the Museum wall.

Only that had been but a cast, whereas this was real. This had slept with the dead from whose features it had been fashioned, the dead who lay, or who had lain, within.

A sudden resolution took hold of Smith. He would explore that tomb, at once and alone. No one should accompany him on this his first visit; it would be a sacrilege that anyone save himself should set foot there until he had looked on what it might contain.

Why should he not enter? His lamp, of what is called the 'hurricane' brand, was very good and bright, and would burn for many hours. Moreover, there had been time for the foul air to escape through the hole that they had cleared. Lastly, something seemed to call on him to come and see. He placed the bronze head in his breast-pocket over his heart, and, thrusting the lamp through the hole, looked down. Here there was no difficulty, since sand had drifted in to the level of the bottom of the aperture. Through it he struggled, to find himself upon a bed of sand that only just left him room to push himself along between it and the roof. A little farther on the passage was almost filled with mud.

Mahomet had been right when, from his knowledge of the bed-rock, he said that any tomb made in this place must be flooded. It *had* been flooded by some ancient rain-storm, and Smith began to fear that he would find it quite filled with soil caked as hard as iron. So, indeed, it was to a certain depth, a result that apparently had been anticipated by those who hollowed it, for this entrance shaft was left quite undecorated.

Indeed, as Smith found afterwards, a hole had been dug beneath the doorway to allow the mud to enter after the burial was completed. Only a miscalculation had been made. The natural level of the mud did not quite reach the roof of the tomb, and therefore still left it open.

After crawling for forty feet or so over this caked mud, Smith suddenly found himself on a rising stair. Then he understood the plan; the tomb itself was on a higher level.

Here began the paintings. Here the Queen Ma-Mee, wearing her crowns and dressed in diaphanous garments, was presented to god after god. Between her figure and those of the divinities the wall was covered with hieroglyphs as fresh today as on that when the artist had limned them. A glance told him that they were extracts from the Book of the Dead. When the thief of bygone ages had broken into the tomb, probably not very long after the interment, the mud over which Smith had just crawled was still wet. This he could tell, since the clay from the rascal's feet remained upon the stairs, and that upon his fingers had stained the paintings on the wall against which he had supported himself; indeed, in one place was an exact impression of his hand, showing its shape and even the lines of the skin.

At the top of the flight of steps ran another passage at a higher level, which the water had never reached, and to right and left were the beginnings of unfinished chambers. It was clear to him that this queen had died young. Her tomb, as she or the king had designed it, was never finished. A few more paces, and the passage enlarged itself into a hall about thirty feet square. The ceiling was decorated with vultures, their wings outspread, the looped Cross of Life hanging from their talons. On one wall her Majesty Ma-Mee stood expectant while Anubis weighed her heart against the feather of truth, and Thoth, the Recorder, wrote down the verdict upon his tablets. All her titles were given to her here, such as 'Great Royal Heiress, Royal Sister, Royal Wife, Royal Mother, Lady of the Two Lands, Palm-branch of Love, Beautiful exceedingly.'

Smith read them hurriedly and noted that nowhere could he see the name of the king who had been her husband. It would almost seem as though this had been purposely omitted. On the other walls Ma-Mee, accompanied by her *Ka*, or Double, made offerings to the various gods, or uttered propitiatory speeches to the hideous demons of the underworld, declaring their names to them and forcing them to say: 'Pass on. Thou art pure!'

Lastly, on the end wall, triumphant, all her trials done, she, the justified Osiris, or Spirit, was received by the god Osiris, Saviour of Spirits.

All these things Smith noted hurriedly as he swung the lamp to and fro in that hallowed place. Then he saw something else which filled him with dismay. On the floor of the chamber where the coffins had been — for this was the burial chamber — lay a heap of black fragments charred with fire. Instantly he understood. After the thief had done his work he had burned the mummy-cases, and with them the body of the queen. There could be no doubt that this was so, for look! among the ashes lay some calcined human bones, while the roof above was black-ened with the smoke and cracked by the heat of the conflagra-tion. There was nothing left for him to find!

Oppressed with the closeness of the atmosphere, he sat down upon a little bench or table cut in the rock that evidently had been meant to receive offerings to the dead. Indeed, on it still lay the scorched remains of some votive flowers. Here, his lamp between his feet, he rested a while, staring at those calcined bones. See, yonder was the lower jaw, and in it some teeth, small, white, regular, and but little worn. Yes, she had died young. Then he turned to go, for disappointment and the holiness of the place overcame him; he could endure no more of it that night.

Leaving the burial hall, he walked along the painted pass-age, the lamp swinging and his eyes fixed upon the floor. He was disheartened, and the paintings could wait till the morrow. He descended the steps and came to the foot of the mud slope. Here suddenly he perceived, projecting from some sand that had drifted down over the mud, what seemed to be the corner of a reed box or basket. To clear away the sand was easy, and — yes, it was a basket, a foot or so in length, such a basket as the old Egyptians used to contain the funeral figures which are called *ushaptis*, or other objects connected with the dead. It looked as though it had been dropped, for it lay upon its side. Smith opened it — not very hopefully, for surely nothing of value would have been abandoned thus.

The first thing that met his eyes was a mummied hand, broken off at the wrist, a woman's little hand, most delicately shaped. It was withered and paper-white, but the contours still remained; the long fingers were perfect, and the almond-shaped nails had been stained with henna, as was the embalmers' fashion. On the hand were two gold rings, and for those rings it had been stolen. Smith looked at it for a long while, and his heart swelled within him, for here was the hand of that royal lady of his dreams.

Indeed, he did more than look; he kissed it, and as his lips touched the holy relic it seemed to him as though a wind, cold but scented, blew upon his brow. Then, growing fearful of the thoughts that arose within him, he hurried his mind back to the world, or rather to the examination of the basket.

Here he found other objects roughly wrapped in fragments of mummy-cloth that had been torn from the body of the queen. These it is needless to describe, for are they not to be seen in the gold room of the Museum, labelled 'Bijouterie de la Reine Ma-Mê, XVIIIème Dynastie. Thebes (Smith's Tomb)'? It may be mentioned, however, that the set was incomplete. For instance, there was but one of the great gold ceremonial ear-rings fashioned like a group of pomegranate blooms, and the most beautiful of the necklaces had been torn in two — half of it was missing.

It was clear to Smith that only a portion of the precious objects which were buried with the mummy had been placed in this basket. Why had these been left where he found them? A little reflection made that clear also. Something had prompted the thief to destroy the desecrated body and its coffin with fire, probably in the hope of hiding his evil handiwork. Then he fled with his spoil. But he had forgotten how fiercely mummies and their trappings can burn. Or perhaps the thing was an accident. He must have had a lamp, and if its flame chanced to touch this bituminous tinder!

At any rate, the smoke overtook the man in that narrow place as he began to climb the slippery slope of clay. In his haste he dropped the basket, and dared not return to search for it. It could wait till the morrow, when the fire would be out and the air pure. Only for this desecrator of the royal dead that morrow never came, as was discovered afterwards.

When at length Smith struggled into the open air the stars were paling before the dawn. An hour later, after the sky was well up, Mahomet (recovered from his sickness) and his myrmidons arrived.

'I have been busy while you slept,' said Smith, showing them the mummied hand (but not the rings which he had removed from the shrunk fingers), and the broken bronze, but not the priceless jewellery which was hidden in his pockets.

For the next ten days they dug till the tomb and its approach were quite clear. In the sand, at the head of a flight of steps which led down to the doorway, they found the skeleton of a man, who evidently had been buried there in a hurried fashion. His skull was shattered by the blow of an axe, and the shaven scalp that still clung to it suggested that he might have been a priest.

Mahomet thought, and Smith agreed with him, that this was the person who had violated the tomb. As he was escaping from it the guards of the holy place surprised him after he had covered up the hole by which he had entered and purposed to return. There they executed him without trail and divided up the plunder, thinking that no more was to be found. Or perhaps his confederates killed him.

Such at least were the theories advanced by Mahomet. Whether they were right or wrong none will ever know. For instance, the skeleton may not have been that of the thief, though probability appears to point the other way.

Nothing more was found in the tomb, not even a scarab or a mummy-bead. Smith spent the remainder of his time in photographing the pictures and copying the inscriptions, which for various reasons proved to be of extraordinary interest. Then, having reverently buried the charred bones of the queen in a secret place of the sepulchre, he handed it over to the care of the local Guardian of Antiquities, paid off Mahomet and the fellaheen, and departed for Cairo. With him went the wonderful jewels of which he had breathed no word, and another relic to him yet more precious — the hand of her Majesty Ma-Mee, Palm-branch of Love.

And now follows the strange sequel of this story of Smith and the queen Ma-Mee.

II

Smith was seated in the sanctum of the distinguished Director-General of Antiquities at the new Cairo Museum. It was a very interesting room. Books piled upon the floor; objects from tombs awaiting examination, lying here and there; a hoard of Ptolemaic silver coins, just dug up at Alexandria, standing on the table in the pot that had hidden them for two thousand years; in the corner the mummy of a royal child, aged six or seven, not long ago discovered, with some inscription scrawled upon the wrappings (brought here to be deciphered by the Master), and the withered lotus-bloom, love's last offering, thrust beneath one of the pink retaining bands.

'A touching object,' thought Smith to himself. 'Really, they might have left the dear little girl in peace.'

Smith had a tender heart, but even as he reflected he became aware that some of the jewellery hidden in an inner pocket of his waistcoat (designed for bank notes) was fretting his skin. He had a tender conscience also.

Just then the Director, a French savant, bustled in, alert, vigorous, full of interest.

'Ah, my dear Mr Smith!' he said, in his excellent English. 'I am indeed glad to see you back again, especially as I understand that you are come rejoicing and bringing your sheaves with you. They tell me you have been extraordinarily successful. What do you say is the name of this queen whose tomb you have found — Ma-Mee? A very unusual name. How do you get the extra vowel? Is it for euphony, eh? Did I not know how good a scholar you are, I should be tempted to believe that you had misread it. Me-Mee, Ma-Mee! That would be pretty in French, would it not? *Ma mie* — my darling! Well, I dare say she was somebody's *mie* in her time. But tell me the story.'

Smith told him shortly and clearly; also he produced his photographs and copies of inscriptions.

'This is interesting — interesting truly,' said the Director, when he had glanced through them. 'You must leave them with me to study. Also you will publish them, is it not so? Perhaps one of the Societies would help you with the cost, for it should be done in facsimile. Look at this vignette! Most unusual. Oh, what a pity that scoundrelly priest got off with the jewellery and burnt her Majesty's body!'

'He didn't get off with all of it.'

'What, Mr Smith? Our inspector reported to me that you found nothing.'

'I dare say, sir; but your inspector did not know what I found.'

'Ah, you are a discreet man! Well, let us see.'

Slowly Smith unbuttoned his waistcoat. From its inner pocket and elsewhere about his person he extracted the jewels wrapped in mummy-cloth as he had found them. First he produced a sceptre-head of gold, in the shape of a pomegranate fruit and engraved with the throne name and titles of Ma-Mee.

'What a beautiful object!' said the Director. 'Look! the handle was of ivory, and that *sacré* thief of a priest smashed it out at the socket. It was fresh ivory then; the robbery must have taken place not long after the burial. See, this magnifying-glass shows it. Is that all?'

Smith handed him the surviving half of the marvellous necklace that had been torn in two.

'I have re-threaded it,' he muttered, 'but every bead is in its place.'

'Oh, heavens! How lovely! Note the cutting of those cornelian heads of Hathor and the gold lotus-blooms between — yes, and the enamelled flies beneath. We have nothing like it in the Museum.'

So it went on.

'Is that all?' gasped the Director at last, when every object from the basket glittered before them on the table.

'Yes,' said Smith. 'That is — no. I found a broken statuette hidden in the sand outside the tomb. It is of the queen, but I thought perhaps you would allow me to keep this.'

'But certainly, Mr Smith; it is yours indeed. We are not niggards here. Still, if I might see it . . .'

From yet another pocket Smith produced the head. The Director gazed at it, then he spoke with feeling.

'I said just now that you were discreet, Mr Smith, and I have been reflecting that you are honest. But now I must add that you are very clever. If you had not made me promise that this bronze should be yours before you showed it to me — well, it would never have gone into that pocket again. And, in the public interest, won't you release me from the promise?'

'*No,*' said Smith.

'You are perhaps not aware,' went on the Director, with a groan, 'that this is a portrait of Mariette's unknown queen whom we are thus able to identify. It seems a pity that the two should be separated; a replica we could let you have.'

'I am quite aware,' said Smith, 'and I will be sure to send *you* a replica, with photographs. Also I promise to leave the original to some museum by will.'

The Director clasped the image tenderly, and, holding it to the light, read the broken cartouche beneath the breasts.

' "Ma-Mé, Great Royal Lady. Beloved of . . ." Beloved of whom? Well, of Smith, for one. Take it, monsieur, and hide it away at once, lest soon there should be another mummy in this collection, a modern mummy called Smith; and, in the name of Justice, let the museum which inherits it be not the British, but that of Cairo, for this queen belongs to Egypt. By the way, I have been told that you are delicate in the lungs. How is your health now? Our cold winds are very trying. Quite good? Ah, that is excellent! I suppose that you have no more articles that you can show me?'

'I have nothing more except a mummied hand, which I found in the basket with the jewels. The two rings off it lie there. Doubtless it was removed to get at that bracelet. I suppose you will not mind my keeping the hand?'

'Of the beloved of Smith,' interrupted the Director drolly. 'No, I suppose not, though for my part I should prefer one that was not quite so old. Still, perhaps *you* will not mind my seeing it. That pocket of yours still looks a little bulky; I thought that it contained books!'

Smith produced a cigar-box; in it was the hand wrapped in cotton wool.

'Ah,' said the Director, 'a pretty, well-bred hand. No doubt this Ma-Mee was the real heiress to the throne, as she describes herself. The Pharaoh was somebody of inferior birth, half-brother — she is called 'Royal Sister', you remember — son of one of the Pharaoh's slave-women, perhaps. Odd that she never mentioned him in the tomb. It looks as though they didn't get on in life, and that she was determined to have done with him in death. Those were the rings upon that hand, were they not?'

He replaced them on the fingers, then took off one, a royal signet in a cartouche, and read the inscription on the other:
' "Bes Ank, Ank Bes." Bes the Living, the living Bes.'

'Your Ma-Mee had some human vanity about her,' he added. 'Bes, among other things, as you know, was the god of beauty and of the adornments of women. She wore that ring that she might remain beautiful, and that her dresses might always fit, and her rouge never cake when she was dancing before the gods. Also it fixes her period pretty closely, but then so do other things. It seems a pity to rob Ma-Mee of her pet ring, does it not? The royal signet will be enough for us.'

With a little bow he gave the hand back to Smith, leaving the Bes ring on the finger that had worn it for more than three thousand years. At least, Smith was so sure it was the Bes ring that at the time he did not look at it again.

Then they parted, Smith promising to return upon the morrow, which, owing to events to be described, he did not do.

'Ah!' said the Master to himself, as the door closed behind his visitor. 'He's in a hurry to be gone. He has fear lest I should change my mind about that ring. Also there is the bronze. Monsieur Smith was *rusé* there. It is worth a thousand pounds, that bronze. Yet I do not believe he was thinking of the money. I believe he is in love with that Ma-Mee and wants to keep her picture. *Mon Dieu!* A well-established affection. At least he is what the English call an odd fish, one whom I could never make out, and of whom no one seems to know anything. Still, honest, I am sure – quite honest. Why, he might have kept every one of those jewels and no one have been the wiser. And what things! What a find! *Ciel!* what a find! There has been nothing like it for years. Benedictions on the head of Odd-fish Smith!'

Then he collected the precious objects, thrust them into an inner compartment of his safe, which he locked and double-locked, and, as it was nearly five o'clock, departed from the Museum to his private residence in the grounds, there to study Smith's copies and photographs, and to tell some friends of the great things that had happened.

When Smith found himself outside the sacred door, and had presented its venerable guardian with a baksheesh of five piastres, he walked a few paces to the right and paused a while to watch some native labourers who were dragging a huge sarcophagus upon an improvised tramway. As they dragged they sang an echoing rhythmic song, whereof each line ended with an invocation to Allah.

Just so, reflected Smith, had their forefathers sung when, millenniums ago, they dragged that very sarcophagus from the quarries to the Nile, and from the Nile to the tomb whence it reappeared today, or when they slid the casing blocks of the pyramids up the great causeway and smooth slope of sand, and laid them in their dizzy resting-places. Only then each line of the immemorial chant of toil ended with an invocation to Amen, now transformed to Allah.

The East may change its masters and its gods, but its customs never change, and if today Allah wore the feathers of Amen one wonders whether the worshippers would find the difference so very great.

Thus thought Smith as he hurried away from the sarcophagus and those blue-robed, dark-skinned fellaheen, down the long gallery that is filled with a thousand sculptures. For a moment he paused before the wonderful white statue of Queen Amenartas, then, remembering that his time was short, hastened on to a certain room, one of those which opened out of the gallery.

In a corner of this room, upon the wall, amongst many other beautiful objects, stood that head which Mariette had found, whereof in past years the cast had fascinated him in London. Now he knew whose head it was; to him it had been given to find the tomb of her who had sat for that statue. Her very hand was in his pocket – yes, the hand that had touched yonder marble, pointing out its defects to the sculptor, or perhaps swearing that he flattered her. Smith wondered who that sculptor was; surely he must have been a happy man. Also he wondered whether the statuette was also this master's work. He thought so, but he wished to make sure.

Near to the end of the room he stopped and looked about him like a thief. He was alone in the place; not a single student or tourist could be seen, and its guardian was somewhere else. He drew out the box that contained the hand. From the hand he slipped the ring which the Director-General had left there as a gift to himself. He would much have preferred the other with the signet, but how could he say so, especially after the episode of the statuette.

Replacing the hand in his pocket without looking at the ring – for his eyes were watching to see whether he was observed

— he set it upon his little finger, which it exactly fitted. (Ma-Mee had worn both of them upon the third finger of her left hand, the Bes ring as a guard to the signet.) He had the fancy to approach the effigy of Ma-Mee wearing a ring which she had worn and that came straight from her finger to his own.

Smith found the head in its accustomed place. Weeks had gone by since he looked upon it, and now, to his eyes, it had grown more beautiful than ever, and its smile was more mystical and loving. He drew out the statuette and began to compare them point by point. Oh, no doubt was possible! Both were like-nesses of the same woman, though the statuette might have been executed two or three years later than the statue. To him the face of it looked a little older and more spiritual. Perhaps illness, or some premonition of her end had then thrown its shadow on the queen. He compared and compared. He made some rough measurements and sketches in his pocket-book, and set himself to work out a canon of proportions.

So hard and earnestly did he work, so lost was his mind that he never heard the accustomed warning sound which announces that the Museum is about to close. Hidden behind an altar as he was, in his distant, shadowed corner, the guardian of the room never saw him as he cast a last perfunctory glance about the place before departing till the Saturday morning; for the morrow was Friday, the Mohammedan Sabbath, on which the Museum remains shut, and he would not be called upon to attend. So he went. Everybody went. The great doors clanged, were locked and bolted, and, save for a watchman outside, no one was left in all that vast place except Smith in his corner, engaged in sketching and in measurements.

The difficulty of seeing, owing to the increase of shadow, first called his attention to the fact that time was slipping away. He glanced at his watch and saw that it was ten minutes to the hour.

'Soon be time to go,' he thought to himself, and resumed his work.

How strangely silent the place seemed! Not a footstep to be heard or the sound of a human voice. He looked at his watch again, and saw that it was six o'clock, not five, or so the thing said. But that was impossible, for the Museum shut at five; evidently the desert sand had got into the works. The room in which he stood was that known as Room I, and he had noticed that its Arab custodian often frequented Room K or the gallery outside. He would find him and ask what was the real time.

Passing round the effigy of the wonderful Hathor cow, perhaps the finest example of an ancient sculpture of a beast in the whole world, Smith came to the doorway and looked up and down the gallery. Not a soul to be seen. He ran to Room K, to Room H, and others. Still not a soul to be seen. Then he made his way as fast as he could go to the great entrance. The doors were locked and bolted.

'Watch must be right after all. I'm shut in,' he said to himself. 'However, there's sure to be someone about somewhere. Probably the *salle des ventes* is still open. Shops don't shut till they are obliged.'

Thither he went, to find its door as firmly closed as a door can be. He knocked on it, but a sepulchral echo was the only answer.

'I know,' he reflected. 'The Director must still be in his room. It will take him a long while to examine all that jewellery and put it away.'

So for the room he headed, and, after losing his path twice, found it by help of the sarcophagus that the Arabs had been dragging, which now stood as deserted as it had done in the tomb, a lonesome and impressive object in the gathering shadows. The Director's door was shut, and again his knockings produced nothing but an echo. He started on a tour round the Museum, and, having searched the ground floors, ascended to the upper galleries by the great stairway.

Presently he found himself in that devoted to the royal mummies, and, being tired, rested there a while. Opposite to him, in a glass case in the middle of the gallery, reposed Rameses II. Near to, on shelves in a side case, were Rameses's son, Meneptah, and above, his son, Seti II, while in other cases were the mortal remains of many more of the royalties of Egypt. He looked at the proud face of Rameses and at the little fringe of white locks turned yellow by the embalmer's spices, also at the raised left arm. He remembered how the Director had told him that when they were unrolling this mighty monarch they went away to lunch, and that presently the man who had been left in charge of the body rushed into the room with his hair on end, and said that the dead king had lifted his arm and pointed at him.

Back they went, and there, true enough, was the arm lifted; nor were they ever able to get it quite into its place again. The explanation given was that the warmth of the sun had contracted the withered muscles, a very natural and correct explanation.

Still, Smith wished that he had not recollected the story just at this moment, especially as the arm seemed to move while he contemplated it — a very little, but still to move.

He turned round and gazed at Meneptah, whose hollow eyes stared at him from between the wrappings carelessly thrown across the parchment-like and ashen face. There, probably, lay the countenance that had frowned on Moses. There was the heart which God had hardened. Well, it was hard enough now, for the doctors said he died of ossification of the arteries, and that the vessels of the heart were full of lime!

Smith stood upon a chair and peeped at Seti II above. His weaker countenance was very peaceful, but it seemed to wear an air of reproach. In getting down Smith managed to upset the heavy chair. The noise it made was terrific. He would not have thought it possible that the fall of such an article could produce so much sound. Satisfied with his inspection of these particular kings, who somehow looked quite different now from what they had ever done before — more real and imminent, so to speak — he renewed his search for a living man.

On he went, mummies to his right, mummies to his left, of every style and period, till be began to feel as though he never wished to see another dried remnant of mortality. He peeped into the room where lay the relics of Iouiya and Touiyou, the father and mother of the great Queen Taia. Cloths had been drawn over these, and really they looked worse and more suggestive thus draped than in their frigid and unadorned blackness. He came to the coffins of the priest-kings of the twentieth dynasty, formidable painted coffins with human faces. There seemed to be a vast number of these priest-kings, but perhaps they were better than the gold masks of the great Ptolemaic ladies which glinted at him through the gathering gloom.

Really, he had seen enough of the upper floors. The statues

downstairs were better than all these dead, although it was true that, according to the Egyptian faith, every one of those statues was haunted eternally by the *Ka* or Double, of the person whom it represented. He descended the great stairway. Was it fancy, or did something run across the bottom step in front of him – an animal of some kind, followed by a swift-moving and indefinite shadow? If so, it must have been the Museum cat hunting a Museum mouse. Only then what on earth was that very peculiar and unpleasant shadow?

He called, 'Puss! puss! puss!' for he would have been quite glad of its company; but there came no friendly 'miau' in response. Perhaps it was only the *Ka* of a cat and the shadow was – oh! never mind what. The Egyptians worshipped cats, and there were plenty of their mummies about on the shelves. But the shadow!

Once he shouted in the hope of attracting attention, for there were no windows to which he could climb. He did not repeat the experiment, for it seemed as though a thousand voices were answering him from every corner and roof of the gigantic edifice.

Well, he must face the thing out. He was shut in a museum, and the question was in what part of it he should camp for the night. Moreover, as it was growing rapidly dark, the problem must be solved at once. He thought with affection of the lavatory, where, before going to see the Director, only that afternoon he had washed his hands with the assistance of a kindly Arab who watched the door and gracefully accepted a piastre. But there was no Arab there now, and the door, like every other in this confounded place, was locked. He marched on to the entrance.

Here, opposite to each other, stood the red sarcophagi of the great Queen Hatshepu and her brother and husband, Thotmes III. He looked at them. Why should not one of these afford him a night's lodging? They were deep and quiet, and would fit the human frame very nicely. For a while Smith wondered which of these monarchs would be the more likely to take offence at such a use of a private sarcophagus, and, acting on general principles, concluded that he would rather throw himself on the mercy of the lady.

Already one of his legs was over the edge of that solemn

coffer, and he was squeezing his body beneath the massive lid that was propped above it on blocks of wood, when he remembered a little, naked, withered thing with long hair that he had seen in a side chamber of the tomb of Amenhotep II in the Valley of Kings at Thebes. This caricature of humanity many thought, and he agreed with them, to be the actual body of the mighty Hatshepu as it appeared after the robbers had done with it.

Supposing now, that when he was lying at the bottom of that sarcophagus, sleeping the sleep of the just, this little personage should peep over its edge and ask him what he was doing there! Of course the idea was absurd; he was tired, and his nerves were a little shaken. Still, the fact remained that for centuries the hallowed dust of Queen Hatshepu had slept where he, a modern man, was proposing to sleep.

He scrambled down from the sarcophagus and looked round him in despair. Opposite to the main entrance was the huge central hall of the Museum. Now the cement roof of this hall had, he knew, gone wrong, with the result that very extensive repairs had become necessary. So extensive were they, indeed, that the Director-General had informed him that they would take several years to complete. Therefore this hall was boarded up, only a little doorway being left by which the workmen could enter. Certain statues, of Seti II and others, too large to be moved, were also roughly boarded over, as were some great funeral boats on either side of the entrance. The rest of the place, which might be two hundred feet long with a proportionate breadth, was empty save for the colossi of Amenhotep III and his queen Taia that stood beneath the gallery at its farther end.

It was an appalling place in which to sleep, but better, reflected Smith, than a sarcophagus or those mummy chambers. If, for instance, he could creep behind the deal boards that enclosed one of the funeral boats he would be quite comfortable there. Lifting the curtain, he slipped into the hall, where the gloom of evening had already settled. Only the skylights and the outline of the towering colossi at the far end remained visible. Close to him were the two funeral boats which he had noted when he looked into the hall earlier on that day, standing at the head of a flight of steps which led to the sunk floor of the centre. He groped his way to that on the right. As he expected, the projecting planks were not quite joined at the bow. He crept in between them and the boat and laid himself down.

Presumably, being altogether tired out, Smith did ultimately fall asleep, for how long he never knew. At any rate, it is certain that, if so, he woke up again. He could not tell the time, because his watch was not a repeater, and the place was as black as the pit. He had some matches in his pocket, and might have struck one and even have lit his pipe. To his credit be it said, however, he remembered that he was the sole tenant of one of the most valuable museums in the world, and his responsibilities with reference to fire. So he refrained from striking that match under the keel of a boat which had become very dry in the course of five thousand years.

Smith found himself very wide awake indeed. Never in all his life did he remember being more so, not even in the hour of its great catastrophe, or when his godfather, Ebenezer, after much hesitation, had promised him a clerkship in the bank of which he was a director. His nerves seemed strung tight as harp-strings, and his every sense was painfully acute. Thus he could even smell the odour of mummies that floated down from the upper galleries and the earthly scent of the boat which had been buried for thousands of years in sand at the foot of the pyramid of one of the fifth dynasty kings.

Moreover, he could hear all sorts of strange sounds, faint and far-away sounds which at first he thought must emanate from Cairo without. Soon, however, he grew sure that their origin was more local. Doubtless the cement work and the cases in the galleries were cracking audibly, as is the unpleasant habit of such things at night.

Yet why should these common manifestations be so universal and affect him so strangely? Really, it seemed as though people were stirring all about him. More, he could have sworn that the great funeral boat beneath which he lay had become repeopled with the crew that once it bore.

He heard them at their business above him. There were trampings and a sound as though something heavy were being laid on the deck, such, for instance, as must have been made when the mummy of Pharaoh was set there for its last journey to the western bank of the Nile. Yes, and now he could have sworn again that the priestly crew were getting out the oars.

Smith began to meditate flight from the neighbourhood of that place when something occurred which determined him to stop where he was.

The huge hall was growing light, but not, as at first he hoped, with the rays of dawn. This light was pale and ghostly, though very penetrating. Also it had a blue tinge, unlike any other he had ever seen. At first it arose in a kind of fan or fountain at the far end of the hall, illumining the steps there and the two noble colossi which sat above.

But what was this that stood at the head of the steps, radiating glory? By heavens! it was Osiris himself or the image of Osiris, god of the Dead, the Egyptian saviour of the world!

There he stood, in his mummy-cloths, wearing the feathered crown, and holding in his hands, which projected from an opening in the wrappings, the crook and the scourge of power. Was he alive, or was he dead? Smith could not tell, since he never moved, only stood there, splendid and fearful, his calm, benignant face staring into nothingness.

Smith became aware that the darkness between him and the vision of this god was peopled; that a great congregation was gathering, or had gathered there. The blue light began to grow; long tongues of it shot forward, which joined themselves together, illumining all that huge hall.

Now, too, he saw the congregation. Before him, rank upon rank of them, stood the kings and queens of Egypt. As though at a given signal, they bowed themselves to the Osiris, and ere the tinkling of their ornaments had died away, lo! Osiris was gone. But in his place stood another, Isis, the Mother of Mystery, her deep eyes looking forth from beneath the jewelled vulture-cap. Again the congregation bowed, and, lo! she was gone. But in her place stood yet another, a radiant, lovely being, who held in her hand the Sign of Life, and wore upon her head the symbol of the shining disc – Hathor, Goddess of Love. A third time the congregation bowed, and she, too, was gone; nor did any other appear in her place.

The Pharaohs and their queens began to move about and speak to each other; their voices came to his ears in one low, sweet murmur.

In his amazement Smith had forgotten fear. From his hiding-place he watched them intently. Some of them he knew by their faces. There, for instance, was the long-necked Khu-en-aten, talking somewhat angrily to the imperial Rameses II. Smith could understand what he said, for this power seemed to have been given to him. He was complaining in a high, weak voice that on this, the one night of the year when they might meet, the gods, or the magic images of the gods who were put up for them to worship, should not include *his* god, symbolized by the 'Aten', or the sun's disc.

'I have heard of your Majesty's god,' replied Rameses; 'the priests used to tell me of him, also that he did not last long after your Majesty flew to heaven. The Fathers of Amen gave you a bad name; they called you 'the heretic' and hammered out your cartouches. They were quite rare in my time. Oh, do not let your Majesty be angry! So many of us have been heretics. My grandson, Seti, there,' – and he pointed to a mild, thoughtful-faced man – 'for example. I am told that he really worshipped the god of those Hebrew slaves whom I used to press to build my cities. Look at that lady with him. Beautiful, isn't she? Observe her large, violet eyes! Well, she was the one who did the mischief, a Hebrew herself. At least, they tell me so.'

'I will talk with him,' answered Khu-en-aten. 'It is more than possible that we may agree on certain points. Meanwhile, let me explain to your Majesty――'

'Oh, I pray you, not now. There is my wife.'

'Your wife?' said Khu-en-aten, drawing himself up. 'Which wife? I am told that your Majesty had many and left a large family; indeed, I see some hundreds of them here tonight. Now, I – but let me introduce Nefertiti to your Majesty. I may explain that she was my *only* wife.'

'So I have understood. Your Majesty was rather an invalid, were you not? Of course, in those circumstances, one prefers the nurse whom one can trust. Oh, pray, no offence! Nefertari, my love – oh, I beg pardon! – Astnefert – Nefertari has gone to speak to some of her children – let me introduce you to your predecessor, the Queen Nefertiti, wife of Amenhotep IV – I mean Khu-en-aten (he changed his name, you know, because half of it was that of the father of the gods). She is interested in the question of plural marriage. Goodbye! I wish to have a word with my grandfather, Rameses I. He was fond of me as a little boy.'

At this moment Smith's interest in that queer conversation died away, for of a sudden he beheld none other than the queen of his dreams, Ma-Mee. Oh! there she stood, without a doubt, only ten times more beautiful than he had ever pictured her. She was tall and somewhat fair-complexioned, with slumbrous, dark eyes, and on her face gleamed the mystic smile he loved. She wore a robe of simple white and a purple-broidered apron, a crown of golden *urœi* with turquoise eyes was set upon her dark hair as in her statue, and on her breast and arms were the very necklace and bracelets that he had taken from her tomb. She appeared to be somewhat moody, or rather thoughtful, for she leaned by herself against a balustrade, watching the throng without much interest.

Presently a Pharaoh, a black-browed, vigorous man with thick lips, drew near.

'I greet your Majesty,' he said.

She started, and answered:

'Oh, it is you! I make my obeisance to your Majesty,' and she curtsied to him, humbly enough, but with a suggestion of mockery in her movements.

'Well, you do not seem to have been very anxious to find me, Ma-Mee, which, considering that we meet so seldom——'

'I saw that your Majesty was engaged with my sister queens,' she interrupted , in a rich, low voice, 'and with some other ladies in the gallery there, whose faces I seem to remember, but who I think were *not* queens. Unless, indeed, you married them after I was drawn away.'

'One must talk to one's relations,' replied the Pharaoh.

'Quite so. But, you see, I have no relations – at least, none whom I know well. My parents, you will remember, died when I was young, leaving me Egypt's heiress, and they are still vexed at the marriage which I made on the advice of my counsellors. But, is it not annoying? I have lost one of my rings, that which had the god Bes on it. Some dweller on the earth must be wearing it today, and that is why I cannot get it back from him.'

'Him! Why 'him'? Hush; the business is about to begin.'

'What business, my lord?'

'Oh, the question of the violation of our tombs, I believe.'

'Indeed! That is a large subject, and not a very profitable one, I should say. Tell me, who is that?' And she pointed to a lady who had stepped forward, a very splendid person, magnificently arrayed.

'Cleopatra the Greek,' he answered, 'the last of Egypt's Sovereigns, one of the Ptolemys. You can always know her by that Roman who walks about after her.'

'Which?' asked Ma-Mee. 'I see several — also other men. She was the wretch who rolled Egypt in the dirt and betrayed her. Oh, if it were not for the law of peace by which we abide when we meet thus!'

'You mean that she would be torn to shreds, Ma-Mee, and her very soul scattered like the limbs of Osiris? Well, if it were not for that law of peace, so perhaps would many of us, for never have I heard a single king among these hundreds speak altogether well of those who went before or followed after him.'

'Especially of those who went before if they happen to have hammered out their cartouches and usurped their monuments,' said the queen, dryly, and looking him in the eyes.

At this home-thrust the Pharaoh seemed to wince. Making no answer, he pointed to the royal woman who had mounted the steps at the end of the hall.

Queen Cleopatra lifted her hand and stood thus for a while. Very splendid she was, and Smith, on his hands and knees behind the boarding of the boat, thanked his stars that alone among modern men it had been his lot to look upon her rich and living loveliness. There she shone, she who had changed the fortunes of the world, she who, whatever she did amiss, at least had known how to die.

Silence fell upon that glittering galaxy of kings and queens and upon all the hundreds of their offspring, their women, and their great officers who crowded the double tier of galleries around the hall.

'Royalties of Egypt,' she began, in a sweet, clear voice which penetrated to the farthest recesses of the place, 'I, Cleopatra, the sixth of that name and the last monarch who ruled over the Upper and the Lower Lands before Egypt became a home of slaves, have a word to say to your Majesties, who, in your mortal days, all of you more worthily filled the throne on which once I sat. I do not speak of Egypt and its fate, or of our sins — whereof mine were not the least — that brought her to the dust. Those sins I and others expiate elsewhere, and of them, from age to age, we hear enough. But on this one night of the year, that of the feast of him whom we call Osiris, but whom other nations have known and know by different names, it is given to us once more to be mortal for an hour, and, though we be but shadows, to renew the loves and hates of our long-perished flesh. Here for an hour we strut in our forgotten pomp; the crowns that were ours still adorn our brows, and once more we seem to listen to our people's praise. Our hopes are the hopes of mortal life, our foes are the foes we feared, our gods grow real again, and our lovers whisper in our ears. Moreover, this joy is given to us — to see each other as we are, to know as the gods know, and therefore to forgive, even where we despise and hate. Now I have done, and I, the youngest of the rulers of ancient Egypt, call upon him who was the first of her kings to take my place.'

She bowed, and the audience bowed back to her. Then she descended the steps and was lost in the throng. Where she had been appeared an old man, simply-clad, long-bearded, wise-faced, and wearing on his grey hair no crown save a plain band of gold, from the centre of which rose the snake-headed *uræus* crest.

'Your Majesties who came after me,' said the old man, 'I am Menes, the first of the accepted Pharaohs of Egypt, although many of those who went before me were more truly kings than I. Yet as the first who joined the Upper and the Lower Lands, and took the royal style and titles, and ruled as well as I could rule, it is given to me to talk with you for a while this night whereon our spirits are permitted to gather from the uttermost parts of the uttermost worlds and see each other face to face. First, in darkness and in secret, let us speak of the mystery of the gods and of its meanings. Next, in darkness and in secret, let us speak of the mystery of our lives, of whence they come, of where they tarry by the road, and whither they go at last. And afterwards, let us speak of other matters face to face in light and openness, as we were wont to do when we were men. Then hence to Thebes, there to celebrate our yearly festival. Is such your will?'

'Such is our will,' they answered.

It seemed to Smith that dense darkness fell upon the place, and with it a silence that was awful. For a time that he could not reckon, that might have been years or might have been moments, he sat there in the utter darkness and the utter silence.

At length the light came again, first as a blue spark, then in upward pouring rays, and lastly pervading all. There stood Menes on the steps, and there in front of him was gathered the same royal throng.

'The mysteries are finished,' said the old king. 'Now, if any have aught to say, let it be said openly.'

A young man dressed in the robes and ornaments of an early dynasty came forward and stood upon the steps between the Pharaoh Menes and all those who had reigned after him. His face seemed familiar to Smith, as was the side lock that hung down behind his right ear in token of his youth. Where had he seen him? Ah, he remembered. Only a few hours ago lying in one of the cases of the Museum, together with the bones of the Pharaoh Unas.

'Your Majesties,' he began, 'I am the King Metesuphis. The matter that I wish to lay before you is that of the violation of our sepulchres by those men who live upon the earth. The mortal bodies of many who are gathered here tonight lie in this place to be stared at and mocked by the curious. I myself am one of them, jawless, broken, hideous to behold. Yonder, day by day, must my *Ka* sit watching my desecrated flesh, torn from the pyramid that, with cost and labour, I raised up to be an eternal house wherein I might hide till the hour of resurrection. Others of us lie in far lands. Thus, as he can tell you, my predecessor, Man-kau-ra, he who built the third of the great pyramids, the Pyramid of Her, sleeps, or rather wakes in a dark city, called London, across the seas, a place of murk where no sun shines. Others have been burnt with fire, others are scattered in small dust. The ornaments that were ours are stole away and sold to the greedy; our sacred writings and our symbols are their jest. Soon there will not be one holy grave in Egypt that remains undefiled.'

'That is so,' said a voice from the company. 'But four months gone the deep, deep pit was opened that I had dug in the shadow of the Pyramid of Cephren, who begat me in the world. There in my chamber I slept alone, two handfuls of white bones, since when I died they did not preserve the body with wrappings and with spices. Now I see those bones of mine, beside which my

Double has watched for these five thousand years, hid in the blackness of a great ship and tossing on a sea that is strewn with ice.'

'It is so.' echoed a hundred other voices.

Then,' went on the young king, turning to Menes, 'I ask of your Majesty whether there is no means whereby we may be avenged on those who do us this foul wrong.'

'Let him who has wisdom speak,' said the old Pharaoh.

A man of middle age, short in stature and of a thoughtful brow, who held in his hand a wand and wore the feathers and insignia of the heir to the throne of Egypt and of a high priest of Amen, moved to the steps. Smith knew him at once from his statues. He was Khaemuas, son of Rameses the Great, the mightiest magician that ever was in Egypt, who of his own will withdrew himself from earth before the time came that he should sit upon the throne.

'I have wisdom, your Majesties, and I will answer,' he said. 'The time draws on when, in the land of Death which is Life, the land that we call Amenti, it will be given to us to lay our wrongs as to this matter before Those who judge, knowing that they will be avenged. On this night of the year also, when we resume the shapes we were, we have certain powers of vengeance, or rather of executing justice. But our time is short, and there is much to say and do before the sun-god Ra arises and we depart each to his place. Therefore it seems best that we should leave these wicked ones in their wickedness till we meet them face to face beyond the world.'

Smith, who had been following the words of Khaemuas with the closest attention and considerable anxiety, breathed again, thanking Heaven that the engagements of these departed monarchs were so numerous and pressing. Still, as a matter of precaution, he drew the cigar-box which contained Ma-Mee's hand from his pocket, and pushed it as far away from him as he could. It was a most unlucky act. Perhaps the cigar-box grated on the floor, or perhaps the fact of his touching the relic put him into psychic communication with all these spirits. At any rate, he became aware that the eyes of that dreadful magician were fixed upon him, and that a bone had a better chance of escaping the search of a Röntgen ray than he of hiding himself from their baleful glare.

'As it happens, however,' went on Khaemuas, in a cold voice, 'I now percieve that there is hidden in this place, and spying on us, one of the worst of these vile thieves. I say to your Majesties that I see him crouched beneath your funeral barge, and that he has with him at this moment the hand of one of your Majesties, stolen by him from her tomb at Thebes.'

Now every queen in the company became visibly agitated (Smith, who was watching Ma-Mee, saw her hold up her hands and look at them), while all the Pharaohs pointed with their fingers and exclaimed together, in a voice that rolled round the hall like thunder:

'Let him be brought forth to judgment!'

Khaemuas raised his wand and, holding it towards the boat where Smith was hidden, said:

'Draw near, Vile One, bringing with thee that thou hast stolen.'

Smith tried hard to remain where he was. He sat himself down and set his heels against the floor. As the reader knows, he was always shy and retiring by disposition, and never had these weaknesses oppressed him more than they did just then. When a child his favourite nightmare had been that the fore-man of a jury was in the act of proclaiming him guilty of some dreadful but unstated crime. Now he understood what that nightmare foreshadowed. He was about to be convicted in a court of which all the kings and queens of Egypt were the jury, Menes was Chief Justice, and the magician Khaemuas played the *rôle* of Attorney-General.

In vain did he sit down and hold fast. Some power took possession of him which forced him first to stretch out his arm and pick up the cigar-box containing the hand of Ma-Mee, and next drew him from the friendly shelter of the deal boards that were about the boat.

Now he was on his feet and walking down the flight of steps opposite to those on which Menes stood far away. Now he was among all that throng of ghosts, which parted to let him pass, looking at him as he went with cold and wondering eyes. They were very majestic ghosts; the ages that had gone by since they laid down their sceptres had taken nothing from their royal dignity. Moreover, save one, none of them seemed to have any pity for his plight. She was a little princess who stood by her mother, that same little princess whose mummy he had seen and pitied in the Director's room with a lotus flower thrust beneath her bandages. As he passed Smith heard her say:

'This Vile One is frightened. Be brave, Vile One!'

Smith understood, and pride come to his aid. He, a gentleman of the modern world, would not show the white feather before a crowd of ancient Egyptian ghosts. Turning to the child, he smiled at her, them drew himself to his full height and walked on quietly. Here it may be stated that Smith was a tall man, still comparatively young, and very good-looking, straight and spare in frame, with dark, pleasant eyes and a little black beard.

'At least he is a well-favoured thief,' said one of the queens to another.

'Yes,' answered she who had been addressed. 'I wonder that a man with such a noble air should find pleasure in disturbing graves and stealing the offerings of the dead,' words that gave Smith much cause for thought. He had never considered the matter in this light.

Now he came to the place where Ma-Mee stood, the black-browed Pharaoh who had been her husband at her side. On his left hand which held the cigar-box was the gold Bes ring, and that box he felt constrained to carry pressed against him just over his heart.

As he went by he turned his head, and his eyes met those of Ma-Mee. She started violently. Then she saw the ring upon his hand and again started still more violently.

'What ails your Majesty?' asked the Pharaoh.

'Oh, naught,' she answered. 'Yet does this earth-dweller remind you of anyone?'

'Yes, he does,' answered the Pharaoh. 'He reminds me very much of that accursed sculptor about whom we had words.'

'Do you mean a certain Horu, the Court artist; he who worked the image that was buried with me, and whom you sent to carve your statues in the deserts of Kush, until he died of fevers – or was it poison?'

'Aye; Horu and no other, may Set take and keep him!' growled the Pharaoh.

Then Smith passed on and heard no more. Now he stood before the venerable Menes. Some instinct caused him to bow to this Pharaoh, who bowed back to him. Then he turned and bowed to the royal company, and they also bowed back to him, coldly, but very gravely and courteously.

'Dweller on the world where once we had our place, and therefore brother of us, the dead,' began Menes, 'this divine priest and magician' – and he pointed to Khaemuas – 'declares that you are one of those who foully violate our sepulchres and desecrate our ashes. He declares, moreover, that at this very moment you have with you a portion of the mortal flesh of a certain Majesty whose spirit is present here. Say, now, are these things true?'

To his astonishment Smith found that he had not the slightest difficulty in answering in the same sweet tongue.

'O King, they are true, and not true. Hear me, rulers of Egypt. It is true that I have searched in your graves, because my heart has been drawn towards you, and I would learn all that I could concerning you, for it comes to me *now* that once I was one of you – no king, indeed, yet perchance of the blood of kings. Also – for I would hide nothing even if I could – I searched for one tomb above all others.'

'Why, O man?' asked the Judge.

'Because a face drew me, a lovely face that was cut in stone.'

Now all that great audience turned their eyes towards him and listened as though his words moved them.

'Did you find that holy tomb?' asked Menes. 'If so, what did you find therein?'

'Aye, Pharaoh, and in it I found these,' and he took from the box the withered hand, from his pocket the broken bronze, and from his finger the ring.

'Also I found other things which I delivered to the keeper of this place, articles of jewellery that I seem to see tonight upon one who is present here among you.'

'Is the face of this figure the face you sought?' asked the Judge.

'It is the lovely face,' he answered.

Menes took the effigy in his hand and read the cartouche that was engraved beneath its breast.

'If there be here among us,' he said, presently, 'one who long after my day ruled as queen in Egypt, one who was named Ma-Mé, let her draw near.'

Now from where she stood glided Ma-Mee and took her

place opposite to Smith.

'Say, O Queen,' asked Menes, 'do you know aught of this matter?'

'I know that hand; it was my own hand,' she answered. 'I know that ring; it was my ring. I know that image in bronze; it was my image. Look on me and judge for yourselves whether this be so. A certain sculptor fashioned it, the son of a king's son, who was named Horu, the first of sculptors and the head artist of my Court. There, clad in strange garments, he stands before you. Horu, or the Double of Horu, he who cut the image when I ruled in Egypt, is he who found the image and the man who stands before you; or, mayhap, his Double cast in the same mould.'

The pharaoh Menes turned to the magician Khaemuas and said:

'Are these things so, O Seer?'

'They are so,' answered Khaemuas. 'This dweller on the earth is he who, long ago, was the sculptor Horu. But what shall that avail? He, once more a living man, is a violator of the hallowed dead. I say, therefore, that judgment should be executed on his flesh, so that when the light comes here tomorrow he himself will again be gathered to the dead.'

Menes bent his head upon his breast and pondered. Smith said nothing. To him the whole play was so curious that he had no wish to interfere with its development. If these ghosts wished to make him of their number, let them do so. He had no ties on earth, and now when he knew full surely that there was a life beyond this of earth he was quite prepared to explore its mysteries. So he folded his arms upon his breast and awaited the sentence.

But Ma-Mee did not wait. She raised her hand so swiftly that the bracelets jingled on her wrists, and spoke out with boldness.

'Royal Khaemuas, prince and magician,' she said, 'hearken to one who, like you, was Egypt's heir centuries before you were born, one also who ruled over the Two Lands, and not so ill — which, Prince, never was your lot. Answer me! Is all wisdom centred in your breast? Answer me! Do you alone know the mysteries of Life and Death? Answer me! Did your god Amen teach you that vengeance went before mercy? Answer me! Did he teach you that men should be judged unheard? That they should be hurried by violence to Osiris ere their time, and thereby separated from the dead ones whom they loved and forced to return to live again upon this evil Earth?

'Listen: when the last moon was near her full my spirit sat in my tomb in the burying-place of queens. My spirit saw this man enter into my tomb, and what he did there. With bowed head he looked upon my bones that a thief of the priesthood of Amen had robbed and burnt within twenty years of their burial, in which he himself had taken part. And what did this man with those bones, he who was once Horu? I tell you that he hid them away there in the tomb where he thought they could not be found again. Who, then, was the thief and the violator? He who robbed and burnt my bones, or he who buried them with reverence? Again, he found the jewels that the priest of your brotherhood had dropped in his flight, when the smoke of the burning flesh and spices overpowered him, and with them the hand which that wicked one had broken off from the body of my Majesty. What did this man then? He took the jewels. Would you have had him leave them to be stolen by some peasant? And the hand? I tell you that he kissed that poor dead hand which once had been part of the body of my Majesty, and that now he treasures it as a holy relic. My spirit saw him do these things and made report thereof to me. I ask you, therefore, Prince, I ask you all, Royalties of Egypt — whether for such deeds this man should die?'

Now Khaemuas, the advocate of vengeance, shrugged his shoulders and smiled meaningly, but the congregation of kings and queens thundered an answer, and it was:

'No!'

Ma-Mee looked to Menes to give judgment. Before he could speak the dark-browed Pharaoh who had named her wife strode forward and addressed them.

'Her Majesty, Heiress of Egypt, Royal Wife, Lady of the Two Lands, has spoken,' he cried. 'Now let me speak who was the husband of her Majesty. Whether this man was once Horu the sculptor I know not. If so he was also an evil-doer who, by my decree, died in banishment in the land of Kush. Whatever be the truth as to that matter, he admits that he violated the tomb of her Majesty and stole what the old thieves had left. Her Majesty says also — and he does not deny it — that he dared to kiss her hand, and for a man to kiss the hand of a wedded Queen of Egypt the punishment is death. I claim that this man should die to the World before his time, that in a day to come again he may live and suffer in the World. Judge, O Menes.'

Menes lifted his head and spoke, saying:

'Repeat to me the law, O Pharaoh, under which a living man must die for the kissing of a dead hand. In my day and in that of those who went before me there was no such law in Egypt. If a living man, who was not her husband, or of her kin, kissed the living hand of a wedded Queen of Egypt, save in ceremony, then perchance he might be called upon to die. Perchance for such a reason a certain Horu once was called upon to die. But in the grave there is no marriage, and therefore even if he had found her alive within the tomb and kissed her hand, or even her lips, why should he die for the crime of love?

'Hear me, all; this is my judgment in the matter. Let the soul of that priest who first violated the tomb of the royal Ma-Mee be hunted down and given to the jaws of the Destroyer, that he may know the last depths of Death, if so the gods declare. But let this man go from among us unharmed, since what he did he did in reverent ignorance and because Hathor, Goddess of Love, guided him from of old. Love rules this world wherein we meet tonight, with all the worlds whence we have gathered or whither we still must go. Who can defy its power? Who can refuse its rites? Now hence to Thebes!'

There was a rushing sound as of a thousand wings, and all were gone.

No, not all, since Smith yet stood before the draped colossi and the empty steps, and beside him, glorious, unearthly, gleamed the vision of Ma-Mee.

'I, too, must away,' she whispered; 'yet ere I go a word with you who once were a sculptor in Egypt. You loved me then, and that love cost you your life, you who once dared to kiss this hand of mine that again you kissed in yonder tomb. For I was Pharaoh's wife in name only; understand me well, in name only; since that title of Royal Mother, which they gave me is but a graven lie. Horu, I never was a wife, and when you died, swiftly I followed you to the grave. Oh, you forget, but I remember! I remember many things. You think that the priestly thief broke

- - -

172

this figure of me which you found in the sand outside my tomb. Not so. *I* broke it, because, daring greatly, you had written thereon, "Beloved " not "of *Horus* the God " as you should have done, but of "*Horu* the Man". So when I came to be buried, Pharaoh, knowing all, took the image from my wrappings and hurled it away. I remember, too, the casting of that image, and how you threw a gold chain I had given you into the crucible with the bronze, saying that gold alone was fit to fashion me. And this signet that I bear — it was you who cut it. Take it, take it, Horu, and in its place give me back that which is on your hand, the Bes ring that I also wore. Take it and wear it ever till you die again, and let it go to the grave with you as once it went to the grave with me.

'Now hearken. When Ra the great sun arises again and you awake you will think that you have dreamed a dream. You will think that in this dream you saw and spoke with a lady of Egypt who died more than three thousand years ago, but whose beauty, carved in stone and bronze, has charmed your heart today. So let it be, yet know, O man, who once was named Horu, that such dreams are oft-times a shadow of the truth. Know that this Glory which shines before you is mine indeed in the land that is both far and near, the land wherein I dwell eternally, and that what is mine has been, is, and shall be yours for ever. Gods may change their kingdoms and their names; men may live and die, and live again once more to die; empires may fall and those who ruled them be turned to forgotten dust. Yet true love endures immortal as the souls in which it was conceived, and from it for you and me, the night of woe and separation done, at the daybreak which draws on, there shall be born the splendour and the peace of union. Till that hour foredoomed seek me no more, though I be ever near you, as I have ever been. Till that most blessed hour, Horu, farewell.'

She bent towards him; her sweet lips touched his brow; the perfume from her breath and hair beat upon him; the light of her wondrous eyes searched out his very soul, reading the answer that was written there.

He stretched out his arms to clasp her, and lo! she was gone.

It was a very cold and a very stiff Smith who awoke on the following morning, to find himself exactly where he had lain down —

namely, on a cement floor beneath the keel of a funeral boat in the central hall of the Cairo Museum. He crept from his shelter shivering, and looked at this hall, to find it quite as empty as it had been on the previous evening. Not a sign or a token was there of Pharaoh Menes and all those kings and queens of whom he had dreamed so vividly.

Reflecting on the strange fantasies that weariness and excited nerves can summon to the mind in sleep, Smith made his way to the great doors and waited in the shadow, praying earnestly that, although it was the Mohammedan Sabbath, someone might visit the Museum to see that all was well.

As a matter of fact, someone did, and before he had been there a minute – a watchman going about his business. He unlocked the place carelessly, looking over his shoulder at a kite fighting with two nesting crows. In an instant Smith, who was not minded to stop and answer questions, had slipped past him and was gliding down the portico, from monument to monument, like a snake between boulders, still keeping in the shadow as he headed for the gates.

The attendant caught sight of him and uttered a yell of fear; then, since it is not good to look upon an *afreet*, appearing from whence no mortal man could be, he turned his head away. When he looked again Smith was through those gates and had mingled with the crowd in the street beyond.

The sunshine was very pleasant to one who was conscious of having contracted a chill of the worst Egyptian order from long contact with a damp stone floor. Smith walked on through it towards his hotel – it was Shepheard's, and more than a mile away – making up a story as he went to tell the hall-porter of how he had gone to dine at Mena House by the Pyramids, missed the last tram, and stopped the night there.

Whilst he was thus engaged his left hand struck somewhat sharply against the corner of the cigar-box in his pocket, that which contained the relic of the queen Ma-Mee. The pain caused him to glance at his fingers to see if they were injured, and to perceive on one of them the ring he wore. Surely, surely it was not the same that the Director-General had given him! *That* ring was engraved with the image of the god Bes. On *this* was cut the cartouche of her Majesty Ma-Mee! And he had dreamed – oh, he had dreamed . . .

To this day Smith is wondering whether, in the hurry of the moment, he made a mistake as to which of those rings the Director-General had given him as part of his share of the spoil of the royal tomb he discovered in the Valley of Queens. Afterwards Smith wrote to ask, but the Director-General could only remember that he gave him one of the two rings, and assured him that that inscribed '*Bes Ank, Ank Bes,*' was with Ma-Mee's other jewels in the Gold Room of the Museum.

Also Smith is wondering whether any other bronze figure of an old Egyptian royalty shows so high a percentage of gold as, on analysis, the broken image of Ma-Mee was proved to do. For had she not seemed to tell him a tale of the melting of a golden chain when that effigy was cast?

Was it all only a dream, or was it — something more — by day and by night he asks of Nothingness?

But, be she near or far, no answer comes from the Queen Ma-Mee, whose proud titles were 'Her Majesty the Good God, the justified Dweller in Osiris; Daughter of Amen, Royal Heiress, Royal Sister, Royal Wife, Royal Mother; Lady of the Two Lands; Wearer of the Double Crown; of the White Crown, of the Red Crown; Sweet Flower of Love, Beautiful Eternally.'

So, like the rest of us, Smith must wait to learn the truth concerning many things, and more particularly as to which of those two circles of ancient gold the Director-General gave him yonder at Cairo.

It seems but a little matter, yet it is more than all the worlds to him!

To the astonishment of his colleagues in antiquarian research, Smith has never returned to Egypt. He explains to them that his health is quite restored, and that he no longer needs this annual change to a more temperate clime.

Now, *which* of the two royal rings did the Director-General return to Smith on the mummied hand of her late Majesty Ma-Mee?

DELENDA EST

by Robert E. Howard

'It's no empire, I tell you! It's only a sham. Empire? Pah! Pirates, that's all we are!' It was Hunegais, of course, the ever moody and gloomy, with his braided black locks and drooping moustaches betraying his Slavonic blood. He sighed gustily, and the Falernian wine slopped over the rim of the jade goblet clenched in his brawny hand, to stain his purple, gilt-embroidered tunic. He drank noisily, after the manner of a horse, and returned with melancholy gusto to his original complaint.

'What have we done in Africa? Destroyed the big land-holders and the priests, set ourselves up as landlords. Who works the land? Vandals? Not at all! The same men who worked it under the Romans. We've merely stepped into Roman shoes. We levy taxes and rents, and are forced to defend the land from the accursed Berbers. Our weakness is in our numbers. We can't amalgamate with the people! We'd be absorbed. We can't make allies and subjects out of them; all we can do is maintain a sort of military prestige – we are a small body of aliens sitting in castles and, for the present, enforcing our rule over a big native population – who, it's true, hates us no worse than they hated the Romans, but—'

'Some of that hate could be done away with,' interrupted Athaulf. He was younger than Hunegais, clean-shaven, and not unhandsome; his manners were less primitive. He was a Suevi, whose youth had been spent as a hostage in the East Roman court. 'They are orthodox; if we could bring ourselves to renounce Arianism—'

'*No!*' Hunegais' heavy jaws came together with a snap

176

that would have splintered lesser teeth than his. His dark eyes flamed with the fanaticism that was, among all the Teutons, the exclusive possession of his race. 'Never! We are the masters! It is theirs to submit – not ours. We *know* the truth of Arian; if the miserable Africans can not realise their mistake, they must be made to see it – by torch and sword and rack, if necessary!' Then his eyes dulled again, and with another gusty sigh from the depths of his belly, he groped for the wine jug.

'In a hundred years the Vandal kingdom will be a memory,' he predicted. 'All that holds it together now is the will of Genseric.' He pronounced it Geiserich.

The individual so named laughed, leaned back in his carven ebony chair, and stretched out his muscular legs before him. Those were the legs of a horseman; but their owner had exchanged the saddle for the deck of a war galley. Within a generation, he had turned a race of horsemen into a race of sea-rovers. He was the king of a race whose name had already become a term for destruction, and he was the possessor of the finest brain in the known world.

Born on the banks of the Danube and grown to manhood on that long trek westward, when the drifts of the nations crushed over the Roman palisades, he had brought to the crown forged for him in Spain all the wild wisdom the times could teach, in the feasting of swords and the surge and crush of races. His wild riders had swept the spears of the Roman rulers of Spain into oblivion. When the Visigoths and the Romans joined hands and began to look southward, it was the intrigues of Genseric which brought Attila's scarred Huns swarming westward, tusking the flaming horizons with their myriad lances. Attila was dead now, and none knew where lay his bones and his treasures, guarded by the ghosts of five hundred slaughtered slaves; his name thundered around the world; but in his day he had been but one of the pawns moved resistlessly by the hand of the Vandal king.

And when, after Chalons, the Gothic hosts moved down through the Pyrenees, Genseric had not waited to be crushed by superior numbers. Men still cursed the name of Boniface, who called on Genseric to aid him against his rival, Aetius, and opened the Vandal's road to Africa. His reconciliation with Rome had been too late; vain as the courage with which he had sought to undo what he had done. Boniface died on a Vandal spear, and a new kingdom rose in the south. And now Aetius, too, was dead, and the great war galleys of the Vandals were moving northward, the long oars dipping and flashing silver in the starlight, the great vessels heeling and rocking to the lift of the waves.

And in the cabin of the foremost galley, Genseric listened to the conversation of his captains, and smiled gently as he combed his unruly yellow beard with his muscular fingers. There was in his veins no trace of the Scythic blood which set his race somewhat aside from the other Teutons, from the long ago when scattered steppes-riders, drifting west-ward before the conquering Sarmatians, had come among the people dwelling on the upper reaches of the Elbe. Genseric was pure German; of medium height, with a magnificent sweep of shoulders and chest, and a massive corded neck, his frame promised as much of physical vitality as his wide blue eyes reflected mental vigor.

He was the strongest man in the known world, and he was a pirate – the first of the Teutonic sea-raiders whom men later called Vikings; but his domain of conquest was not the Baltic nor the blue North Sea, but the sunlit shores of the Mediterranean.

'And the will of Genseric,' he laughed, in reply to Hunegais' last remark, 'is that we drink and feast and let tomorrow take care of itself.'

'So you say!' snorted Hunegais, with the freedom that still existed among the barbarians. 'When did you ever let a tomorrow take care of itself? You plot and plot, not for tomorrow alone, but for a thousand tomorrows to come! You need not masquerade with us! We are not Romans to be fooled into thinking *you* are a fool – as Boniface was!'

'Aetius was no fool,' muttered Thrasamund.

'But he's dead, and we are sailing on Rome,' answered Hunegais, with the first sign of satisfaction he had yet evinced. 'Alaric didn't get all the loot, thank God! And I'm glad Attila lost his nerve at the last minute – the more plunder for us.'

'Attila remembered Chalons,' drawled Athaulf. 'There is something about Rome that lives – by the saints, it is strange. Even when the empire seems most ruined – torn, befouled, and tattered – some part of it springs into life again. Stilicho, Theodosius, Aetius – who can tell? Tonight in Rome there may be a man sleeping who will overthrow us all.'

Hunegais snorted and hammered on the wine-stained board.

'Rome is as dead as the white mare I rode at the taking of Carthage! We have but to stretch out our hands and grasp the plunder of her!'

'There was a great general once who thought as much,' said Thrasamund drowsily. 'A Carthaginian, too, by God! I have forgotten his name. But he beat the Romans at every turn. Cut, slash, that was his way!'

'Well,' remarked Hunegais, 'he must have lost at last, or he would have destroyed Rome.'

'That's so!' ejaculated Thrasamund.

'We are not Carthaginians,' laughed Genseric. 'And who said aught of plundering Rome? Are we not merely sailing to the imperial city in answer to the appeal of the Empress who is beset by jealous foes? And now, get out of here, all of you. I want to sleep.'

The cabin door slammed on the morose predictions of Hunegais, the witty retorts of Athaulf, the mumble of the others. Genseric rose and moved over to the table, to pour himself a last glass of wine. He walked with a limp; a Frankish spear had girded him in the leg long years ago.

He lifted the jeweled goblet to his lips – wheeled with a startled oath. He had not heard the cabin door open, but a man was standing across the table from him.

'By Odin!' Genseric's Arianism was scarcely skin-deep. 'What do you in my cabin?'

The voice was calm, almost placid, after the first startled oath. The king was too shrewd to often evince his real emotions. His hand stealthily closed on the hilt of his sword. A sudden and unexpected stroke—

But the man made no hostile movement. He was a stranger to Genseric, and the Vandal knew he was neither Teuton nor Roman. He was tall, dark, with a stately head, his flowing locks confined by a dark crimson band. A curling, patriarchal beard swept his breast. A dim, misplaced familiarity twitched at the Vandal's mind as he looked.

'I have not come to harm you!' The voice was deep, strong, and resonant. Genseric could tell little of his attire, since he was masked in a wide dark cloak. The Vandal wondered if he grasped a weapon under that cloak.

'Who are you, and how did you get into my cabin?' he demanded.

'Who I am, it matters not,' returned the other. 'I have been on this ship since you sailed from Carthage. You sailed at night; I came aboard then.'

'I never saw you in Carthage,' muttered Genseric. 'And you are a man who would stand out in a crowd.'

'I dwell in Carthage,' the stranger replied. 'I have dwelt there for many years. I was born there, and my forefathers before me. Carthage is my life!' The last sentence was uttered in a voice so passionate and fierce that Genseric involuntarily stepped back, his eyes narrowing.

'The folk of the city have some cause of complaint against us,' said he. 'But the looting and destruction was not by my orders. Even then it was my intention to make Carthage my capital. If you suffered loss by the sack, why—'

'Not from your wolves,' grimly answered the other. 'Sack of the city? I have seen such a sack as not even you, barbarian, have dreamed of! They call you barbaric. I have seen what civilised Romans can do.'

'Romans have not plundered Carthage in my memory,' muttered Genseric, frowning in some perplexity.

'Poetic justice!' cried the stranger, his hand emerging from his cloak to strike down on the table. Genseric noted that the hand was muscular yet white, the hand of an aristocrat. 'Roman greed and treachery destroyed Carthage, trade rebuilt her in another guise. Now you, barbarian, sail from her harbors to humble her conqueror! Is it any wonder that old dreams silver the cords of your ships and creep amidst the holds, and that forgotten ghosts burst their immemorial tombs to glide upon your decks?'

'Who said anything of humbling Rome?' uneasily demanded Genseric. 'I merely sail to arbitrate a dispute as to succession—'

'Pah!' Again the hand slammed down on the table. 'If you knew what I know, you would sweep that accursed city clean of life before you turn your prows southward again. Even now, those you sail to aid plot your ruin – and a traitor is on board your ship!'

'What do you mean?' Still there was neither excitement nor passion in the Vandal's voice.

'Suppose I gave you proof that your most trusted companion and vassal plots your ruin with those to whose aid you lift your sails?'

'Give me that proof; then ask what you will,' answered Genseric with a touch of grimness.

'Take this in token of faith!' The stranger rang a coin on the table, and caught up a silken girdle which Genseric himself had carelessly thrown down.

'Follow me to the cabin of your counsellor and scribe, the handsomest man among the barbarians—'

'Athaulf?' In spite of himself, Genseric started. 'I trust him beyond all others.'

'Then you are not as wise as I deemed you,' grimly answered the other. 'The traitor within is to be feared more than the foe without. It was not the legions of Rome which conquered *me* – it was the traitors within my gates. Not alone in swords and ships does Rome deal, but with the souls of men. I have come from a far land to save your empire and your life. In return I ask but one thing: drench Rome in blood!'

For an instant the stranger stood transfigured, mighty arm lifted, fist clenched, dark eyes flashing fire. An aura of terrific power emanated from him, awing even the wild Vandal. Then sweeping his purple cloak about him with a kingly gesture, the man stalked to the door and through it, despite Genseric's exclamation and effort to detain him.

Swearing in bewilderment, the king limped to the door, opened it, and glared out on the deck. A lamp burned on the poop. A reek of unwashed bodies came up from the hold where the weary rowers toiled at their oars. The rhythmic clack vied with a dwindling chorus from the ships which followed in a long ghostly line. The moon struck silver from the waves, shone white on the deck. A single warrior stood on guard outside Genseric's door, the moonlight sparkling on his crested golden helmet and Roman corselet. He lifted his javelin in salute.

'Where did he go?' demanded the king.

'Who, my lord?' inquired the warrior stupidly.

'The tall man, dolt,' exclaimed Genseric impatiently. 'The man in the purple cloak who just left my cabin.'

'None has left your cabin since the lord Hugenais and the others went forth, my lord,' replied the Vandal in bewilderment.

'Liar!' Genseric's sword was a ripple of silver in his hand as it slid from its sheath. The warrior paled and shrank back.

'As God is my witness, king,' he swore, 'no such man have I seen this night.'

Genseric glared at him; the Vandal king was a judge of men and he knew this one was not lying. He felt a peculiar twitching of his scalp, and turning without a word, limped hurriedly to Athaulf's cabin. There he hesitated, then threw open the door.

Athaulf lay sprawled across a table in an attitude which needed no second glance to classify. His face was purple, his glassy eyes distended, and his tongue lolled out blackly. About his neck, knotted in such a knot as seamen make, was Genseric's silken girdle. Near one hand lay a quill, near the other, ink and a piece of parchment. Catching it up, Genseric read laboriously.

To her majesty, the empress of Rome:

I, thy faithful servant, have done thy bidding, and am prepared to persuade the barbarian I serve to delay his onset on the imperial city until the aid you expect from Byzantium has arrived. Then I will guide him into the bay I mentioned, where he can be caught as in a vise and destroyed with his whole fleet, and—

The writing ceased with an erratic scrawl. Genseric glared down at him, and again the short hairs lifted on his scalp. There was no sign of the tall stranger, and the Vandal knew he would never be seen again.

'Rome shall pay for this,' he muttered. The mask he wore in public had fallen away; the Vandal's face was that of a hungry wolf. In his glare, in the knotting of his mighty hand, it took no sage to read the doom of Rome. He suddenly remembered that he still clutched in his hand the coin the stranger had dropped on his table. He glanced at it, and his breath hissed between his teeth, as he recognised the characters of an old, forgotten language, the features of a man which he had often seen carved in ancient marble in old Carthage, preserved from Roman hate.

'Hannibal!' muttered Genseric.

EYES OF TERROR

by Mrs. L. T. Meade

~~~~~~

The strange story which I am about to tell happened just when the late war in South Africa was at its height. I was in a very nervous condition at the time, having lost my dear father, who was killed in action shortly before the taking of Pretoria. The news of my father's death reached us on a certain evening in May, just when the days were approaching their longest, and summer, with all its beauties, was about to visit the land. It was immediately afterwards that the visitations which I am about to describe took place. They were of a very alarming character, and so much did they upset my mental equilibrium that I determined to put my case into the hands of a certain Professor Ellicott, who was not only a physician and surgeon in the ordinary sense, but was also a man of great learning and keen original research.

I had met the Professor once at the house of a neighbour, and on that occasion had admired him, not only for his intellectual appearance, but also for the massive strength of his face and the calmness of his bearing. I knew that a strong man, who was also sympathetic and tactful, would not laugh at a girl's fears, however unreasonable he might consider them, and had not the least doubt that I should receive a patient hearing when I told him my story.

My name is Nora Dallas. I am twenty-one years of age. I have lived all my life in a beautiful old place about a mile and a half from the town of Ashingford. Professor Ellicott lived in the High Street, and I was fortunate enough to find him at home.

I sent in my card and was immediately admitted into his presence. He was a man of about thirty, with resolute grey eyes and a determined chin. He gave me a quick glance when I entered the room; then, without uttering a word, pointed to a chair.

"I am called Nora Dallas," I said.

"I know," he replied, in a gentle voice. "You are the daughter of that Colonel Dallas whose gallant action, when he sacrificed his life for his country on the march to Pretoria, is the talk and admiration of the country."

My eyes filled with tears.

"It is only three weeks since I heard of my father's death," I said. "You will forgive me sir, but I cannot bear any sympathetic reference to the subject, at least for the present."

"I understand," he replied, his hard face softening. "And now, what can I do for you?"

"I want to consult you as a doctor."

"But I am not a consultant—I mean that I do not practise medicine in the ordinary sense."

"I am aware of that fact," I answered. "And just for that very reason, Professor Ellicott, I have been compelled to come to you."

"I do not quite understand."

He looked at me with the dawn of a smile on his lips.

"I think you will give me a frank opinion, and be unbiased by the red-tapism which causes many medical men to hide the truth from their patients."

"Ah, you think well of me," he said, with a smile, "and I perceive that you are a brave woman. Nevertheless, I must inform you that I am scarcely qualified to enter into your case. My work lies altogether in the regions of original research."

"May I at least tell you my story?" I insisted. "You can make up your mind afterwards whether you will help me or not."

His reply to this was to get up and pace the room, stopping once or twice to look at me, then continuing his slow, measured tread up and down. I did not interrupt him. I sat as still as though carved in marble.

"You must forgive my apparent rudeness, Miss Dallas," he said, "but I was endeavouring to recall what I had already heard about you. I remember everything now. I met you a month ago at Sir John Newcome's. You live at Courtlands, one of the finest places in the neighbourhood. You are an only child. Doubtless, now that your father is dead, you are wealthy. You have lived at Courtlands almost all your life. Of course, Miss Dallas, you have your own family physician?"

"Yes," I answered.

"Will you not consult him?"

"No; for he is not the man for my purpose."

He smiled.

"You think that I am?"

"If anyone can help me, you can."

"How like a woman!" he said, somewhat impatiently. "And yet you know nothing about me. As I said just now, I am not a consultant. I have come to Ashingford for quiet, and for the opportunity to examine into the length and breadth of a problem which, if I can bring it to a successful issue, will mean health and happiness to millions. And yet a girl, little more than a child, wants to interrupt my train of thought. Do you think you are fair to me?"

"I don't know anything about that," I replied, with vehemence. "I only know that I want help. Will you give it to me?"

My voice broke.

"Of course I will," he said, cordially, and his whole manner completely altered. "I only said what I did to test you. Now we will preamble no more. Tell me your story."

"I was twenty-one last March," I began, immediately, "and now that my dear father is dead I am absolutely my own mistress. With the exception of my Aunt Sophia, my father's sister, who lives with me, and my two cousins, I am without relations. It is about these cousins that I wish specially to speak. They are the sons of my father's younger brother, who has long been dead. My father adopted them in their infancy, brought them up, sent them to school, and gave them all they required. They are twins and are now five-and twenty years of age. Rudolf has been called to the Bar and Lionel is a solicitor. Professor Ellicott, I must be truthful—I must be truthful even at the risk of failing in charity. My cousins are not good men. I have nothing to say against them—I have no means at present of proving my words—nevertheless, instinct tells me that I am right. Rudolf is the sort of man who imposes on people. I have seen him rhapsodize over poetry or a sunset, and his friends then imagine that he has a great love for the beautiful. But I know better. The only love in his wicked heart is the love of money. Lionel is his weak shadow—his dupe and tool."

"Surely you are hard on your cousins?"

"You would naturally think so; and yet I hope to convince you that I have read their characters aright.

"My father, before he went to South Africa, made a will, the contents of which he fully explained to me. In the event of his death I was to inherit the house and estate and also the bulk of his money, with the exception of a sum of sixty thousand pounds, which was to be divided between my two cousins. He fully explained all that he wanted to tell me with regard to his last will, and gave me directions as to certain affairs which he wished to be specially attended to. My dear father then continued to say some words which astonished and distressed me very much. He declared that it was the darling wish of his heart that Rudolf and I should marry. My father said that he had the highest opinion of my cousin and assured me that nothing would make him happier than such a marriage. Rudolf had told him of his attachment to me—an attachment which I knew well did not exist.

"I heard my father in silence. Then I gave an emphatic negative to the whole proposal. My father listened in amazement. I said that I neither liked nor trusted my cousin, and that nothing—no words, no conditions—would make me accept him. After a pause my father said that my feelings must be my guide, but he continued:

" 'I cannot agree with your opinion, and I sincerely hope that time may alter it.'

"From the hour of his depature there began for me a detestable period, during which I was persecuted by Rudolf's odious attentions. As he and Lionel practically lived in our house, you can imagine that it was impossible for me to escape altogether from his presence. But at last it became so intolerable that I wrote to my father on the subject. I told Rudolf quite frankly that I was doing so, and even made him acquainted with the greater part of my letter. In that letter I told my father that he did not rightly gauge his nephew's character, that he was not what he believed him to be, and, in order to prove my words, I mentioned a few instances which, unconvincing to a stranger like yourself, might have the effect of opening his eyes.

"That letter was posted two months ago. Up to the present I have had no reply to it, but am even now waiting and hoping to hear my father's views on the subject. Important letters must be on the road from South Africa for me. I have only received the news of my dear father's death by cablegram."

My voice broke. I paused, struggling with emotion; then I continued:

"I am sorry to trouble you, Professor Ellicott, with this long preamble. I am now approaching that strange thing about which I wish to consult you.

"We received the cablegram acquainting us with the news of my father's death on a certain morning towards the end of last month. On the evening of that same day another long cablegram from South Africa was put into Rudolf's hands. He was sitting with my aunt and me in the drawing-room when he received it. He opened it, was evidently very much upset, but refused to divulge its contents. He called Lionel to his side, and they left the room together. I saw them pacing up and down in the shrubbery, evidently consulting with regard to the contents of the cablegram, but never from that hour till now have I heard the slightest inkling of what it was about.

"Three days later my father's will was read and my cousins heard of the large sums of money which would fall to their share. They fully expected to be remembered in my father's will, but not to such a generous extent, and their satisfaction was very great. As to Rudolf, his face quite beamed with delight, and they were both in feverish haste to possess themselves of the money. Mr. Brewster, our family lawyer, however, said that it would be impossible for them to receive their legacies for several weeks, as probate would have to be taken and other preliminaries attended to. Finally he made the remark:

"Nothing can really be done until Colonel Dallas's letters and papers arrive from South Africa. This can scarcely be expected until a month from the present date.'

"On that very evening my elder cousin came to me again and once more implored me to become his wife. He spoke of my father and his well-known wishes on the subject, and pleaded with such power that had I not known him well I might have been touched into a semblance of kindness by his manner. I did know my cousin, however, and told him so in unmistakable terms. He seemed to struggle with emotion for a minute; then he said, rising as he spoke:

" 'All right, Nora, I see I must accept your verdict. You may be sure that I will not trouble you on this subject again. It would be brutal to do so," he added, "for you are looking very ill. I see it in your eyes. '

" 'I am not exactly ill,' I answered. 'I am naturally in very great trouble, but I am no more really ill than you are.'

" 'I am all right, ' he said, with a shrug of his shoulders. 'But your nerves, poor Nora, are in a sad condition. You have received a most serious shock, and it is telling on you. You ought to be exceedingly careful. I mean it is your duty to be much more careful than most women. '

" 'I don't understand you,' I answered. 'And I wish,' I added, 'that you would leave me now.'

" 'I will in a minute,' he said, and then he approached quite close to my side.

" 'One word before I go,' he went on, and he fixed his great, strong, dark eyes on mine. 'Whether you like me or whether you hate me we are cousins, Nora. Our family history is well known to each of us. I in particular, however, have studied medicine, and am therefore in a position to speak. I only gave up medicine for the Bar because I thought I saw a more speedy way of earning money in that profession. Now, Nora, listen. Raise your eyes to mine. Don't shrink, child. If you encourage the morbid fancies which are now filling your brain you will share the fate of poor Aunt Ethel. I know what I am talking about. The pupils of your eyes point to a disordered brain.'

"He left me. I sat still for a minute, feeling more nervous and disturbed than I cared to own. Then I went to Aunt Sophia.

" 'What is the matter, Nora?' she said, when I found her. 'You are trembling all over and looking so ill. What is wrong child?'

" 'I want to ask you a straight question,' I replied. 'Who was, or who is, Aunt Ethel? I have never heard of her.'

"Aunt Sophia looked startled. She did not speak for a minute; then she said, with considerable reluctance:

" 'It doesn't matter about your Aunt Ethel. She has been long in her grave. Let her memory rest in peace.'

" 'But what about her?' I said. 'I *will* know,' I continued, and then I repeated what Rudolf had told me.

"Aunt Sophia looked very queer. After a futher pause she said:

" 'Rudolf has done wrong, but as you know so much you may as well know all. Your Aunt Ethel was your father's eldest sister. She went mad when about your age, and eventually ended her days by suicide.'

" 'And I was never told,' I said, turning white.

" 'Why should you be told?'

" 'But there must be insanity in our family.'

" 'Hers was the only case. Don't think about it again, child. Busy yourself with those active employments which a woman in your position has naturally so much to do with.'

"I left Aunt Sophia and returned to my room. There was a moon in the sky. My bedroom windows were open. I lit a pair of candles at each side of the long mirror at one end of the room, and deliberately studied my face. I had always known that my eyes were somewhat peculiar, my pupils being more dilated than those of most women."

"That fact merely betokens a high degree of nervous sensibility," said the Professor.

"I examined my eyes that night," I continued, "and it did seem to me that they had a wild and startled glance. I called my courage to my aid, however, and determined not to be fanciful, and to try to forget my cousin's words. That was easily said, but very difficult to act upon. My courage certainly did ebb as night went on. I found that my thoughts dwelt on Aunt Ethel and her horrible fate, and also found that I could turn them in no other direction. Presently I went to the window and looked out into the beautiful night. The moonlight was falling across the grass and causing black shadows under the trees.

"Suddenly I uttered a scream and fell back, too startled to keep my self-control. For gazing at me fixedly out of the deep mass of foliage were two very bright, luminous eyes, eyes full of a strange and terrifying gleam. I saw them as distinctly as I now see you. I watched them move, and saw them glitter as they disappeared into the darkness. When they had quite vanished I knew that I was cold all over. I shivered with a most awful sense of dread. My first desire was to run straight to Aunt Sophia, tell her the whole truth, and beg of her to share my room for the night. But on reflection I resolved not to do this. I did not want Aunt Sophia to know. She would certainly not have believed my tale, and she would put down the vision which I had seen to the same cause of which Rudolf would doubtless attribute it.

"There was no repose for me that night. The thought of those eyes kept me company—the eyes themselves and Rudolf's significant words: 'If you encourage those morbid fancies you will share the fate of poor Aunt Ethel. The pupils of your eyes point to a disordered brain.'

"In the afternoon of the next day I went for a solitary walk by myself. We have pine woods at the back of our house. From there I could see at intervals the tower which is the oldest part of the mansion. It is situated at the end of a long, rambling building, and was in existence at least four centuries ago. It is a curious Old Norman tower, with arches over the windows and a castellated roof. The tower contains only two rooms, the lower one being the library of our house and the upper my father's study. Since his death no one has been near that part of the building. I felt a sense of reproach as I remembered his room now. Was his study neglected and covered with dust? Were the flowers in the vases dried up and dead? I would go to the study tomorrow and see that it was made fresh and clean. I would open the windows and let in the sweet air. Nay, more, when the long-looked-for and eagerly expected letters arrived from South Africa I would read them in my father's study.

"That evening I paced up and down for a long time in the pine woods, then I returned to the house. I took up a novel and tried to read, but the book did not suit my mood. I remembered another which had begun to interest me, and which I had left in one of the drawing-rooms. I went downstairs to fetch it. There was no one in the room. I found the book in a distant corner and returned slowly to my bedroom. To do this I had to go down a long corridor into which many opened. For some extraordinary reason the electric light in this corridor was not turned on. I noticed how dark it was, and just as I reached my own door I looked back, impelled, I suppose, by instinct. In the darkness at the father end of the corridor I again saw the gleaming eyes. They stared fixedly at me without blinking, and with a horrible leering expression in their gaze. Again I screamed, rushed into my room, and locked the door. I could scarcely endure my misery.

" 'Am I going mad or am I the victim of an apparition?' I said to myself. 'Is my brain giving way? What am I to do? How am I to endure this? How am I to live?'

"The next week or ten days passed without any futher disturbance, and I was beginning to recover my mental balance. Rudolf was away from home during the greater part of that time, engaged on some very special business in the North of England. I was undoubtedly happier and less nervous when he was absent, but when he returned his affectionate and concerned manner about me made me self-reproachful, and I almost wondered at myself for the intolerable feeling of repugnance which I always felt towards him.

"Two or three nights after his return I saw the eyes again. On this occasion they stared at me from the centre of the rose-lawn. The night was black as pitch, and there were the eyes raised between five and six feet above the ground, and staring full at me with unblinking directness. After this visitation I determined to see you at once. Now, can you help me? Have I been visited by an apparition or am I mad? Tell me what you really think."

For reply the Professor said, quietly:

"I will examine your own eyes before I pronounce an opinion."

I rose at once. He placed me in a chair in front of a large window and, taking up some powerful lenses, carefully looked into both my eyes. When the examination was over he said:—

"You are very nervous. Some of the higher nerve centres are in a state of irritation. Your Father's death, joined to the shock of this apparition, trick, or what you like to call it, has been too much for you. You ought really to leave home."

"But am I going mad?"

"There is no trace of a disordered brain. Nevertheless you are nervous, and nerves are kittle cattle, and ought to be attended to."

"But, Dr. Ellicott, why should I be nervous? Why should I see those ghastly eyes? What is the mystery?"

"I should like much to unravel it," he said, with a shrug of his shoulders.

"How I wish you would!"

He looked thoughtful for a minute or two; then he said:

"Would it be possible for you to invite me to stay at Courtlands?"

"Would you come?"

"Could you give me a room where I could continue my business without interruption?"

"I could hand you over the library in the old tower. There you need never hear a footfall, for the tower is at the end of an unused wing at a remote part of the building."

"In that case I will bring my things and spend a few days at Courtlands. I do not believe in your apparition as an apparition, nor do I think that you are becoming insane. Your case interests me. May I arrive in time for dinner this evening?"

"I don't know how to thank you," was my answer.

"Expect me at Courtlands about seven o'clock. And now leave me, like a good girl, for I have many things to attend to."

I returned home with a great sense of relief, just in time for lunch. The only people at table were Aunt Sophia and my Cousin Lionel.

"Why, Nora," cried my aunt, "how much better you look! Have you had good news?"

"Yes and no," I replied. "By the way, Aunt Sophy, can we entertain a visitor for the next few days?'

"A visitor now?" she said, raising her brows in astonishment.

Lionel laid down his knife and fork and looked hard at me.

"To receive a visitor in the house now would be unusual, would it not, Nora?" he said, gently. "My uncle has not been dead a month yet."

I took no notice of him, but turned again to Aunt Sophia.

"Dr. Ellicott, the well-known Professor, is staying at Ashingford," I said. "I met him some time ago at the Newcomes'. He is a remarkably clever man, and I may as well confess that I consulted him medically this morning. No more Dr. Jessops for me. I preferred to consult one who was well up-to-date on medical matters. The Professor interests me and I interest him. He wishes to come here for a few days in order to watch my symptoms. He will arrive in time for dinner. Please, Aunt Sophy, will you order the green room to be got ready for him, and also the library in the old tower?"

I spoke in a decided manner, and neither my aunt nor Lionel ventured to remonstrate, for, after all, I was really mistress.

Suddenly I turned to my cousin.

"Is Rudolf away again?" I asked.

"No," he replied; "Rudolf is unwell. His eyes are hurting him. He is obliged to stay in a darkened room."

"I did not know that Rudolf suffered from his eyes."

"He never did until lately. We neither of us can imagine what is the matter with them," was Lionel's response.

I said a word or two of commonplace condolence, and then left the room.

That evening the Professor arrived, and when I entered the drawing-room before dinner I noticed that my aunt and both my cousins were waiting to receive him. During dinner he made himself generally agreeable, and Rudolf in especial seemed to be attracted by his manner and powers of conversation. I noticed, however, rather to my amazement, that my elder cousin wore a shade over his eyes, and in the course of dinner I inquired what really ailed them.

"I don't know," he said. "I am in considerable pain. My eyes are very much inflamed."

"Will you permit me to do something to relieve your symptoms?" said Professor Ellicott, suddenly, turning as he spoke, raising his pince-nez, and fixing his gaze on Rudolf's face.

"I wish you would," was the reply.

"I will look at your eyes after dinner. And now, Miss Dallas," he continued, turning with courtesy to my aunt, "let me explain that knotty point to you."

He was discussing a little matter with regard to the growth of ferns, and Aunt Sophia, a keen botanist, was listening to him with rapt attention.

By-and-by I made the signal to leave the room, and the gentlemen were left to themselves. In the course of that same evening the Professor came to sit near me.

"I have examined your cousin's eyes. There is considerable inflammation both in the eyelids and the eyes themselves. Their condition points to a strange diagnosis, but as it seems impossible that it can be the right one I am not prepared to say anything further on the subject—at least now. Tell me are you going to have a good sleep tonight?"

"I hope so."

"I think you will, for I have prepared a small, but effectual, draught, which I want you to take just as you are lying down. Get your maid to sleep in your room, and believe me that, eyes or no eyes, you will be in a state of oblivion five minutes after you take my draught."

I smiled, with a sense of relief.

"I believe," I said, "that in any case I should sleep well with you in the house."

The next few days passed without anything fresh occurring. We saw but little of the Professor. He was absorbed with his own work in the old library in the tower.

At last the day arrived when we expected letters and news from the beloved dead. Even Aunt Sophia was agitated, and Lionel and Rudolf were like restless ghosts, hovering here, there and everywhere. Rudolf's eyes looked worse than ever, and he also complained of a strange sore at his side. At dinner that evening the Professor said, abruptly:

"By the way, Dallas, do you happen to know anything about that new substance—radium?"

"I have heard of it," was the reply.

Lionel's face became suddenly rigid and very pale. Rudolf, on the contrary, looked with the utmost composure at Professor Ellicott.

"You, of course, have studied its properties," he said. "Tell me about them. I dabble in many things, and, above all enjoyments, to peer into the mysteries of science delights me most. But give me an account of the properties of radium."

"They are too varied to mention here. I will but allude to one or two. In close contact with the skin, radium has the effect of absolutely destroying the epidermis and the true skin beneath, thus in time producing an open sore. Moreover," said the Professor, "were you really dabbling with this strange substance the state of your eyes would be accounted for."

"I have never even seen the thing," was the abrupt answer.

The conversation turned to other matters. After dinner we all went to the drawing-room. Professor Ellicott came and seated himself near me.

"You will receive a letter from your father by the next post?" he asked.

"Yes."

"Where will you read it?"

"In his study. I have always read his letters there. I made him a promise that I would do so. He said he would like to think of me sitting under my mother's portrait, reading his letters and thinking of him."

A few minutes afterwards the postman's ring was heard, and a servant entered with several letters on a salver. The one I had expected was handed to me, and there was also a foreign letter for Aunt Sophia. Rudolf, who had come into the room just before the servant brought the letters, came up to me.

"You will go away by yourself and read your letter," he said, kindly. "You will read it in your father's study, won't you?"

I nodded. He smiled.

"I felt sure you would go there, Nora. He will be with you in spirit."

As Rudolf uttered the last words he glanced towards Lionel, and the two left the room a minute or two before I did.

To reach the tower I had to go down a long corridor which was seldom used. At the farther end of the corridor was a baize door which opened on to some narrow stone stairs. They were worn with age. Mounting them, I soon reached my father's study on the top floor of the tower. It was octagonal in shape, with many windows. These windows were closely barred and the panes of glass were small. When I entered the room I gave a start of surprise. I expected to see it in darkness, but instead of that a small table had been drawn up within a foot or two of the high, old-fashioned grate, and on it were placed a pair of brass candlesticks with candles in them already lighted. But why were the blinds not drawn down at the windows? I felt a momentary inclination to repair this omission myself, but my father's letter occupied all my thoughts and I soon forgot everything but the fact that I was about to read the beloved words—in short, to receive a message from the dead.

The contents of my father's letter absorbed my complete attention, and I soon perceived that only the very early portion was written by himself; most of it had evidently been dictated to a certain Edward Vincent, whose name, as one of the young lieutenants in my father's regiment, was already familiar to me. The letter told me that my father was mortally wounded, and that he was now partly writing, partly dictating his last good-bye to me in the tent where they had removed him after the skirmish with the enemy. In the letter he told me that he had received my last communication, and, in consequence, had made inquiries, which took some little time to come to fruition. On that very morning, however, he had received a long letter from London, which contained a complete confirmation of what I had told him, and also many other revelations had been forthcoming, which filled him with the utmost displeasure and horror. He therefore resolved immediately to change his will, leaving none of his property to my cousins, but all to me. The last words of his letter desired me to turn to the opposite page, on which a formally-worded will was written. This will left everything to me. I turned to it and read it. It was very short, and was signed by my father, and had also the signatures of two witnesses.

Tears flowed from my eyes. In one sense I was relieved, and yet my heart was torn. I covered my face. Just then a slight noise, which might have been attributed to the tapping of a bough against the window-pane, caused me to turn my head. I did so tremblingly. I felt convinced that I was not alone. Something, or someone, was looking at me. Fascinated, I gazed straight before me. Again came that ghastly tap, which I felt sure, proceeded from no human hand. I looked towards the upper panes of one of the windows, and there were the eyes. Never had they seemed more malicious or horrible. I lost my nerve, gave one shrill and terrified scream, and rushed towards the door, altogether forgetting my letter, which lay upon the table.

I had just reached the door when a fresh thing happened. The room became full of a sudden and terrible wind. It caught at the table-cloth, flapping it violently. The letter, written on thin foreign paper and consequently light as air, floated off the table with one or two other loose letters, was carried straight to the fireplace, and then up the chimney. The next instant I felt my dress dragged as by an unseen power. Something seemed to draw me back into the room, and the candles on the table flickered and went out. I was in the dark and alone, yet not alone. What awful thing had happened? My brain swam for a minute. I felt sick and cold; then I lost consciousness.

When I returned to my senses I was lying on the sofa and Professor Ellicott was bending over me.

"Now, control yourself, Miss Dallas," he said. "We have not a moment to lose. Tell me exactly what occurred."

I pressed my hand to my face. There was a light again in the room.

"Be quick," said the Professor. "What did you see? Why did you cry out? I was coming into the house in a hurry—in fact, I was on my way to this room—when I heard your shriek. I had been smoking and walking up and down in the grounds. Something induced me to look towards the tower. All of a sudden I saw—but tell me first what did you see?"

"The eyes," I answered. "They looked at me through one of the windows—that one exactly facing the table."

"Through what part of the window did they look?"

"Through one of the topmost panes."

"Good! I thought so. Now go on. Tell me the rest."

"I lost my nerve. I rushed towards the door, and just as I got there I turned, for the room was full of wind."

"Wind!" said the Professor. "Why, the night is as calm as death."

"Nevertheless, the room was full of a sort of gale, and the letter—my father's letter—was lifted and carried towards the chimney, up which it disappeared, and I myself was dragged back into the room. Then the candles were put out. Oh, I do believe at last in the ghost. Professor Ellicott, I wish I were dead."

"Don't be so silly, child. I assure you there is no ghost. Now, listen. I also saw something."

"The eyes?"

He nodded.

"They flashed at me for an instant. I fancy, Miss Dallas, this is a very tangible ghost. I saw a figure crouching on the roof, bending down over the turret towards that very window. I was just under the tower, hastening in, when you screamed, and I looked up and saw it disappear behind the parapet. The eyes were visible for about half a second. We shall catch your ghost, don't be afraid, and solve your mystery. I shall remain here for the present, but we must have the roof examined, and at once. Do you know of any other way to get to it except by a ladder from the ground? There surely must be a trap-door somewhere."

"There is, " I answered, "There's a trap-door at the end of this very wing."

"Good!" said the Professor. "Go downstairs at once and get several men, your cousins amongst them, to examine the roof from end to end, and in especial to look on the roof of this tower. I will stay here. Don't be long."

I ran away. The Professor's words had excited me, and my courage had returned. I gave the alarm. I could not find my cousins, but soon the rest of the house was in a state of ferment. Some of the men-servants and two of the gardeners immediately ascended to the roof. They carefully examined not only the roof of the house, but that of the tower. But look as they would they could not see a single trace of any individual hiding there. It is true that a rope, fastened to one of the chimneys, was hanging close to one of the parapets of the tower. This alone pointed conclusively to the fact that someone had been there. Nothing else, however, was to be discovered.

Accompanied by Aunt Sophia I returned to the Professor.

"Four of our men have been on the roof," I said, "and they brought away this rope. You can see it, There was no one there."

"Ah!" He shrugged his shoulders. "I thought there must have been a rope. He could not have bent over so far without being secured against the possibility of falling."

"The rope was fastened round one of the chimneys," I continued.

"Profesor, what does this mean?" said poor Aunt Sophia.

"Where are your nephews, madam?" was his answer. "Why are they not helping in this search?"

"We cannot find my cousins anywhere," I answered. "The last I saw of them was when I was going upstairs to read my father's letter. They then left the drawing-room and went out of the house arm-in-arm."

"I will go and have a further search made for them," said my aunt. "They certainly ought to be acquainted with this most remarkable occurrence."

She gave me a suspicious and, I fancied, unbelieving glance. Did she really think that I was imagining the whole thing? The Professor's attitude, however, comforted me.

"Don't be alarmed, child," he said. "The clue which we seek is close at hand. I am convinced of it. Now we must do something. I shall remain in this room for the night, and one or two of the servants must watch on the roof of the tower. But you must go to bed and rest, otherwise you will be down with nervous fever. Now, tell me, please, Miss Dallas, who are the most trustworthy and absolutely reliable servants in your house?"

"Harris, the old gardener, for one," I answered. "He has been with us since before I was born."

"Who else?"

"Franks, the butler."

"Then Harris and Franks shall watch on the roof of the tower tonight. Now go to bed."

Against my will I was forced to go to my room. Another sleeping-draught, administered by the Professor, ensured my repose, and in the morning I was sufficiently calm even to defy Aunt Sophia's looks of suspicion, for suspect me now of incipient insanity she evidently did.

The mysterious disappearance of both my cousins caused a great deal of talk and speculation on the following morning, and I went to the tower to visit the Professor in a state of great excitement on the subject. His manners were absolutely non-committal. He refused to say anything about my cousins, and he also refused to leave the study.

"When I go someone else must take my place," he said. "This room must not be left unguarded for a single moment, nor must the roof above."

Towards the latter part of the day he suggested that I should take his place in the study while he himself examined the roof. In about half an hour he returned to me. I saw that he held a tiny glass tube in his hand.

"Can you make anything of this?" he said, laying it on the table before me.

"Nothing," I answered. "What is it?"

"A very valuable piece of evidence, I take it."

"What do you mean?"

"I will try to tell you. I found this tube in the gutter just above the window. It is, as you see, sealed up at each end. It looks innocent enough; nevertheless, it contains a very minute portion of that new substance—radium. You heard what I said to your Cousin Rudolf with regard to the effect of radium on the human skin, but I did not tell him that it does something else. When held for a short time in front of the eyes, the eyes take to themselves a certain amount of its properties, and they glow in the dark with a great luminosity which gives them a most terrifying appearance. It strikes me, Miss Dallas, that in this little bottle I hold the solution of your ghost. The eyes of a man who held radium a short distance from his pupils would also become very much inflamed. Consider the condition of your Cousin Rudolf's eyes. I found this tube in the gutter. We are getting near the clue; eh, don't you think so?"

I felt myself turning pale. I know that I trembled.

"Could any man living be so wicked?" was my next remark.

"Men will do strange things for money," was his answer. "But how your cousin would know that your father intended to change his will is a mystery which I cannot fathom."

"What do you mean to do next?" I asked.

"Watch for the scoundrels. They are hiding somewhere, and all in good time they will reappear. By the way, you say that your father's letter, containing the will, was blown up the chimney. James," he continued, turning to the servant who had just entered the room, "you and Andrews must come up here within an hour and take my place while I visit the roof. I may have to remain there for some hours this evening. Meanwhile, Miss Dallas," he continued, giving me a quick smile, "you shall go and take a constitutional."

I did not want to go out, but the Professor's word just then was my law. The evening was a lovely one, and I walked for some little time. As I returned I looked towards the tower. Suddenly I perceived the tall figure of the Professor. He was standing absolutely motionless near one of the chimneys. He evidently saw me, but did not make the slightest movement. A wild desire to be with him and to share his watch came over me. Quick as thought I entered the house, reached the trap-door, which was open, and soon was standing on the low roof of Courtlands. I walked warily and presently reached the edge of the parapet. There were two steps here leading from the roof of the house to the roof of the tower. I mounted them and stood by the Professor's side.

"Child," he said, in a whisper, "what are you doing?"

"I must share your watch," I said.

"I would rather be alone."

I shook my head.

"Something forces me to remain with you. Don't deny me my wish."

He held up his hand with a warning gesture to me.

"Then you must crouch by this parapet," he said, "and remain motionless. I shall hide behind the chimney. My suspicions are confirmed. There are men not far from here. I heard a movement not along ago. Absolute quiet will force the scoundrels from their lair."

I now perceived that he carried a revolver. Moving away from him a few paces I crouched down behind the parapet. He did likewise a little way off. We were the only watchers on the silent tower, but I knew that there were servants also on guard in the room below.

By-and-by the sun sank towards the west and twilight reigned over the scene. Twilight deepened into night.

The Professor and I had remained motionless, as though we were dead, for from two to three hours.

All of a sudden I saw Professor Ellicot raise himself and glance towards me. I could but dimly see his face, but I knew that something was about to happen. The next minute, peering hard towards the stack of chimneys, I noticed, to my unbounded horror, the head of my Cousin Rudolf show itself. He did not see us, and cautiously began to descend from the chimney on to the roof. Just as he was about to place his feet on the roof, Professor Ellicott, strong as steel, sprang upon him and dragged him by the shoulders and arms down upon his knees.

"I have been waiting for you," he said. As he spoke he held his revolver to my cousin's ear. "If you stir you are a dead man. Confess your crime at once. Your game is up! Now, then, what does this mean?"

Rudolf groaned.

"The agony in my eyes is past bearing," he said.

"Call to your brother to come out of his hiding-place. I will take you both to the Colonel's study. There you shall explain your villainies."

"Let me rise, and I promise you I will not try to escape," answered Rudolf. "I am in such pain that I am past caring for anything but the chance of relief. I will shout to Lionel. We have been starving and have been in the dark. Oh, the agony in my eyes!"

The Professor allowed Rudolf to rise. He went to the chimney and called down. In a moment Lionel made his appearance. Professor Ellicott then escorted the two men across the roof, down through the trap-door, and back again to my father's study.

"I cannot face the light," said Rudolf at once, covering his eyes with his hands. "I have endured more than I bargained for. If I am happy enough to escape without the punishment of the law, I will confess everything."

"That remains with Miss Dallas, for she is the person you have injured," said the Professor.

"Tell the truth, Rudolf. I won't be too hard on you," I answered, my voice trembling. I saw him shiver slightly. His tall, athletic figure was bowed. He still kept his face covered with his hand. As to Lionel, he was crouching in the attitude of an unmistakable cur in a distant corner.

"This is the story," said Rudolf. "There is no use any longer hiding things. I was in serious money trouble—Stock Exchange debts, the usual thing. The money left to me in my uncle's will would, however, have put me again on my feet. Were it for any reason withdrawn, nothing remained for me but open disgrace and ruin.

"For years it has been my one effort to keep my transgressions from my uncle's ears, and only for the extraordinary instinct which you, Nora, possessed, and which caused you to watch me as a cat watches a mouse, I should have succeeded in securing the fortune which he meant to leave me. Lionel was much in the same boat. We decided, therefore, to act together. For a long time we have been in league with a certain Lieutenant Vincent, a young officer in the same regiment as my uncle. My uncle was much attached to Vincent. In the hour of his death Vincent happened to be near, and it was to him my uncle dictated his letter, the letter which you received last night. On the afternoon of the day when the news of my uncle's death was received here I had a long cablegram from Vincent, in which he gave me briefly the contents of the new will, which was already on its way to England, and also said that both the witnesses, privates in my uncle's regiment, had been shot dead shortly after he breathed his last. Thus there were no witnesses to prove this will. He said we must make the best of his information, and we had a month to mature our plans in. We put our heads together and re-solved on a course of action. We knew the history of Aunt Ethel. Nora has always had very highly strung nerves, and we perceived to our satisfaction that they were terribly upset by her father's death. I had been reading a good deal about the newly discovered substance —radium, and thought it possible that it might serve my purpose. I purchased a minute portion and began at once to work on my cousin's fears. Radium, as you know, when held near the eyes, can give them a luminous and very ghastly appearance. I got Nora to believe that she was the victim of a terrifying disorder, and you are aware how successfully my purpose worked. I further arranged, with Lionel's help, to deprive Nora of the fresh will as soon as she had read it; our belief being that her story would not be credited, and that when she spoke of a new will having been sent to her the whole thing, in combination with her story of the ghostly eyes, would be put down to insanity.

"Now, this was our plan: We knew that her habit was to read all letters received from her father in his study. We investigated this room thoroughly and made an important discovery. A few feet up the wide chimney was a secret chamber. The entrance to this chamber was approached by climbing down the inside of the chimney from the roof. This mode of entrance was facilitated by projecting bricks left for the purpose. We resolved to utilise the chamber for our requirements.

"As soon, therefore, as the post arrived from South Africa, Lionel and I left the drawing-room. We immediately went by the trap-door on to the roof. Lionel disappeared down the chimney into the secret chamber, where we had previously taken an immensely powerful exhaust-pump. In the bottom of the chimney there was placed a short time ago a large register, thus closing up the space except for a small hole in the centre, in order to let the smoke pass up. Leading from the exhaust-pump we had arranged a large tube, the mouth of which fitted exactly into the hole in the register. We had also put in order a small electric bell which communicated from the roof to the chamber. After Lionel had disappeared down the chimney I prepared my eyes, and at the right moment bent over the parapet.

"All the time Nora was reading her letter I was looking at her, and when I perceived that she had quite taken in its contents I attracted her attention by gently tapping on the window with a spray of ivy. She turned instinctively. Again I tapped, and she looked up and saw me. As my brother and I guessed she would, she uttered a scream and immediately tried to leave the room, forgetting the letter, which still lay on the table. I immediately rang the bell. Nora was too terrified to hear it. At the signal Lionel began to work the exhaust-pump by means of a hand wheel. It sucked the air out of the study, and drew the letter and other small papers up the chimney right into the tube. Thus we secured the letter and the new will.

"I then joined Lionel in the secret room, not forgetting to take with me the wires from the electric bell. We both immediately set to work to draw back the tube into the secret chamber, and by the time Nora had recovered consciousness all trace of our plot had virtually disappeared."

"What about the will? Have you destroyed it?" said the Professor.

"Strange to say, we have not," replied Lionel. "The fact is, we were in the dark and starving. We had hoped, but for your interference to get away in a few minutes. We have been incarcerated for twenty-four hours. Rudolf was in agony with his eyes. We wanted to read the will before tearing it up."

"Then you can give it to me?"

"Yes. We have it here intact, and, if our cousin will permit us, we will leave the country tomorrow and never trouble her again."

They did so. I did not wish to pursue them, as I doubtless could, with the punishment of the law. My terrors were over. Never more would the ghastly eyes alarm me.

Hunter Quatermain's Story

Sir Henry Curtis, as everybody acquainted with him knows, is one of the most hospitable men on earth. It was in the course of the enjoyment of his hospitality at his place in Yorkshire the other day that I heard the hunting story which I am now about to transcribe. Many of those who read it will no doubt have heard some of the strange rumours that are flying about to the effect that Sir Henry Curtis and his friend Captain Good, R.N., recently found a vast treasure of diamonds out in the heart of Africa, supposed to have been hidden by the Egyptians, or King Solomon, or some other antique person. I first saw the matter alluded to in a paragraph in one of the society papers the day before I started for Yorkshire to pay my visit to Curtis, and arrived, needless to say, burning with curiosity; for there is something very fascinating to the mind in the idea of hidden treasure. When I reached the Hall, I at once asked Curtis about it, and he did not deny the truth of the story; but on my pressing him to tell it he would not, nor would Captain Good, who was also staying in the house.

'You would not believe me if I did,' Sir Henry said, with one of the hearty laughs which seem to come right out of his great lungs. 'You must wait till Hunter Quatermain comes; he will arrive here from Africa tonight, and I am not going to say a word about the matter, or Good either, until he turns up. Quatermain was with us all through; he has known about the business for years and years, and if it had not been for him we should not have been here today. I am going to meet him presently.'

I could not get a word more out of him, nor could anybody else, though we were all dying of curiosity, especially some of the ladies. I shall never forget how they looked in the drawing-room before dinner when Captain Good produced a great rough diamond, weighing fifty carats or more, and told them that he had many larger than that. If ever I saw curiosity and envy printed on fair faces, I saw them then.

It was just at this moment that the door was opened, and Mr Allan Quatermain announced, whereupon Good put the diamond into his pocket, and sprang at a little man who limped shyly into the room, convoyed by Sir Henry Curtis himself.

'Here he is, Good, safe and sound,' said Sir Henry, gleefully. 'Ladies and gentlemen, let me introduce you to one of the oldest hunters and the very best shot in Africa, who has killed more elephants and lions than any other man alive.'

Everybody turned and stared politely at the curious-looking little lame man, and though his size was insignificant, he was quite worth staring at. He had short grizzled hair, which stood about an inch above his head like the bristles of a brush, gentle brown eyes that seemed to notice everything, and a withered face, tanned to the colour of mahogany from exposure to the weather. He spoke, too, when he returned Good's enthusiastic greeting, with a curious little accent, which made his speech noticeable.

It so happened that I sat next to Mr Allan Quatermain at dinner, and, of course, did my best to 'draw' him; but he was not to be drawn. He admitted that he had recently been a long journey into the interior of Africa with Sir Henry Curtis and Captain Good, and that they had found treasure; then he politely turned the subject and began to ask me questions about England, where he had never been before – that is, since he came to years of discretion.[1] Of course, I did not find this very interesting, and so cast about for some means to bring the conversation round again.

Now, we were dining in an oak-panelled vestibule, and on the wall opposite to me were fixed two gigantic elephant tusks, and under them a pair of buffalo horns, very rough and knotted, showing that they came off an old bull, and having the tip of one horn split and chipped. I noticed that Hunter Quatermain's eyes kept glancing at these trophies, and took an occasion to ask him if he knew anything about them.

'I ought to,' he answered, with a little laugh; 'the elephant to which those tusks belonged tore one of our party right in two about eighteen months ago, and as for the buffalo horns, they

---

[1] For a full account of the adventures of Mr Quatermain and his companions upon this journey the reader is referred to the book called *King Solomon's Mines* by H. Rider Haggard.

were nearly my death, and were the end of a servant of mine to whom I was much attached. I gave them to Sir Henry when he left Natal some months ago;' and Mr Quatermain sighed and turned to answer a question from the lady whom he had taken down to dinner, and who, needless to say, was also employed in trying to pump him about the diamonds.

Indeed, all around the table there was a simmer of scarcely suppressed excitement, which, when the servants had left the room, could no longer be restrained.

'Now, Mr Quatermain,' said the lady next to him, 'we have been kept in an agony of suspense by Sir Henry and Captain Good, who have persistently refused to tell us a word of this story about the hidden treasure till you came, and we simply can bear it no longer; so, please, begin at once.'

'Yes,' said everybody, 'go on, please.'

Hunter Quatermain glanced round the table apprehensively; he did not seem to appreciate finding himself the object of so much curiosity.

'Ladies and gentlemen,' he said at last, with a shake of his grizzled head, 'I am very sorry to disappoint you, but I cannot do it. It is this way. At the request of Sir Henry and Captain Good I have written down a true and plain account of King Solomon's Mines and how we found them, so you will soon all be able to learn all about that wonderful adventure for yourselves; but until then I will say nothing about it, not from any wish to disappoint your curiosity, or to make myself important, but simply because the whole story partakes so much of the marvellous, that I am afraid to tell it in a piecemeal, hasty fashion, for fear I should be set down as one of those common fellows of whom there are so many in my profession, who are not ashamed to narrate things they have not seen, and even to tell wonderful stories about wild animals they have never killed. And I think that my companions in adventure, Sir Henry Curtis and Captain Good, will bear me out in what I say.'

'Yes, Quatermain, I think you are quite right,' said Sir Henry. 'Precisely the same considerations have forced Good and myself to hold our tongues. We did not wish to be bracketed with — well, with other famous travellers.'

There was a murmur of disappointment at these announcements.

'I believe you are all hoaxing us,' said the young lady next to Mr Quatermain, rather sharply.

'Believe me,' answered the old hunter, with a quaint courtesy and a little bow of his grizzled head; 'though I have lived all my life in the wilderness, and amongst savages, I have neither the heart, nor the want of manners, to wish to deceive one so lovely.'

Whereat the young lady, who was pretty, looked appeased.

'This is very dreadful,' I broke in. 'We ask for bread and you give us a stone, Mr Quatermain. The least that you can do is to tell us the story of the tusks opposite and the buffalo horns underneath. We won't let you off with less.'

'I am but a poor storyteller,' put in the old hunter, 'but if you will forgive my want of skill, I shall be happy to tell you, not the story of the tusks, for it is part of the history of our journey to King Solomon's Mines, but that of the buffalo horns beneath them, which is now ten years old.'

'Bravo, Quatermain!' said Sir Henry. 'We shall all be delighted. Fire away! Fill up your glass first.'

The little man did as he was bid, took a sip of claret, and began:

About ten years ago I was hunting up in the far interior of Africa, at a place called Gatgarra, not a great way from the Chobe River. I had with me four native servants, namely, a driver and voorlooper, or leader who were natives of Matabeleland, a Hottentot called Hans, who had once been the slave of a Transvaal Boer, and a Zulu hunter, who for five years had accompanied me upon my trips, and whose name was Mashune. Now near Gatgarra I found a fine piece of healthy, park-like country, where the grass was very good, considering the time of year; and here I made a little camp or headquarter settlement, from whence I went on expeditions on all sides in search of game, especially elephant. My luck, however, was bad; I got but little ivory. I was therefore very glad when some natives brought me news that a large herd of elephants were feeding in a valley about thirty miles away. At first I thought of trekking down to the valley, waggon and all, but gave up the idea on hearing that it was infested with the deadly 'tsetse' fly, which is certain death to all animals, except men, donkeys, and wild game. So I reluctantly determined to leave the waggon in the charge of the Matabele leader and driver, and to start on a trip into the thorn country, accompanied only by the Hottentot Hans, and Mashune.

Accordingly on the following morning we started, and on the evening of the next day reached the spot where the elephants were reported to be. But here again we were met by ill luck. That the elephants had been there was evident enough, for their spoor was plentiful, and so were other traces of their presence in the shape of mimosa trees torn out of the ground, and placed topsy-turvy on their flat crowns, in order to enable the great beasts to feed on their sweet roots; but the elephants themselves were conspicuous by their absence. They had elected to move on. This being so, there was only one thing to do, and that was to move after them, which we did, and a pretty hunt they led us. For a fortnight or more we dodged about after those elephants, coming up with them on two occasions, and a splendid herd they were – only, however, to lose them again. At length we came up with them a third time, and I managed to shoot one bull, and then they started off again, where it was useless to try to follow them. After this I gave it up in disgust, and we made the best of our way back to the camp, not in the sweetest of tempers, carrying the tusks of the elephant I had shot.

It was on the afternoon of the fifth day of our tramp that we reached the little koppie overlooking the spot where the waggon stood, and I confess that I climbed it with a pleasurable sense of home-coming, for his waggon is the hunter's home, as much as his house is that of a civilized person. I reached the top of the koppie, and looked in the direction where the friendly white tent of the waggon should be, but there was no waggon, only a black burnt plain stretching away far as the eye could reach. I rubbed my eyes, looked again, and made out on the spot of the camp, not my waggon, but some charred beams of wood. Half wild with grief and anxiety, followed by Hans and Mashune, I ran at full speed down the slope of the koppie, and across the space of plain below to the spring of water, where my camp had been. I was soon there, only to find that my suspicions were confirmed.

The waggon and all its contents, including my spare guns and ammunition, had been destroyed by a grass fire.

Now before I started, I had left orders with the driver to

burn off the grass round the camp, in order to guard against accidents of this nature, and here was the reward of my folly: a very proper illustration of the necessity, especially where natives are concerned, of doing a thing one's self if one wants it done at all. Evidently the lazy rascals had not burnt round the waggon; most probably, indeed, they had themselves carelessly fired the tall and resinous tambouki grass near by; the wind had driven the flames on to the waggon tent, and there was quickly an end of the matter. As for the driver and leader, I know not what became of them: probably fearing my anger, they bolted, taking the oxen with them. I have never seen them from that hour to this.

I sat down on the black veldt by the spring, and gazed at the charred axles and disselboom of my waggon, and I can assure you, ladies and gentlemen, I felt inclined to weep. As for Mashune and Hans they cursed away vigorously, one in Zulu and the other in Dutch. Ours was a pretty position. We were nearly three hundred miles away from Bamangwato, the capital of Khama's country, which was the nearest spot where we could get any help, and our ammunition, spare guns, clothing, food, and everything else, were all totally destroyed. I had just what I stood in, which was a flannel shirt, a pair of 'veldt-schoons', or shoes of raw hide, my eight-bore rifle, and a few cartridges. Hans and Mashune had also each a Martini rifle and some cart-ridges, not many. And it was with this equipment that we had to undertake a journey of three hundred miles through a desolate and almost uninhabited region. I can assure you that I have rarely been in a worse position, and I have been in some queer ones. However, these accidents are natural to a hunter's life, and the only thing to do was to make the best of them.

Accordingly, after passing a comfortless night by the remains of my waggon, we started next morning on our long journey towards civilization. Now if I were to set to work to tell you all the troubles and incidents of that dreadful journey I should keep you listening here till midnight; so I will, with your permission, pass on to the particular adventure of which the pair of buffalo horns opposite are a melancholy memento.

We had been travelling for about a month, living and get-ting along as best we could, when one evening we camped some forty miles from Bamangwato. By this time we were indeed in a melancholy plight, footsore, half starved, and utterly worn out; and, in addition, I was suffering from a sharp attack of fever, which half blinded me and made me as weak as a babe. Our ammunition, too, was exhausted; I had only one cartridge left for my eight-bore rifle, and Hans and Mashune, who were armed with Martini Henrys, had three between them. It was about an hour from sundown when we halted and lit a fire – for luckily we had still a few matches. It was a charming spot to camp, I remember. Just off the game track we were following was a little hollow, fringed about with flat-crowned mimosa trees, and at the bottom of the hollow, a spring of clear water welled up out of the earth, and formed a pool, round the edges of which grew an abundance of watercresses of an exactly similar kind to those which were handed round the table just now. Now we had no food of any kind left, having that morning devoured the last remains of a little oribe antelope, which I had shot two days previously. Accordingly Hans, who was a better shot than Mashune, took two of the three remaining Martini cartridges, and started out to see if he could not kill a buck for supper. I was too weak to go myself.

Meanwhile Mashune employed himself in dragging together some dead boughs from the mimosa trees to make a sort of 'skerm', or shelter for us to sleep in, about forty yards from the edge of the pool of water. We had been greatly troubled with lions in the course of our long tramp, and only on the previous night had very nearly been attacked by them, which made me nervous, especially in my weak state. Just as we had finished the skerm, or rather something which did duty for one, Mashune and I heard a shot apparently fired about a mile away.

'Hark to it!' sung out Mashune in Zulu, more, I fancy, by way of keeping his spirits up than for any other reason – for he was a sort of black Mark Tapley, and very cheerful under difficulties. 'Hark to the wonderful sound with which the "Maboona" (the Boers) shook our fathers to the ground at the battle of the Blood River. We are hungry now, my father; our stomachs are small and withered up like a dried ox's paunch, but they will soon be full of good meat. Hans is a Hottentot, and an *umfagozan* (that is, a low fellow), but he shoots straight – ah! he certainly shoots straight. Be of a good heart, my father, there will soon be meat upon the fire, and we shall rise up men.'

And so he went on talking nonsense till I told him to stop, because he made my head ache with his empty words.

Shortly after we heard the shot, the sun sank in his red splendour, and there fell upon earth and sky the great hush of the African wilderness. The lions were not up as yet, they would probably wait for the moon, and the birds and beasts were all at rest. I cannot describe the intensity of the quiet of the night: to me in my weak state, and fretting as I was over the non-return of the Hottentot Hans, it seemed almost ominous – as though Nature were brooding over some tragedy which was being enacted in her sight.

It was quiet – quiet as death, and lonely as the grave.

'Mashune,' I said at last, 'where is Hans? my heart is heavy for him.'

'Nay, my father, I know not; mayhap he is weary, and sleeps, or mayhap he has lost his way.'

'Mashune, art thou a boy to talk folly to me?' I answered. 'Tell me, in all the years thou hast hunted by my side, didst thou ever know a Hottentot to lose his path or to sleep upon the way to camp?'

'Nay, Macumazahn,' (that, ladies, is my native name, and means the man who 'gets up by night,' or who 'is always awake') 'I know not where he is.'

But though we talked thus, we neither of us liked to hint at what was in both our minds, namely, that misfortune had over-taken the poor Hottentot.

'Mashune,' I said at last, 'go down to the water and bring me of those green herbs that grow there. I am hungered, and must eat something.'

'Nay, my father; surely the ghosts are there; they come out of the water at the night, and sit upon the banks to dry them-selves. An Isanusi[1] told it me.'

Mashune was, I think, one of the bravest men I ever knew in the daytime, but he had a more than civilized dread of the supernatural.

'Must I go myself, thou fool?' I said, sternly.

'Nay, Macumazahn, if thy heart yearns for strange things like a sick woman, I go, even if the ghosts devour me.'

And accordingly he went, and soon returned with a large bundle of watercresses, of which I ate greedily.

'Art thou not hungry?' I asked the great Zulu presently, as he sat eyeing me eating.

'Never was I hungrier, my father.'

'Then eat,' and I pointed to the watercresses.

'Nay, Macumazahn, I cannot eat those herbs.'

'If thou dost not eat thou wilt starve: eat, Mashune.'

He stared at the watercresses doubtfully for a while, and at last seized a handful and crammed them into his mouth, crying out as he did so, 'Oh, why was I born that I should live to feed on green weeds like an ox? Surely if my mother could have known it she would have killed me when I was born!' and so he went on lamenting between each fistful of watercresses till all were finished, when he declared that he was full indeed of stuff, but it lay very cold on his stomach, 'like snow upon a mountain'. At any other time I should have laughed, for it must be admitted he had a ludicrous way of putting things. Zulus do not like green food.

Just after Mashune had finished his watercress, we heard the loud 'woof! woof!' of a lion, who was evidently promenading much nearer to our little skerm than was pleasant. Indeed, on looking into the darkness and listening intently, I could hear his snoring breath, and catch the light of his great yellow eyes. We shouted loudly, and Mashune threw some sticks on the fire to frighten him, which apparently had the desired effect, for we saw no more of him for a while.

Just after we had had this fright from the lion, the moon rose in her fullest splendour, throwing a robe of silver light over all the earth. I have rarely seen a more beautiful moonrise. I remember that sitting in the skerm I could with ease read faint pencil notes in my pocketbook. As soon as the moon was up game began to trek down to the water just below us. I could, from where I sat, see all sorts of them passing along a little ridge that ran to our right, on their way to the drinking place. Indeed, one buck – a large eland – came within twenty yards of the skerm, and stood at gaze, staring at it suspiciously, his beautiful head and twisted horns standing out clearly against the sky. I had, I recollect, every mind to have a pull at him on the chance of providing ourselves with a good supply of beef; but remembering that we had but two cartridges left, and the extreme uncertainty of a shot by moonlight, I at length decided to refrain. The eland presently moved on to the water, and a minute or two afterwards there arose a great sound of splashing followed by the quick fall of galloping hoofs.

'What's that, Mashune?' I asked.

'That damn lion; buck smell him,' replied the Zulu in English, of which he had a very superficial knowledge.

Scarcely were the words out of his mouth before we heard a sort of whine over the other side of the pool, which was instantly answered by a loud coughing roar close to us.

'By Jove!' I said, 'there are two of them. They have lost the buck; we must look out they don't catch us.' And again we made up the fire, and shouted, with the result that the lions moved off.

'Mashune,' I said, 'do you watch till the moon gets over that tree, when it will be the middle of the night. Then wake me. Watch well, now, or the lions will be picking those worthless bones of yours before you are three hours older. I must rest a little, or I shall die.'

'Koos!' (chief), answered the Zulu. 'Sleep, my father, sleep in peace; my eyes shall be open as the stars; and like the stars shall watch over you.'

Although I was so weak, I could not at once follow his poetical advice. To begin with, my head ached with fever, and I was torn with anxiety as to the fate of the Hottentot Hans; and, indeed, as to our own fate, left with sore feet, empty stomachs, and two cartridges, to find our way to Bamangwato, forty miles off. Then the mere sensation of knowing that there are one or more hungry lions prowling round you somewhere in the dark is disquieting, however well one may be used to it, and, by keeping the attention on the stretch, tends to prevent one from sleeping. In addition to all these troubles, too, I was, I remember, seized with a dreadful longing for a pipe of tobacco, whereas, under the circumstances, I might as well have longed for the moon.

At last, however, I fell into an uneasy sleep as full of bad dreams as a prickly pear is of points, one of which, I recollect, was that I was setting my naked foot upon a cobra which rose upon its tail and hissed my name, 'Macumazahn,' into my ear. Indeed, the cobra hissed with such persistency that at last I roused myself.

'*Macumazahn, nanzia, nanzia!*' (there, there!) whispered Mashune's voice into my drowsy ears. Raising myself, I opened my eyes, and I saw Mashune kneeling by my side and pointing towards the water. Following the line of his outstretched hand, my eyes fell upon a sight that made me jump, old hunter as I was even in those days. About twenty paces from the little skerm was a large ant-heap, and on the summit of the ant-heap, her four feet rather close together, so as to find standing space, stood the massive form of a big lioness. Her head was towards the skerm, and in the bright moonlight I saw her lower it and lick her paws.

Mashune thrust the Martini rifle into my hands, whispering that it was loaded. I lifted it and covered the lioness, but found that even in that light I could not make out the foresight of the Martini. As it would be madness to fire without doing so, for the result would probably be that I should wound the lioness, if, indeed, I did not miss her altogether, I lowered the rifle; and, hastily tearing a fragment of paper from one of the leaves of my pocketbook, which I had been consulting just before I went to sleep, I proceeded to fix it on to the front sight. But all this took a little time, and before the paper was satisfactorily arranged, Mashune again gripped me by the arm, and pointed to a dark heap under the shade of a small mimosa tree which grew not more than ten paces from the skerm.

'Well, what is it?' I whispered; 'I can see nothing.'

'It is another lion,' he answered.

'Nonsense! thy heart is dead with fear, thou seest double;' and I bent forward over the edge of the surrounding fence, and stared at the heap.

Even as I said the words, the dark mass rose and stalked out into the moonlight. It was a magnificent, black-maned lion, one of the largest I had ever seen. When he had gone two or three steps he caught sight of me, halted, and stood there gazing straight towards us; he was so close that I could see the firelight reflected in his wicked, greenish eyes.

'Shoot, shoot!' said Mashune. 'The devil is coming – he is going to spring!'

I raised the rifle, and got the bit of paper on the foresight straight on to a little patch of white hair just where the throat is set into the chest and shoulders. As I did so, the lion glanced back over his shoulders, as, according to my experience, a lion nearly always does before he springs. Then he dropped his body a little, and I saw his big paws spread out upon the ground as he put his weight on them to gather purchase. In haste I pressed the trigger of the Martini, and not an instant too soon; for, as I did so, he was in the act of springing. The report of the rifle rang out sharp and clear on the intense silence of the night, and in another second the great brute had landed on his head within four feet of us, and rolling over and over towards us, was sending the bushes which composed our little fence flying with convulsive strokes of his great paws. We sprang out of the other side of the skerm, and he rolled on to it and into it and then right through the fire. Next he raised himself and sat upon his haunches like a great dog, and began to roar. Heavens! how he roared! I never heard anything like it before or since. He kept filling his lungs with air, and then emitting it in the most heart-shaking volumes of sound. Suddenly, in the middle of one of the loudest roars, he rolled over on to his side and lay still, and I knew that he was dead. A lion generally dies upon his side.

With a sigh of relief I looked up towards his mate upon the ant-heap. She was standing there apparently petrified with astonishment, looking over her shoulder, and lashing her tail; but to our intense joy, when the dying beast ceased roaring, she turned, and, with one enormous bound, vanished into the night.

Then we advanced cautiously towards the prostrate brute, Mashune droning an improvised Zulu song as he went, about how Macumazahn, the hunter of hunters, whose eyes are open by night as well as by day, put his hand down the lion's stomach when it came to devour him and pulled out his heart by the roots, etc., etc., by way of expressing his satisfaction, in his hyperbolical Zulu way, at the turn events had taken.

There was no need for caution; the lion was as dead as though he had already been stuffed with straw. The Martini bullet had entered within an inch of the white spot I had aimed at, and travelled right through him, passing out at the right buttock, near the root of the tail. The Martini has wonderful driving power, though the shock it gives to the system is, comparatively speaking, slight, owing to the smallness of the hole it makes. But fortunately the lion is an easy beast to kill.

I passed the rest of that night in a profound slumber, my

head reposing upon the deceased lion's flank, a position that had, I thought, a beautiful touch of irony about it, though the smell of his singed hair was disagreeable. When I woke again the faint primrose lights of dawn were flushing in the eastern sky. For a moment I could not understand the chill sense of anxiety that lay like a lump of ice at my heart, till the feel and smell of the skin of the dead lion beneath my head recalled the circumstances in which we were placed. I rose, and eagerly looked round to see if I could discover any signs of Hans, who, if he had escaped accident, would surely return to us at dawn, but there were none. Then hope grew faint, and I felt that it was not well with the poor fellow. Setting Mashune to build up the fire I hastily removed the hide from the flank of the lion, which was indeed a splendid beast, and cutting off some lumps of flesh, we toasted and ate them greedily. Lions' flesh, strange as it may seem, is very good eating, and tastes more like veal than anything else.

By the time that we had finished our much-needed meal the sun was getting up, and after a drink of water and a wash at the pool, we started to try and find Hans leaving the dead lion to the tender mercies of the hyenas. Both Mashune and myself were, by constant practice, pretty good hands at tracking, and we had not much difficulty in following the Hottentot's spoor, faint as it was. We had gone on in this way for half-an-hour or so, and were, perhaps, a mile or more from the site of our camping-place, when we discovered the spoor of a solitary bull buffalo mixed up with the spoor of Hans, and were able from various indications, to make out that he had been tracking the buffalo. At length we reached a little glade in which there grew a stunted old mimosa thorn, with a peculiar and overhanging formation of root, under which a porcupine, or an ant-bear, or some such animal, had hollowed out a wide-lipped hole. About ten or fifteen paces from this thorn-tree there was a thick patch of bush.

'See, Macumazahn! see!' said Mashune, excitedly, as we drew near the thorn; 'the buffalo has charged him. Look, here he stood to fire at him; see how firmly he planted his feet upon the earth; there is the mark of his crooked toe (Hans had one bent toe). Look! here the bull came like a boulder down the hill, his hoofs turning up the earth like a hoe. Hans had hit him: he bled as he came; there are the blood spots. It is all written down there, my father – there upon the earth.'

'Yes,' I said; 'yes; but *where is Hans?*'

Even as I said it Mashune clutched my arm, and pointèd to the stunted thorn just by us. Even now, gentlemen, it makes me feel sick when I think of what I saw.

For fixed in a stout fork of the tree some eight feet from the ground was Hans himself, or rather his dead body, evidently tossed there by the furious buffalo. One leg was twisted round the fork, probably in a dying convulsion. In the side, just beneath the ribs, was a great hole, from which the entrails protruded. But this was not all. The other leg hung down to within five feet of the ground. The skin and most of the flesh were gone from it. For a moment we stood aghast, and gazed at this horrifying sight. Then I understood what had happened. The buffalo, with that devilish cruelty which distinguishes the animal, after his enemy was dead, had stood underneath his body, and licked the flesh off the pendant leg with his file-like tongue. I had heard of such a thing before, but had always treated the stories as hunters' yarns; but I had no doubt about it now. Poor Hans' skeleton foot and ankle were an ample proof.

We stood aghast under the tree, and stared and stared at this awful sight, when suddenly our cogitations were interrupted in a painful manner. The thick bush about fifteen paces off burst asunder with a crashing sound, and uttering a series of ferocious pig-like grunts, the bull buffalo himself came charging out straight at us. Even as he came I saw the blood mark on his side where poor Hans' bullet had struck him, and also, as is often the case with particularly savage buffaloes, that his flanks had recently been terribly torn in an encounter with a lion.

On he came, his head well up (a buffalo does not generally lower his head till he does so to strike); those great black horns – as I look at them before me, gentlemen, I seem to see them come charging at me as I did ten years ago, silhouetted against the green bush behind; – on, on!

With a shout Mashune bolted off sideways towards the bush. I had instinctively lifted my eight-bore, which I had in my hand. It would have been useless to fire at the buffalo's head, for the dense horns must have turned the bullet; but as Mashune bolted, the bull slewed a little, with the momentary idea of following him, and as this gave me a ghost of a chance, I let drive my only cartridge at his shoulder. The bullet struck the shoulder-blade and smashed it up, and then travelled on under the skin into his flank; but it did not stop him, though for a second he staggered.

Throwing myself on to the ground with the energy of despair, I rolled under the shelter of the projecting root of the thorn, crushing myself as far into the mouth of the ant-bear hole as I could. In a single instant the buffalo was after me. Kneeling down on his uninjured knee — for one leg, that of which I had broken the shoulder, was swinging helplessly to and fro — he set to work to try and hook me out of the hole with his crooked horn. At first he struck at me furiously, and it was one of the blows against the base of the tree which splintered the tip of the horn in the way that you see. Then he grew more cunning, and pushing his head as far under the root as possible, made long semi-circular sweeps at me, grunting furiously and blowing saliva and hot steamy breath all over me. I was just out of reach of the horn, though every stroke, by widening the hole and making more room for his head, brought it closer to me, but every now and again I received heavy blows in the ribs from his muzzle. Feeling that I was being knocked silly, I made an effort and seizing his rough tongue, which was hanging from his jaws, I twisted it with all my force. The great brute bellowed with pain and fury, and jerked himself backwards so strongly, that he dragged me some inches further from the mouth of the hole, and again made a sweep at me, catching me this time round the shoulder-joint in the hook of his horn.

I felt that it was all up now, and began to holloa.

'He has got me!' I shouted in mortal terror. '*Gwasa, Mashune, gwasa!*' ('Stab, Mashune, stab!')

One hoist of the great head, and out of the hole I came like a periwinkle out of his shell. But even as I did so, I caught sight of Mashune's stalwart form advancing with his 'bangwan,' or broad stabbing assegai, raised above his head. In another quarter of a second I had fallen from the horn, and heard the blow of the spear, followed by the indescribable sound of steel shearing its way through flesh. I had fallen on my back, and, looking up, I saw that the gallant Mashune had driven the assegai a foot or more into the carcass of the buffalo, and was turning to fly.

Alas! it was too late. Bellowing madly, and spouting blood from mouth and nostrils, the devilish brute was on him, and had thrown him high like a feather, and then gored him twice as he lay. I struggled up with some wild idea of affording help, but before I had gone a step the buffalo gave one long sighing bellow, and rolled over dead by the side of his victim.

Mashune was still living, but a single glance at him told me that his hour had come. The buffalo's horn had driven a great hole in his right lung, and inflicted other injuries.

I knelt down beside him in the uttermost distress, and took his hand.

'Is he dead, Macumazahn?' he whispered. 'My eyes are blind; I cannot see.'

'Yes, he is dead.'

'Did the black devil hurt thee, Macumazahn?'

'No, my poor fellow, I am not much hurt.'

'Ow! I am glad.'

Then came a long silence, broken only by the sound of the air whistling through the hole in his lung as he breathed.

'Macumazah, art thou there? I cannot feel thee.'

'I am here, Mashune.'

'I die, Macumazahn — the world flies round and round. I go — I go out into the dark! Surely, my father, at times in days to come — thou wilt think of Mashune who stood by thy side — when thou killest elephants, as we used — as we used——'

They were his last words, his brave spirit passed with them. I dragged his body to the hole under the tree, and pushed it in, placing his broad assegai by him, according to the custom of his people, that he might not go defenceless on his long journey; and then, ladies — I am not ashamed to confess — I stood alone there before it, and wept like a woman.

The Fate of the 'Senegambian Queen'

Wardon Allan Curtis

It was off the east coast of Madagascar, seat of pirate lairs, where no honest vessel ever ventured voluntarily, yet the clumsy little Dutch brig, labouring slowly southward before a fair north wind, with the mangrove swamps of the shore not three miles off its starboard quarter, could hardly be a vessel which storms had driven into that neighbourhood, for fair weather had prevailed for several weeks. Storm driven she was not, honest she could not but be, for no pirate would sail in such a wagon of the deep, and so the pirate lookout in the tall tree at the entrance of the cove where lay ambushed the *Senegambian Queen*, Captain William Avery, conjectured that it was in search of water that the stranger had approached the pirate-haunted coast. So little had the crew of the *Senegambian Queen* expected any quarry to come their way while they were on the island, and so little did they fear the advent of warships, that it was a full three hours after the brig was sighted before they were collected from the retreats to which they had scattered. Slowly the *Senegambian Queen* poked her black nose out from behind the forest-covered point of the cove, like some lank beast of prey reconnoitering the fat little vessel in the offing. Then, catching the wind, she began to skim the water. Such a poor prize the brig looked to be. The men cursed Captain Avery for calling them from their naps and sports to the pursuit of this little square-nosed Dutchman. But as they overhauled it, a languid interest and finally a keen surprise took the place of their complaining, for on the doomed vessel no preparations for flight or fight were being made. Indeed, there was no sign of alarm, and the crew of the brig were apparently oblivious to the existence of aught but themselves. Through a glass could be seen the captain sitting on the deck, reading a big tome. Along the bulwarks leaned a score of men, gazing at the coast. Not a glass, not an eye, even, was turned on the pursuing *Senegambian Queen.*

'Wake them up, quartermaster,' said Captain William Avery. 'Send a shot through their rigging and let them show that they are alive, or know that we are.'

The long twelve spoke, the shot passed harmlessly through the rigging of the brig, and then, like puppets in a show, the men leaning on the bulwarks turned about, the captain closed his book, and all gazed at the pirate ship, calmly and in no alarm.

'Well, the shot half awakened them,' said Captain William Avery. 'We will see if we cannot drive all the drowsiness from their eyes by boarding them. Ready for boarders!'

As if to aid the design of the captain, came a sudden freshening of the breeze, carrying the *Senegambian Queen* almost to the stranger before it shook the latter's sails at all. And then the eyes of the pirates fell upon what deprived them of speech, and the misgivings that invaded their minds would have made them turn tail and away, but that they were deprived of the power of motion, too. From the open mouth of Captain

William Avery came naught but a gasp, the helmsman stood frozen at the wheel, and like statues stood the boarders with their gleaming cutlasses and pikes, while swiftly closed the distance between the well-groomed *Senegambian Queen* and the decaying hulk, along which ran phosphorescent gleams down near the water in the shadow that the two vessels made. On weather-blackened masts hung yellow, tattered, mildewed sails, and over the crumbling bulwarks looked a crew of ancient, hoary men, clad in ragged, faded garments of a past century. It was not the crew of the *Senegambian Queen* that sprang to lash the two vessels together as they touched, but the greybeard crew of the stranger, whose agility and strength belied their age-worn appearance.

'The *Flying Dutchman*! Cut the lashings! Port the helm!' cried Captain William Avery, finding his voice at last, and at last spun the wheel in the helmsman's hands, and a dozen men sprang to do their commander's bidding, but leaped back in dread as a venerable old man appeared, drawing himself over the bulwarks and dropped upon the deck of the *Senegambian Queen*.

'Who is it that thus rudely lies aboard of the ship of Vanderdecken?' he cried in a quavering, yet deep and powerful voice. Not an answer had he save in the clanging of arms dropped by the pirates nearest him as they scurried back into the ranks of their comrades. 'But whatever your errand, I am ready to forgive the first men who have not fled from us in a century. Pirates you may be, but you are also men, and the first we have seen face to face in an hundred years. Like lords shall you be treated. Come aboard of us. Malvoisie, Chianti, sherry and the juices of the Rhine, mellowed by the flight of time until there is nowhere its like in this terrestrial globe, shall be yours. Not even kings can drink such wine as you shall have with us. Come, we bear you no ill-will, but love you like brothers, so pleasant it is to see the faces and hear the voices of men once more. Afar off in storms, afar off in fair weather, but always fleeing from our accursed ship, have we seen other ships, so unreal that we have wondered if time had not slain all mankind and we alone be left in the world in the midst of flitting spectres. Blessed be your dishonesty, your temerity, whatever has made you board us to-day. Pursue a ship we cannot, so slow are we. You are the first who have pursued us. Come, the good cheer waits.'

The pirates stood astonished for a time, silent and amazed, but at length Captain William Avery raised his voice and said: 'These men be preserved beyond their natural span by a curse, and nothing that is of this world has ever harmed them, but I do not believe that they are by reason of this curse more enabled to injure other men than before. They are weak old men. I fear them not. Let us cheer their cold hearts by accepting their hospitality, doing one good deed in our lives. Moreover, the marvels they can tell us will indeed be strange and pleasant to hear.'

The breeze lay dead on the water, the sun shone out of a cloudless sky and need of a watch on the *Senegambian Queen* there was none, and all of her crew save Sanchez at the wheel and Scipio and Libya, the two blacks, swarmed on to the vessel of Vanderdecken. That so old a ship should keep the seas caused them much astonishment, yet her frame seemed stout and sound withal, despite the gnawings of worms and time that were evident in the outer sheathings of her hull and decks. And her company, too, had in like manner been used by the years that had rolled over them. White were their hair and beards, ragged their garments, yet ruddy were their cheeks, bright their eyes, firm their step, straight their backs, and sonorous their voices. Indeed, Captain William Avery remarked upon these incongruities to Mynheer Vanderdecken, who eyed him narrowly, coughed once or twice and ordered that the wine be brought. Sorely were the pirates disappointed in the wine. Good it was and that was all. The flavour that the years had imparted to it was to be told in a slight suspicion of mawkishness, yet this was not what the rovers had found in other old wines, nor did they think it pleasant. Yet they quaffed it copiously, for after all it was wine, and as their spirits rose, they glanced at the silver flagons in the cabin and began to whisper among themselves that it would be but an act of charity to knock the Dutchmen on the head and send them out of the world of which they must be so weary, and, in default of any who could prove kinship, become their heirs. Such thoughts, ere long, Captain William Avery put into jocose words and addressed to Mynheer Vanderdecken, who for a moment grew grave, and then jolly, and cried:

'Done! But have one more cup of wine to our release,' and telling all of his men what Captain Avery had proposed, he ordered that the very oldest cask of wine be broached. The rovers gaily drained their beakers, though the sweet mawkishness was more than ever to be tasted in this, the oldest wine.

'Again,' shouted Mynheer Vanderdecken, and some of the pirates held forth their beakers, but others lolled against the masts and bulwarks, or fell dozing to the deck.

'Let the stroke fall,' said Vanderdecken, but no stroke fell, only the last of the pirates, down to the deck among his prone comrades, sleeping heavily all, snoring and snorting, hard at it, as if striving to compress the slumbers of a week into a few hours' space.

'Van Steenwyck, do you shoot down the Spaniard at the wheel,' whispered the Dutch captain. 'Marnitz and Wynkoop, level your blunderbusses at the heads of the blacks, and bid them throw up their hands. We will spare them. As for these swine on the deck, tie weights to their feet and roll them into the sea before they begin to arouse.'

Into the quiet depths, one after another shot the crew of the *Senegambian Queen*, and when the last one had sunk beneath the glassy rollers, off came white beards and wigs and ragged coats and the Dutch crew piled aboard the pirate ship and took stock of the great treasure that was now theirs.

'Mynheer Van Oosterzee,' said the Dutch captain, addressing a richly dressed man who had not been visible while the pirates were on the brig, 'the two years for which I engaged with you are up. Play acting on the seas is more profitable than in Amsterdam, but I yearn for the boards once more. The promise I made you that this slow brig, under my direction, should bring more fortune than the swiftest keel ever laid in England or France, has been made good. The ragged sails and worm-eaten sheathing of the hull have brought more prey to us than ever this sea greyhound, with all of its top-hamper and its clean lines, overtook in like time. These white beards were more protection than coats of mail, superstition kept all cannon shot from our sides, and the wine with mandragora made easy the slaying of those who found it in their hearts to slay others. We have cleared the Indian Ocean of its last pirate. The robbers of England and France, with their jibes at the slow-going Dutch, have been overcome. Now for home.'

White Zombie

Vivian Meik

Geoffrey Aylett, acting commissioner of the district of Nswadzi, was frightened. During his twenty years of Africa never before had he experienced the sensation of being so definitely baffled. He felt as if something was pressing against him, something that he could neither see nor locate, but, nevertheless, something that seemed to envelop him, and, in some inexplicable way, threaten to stifle him. Lately he had begun to wake suddenly at nights, struggling for breath and almost overcome by a feeling of nausea. After the nausea had disappeared there still remained a strange suggestion of some nameless horrible odour, an odour that was strongly reminiscent of the aftermath of the earlier battles of the Mesopotamia campaign. Those had been days of foul disease, when cholera and dysentery, sunstroke, typhoid and gangrene had raged unchecked; where hundreds had lain where they had fallen; when, pressed by enemies and forgotten by friends, the survivors were forced to let even the elementary decencies of death go by the board. . . . He remembered the flies and the corruption, and the temperature of a hundred and twenty degrees. . . .

And now, eighteen years later, that same smell of fetid corruption seemed to hover about him like some evil presence when he woke at nights.

Aylett was, first and foremost, a rational man, accustomed to face facts. His knowledge of the mystery of Africa, of its depths and jungles, of its eerie atmosphere, was as complete as that of any white man – he smiled whimsically as he emphasised to himself how little that was – and he looked for some concrete reason that would explain the bridging of the years by this horrible harmonic. Failing a satisfactory solution he would be forced to conclude that it was about time he went home on long leave.

Carefully, as befitted a man of his experience of the ways of the dark gods, he searched his innermost soul, but failed to find the answer he sought.

There was only one connection in the district between him and the Mesopotamia of 1915 – a certain John Sinclair, late of the Indian Army – but that connection was already a broken link long before the first occurrence of these nauseating nightmares.

Sinclair had been a brother officer in the old days, and, mainly on Aylett's advice, had taken up a few thousand acres of virgin country in the comparatively unknown Nswadzi district immediately after the War. But he had died more than a year previously – and, what was more to the point, had died a natural death. Aylett himself had been present at the passing of his friend.

Being both a mystic as the result of his knowledge of Africa, and a logician as a result of his Western upbringing, Aylett methodically considered the platitudinous truth that there are more things in heaven and earth than are dreamed of in our philosophy, and went over the entire period of his association with Sinclair in every detail.

At the end of it all he was forced to admit failure, and, indeed, judged either logically or mystically, there was no adequate reason for linking Sinclair with his present troubles. Sinclair had died peacefully. He even remembered the utter content of the last sigh . . . as if some great burden had been lifted.

It was true that before this, Sinclair – and Aylett himself for that matter – during the first two years of the War, had been through a hell that only those who had experienced it could appreciate. It was also true that Sinclair had saved Aylett's life at a great risk to his own, on a certain memorable occasion, when Aylett, left for dead, had been lying badly wounded in the sun. Aylett had, naturally, never forgotten that, but being a typical Englishman, had done very little more than shake his friend's hand, and mumble something to the effect that he hoped that one day there would be an opportunity to repay. Sinclair had waved the matter aside, with a laugh, as one of no account – merely a job in the day's work. There the incident had ended, and each went about his own lawful occasions.

As a settler Sinclair had been a complete success. In due course he had married a very capable woman, who, it appeared to Aylett, whenever he had broken journey at the homestead, was eminently suited to the hard existence of a planter's wife.

At first Sinclair had seemed very happy, but as the years went by Aylett had not been quite so sure. He had had occasion more than once to notice the subtle change for the worse in his old friend. Staleness, he diagnosed, and recommended a holiday in England. Lonely plantations, far from one's own kind, are apt to get on the nerves. Nothing came of his suggestion, however, and the Sinclairs stayed on. They had grown to love the place too well, they said, though he thought that Sinclair's enthusiasm did not ring true. Anyway, it had not been his business.

That was all that he could recall in his contemplation, and he repeated again how it had all finished over a year ago. But old memories cling. He found himself living over again that ghastly day after Ctesiphon when Sinclair had literally brought him back to life.

He began to wonder – idly, fantastically. The afternoon

dimmed to sundown, sundown gave way to the magic of the night. Still Aylett made no move to leave the camp-chair under the awning of his tent and go to bed. After a while the last of his 'boys' came up to ask him whether he might retire. Aylett answered him absently, his eyes on the glowing logs of the camp-fire.

As the hours wore on he could hear the sound of the night drums more distinctly. From all the points of the compass the sounds came and went, drum answering drum . . . the telegraph of the trackless miles that the world calls Africa. Lazily he wondered what they were saying, and how exactly they transmitted their news. Strange, he thought, that no white man has ever mastered the secret of the drums.

Subconsciously he followed their throbbing monotony. He gradually became aware that the beat had changed. No more were simple news or opinions being transmitted. That much he could understand. There was something else being sent out, something of importance. He suddenly realized that whatever this something was, it was apparently regarded as being of vital urgency, and that, for at least an hour, the same short rhythm had been repeated. North, south, east and west, the echoes throbbed and throbbed again.

The drums began to madden him, but there was no way to stop them. He decided to go to bed, but he had been listening too long, and the rhythm followed him. Eventually he dropped off into a listless disturbed sleep, during which the implacable staccato throbbing kept hammering away its unreadable message into his subconsciousness.

It seemed only a moment later that he awoke. A malarious mist had rolled up from the swamps below and had pervaded his camp. He found himself gasping for breath. He tried to sit up, but the mist seemed to be pressing him down where he lay. No sound issued from his lips when he endeavoured to call his 'boys'. He felt himself being steadily submerged – down, down, down and still down.

Just before he lost consciousness he realized that he was being suffocated, not by the heavy mist, but by a foul miasma reeking with all the horror of corruption. . . .

Aylett looked about him in a bewildered fashion when he opened his eyes again. A kindly bearded face was bending over him, and he heard a voice that seemed to be coming from a great distance encouraging him to drink something. His head was throbbing violently, and his breath came in deep gasps. But the cool water cleared in some measure the foul odour that seemed to cling to his brain.

'Ah, *mon ami, c'est bon.* We thought you were dead when the "boys" brought you in.' The bearded face broke into a grin: 'But now you will be well, *hein?* You are – what you say? – a tough, *hein?*'

Aylett laughed in spite of himself. Why, of course, this was the mission station of the White Fathers, and his old friend, Padre Vaneken, placid and reliable, was looking after him. He closed his eyes happily. Now there was nothing more to fear, everything would soon be well. Then, as suddenly as it had come, that terrible clinging odour of death and decay left him. . . .

'But, padre man,' he discussed his horrible experience later, 'what could have happened? We are both men of some experience of Africa – '

The missionary shrugged his shoulders. '*Mon ami,* as you imply, this is Africa . . . and I have no evidence that the curse on Ham, the son of Noah, has ever been lifted. The dark forests, they are the stronghold of such whose unconscious spirits have rebelled and have not yet come out to serve as was first ordained. Who knows? . . . We – I – do not look too deeply there. When I first came out, in my early idealism I sought but the convert, now I – I am content to do mostly the cures for fevers and wounds, and hope that *le bon Dieu* will understand. It is the same everywhere where the curse of Noah carries. Civilisation counts not. Regard Haiti – I spent twelve years there – Sierra Leone, the Congo, and here. What can I say about your attack by the mist? Nothings, *hein?* You – you thank God you live, for here, *mon ami* – here is the cradle of Africa, the oldest stronghold of the sons of Ham. . . .'

Aylett regarded the missionary intently. 'Padre,' he spoke deliberately, 'what exactly are you trying to make me understand?'

The two men, old in the ways of the black jungle, faced each other steadily. *'Mon ami,'* the priest said quietly, 'you are my old friend. On the forms of religion we think differently, you and I, but this is not conventional Europe, thank God, and, side by side, we have done our best according to our lights. God himself cannot do more. So I will tell you. *I have seen the mist before . . . twice. Once in Haiti and once in this district.'*

'Here?'

The padre nodded. 'I was in camp at the catechumen's school by Mrs Sinclair's estate – '

'Go on.' Aylett's voice was low.

'As you know, Mrs Sinclair has run the plantation since her husband's death. She refused to go home. At first you, I – all the countryside – thought she was mad to stay there alone, but – ' the missionary shrugged his shoulders – *'que voulez-vous?* A woman is a law unto herself. Anyway, she has made it a greater success than ever, and we are silenced, *hein?'*

'But the mist?'

'I was coming to that. It caught me by the throat that night. I was living at the house, as we all do who pass that way – Central Africa is not a cathedral close – but beyond not knowing anything of what happened for several hours nothing happened to me.' He touched the emblem of his faith on the rosary that was part of his dress. 'Mrs Sinclair said that I had been overcome by the heat, but to me that explanation would not do. . . .'

'But that doesn't explain anything.'

'Perhaps not – *but Mrs Sinclair said that she had not noticed anything peculiar . . .!*

'How was that?'

The priest shrugged his shoulders. 'I am not Mrs Sinclair,' he said abruptly, and Aylett knew that not another word about her would the missionary say.

'Tell me about Haiti, padre,' he asked.

The priest replied quietly. 'We understood it there to mean that it was artifically produced by *voodoo* black magic – a very real thing, *mon ami*, which my church readily admits, as you probably know – and there they call it "the breath of the dead." Why? . . .' He shrugged his shoulders again.

Aylett turned away and looked out steadily into the distance. For a long time he fixed his gaze on the line of distant hills, thinking deeply. He recalled a picture where just such hills appeared in the background – a photograph taken by a man who had been almost beyond the borderline to give the truth to the world. But he had failed. The picture showed a group of figures. That was all until one studied them, and even then no one would believe that this was a photograph of dead men – *who were not allowed to die.*

For hours the two men sat silently, each busy with his own thoughts. Night mantled the tiny mission station, and from afar the sound of drums came through on the soft breeze. Aylett turned suddenly to the missionary. 'Padre man,' he said quietly, 'it's only twenty miles from here to the Sinclair's estate. . . .'

The padre nodded. 'I understand, *mon ami*,' he replied. Then after a moment, 'Would you think it an impertinence if I asked you to keep this in your pocket – till you come back?' He produced a small silver crucifix.

Aylett held out his hand. 'Thank you,' he said simply.

The sun had set when Aylett's *machila** was set down on Mrs Sinclair's verandah. She came forward to welcome him. 'I wondered if I should ever see you again.' She looked

* *Machila* – a stretcher slung on a pole – the standard means of transport in the 'bush'.

at him quietly. 'You haven't been here since – for over a year now.' Then she changed her tone. She laughed. 'As a district officer,' she said, 'you've neglected your duties shamefully!'

Aylett smilingly pleaded guilty, excusing himself on the ground that everything had gone so well in this section, that he had hesitated to intrude on perfection.

'Has it fallen from perfection now?' she countered.

'Not at all,' he replied, 'this visit is merely routine.'

'Er – thank you,' she said dryly, 'anyway, come in and make yourself comfortable, and tomorrow I'll show you a perfect estate.'

Aylett studied his hostess carefully through dinner. He felt uneasy at what he saw whenever he caught her off her guard. He could hardly believe that this was the same woman whom he had welcomed as a bride only a few years ago. The lonely life had hardened her, but he had expected that. There was something more, though – a kind of bitter hardness, he called it, for want of a better term.

After her formal welcome Mrs Sinclair spoke very little. She seemed preoccupied with the affairs of the plantation. 'My very own stake in Africa,' she said. 'Oh, how I love the country, its magic and mystery and its vast grandeur.' She reminded him how she had refused to go home. But tomorrow, she said, when he saw *her* Africa – the plantation – he would understand.

Aylett retired early, distinctly puzzled. He had noticed her looking over the swept and garnished tidiness of the plantation before she had said goodnight. She had unconsciously stretched out her hands to it in a kind of adoring supplication and yet, in the brilliant moonlight under this sensual adoration, he distinctly noticed the contrast of the hard lines on her face and the bitterness of the mouth. Africa. . . .

Exhausted as he was, he slept well. Whether the little cross the padre had given him had anything to do with it or not, he did not know, but in the morning he had waked more refreshed than he had been for weeks. He looked forward to the visit over the estate.

Mrs Sinclair had not exaggerated when she had used the word perfection. Fields had been hoed till not a stray blade of grass grew among the crops; barns stood in serried rows; wood fuel was stacked in the neatest of 'cords'; the orchard and the kitchen garden were luxurious, and the pasture in the miniature home farm was the greenest he had seen in the tropics.

'For what?' his subconscious brain kept hammering at him. 'Why – and above all, *how?*'

Aylett had noticed what only an expert would have seen. There was a great shortage of labour, though such workers as were dotted about seemed to be very busy.

As if she divined his thoughts, Mrs Sinclair answered them. 'My "boys" *work*,' she said, in even tones as she flicked the hippo hide whip she carried.

Aylett raised his eyebrows. 'Portuguese methods?' he asked quietly, and looked at the whip.

Mrs Sinclair turned to him. For the first time he noticed her deliberate antagonism. 'Not at all,' she said evenly, 'a knowledge of how to get the most out of a native, a faculty which I notice officialdom has not yet acquired.'

The district officer took the rapier-like thrust without faltering. *'Touché,'* he answered, but nevertheless he knew he had not been wrong about the labour. 'Queer,' he thought, 'damnably queer. . . .'

Mrs Sinclair took no notice of his acknowledgement of her point. Her lips were set hard and she spoke coldly. She continued, 'It's only a matter of getting to the heart of Africa – the throbbing beating heart below all this – Africa has no use for those who do not join their own souls.' Suddenly she realized what she was saying, but before she could change the subject Aylett took up the question. He matched her tone.

'Very interesting . . .' he said, 'but we don't encourage Europeans, especially European women, to go "native".'

The last word, however, was with the woman. 'All the perspicacity of officialdom!' she murmured. Then she looked Aylett full in the face. 'Do I sound native,' she said harshly, 'or *look* native?'

Aylett was hardly listening. He was staring at her. Her eyes belied her words, for if ever he saw an expression of masterful, baleful perversion in any human face, he saw it then. He began to understand. . . .

He was thankful when the inspection was over, and felt relieved that she did not offer the formal suggestion that he should stay a little longer.

Five miles beyond her boundary he had a bivouac tent pitched behind a thorn-bush, and stored two days' rations in its shade. He sent his *safari* on at the double to the mission station, and watched it till it was out of sight. Then he sat down to wait for the night.

'The heart of Africa . . .' he repeated to himself, but his voice was grim, and his eyes flashed in cold anger.

It was not till he heard the news drums throb that Aylett retraced his steps along the ill-defined track to the plantation. At the edge of the estate he merged himself in the shadows of the forest fringe, and gradually worked his way along the eucalyptus wind breaks. He crawled noiselessly as far as the tree which grew in the garden before the homestead.

In a little while he saw Mrs Sinclair come out on to the verandah. Beside her stood a gigantic native who looked like some obscene devil, a witch doctor, sinister and grotesque, and naked but for a necklace of human bones dangling and rattling on his enormous chest. Daubs of white clay and red ochre plastered his face.

Only partly covered by a magnificent leopard skin, the white woman stepped down into the clearing and snapped the whip she had in her hands. It sounded like a revolver shot. As if it were a signal Aylett heard the roll of drums near at hand. From one of the barns began the most grotesque procession he had ever seen. The drums throbbed malevolently – the short staccato throb that had preceded the fetid mist which had almost suffocated him. Louder they grew and louder. The message rolled through the jungles, was caught up and answered again. There was no doubt as to its meaning.

He crouched lower as the drums approached, his eyes fixed on the macabre scene before him. Following the drums, as regularly as a column on the march, moved the men who worked the perfect plantation. In columns of four they moved, heavy footed and automatic – but they moved. Every now and then the crack of that terrible whip sounded like a pistol-shot through the roll of drums, and every now and then Aylett could see that cruel thong cut through naked flesh, and a figure drop silently, only to pick itself up again and rejoin the column.

They marched round the garden. As they came near Aylett held his breath. He had to strain every nerve in his body to prevent himself screaming. Almost as if he were hypnotised he looked on the dull expressionless faces of the silent, slow-moving automatons – faces on which there was not even despair. They simply moved to the command of that merciless whip, as they would shortly move off to their allotted task in the fields. Bowed and crushed they passed by him without a sound.

The nervous tension almost broke Aylett. Then the realisation came to him – *these pitiful automatons were dead – and they were not allowed to die.* . . .

The figures in the unbelievable photograph came back to him; the padre's words; the magic of the *voodoo*, acknowledged as fact by the greatest Christian Church in history. The dead . . . who were not allowed to die . . . Zombies, the natives called them in hushed voices, wherever the curse of Noah was borne . . . and *she* called it knowing Africa.

A cold terror came over Aylett. The long column was nearing its end. Mrs Sinclair was walking down the line, her whip cracking mercilessly, her face distorted with perverted lust, the foul witch doctor leering over her naked shoulder.

She stopped by the tree behind which he crouched. A single bent figure followed the column. With a gasp of horror Aylett recognized Sinclair. Then the whip crashed across the poor thing who had once died in his arms.

'My God!' Aylett muttered helplessly. 'It's not possible – ' but he knew that the witch doctor's *voodoo* had thrown the impossibility in his face. The whip cracked again, hurling the lone white Zombie to the ground. Slowly it picked itself up – without a sound, without expression – and automatically followed the column. He heard, as in a nightmare, unbelievably foul obscenities fall from the woman's lips – cruel taunts. . . . And the whip cracked and bit and tore, again and yet again. At the head of the column the drums throbbed on.

Horror gave way at last. Aylett found himself desperately clutching the tiny cross the padre had given him. With the other hand he found his revolver and took aim with icy coolness. . . . Four times he fired at a point above the leopard skin and twice into the ochred face of the witch doctor. . . . Then he leapt forward, cross in hand, to what had once died as Sinclair.

The figure was standing silently, bent and expressionless. It made no sign as Aylett approached, but as the crucifix touched it a tremor shook the frame. The drooping eyelids lifted and the lips moved. 'You have repaid,' they whispered gently. The body swayed slightly and toppled over. 'Dust to dust. . . .' Aylett prayed. In a few moments all that remained was a little greyish powder. A tropical year had passed, Aylett remembered with a shudder. . . . . Then he turned, and, crucifix in hand, walked along the column. . . .

LORD DUNSANY

Lord Dunsany was born Edward John Moreton Drax Plunkett in London in 1878. Dunsany's youth was spent in Dunsany, Ireland – his family home – and Kent. He attended school at Cheam and Eton, before entering the Royal Military Academy Sandhurst in 1896. He inherited his father's title shortly before fighting in the Second Anglo-Boer War between 1899 and 1901. Dunsany published his first book a collection of Anglo-Irish fantasy stories entitled *The Gods of Pegana*, in 1905.

Over the course of his life, Dunsany was a prolific writer, penning short stories, novels, plays, poetry, essays and autobiography. During the peak of his career he was something of a literary celebrity, spending time with authors such as W. B. Yeats and

Rudyard Kipling. He published over sixty books, and his plays were highly successful; at one point, five Dunsany works were running simultaneously in New York. His most notable fantasy short stories were published between 1905 and 1919, in collections such as *The Sword of Welleran and Other Stories* (1908), *A Dreamer's Tales* (1910), *The Book of Wonder* (1912) and *Tales of Wonder* (1916). Amongst his best-regarded novels are *Don Rodriguez: Chronicles of Shadow Valley* (1922), *The King of Elfland's Daughter* (1924), and *The Charwoman's Shadow* (1926).

Dunsany died in old age, following an attack of appendicitis. Over the course of his writing life, he greatly influenced a wide range of authors. Arthur C. Clarke called him "one of the greatest writers of [the 20th] century," and H. P. Lovecraft described him as being "unexcelled in the sorcery of crystalline singing prose, and supreme in the creation of a gorgeous and languorous world of incandescently exotic vision."

Rider Haggard

Henry Rider Haggard was born in Bradenham, Norfolk, England in 1856. He had an inconsistent education, moving between various schools and failing to gain entrance to both the army and Foreign Office. Haggard was in South Africa between 1875 and 1882, before returning to England, where he studied law and was called to the bar in 1884. However, by this stage his attention had already turned to the writing of novels, and in September of 1885 he published the novel for which he is most famous, *King Solomon's Mines*. Two years later, Haggard published *She* (1887), which was extraordinarily popular, and remains one of the best-selling books of all time, having never been out of print. Haggard followed this with eight more novels, all of which were highly popular. He was made a Knight Bachelor in 1912, and a Knight Commander of the Order of the British Empire in 1919. Haggard died in London, England in 1925, aged 68.

H. P. Lovecraft

Howard Phillips Lovecraft was born in 1890 in Rhode Island, USA. Although a sickly boy, Lovecraft began writing at a very young age, quickly developing a deep and abiding interest in science. At just sixteen he was writing a monthly astronomy column for his local newspaper. However, in 1908, Lovecraft suffered a nervous breakdown and failed to get into university, sparking a period of five years in which he all but vanished.

In 1913, Lovecraft was invited to join the UAPA (United Amateur Press Association) – a development which re-invigorated his writing. In 1917, he began to focus on fiction, producing such well-known early stories as 'Dagon' and 'A Reminiscence of Dr. Samuel Johnson'. In 1924,

Lovecraft married and moved to New York, but he disliked life there intensely, and struggled to find work. A few years later, penniless and now divorced, he returned to Rhode Island. It was here, during the last decade of his life, that Lovecraft produced the vast majority of his best-known fiction, including 'The Dunwich Horror', 'The Shadow over Innsmouth', 'The Thing on the Doorstep' and arguably his most famous story, 'The Call of Cthulhu'. Having suffered from cancer of the small intestine for more than a year, Lovecraft died in March of 1937.

E.F. Benson

Edward Frederic Benson was born at Wellington College (where his father was headmaster) in Berkshire, England in 1867.He was educated at Marlborough College, where he proved himself as an excellent athlete, representing England at figure skating, and published his first novel, *Dodo* (1893), when he was 26.The novel was quite popular, and Benson eventually expanded it into a trilogy (*Dodo the Second*, in 1914, and *Dodo Wonders*, in 1921).Nowadays, Benson is principally known for his 'Mapp and Lucia' series about Emmeline "Lucia" Lucas and Elizabeth Mapp.The series consists of six novels and two short stories, and remains popular to this day, being serialized for Radio 4 as recently as 2008.Benson was also a respected writer of ghost stories – indeed, H. P. Lovecraft spoke very highly of him, especially his story 'The Man Who Went Too Far'.Benson died of throat cancer in 1940, aged 72.

GUY BOOTHBY

Guy Newell Boothby was born in Adelaide, Australia in 1867.Aged twenty-three, he wrote the libretto for a comic opera, *Sylvia,* which was published and produced in Adelaide in 1890.Some years later, looking for greater literary opportunity, Boothby emigrated to London, arriving in 1894.In that same year, he published *On the Wallaby or Through the East and Across Australia* (1894) – a travelogue of his time in Australia – and his first novel, *In Strange Company.*Both were critical and commercial successes.Over the rest of his life, Boothby published more than fifty books, in a variety of genres.Arguably his most successful were a five-novel series featuring 'Doctor Nikola', an occultist anti-hero seeking immortality and world domination.Boothby died in 1905, aged 37.

GRANT ALLEN

Charles Grant Blairfindie Allen was born near Kingston, Canada in 1848.His family moved to the United Kingdom in his teens, and Allen studied at Merton College in Oxford.During his time at university, he became a committed agnostic and socialist, and began to d develop some unique scientific viewpoints. After a brief stint teaching in France and Jamaica, Allen turned to writing as a way to express his (then fairly radical) worldview.

His early works, such as Physiological *Æsthetics* (1877) and *Flowers and Their Pedigrees* (1886), were scientific ones, but in the mid 1880s he turned to fiction.Between 1884 and 1880, Allen produced almost thirty novels.His 1895 title *The Woman Who Did* was a bestseller, not least due to its scandalous portrayal of a young woman living with a man out of wedlock. Allen was a fierce advocate of women's rights, and occasionally wrote under a female pseudonym during his life.He was also a pioneer of science-fiction; his novel *The British Barbarians* (1895) appeared at the same time as H. G. Wells' *The Time*

Machine, and touches on similar themes.His 1901 short story 'The Thames Valley Catastrophe', meanwhile, is an early example of modern disaster fiction, featuring the destruction of London by a sudden volcanic eruption.Allen is even credited with innovation in the field of detective fiction.

Allen died in 1899, aged 51.In his memory, an annual festival celebrating Canadian mystery fiction is now held annually on Wolfe Island, near Kingston, Allen's birthplace.

ROBERT E. HOWARD

Robert Ervin Howard was born in Peaster, Texas in 1906. During his youth, his family moved between a variety of Texan boomtowns, and Howard – a bookish and somewhat introverted child – was steeped in the violent myths and legends of the Old South. Although he loved reading and learning, Howard developed a distinctly Texan, hardboiled outlook on the world. He became a passionate fan of boxing, taking it up at an amateur level, and from the age of nine began to write adventure tales of semi-historical bloodshed. In 1919, when Howard was thirteen, his family moved to the Central Texas hamlet of Cross Plains, where he would stay for the rest of his life.

At fifteen Howard began to read the pulp magazines of the day, and to write more seriously. The December 1922 issue of his high school newspaper featured two of his stories, 'Golden Hope Christmas' and 'West is West'. In

1924 he sold his first piece – a short caveman tale titled 'Spear and Fang' – for $16 to the not-yet-famous *Weird Tales* magazine. He published with the magazine regularly over the next few years. 1929 was a breakout year for Howard, in that the 23-year-old writer began to sell to other magazines, such as *Ghost Stories* and *Argosy*, both of whom had previously sent him hundreds of rejection slips. In 1930, he began a correspondence with weird fiction master H. P. Lovecraft which ran up to his death six years later, and is regarded as one of the great correspondence cycles in all of fantasy literature.

It was partly due to Lovecraft's encouragement that Howard created his most famous character, Conan the Cimmerian. Conan – a barbarian-turned-King during the Hyborian Age, a mythical period of some 12,000 years ago – featured in seventeen *Weird Tales* stories between 1933 and 1936, and is now regarded as having spawned the 'sword and sorcery' genre, making Howard's influence on fantasy literature comparable to that of J. R. R. Tolkien's. The Conan stories have since been adapted many times, most famously in the series of films starring Arnold Schwarzenegger.

Howard was enjoying an all-time high in sales by the beginning of 1936, but he was also deeply upset by the ill health of his mother, who had fallen into a coma. On the morning of June 11, 1936, he asked an attending nurse whether she would ever recover, and the nurse replied negatively. Howard walked to his car, parked outside the family home in Cross Plains, and shot himself. He died eight hours later, aged just thirty.

Mrs. L. T. Meade

Elizabeth Thomasina Meade was born in County Cork, Ireland in 1844. She started writing speculative fiction at a very young age, which horrified her father, a Protestant clergyman. Upon the death of her mother, Meade moved to London, where she spent much time in the Reading Room of the British Museum. In 1879, she married Alfred Toulim Smith. Over the course of her life, Meade was a prolific author, producing more than 280 books and numerous short stories and articles for magazines such as *The Strand Magazine* and *Lady's Pictorial.* At her peak, she was publishing more than ten novels a year. She was best known for her female adventure novels, of which she penned more than thirty, but wrote in a number of genres, from romantic to detective fiction. Meade also co-edited *Atalanta,* a girl's magazine, and was an active feminist. She died in 1914.

VIVIAN MEIK

Vivian Bernard Meik was born in 1894, supposedly while at sea onboard a British vessel off the coast of Calcutta, India.In his early life, Meik worked as a railway engineer, before becoming a keen traveller and spending extended spells of time in Africa, India and the Far East.Meik published most of his fiction during the thirties, with his better-known novels being *Veils of Fear* (1934) and *The Curse of the Red Shiva* (1936).He also published two fairly popular short stories collections, entitled *Devils' Drums* (1933) and *Monsters* (1934).Meik's travelogues – notably *The People of the Leaves* (1931) and *Zambezi Interlude* (1932) – are regarded as valuable accounts of otherwise relatively undocumented groups, such as the Juang or Patuas people of Orissa, India. He was wounded in both World Wars, working as a war correspondent in the Second.In 1943, Meik falsely claimed to have been employed by British Intelligence and was convicted under the Official Secrets Act in 1943 for improperly obtaining documents from a Foreign Office employee.He died some years later.